ooks by *April Alisa Marquette*:

Fiction

~The Cohort Trilogy
Absolution
Progression
Iniquities

I0629721

~The Cohorts, Generation Next
Improbable

~The Sea Isles Series - A Trilogy
Exodus
Affinity
To Be Announced

Turnabout

~A Tranquility Tale
Rebuke

*

Non-Fiction
Co-Authored with Jessica Janna

~The Relinquish & Reap Series
Seedling
Sowing
Yielding

**Ask for them ... at your local Barnes & Noble,
or Books-A-Million bookstore!**

One should always be a little improbable ~Oscar Wilde

Improbable

Highly unlikely or doubtful …

The Cohorts, Generation Next

Book I

by

April Alisa Marquette

Books that captivate

Improbable
2nd Edition
© Copyright 2013 by A. A. Marquette
Cover Design by April A. Marquette

ISBN 978-0-9837206-3-8
Printed in the United States of America

Visit the author at www.aprilalisamarquette.com
Library of Congress Catalog Card No.: On File

Publisher's note:
The novel *Improbable* is a work of fiction – for adults, only.

Prologue

Nowadays, people spoke of his daughter the way they'd spoken of the Priestess in times past. People believed the phenomenal woman had once controlled the wind and even waves.

In one of his highly acclaimed movies, Beau based a character on the beautiful brown Priestess. At the time, his daughter hadn't been born. After she was, Beau still would not have dreamt that people would speak of his baby and the renowned Priestess in the same breath, but it was happening.

The talk was all over the island. However, some dismissed the stories as improbable. They said it wasn't likely that the blond, moody, Home Wares heir, the caramel-brown sheriff, *and* one of Hollywood's hottest actors were all madly in love with the same woman, Beau's daughter. Others dismissed the notion that long-limbed, shapely Gemma Janelle could actually love each of the men.

However, Beau didn't find any of it far-fetched. In fact, he believed the stories, to some degree, the way others believed tales about the Priestess. The Priestess and the men with whom rumor had linked her.

Why did Beau believe? –Because he knew his daughter. Beau knew Gemma Janelle was used to being loved and adored.

Early in the child's life, he and her mother had noticed. Back then, they, nor her other gay male father, attributed the tendency to anything special. For her mother, Gemma was the youngest of five. For her fathers, she was the firstborn. Therefore, the parental triumvirate had just known; Gemma Janelle was often the center of attention.

Beau simply realized, his daughter, nearing thirty, had always been the sun, while others were the moon and the lesser stars. *And* it was improbable, Beau further mused, to think things would ever change.

Forseen

What will happen...

Chapter 1

Gemma Janelle's unblemished skin was a creamy *café au lait* color. Her grandmother said coffee with a liberal dose of cream. Gemma had her mother's tilt-tipped eyes and curves. Gemma's sunlit, sandy brown hair came from her biological father. Yet she thought of herself as what she had been called for most of her life, Beau's baby. Before she had been conceived, her dad had *so* wanted a baby.

While growing up, Gemma always heard remarks about her looks. People even spoke of her extremities. They said that in addition to the rest of her, her hands and feet were lovely. Older people mentioned her vivacious personality before they inevitably swore; that girl was born to break hearts. Perhaps that was why her photo was often splashed across the tabloids. Inquiring magazines, those that stretched a smidgen of truth, alleged things. They claimed she slept with all of her male co-stars—and sexy directors, just because. They declared the late twenty-something looked at sex the way a man did; for her, it was just an activity and not an emotional affair. Now how would they know?

Gemma remembered. She was second-generation Hollywood. Thus, she had been taught not to care. Those rags were trash; Gemma's father, a director/actor, had often said. He reminded her that tales went with the territory. Still, Gemma tried to explain; she didn't read that mess, but those closest to her did, and the lies bothered them. The lies upset über-sexy, strawberry blond Jeremy, heir to the Baptiste and the Harden fortunes. Tales made it hard for him to trust, yet Gemma was crazy about him. She just didn't like Jeremy groaning about the paparazzi and flashbulbs going off in his face. She abhorred hearing how loathsome the catcalls were and the jostling just to get her photo. Sure, her life was complicated, but for her, it was *de rigueur*. That, Jeremy actually got, and *her*. Perhaps those were the reasons Gemma loved him. As a 'person of interest' too, Jeremy knew turmoil would often surround them, but he dealt with it.

Gemma did the same. Hoopla sometimes surrounded Jeremy, 'the heir,' but never would she willingly give him up.

Chapter 2

Jeremy decided. He didn't want to love her anymore. Then again, how could he not? She had been one of his first friends, and she had also been his most intense young love. Now, as twenty-somethings, they were in so deep. Still, a few things had to change. Jeremy wanted him and Gemma to be more. Somehow though, it seemed like he and she just could not get things right; not for too long, anyway

Why? Jeremy didn't know. That was a lie. He knew. Gemma had another man, the sheriff. And another in L.A, that actor, the Nile. If Gemma didn't have those characters, she and Jeremy could make a go of things.

Jeremy had to acknowledge the truth; he and Gemma *were* making it. Their thing worked—until she did something to remind him that she loved the others. Then Jeremy would remind himself, Gem couldn't love any other man as much as she did him.

Sure, he, bi-racial Jeremy Baptiste Harden, had loved other women. Nevertheless, he had never loved anyone else with the same intensity. No other woman made him as crazy. In little ways, Gemma drove Jeremy nuts. Then she drove him nucking futs with lust. Sometimes he wanted more or something different from her. Still, Jeremy honestly didn't know how he and the world-famous lingerie model could have any other existence. The truth was they'd been doing the same dance for so long until, with Gemma, Jeremy knew what to expect –drama, angst, highs, and devastating lows. With his penchant for the same things, Jeremy realized he would not have wanted things any other way. Not with Gemma Janelle.

That was what other women did not understand. As a matter of fact, Jeremy had one who would soon need her walking papers. The side-chick was attempting to put the pieces together –like his and Gemma's love life was a puzzle. Jeremy knew Ashlee was trying to figure out where she could fit. So, soon, he would tell her, she didn't, and she wouldn't, ever.

Jeremy had Gemma Janelle, and for him, it just wasn't that kind of party.

Chapter 3

Ashlee Caro Durham was a bottled-blond, a bimbo. Well, that was how people saw her. Ashlee didn't care, though, because she knew differently. She was smarter than the average person. However, one thing wasn't okay. Although she'd tried to hide it, people on the small isle of Karina Cay knew she had grown up in a trailer park, on the mainland.

Hopefully, islanders didn't know that her home was near Durham, North Carolina, or they'd suspect the truth, the twist. Her middle and last names were an ode to the place whence she'd hailed. Ashlee Caro Durham hated that Karinians—that's what the people on the island were called—considered her an outsider. Most were polite, but they never let her forget. She was an interloper. Their very auras seemed to scream, *you don't belong*! Or maybe she just felt that way. But she did belong. Well, she wanted to because Jeremy B. Harden, of the Baptiste Hardens, had sort of invited her to the island. She'd met him on a ski weekend.

The thing was: she needed to get him to commit—to her. But his mind was always on that black chick. The slinky, coffee-with-milk-colored one, and Ashlee wanted that beeyotch gone!

Why was Jeremy with her, anyway? Sure, he had some Negro in him, as Mam-maw, Ashlee's prejudiced gran, would say. Still, the nigger-ism was so far back in Jeremy's family until his genes had probably rid themselves of the impurity. To Ashlee, the man sure looked white, and was he gorgeous! Ah, and Jeremy had been born into wealth; *that* was most important.

Therefore, it was time to get to work. It was time to plan. Ashlee had to make her new name and her new tits count; she didn't care what she had to do. Heck, to get to this point, she had already done so much. Ashlee had given up her family and her friends. She'd left her home and all she had ever known, so she knew she could go the distance. The truth was, at this point, she would destroy any obstacle that wound up in her way—and those 'obstacles' included that uppity Gemma Janelle.

Ashlee would gladly destroy that nigger chit because there was just no way she would ever go back. Ashlee would never again live in the shadow of the mountains.

What already happened...
Chapter 4

Gemma Janelle Kennings-DeVeaux remembered her upbringing. She knew it was different from that of others. First off, her father was Beau DeVeaux, a wildly successful actor turned filmmaker. Tall, buff, brown, and still beautiful in his sixties, Beau had also been the lead singer in a quasi-renowned band. Infusion, it had been called.

However, shortly after his daughter was born, Gemma's Dad, who could pass for someone in his early forties, had given up touring. He gave up the band, too, so that Gemma could have a stable life.

Gemma's other father was Saavion Kennings. She called the retired optician, Pops. Lean, with sunlit sandy brown hair, he had always been the fun father. That was because Saavion hadn't been dying to have a kid. However, Saavion, Beau's man, had donated his seed, 'the fun part' Saavion often called it. He did it so Beau could get his baby.

Thirty years prior, Gemma's mom had known that her cousin, a gay male, wanted a child. When he'd sought surrogates, Kismet volunteered with one stipulation. She had to use her own eggs. "But," Kismet had pointed out, "Beau, your child will still get some of your family DNA—from me."

Every step of Beau and Kismet Staar's journey was documented in Beau's biography ***Iniquities***. The book described how baby Gemma had been conceived through in vitro fertilization. It was to the dismay of her mother's husband, but that was another story.

Now that she was a woman, Gemma often recalled her youngest years. Despite her non-traditional conception, man had she had fun! During the school year, she'd lived with her fathers, Daddy, and Pops, but summers had been spent with her mom. Spending time with Momma had allowed Gemma to spend unlimited hours with her grandmother. All the grandkids called Nell, Nannie. As the youngest, Gemma also got to be spoiled by Nannie's husband, Paw-Paw. God rest his sweet soul.

With Daddy and Pops, Gemma had lived on the little-known U.S. barrier island of Karina Cay. Holidays, though, had been spent in New York. In the fall and winter, Beau opened his magnificent abode. It was in the exclusive Long Island town of Icebury Court. There, and at

Momma's big gabled colonial, not far away, Thanksgiving and Christmas had been huge affairs. All four of Gemma's older siblings had been present, and all spoiled her. Holidays had been loud, colorful affairs that included aunts, uncles, Nannie and Paw-Paw, and other family and friends. Gemma remembered it with fondness.

Celebrations for the New Year had been even more extensive. Fashionably bundled against the cold, the whole family would pile into a heap of cars. On New Year's Eve, at Mount Hebron, the gray stone family church, they would attend what was known as Watch Night Services. Nannie said they it did to ring in the New Year with the Lord.

At the crowded, huge African Methodist Episcopal church, the choir would sing. The preacher would exhort all to remember those who hadn't made it thus far and give thanks for those who had. At midnight, there had been prayer and praise, the likes of which Gemma believed also went on in Heaven. It had been glorious.

Shortly after midnight, people streamed from the church's massive wooden doors. Outside, they offered hearty greetings, "Happy New Year!" Many would pull on gloves and adjust wool scarves. In the cold night, laughter and conversation rose. Many people flowed through the church's tall, spiked, wrought iron gates. Some briskly went out to the busy Brooklyn street, while others poured into the jam-packed parking lot. As a youngster, Gemma would lift her face to the night sky. With her eyes on indigo pierced by stars, she'd gulp crisp cold air until her chilled lungs burned. "Come on, Munchkin!" Someone would inevitably yell. Racing to the car, they'd yowl, "It's freezing out here!"

Then the fam would arrive at her Dad's house. In exclusive Icebury Court, the home would be ablaze with light and color. It would be open to all the people in Beau's life. Beau's brother Thomas and his lady, Gina, would appear; so would Beau's handlers, business associates, lawyers, and moviemaking chums. His young, red-haired assistant Tatum, and Beau's best friends, Mireya, and transgender Brett, would show up, prettily attired. Beau's former band members and backup vocalists would appear, as would his security team. His head of security, the massive demi-god, Boulder, was ever-present. Beau's celebrity friends would turn up. Then all would marvel at the feast prepared by Beau's longtime chef, JeRell, and his restaurateur wife.

On those festive occasions, Gemma, her siblings, her cousins, and other children would eat, dance, play, and chase each other until they dropped. With pop, reggae, rock, hip-hop, and sultry jazz pulsing in the background, the adults would schmooze, booze, and reminisce.

Then at dawn, collapsed and seated on her daddy's knee, Gemma would doze. Yet she always strove to wake because she loved to hear Beau and his band members speak of Gypsy. He'd been their drummer. Shortly before Gemma had been born, misfortune had befallen Gypsy. Still, she felt like she had actually known the man due to all the stories.

However, there had been one not-so-bright spot. Momma's husband, Lyle. He had never liked Gemma, and he hated her fathers, too. The man with the long dreadlocked hair resented all of them for some reason. Gemma had not known why; she had only known that Lyle wished she'd never been born.

Gemma remembered seeing Lyle and her mother argue. They'd done so on numerous occasions. Not about to take Lyle's mess, Momma gave as good as she got. For that reason, small Gemma felt a little safer around Lyle *and* because her Dad boxed. Even when Gemma had been small, she'd known; Beau's fists were considered lethal. She had also learned that had Lyle hurt her physically, her parents and others would have sought her mother's husband to the ends of the earth. However, Lyle had sneakily attacked her in psychological ways. About that, the parents hadn't been able to do much.

Forgetting Lyle, remembrance speared Gemma's heart. Although she didn't often think about it, Nannie—the family matriarch—died. In Gemma's fifteenth year, at ninety, Nannie transitioned.

After her grandmother's passing, everything changed.

Chapter 5

Jeremy Baptiste Harden didn't recall much about being a kid. However, he remembered the third grade. That was when he'd become fully conscious of Gemma. Sure, they'd attended *Printemps* Academy; both had been enrolled before birth. At their island school, Pre-K through the twelfth grade was taught. Gemma and Jeremy had also lived close by. She resided at DeVeaux House, and his home was Windsor Pines.

On his mother's side, he was of Afro-French ancestry. Thus, while very young, Jeremy knew what the French word *Printemps* meant. Springtime. Still, he couldn't figure out the Academy's motto. 'Building a love for learning in the springtime of your child's life.'

High on the cliffs, small Jeremy had lived in a massive house. It was called the manse. A century back, it had been inhabited by a Methodist cleric. At the manse, Jeremy felt like an only child. He had older sisters, but they were attending a famed university in England. Short for his age, Jeremy was introverted, moody, and not like a child. Due to being bi-racial, he often felt he did not really fit with others. Thus, he didn't have many friends.

There was only curly-haired African-American Colin and blond Jay. There was dark-haired Lance, too. Lance's family owned a Karina Cay summerhouse. Still, Jeremy's three friends rarely visited the vast, spooky structure up on Hollow Well Lane. Tales deemed the place unsafe. The cliff-side on which it sat was disintegrating, too, a few pebbles at a time. When down on the beach, one could look up and see free-flowing rocks. At times, showers of them tumbled down and into the restless ocean below. Then when the tide was out, other rocks, jagged cruel ones, could be seen jutting up from the sea floor. Karinians, those who lived on the island, knew those rocks, the jetty, meant destruction and perhaps even death if one slipped and fell.

However, other tales weren't about Jeremy's home or its foundation. These were about a well on the property behind it. A mass of crumbling bricks, the well was nearly shrouded. Around it, a beautiful old thicket of fragrant morning glory vines had grown up. There were huge, hanging trumpet flowers near the well, too. To small Jeremy, both species appeared eerie, like something for the dead. And both plants seemed to protect the well, of which legend spoke.

Nevertheless, on the U.S. barrier island of Karina Cay, it was common knowledge that the cistern was empty. Still, it was often said that human howls emanated from the well on full moon evenings.

Most Karinians believed the unnerving commotion was made by the ghost of a woman. A century prior, when the property belonged to the Methodist church, a male parishioner had allegedly murdered his wife. The angry husband believed she carried the cleric's baby. After a massive search, the wife's body was found—in the well. The coroner's report cited strangulation as the cause of death. The report stated marks consistent with the finding were on the victim's neck.

However, *legend* claimed the woman was alive when she'd been trapped in the hollow well. It said she began to wail but to no avail.

Adding insult to injury, eighty years later, another man acted similarly. Using blunt force, he, too, allegedly killed and dumped his wife—in the same well. Thus, legend claimed that on certain full moon evenings, both women could be heard howling... about fatal injustices.

Jeremy did not know how true any of that was. But the stories spooked kids, and not many wanted to play on the property. His grandfather, the French mulatto, Gentry Baptiste, had purchased it. At school, the curriculum was English and French. Since kids at the Academy knew the tales, Jeremy only spoke to them when necessary and only in French. He'd wanted it known; he preferred books to people.

Yet Jeremy's mother, who looked white, often said Jere was like her father, his *grand-père*. Petite, blond Giselle said it more when her alabaster-skinned son became infatuated with little brown Gemma Janelle. That child had the most beautiful eyes. Long-lashed, they tilted upward above her sculpted cheekbones. Giselle didn't wonder why her son was smitten, not when it had been the same for her father, Afro-French.

Jeremy's grandfather, who also appeared Caucasian, had been besotted by the beautiful brown island priestess.

However, small Jeremy ignored his mother the same way he ignored island lore. Yet, in class, he often composed poems, and they were about the mysterious girl of his dreams. He wrote in French and kept all guarded in a private notebook. Until one day in third grade...

The Friday afternoon bell rang, signaling the day's end. Popping up from her desk, Gemma raced toward the hall. There perky redheaded Heather Garrahan waited—along with sweet freedom.

Seated behind Gemma, Jeremy slowly rose. More reticent than the girl, Jeremy leisurely started for the door.

Calling to freckle-nosed Heather saying she'd left something, Gemma spun. She knocked Jeremy's books from his arms. "Ooh! Sorry," Gemma apologized. Dropping to her knees, she aided the Dresden doll-boy. Helping to retrieve his things, eight-year-old Gemma noticed his beautiful hands. Then her eyes fell on Jeremy's open notebook. He'd written poems, like those they'd learned, those of *Baudelaire*. Hurriedly, the boy gathered his papers, and it hit Gemma. He had a poet's hands.

Small Jeremy noticed the girl. Her skin was smooth, and it was precisely the color of coffee that had been liberally dashed with cream.

Gemma noticed the boy's lips, bubble gum pink, the lower lush.

When she rose, Jeremy caught the girl's scent, baby soft, as shyly he thanked her. Gemma noticed the boy's mesmerizing eyes, the blue-gray of turbulent skies. Momentarily lost in them, she shook herself free. With a wave for Jeremy, Gemma hurried to her desk. Then she returned to the hall and her freckle-nosed friend.

Jeremy had noticed the brown girl's eyes, too. They were slightly tilted and fringed with the longest lashes. He tried to blink visions of her away, but he knew. She who had bumped him would never leave his mind because… she was no longer shrouded in mystery.

She, Gemma Janelle, was the girl of his dreams.

The next day and those to follow saw the children sneaking glances at each other. Outgoing, Gemma wondered about the intriguing blond boy. He stared intently. At home, she questioned Ina, the longtime housekeeper. "EYE-na, when a boy stares at me, what does that mean? He never says anything. But he keeps looking. Why?"

Sweet round Ina dusted. She bustled about, forgetting her Jewish grandparents who'd lived in a settlement in Poland. Stopping, she yelped, "Oy Vey! My Gem, is this staring boy older than you are?"

"No…he's in my class. We're both eight, or maybe he's nine."

"Oh." the woman who had loved Gemma since she'd been a baby felt relieved. "Bubbe," Ina began, her New York accent apparent. "Boys and staring can mean many things. Little boys are strange. Big ones, too.

Shuggie, stop wondering. Just get your studies. There'll be time to worry about boys, late-uh." Later, Ina waved, "Much late-uh, ya hear that?"

Still, Gemma felt inexplicably drawn to the quiet boy. Infatuated, the introverted strawberry blond—whose hair was neither truly red nor blond but a cross between the two—watched the girl. Jeremy often sketched her and composed odes to her because she was special. Most people ignored him, but she did not. Bigger boys even called him a turtle, and they claimed Jeremy retreated into a shell if anyone spoke to him.

Nevertheless, Gemma didn't see small Jeremy that way. That, he liked, and the way she entered class hugging her books to her chest. Before she took her seat in front of him, she always said hi. Although, most times, paralyzed with awe, Jeremy could not respond. Still, as the years passed, Gemma was consistent. Sometimes at lunch, the two managed to sit side by side. They did so like it was casual, yet they knew better. There had been that first time in the school cafeteria. Jeremy had stood over Gemma while saying nothing. She hadn't called him creepy. She'd only glanced up. Eating, she'd been getting a jump on that night's homework. Sweetly she'd spoken. "Have a seat, Jere. Put your tray down." His heart pounded; she'd used his mom's nickname for him!

"Otherwise," ten-year-old Gemma continued, "how will you eat?"

She was right. Therefore, Jeremy didn't think. He just awkwardly stepped over the bench attached to the table. Without a word, he pushed in beside Gemma, who took it all in stride. Sliding over, she moved books, fries, and her milk. Reassuringly, she patted Jeremy's hand, like Nannie had often done hers. As Gemma's bestie, red-haired Heather, and other girls watched, briskly, Gemma said, "See? All better."

Then smooth as you please, Gemma drew everyone's attention from Jeremy's flaming face. She told a totally unrelated tale about biology class. In seconds, the girls and the boys cracked up and forgot him.

That was when Jeremy knew. He was a kid, maybe even a strange one; he lived in a house deemed haunted, but at eleven, he…was in love.

He progressed to talking to Gemma. Well, they had stilted discussions about race, poetry, and whatever. Jeremy told her that being bi-racial, he felt closest to African-American Colin; the boys shared cultural similarities. Gemma understood. She even visited the manse when most other kids would not. The grounds, their elders said, were inhabited by evil. However, unafraid, Gemma walked around the big imposing old house. She said she liked that his grandfather had named it Windsor

Pines back when he'd gifted it to his bride, Gwendolyn Windsor. Lightly, touching things, Gemma murmured, "Wow, this" or that "is so cool."

Jeremy visited DeVeaux House, too, Gemma's home. It was smaller and felt different, lighter somehow. Hers was indeed an island home, with the beach out back, like his. Yet hers wasn't high up on a cliff, and it was cozy and welcoming. At Gemma's house, Jeremy sat at the breakfast bar on a stool. He wrote secret poems about Gemma while her family's bossy male chef clashed about. Sweet, sturdy Ina, the housekeeper, was always near to mother Gemma, Heather, and Jeremy.

Then Jeremy's friends, brown, curly-haired Colin and blond surf boy Jay, got wind of where Jeremy spent time. Jeremy's best friend Colin got to poking about, and curly-hair pulled Jay along, and Gemma included them. Then Lance, who was only on island during the summer, reappeared. Gemma made room for him, too, as she said, "Now the whole gang is all together." Remembering her dad and his friends—his cohorts—Gemma told the gang they were the cohorts, generation next.

Wow. They were *cohorts*, a group of people banded together! As years passed, none of them forgot it or that lanky brown Gemma had made them so. Slowly, she turned the rag-tag bunch of kids into a family of friends. The self-designated Momma, she was a protector, too. The little lioness punched boys who bothered Jeremy. He figured she was unafraid because she was growing up in a house of men. Along with her fathers, there was male help, including Chef JeRell, who went home to his wife nightly. Jeremy figured Gemma was ferocious, because, in New York, she was the youngest. As such, she probably never got to tell anyone what to do. However, she had five cohorts to boss around. Jeremy, Heather, Jay, Colin, and summerhouse Lance. Sometimes the kids did as Gemma said. Other times the boys were boys. Gemma didn't mind. She only cared that they were friends—forever. Each of them believed it so much that they'd have done anything for her, perhaps because she did nice things for them. She bought cards and made them all sign. She used her allowance to buy presents or asked the gang to chip in. Occasionally she told them, "We're gonna sing Happy Birthday to Heather," or to whomever. Gemma made the cohorts remember one another and others. She forced their focus outward and kept them from being self-centered. Jeremy, whom adults said had an old soul, believed Gemma made them all more human. He had grown to love those things and others about Gemma now that they were double-digit kids.

Yet it was during their sixth-year lessons that he received terrible news. One weekend, Jeremy's mother, petite elegant Giselle, informed him he would be sent to Canada. That Monday, twelve-year-old Jeremy told Gemma. She cried. "Why? Why do you have to go?"

Jeremy said what had been told to him many times. *Grand-père* deemed it so. It was imperative that in Montreal, he attend a school where only French was spoken. Then as an undergrad, he would go to *université* in France. Jeremy was further expected to matriculate to graduate studies in Paris. "It is all settled," young Jeremy told Gemma.

"But why? Why would Mr. Baptiste do that?" eleven-year-old Gemma inquired, feeling crushed, for reasons she could not name. "Jere, do you *want* to go?"

Jeremy's blue-gray eyes appeared unusually stormy as he replied, his accent slightly French. "It is not about what I want. He is *grand-père*. He deems it. Therefore, it is done. I do it."

"That's so *archaic*," lanky pre-teen Gemma stated, thinking aloud. "It's just so old-fashioned." Then in silence, she struggled to understand.

Jeremy shrugged, although he felt like howling, like the ghostly women in the well. Nevertheless, Jeremy managed to sound calm as he said what he had long known. "*I am the heir.*" Jeremy did not speak of his mixed-race heritage or what his grandfather sought to build. Jeremy didn't mention the ethnically diverse school chosen for him. Unlike his and Gemma's small island academy, his new school was better known for its language and literature programs. Therefore, Jeremy modified the truth. He paraphrased what his grandfather had always said to him. "I must learn to manage. To do so, I must first learn to follow instructions. I must take orders," *grand-père's* orders, Jeremy miserably thought but did not say.

Unable to understand that rigid way of thinking or behaving, Gemma shook her head.

Then before either of them could ask further questions, twelve-year-old Jeremy was gone, whisked away. He, however, never forgot Gemma Janelle. At eleven years of age, she did not forget Jeremy Baptiste-Harden, either.

Chapter 6

As an adult, Gemma Janelle remembered 'that summer' in New York... She'd been twelve and already six feet tall. She'd done what she had all her life back then. She hung out with her older sister.

A fraternal twin, Belize, had been eighteen. Leez had their mother's just-beginning-to-brown biscuit-colored skin. Belize had her father's thick curly hair; long, it had never been processed. Belize wasn't even five feet tall. Vertically challenged was what she called it. However, Momma said pint-sized Belize had simply received her height from Nannie. Their grandmother Nell was a half-pint, too. Also, to Belize's dismay, she could never hide the curves or the tiny waist that caused some to refer to her as stacked. Yet the girls' mom said she'd had the same issues back in the day. Now though, Gemma recalled, Momma's waist wasn't so small. Nevertheless, Momma was still quite curvaceous.

One morning 'that summer,' Kismet gave her attractive girls permission. She said they could leave the town of Winter Creek, New York. With a few stipulations, she said, they could shop in Manhattan.

However, once there, the girls conspired. Gemma wanted to ditch security, the man whose job was to make sure no harm befell them. When the sisters chucked the man who'd surely receive a reprimand, a photographer approached them. "I like your look," he told Gemma. Over blaring Manhattan traffic, he asked, "You done any print work?" Before Gemma could reply, the man squinted in the sweltering afternoon sunlight. "Hey—aren't you *that guy's* kid?" The man snapped his fingers. "He played a TV detective, then he made all those movies..."

Later, as she and her sister rode the Long Island Rail Road, Gemma felt giddy. Excited, she loved the idea that she could start modeling. Then she and Belize were back in Winter Creek, surrounded by shopping bags. Calling home, Belize asked their mom to send someone to the train station to pick them up.

Belize's twin Bonaire [Bo-NAR] met them. With a male friend also in the car, tall, dark, handsome Bonaire did not tell the girls. He knew they'd soon find out, though. They were in trouble, deep dog-stuff.

Unable to wait to tell her mother about her new 'modeling career,' Gemma jumped from the car. "Momma!" she yelled, dashing into the big kitchen. Gemma stopped short, not seeing maple cabinetry, splashes of cream, or refreshing Granny Smith Apple green.

Silver-haired Kismet waited with arms folded over her formidable bazooms. "Before you say one thing," she began, "I am aware of what you two did. Gemma Janelle, your Dad," Beau, "knows too."

The twelve-year-old groaned but claimed she could explain.

Kismet, whose hair was always stylishly cut, stood there. She listened as her girls told her and Nannie about 'the adventure.' Then, patiently, The Momma explained why the girls should not have ditched security.

"Gemma, people are not always nice. They won't always have your best interest at heart. That you need to learn." The Momma reminded her youngest, "Your father has garnered fame and money. Due to that, some people will only see *you* as a target—a way to get what they want from him. They may even hurt you…" Kismet's heart pounded at the thought. Placing a hand on her chest, she said, "People have been known to do worse to children of privilege. It's something I need you both to understand." Silver-haired Kismet then reprimanded pint-sized Belize.

"You're eighteen, Leez, so *you* should know better." Despite her older daughter's mewls, curvaceous, silver-haired Kismet continued. "No more co-signing Gem's silly schemes. Sure, they may seem like fun, but some things can become dire. You understand, right, Leez…"

Old enough to remember a few bad things, Belize nodded. Uncle Beau's drummer Gypsy had met an untimely end.

Again, silver-haired Kismet addressed her youngest, "Gemma Janelle, if you were smaller, I'd spank your butt." Lord knew the child raised her pressure. That, Kismet had just told her mother, who was visiting. Kismet had also divulged, "Mama, at fifty-six, maybe I'm too old to be raising a child. Maybe my hair's all white because it's a sign."

Eighty-seven, Nell had chuckled. "You'll be okay, sugar."

"You say that, Nannie because over at your cute lil bungalow, you're mostly removed from all this insanity."

Forgetting the conversation with her children's grandmother, Kismet caught Gemma's eye. "You, young lady, are headstrong, and you don't hear when we tell you things for your own good. So… you're grounded."

"But Momma—"

"But, nothing; grounded, two days. Leave all your stuff in my study." Kismet spoke louder, "Keep talking, Munchkin, and it'll be longer. Tomorrow, no outings and no phone. The same goes for you, Belize."

Kismet knew it wasn't the worst punishment, but her girls hadn't done the worst. As their mom, she just wanted them to become more responsible decision-makers.

"But how will I *live*?" Gemma wailed.

Kismet nearly laughed. That child of hers was indeed an actor—just like her Dad. "You'll manage," The Momma dryly stated, hiding her smirk. When her youngest sputtered, Kismet shook her head. Then both girls knew. Their mom would brook no more arguing. Kismet pointed, "Upstairs. Now," so she could know a moment's peace.

Passing the family room, shorter Belize called her sister. "Come on, Munch." Belize also noticed her father. Lyle was on the sectional. Again. Named for the country in Central America where he'd been born, the older girl saw. Her father had muted the TV, probably to better hear them being reprimanded. Bet he'd been gloating, too, Belize thought, sick of her father's sly antics. Cutting her eyes, the older girl ran upstairs.

When Gemma passed, Lyle stood in the doorway. "You're no Munchkin," he menacingly whispered. "I don't even know why they call you that." His Belizean accent was apparent as he breathed alcoholic fire. "You're a big, tall doofus –a bad seed, and you know it."

The dark man with the long graying locks pulled back into a ponytail continued as he blocked the twelve-year-old's path. "I'll bet now your mother regrets having you. You do know," Lyle sneered, leaning closer, in the near-empty hallway, "if I had my way, you wouldn't be here."

Gemma stared. To her, Lyle looked like an old hippie. Although she said nothing, she knew what he meant. All her life, he had made sure she knew. *He wished she had never been born.* Dismissing Lyle, Gemma put one foot before the other, but the man grabbed her arm.

Creeped out, Gemma pulled away, hissing, "Don't touch me!"

Lyle leered. "You think you're grown, lil girl. You know nothing about grown. You know nothing about touch, either—but I'll teach you." Lyle nearly salivated in anticipation of getting his hands on her. "I'm gonna wear you out. I'll teach you a lesson you'll never forget. Bitch."

Gemma's blood ran cold. She wanted to race upstairs behind her older sister, but Lyle blocked her way, licking parched lips. "When I'm done—fucking you—you'll wish what I wish. That you were dead."

Gemma had enough. Blindly she spun, but strong arms caught her. She would have screamed, but she quickly realized. Lyle was behind her. The person holding her was in front. The body was short and stout. Lyle was tall and flabby. Gemma smelled lavender and a hint of spearmint. Lyle only smelled of liquor. Thus, Gemma knew profound relief when she sobbed, "Nannieee!"

With old, knowing eyes boring into Lyle's, Gemma's grandmother rubbed her back. Nell spoke soothingly, "It's alright, baby." Nell's eyes never left Lyle's, and he remembered what he'd heard for many years. The matriarch didn't allow anyone to mistreat her family. It was why she'd rescued her nephew from his drug-addicted mother. At the time, the druggie had abused and often endangered small Beau's life.

Lyle knew that, in essence, he had slyly done the same to Beau's daughter. Still, Lyle strove for fleeting courage when he scoffed, "What you gonna do, old lady?" Raising his liquor bottle, he mock saluted his mother-in-law, Nell. Taking a swig of rotgut, his eyes fell on…his wife.

Kismet appeared disgusted, but she didn't say a word as she pointed.

He knew she meant for him to go, but hell, not without a fight. The gabled colonial was his home, too, even if he hadn't paid a bill in years.

Knowing he was gearing up for a fight, Kismet snarled. "Go—now!"

Becoming belligerent, Lyle yelled, "Who gonna make me?" When his son Bonaire stepped forward, Lyle's eyes widened.

The eighteen-year-old sidestepped his grandmother, still holding his baby sister. Bonaire, Belize's twin, bypassed his mother. Tall and slender but muscular, Bonaire grabbed his father's nape. "You're out of here."

Lyle struggled against his son's firm grip. "Yo, you *my* boy!"

Forcefully, Bonaire walked his father away. "I'm not a boy anymore, and I'm sick of this. You can't keep terrorizing people here."

Lyle tried to plant his feet. "How you doing me like this?" Lyle yelled, realizing he was actually being removed. "Where'm I gonna go?"

"Should've thought about that," Bonaire shrugged, "before." The younger man leaned to unlock the kitchen door and shoved his struggling father out onto the deck. While Lyle ranted, Bonaire shook his head. For thirteen years, it had been the same thing; the fam enduring alcoholism. Lyle had been a tyrant, and when they'd been small, Lyle's children had cowered as he'd destroyed things. Now, son Bonaire stated, *"No more."*

The ladies watched. Followed by his friend, Bonaire put out a hand to signal. He would handle his angry drunken father by himself.

Hours later, Kismet felt a presence as someone leaned against the doorframe of her study. She raised her eyes, "Bo-NAR." Crossing the room, she grasped her son's smooth dark face. Looking up, she appeared sad. "My handsome young man...thank you."

Bonaire accepted a kiss. Then with arms around his mother, he said, "It was nothing, Momma." With his chin atop Kismet's silver head, Bonaire squeezed. "Actually, it's what we should have done years ago."

Aware that her son was right, Kismet asked, "Where is he?" Lyle.

"Where else?" Bonaire rhetorically inquired. "I couldn't leave him on the street, so I took him to Gran's."

Oh. Lyle's mother. Sweet Collette would be so disappointed.

Kismet's son released her. "Since Leez," his twin, "let me in, I assume you reset the security code."

Kismet nodded, recalling that her errant, soon-to-be ex-husband had once been as good-looking as their young man was now.

"You called them people too, right; the ones who change locks?"

Kismet nodded. "I did." She sighed, "Again." Then she vowed, "I've called them for the last time. I'm done. I can't do this anymore, son. Your father and I are through. I just signed the papers."

"Good." Bonaire squeezed his mom again. The young man revealed something that he had not in a while. "I still love Dad, a little, but I'm done, too. I mean, I would *really* have to *kill* him if—"

"Shhh," Kismet reached out. "Don't speak that way." She hated to think about what would mean lost futures for all.

"I'm just telling you, Mom. If that man hurt you, or Nannie...or one of the girls—especially Munch, because we all know he hates her—there would be powder up in here, 357, for sho."

Kismet's cousin, Gemma's dad, also wouldn't hesitate to kill Lyle.

Bonaire looked into his mother's eyes. "You know I'd have to off Dad before *Beau* got to him." Kismet's son shrugged, "So, all of those are reasons enough for him to *stay* gone, this time." Bonaire turned, and called over a shoulder. "Oh 'n I told Dad the same thing." Kismet's young man pivoted, appearing sardonic. "I just didn't use them little ladylike words."

Chapter 7

Every summer, Jeremy went home to Karina Cay. All during the school year, he thought about it. He would have to work at Home Wares, his father's company. Still, while at home, he could hang with his friend Jay, now known as surfer dude. They'd pal around with dark-haired Lance, whose family owned a summerhouse. They'd hang out with curly-haired Colin. Centuries ago, as slaves, Colin's African ancestors were dragged to nearby islands to unwillingly farm rice and other crops.

Yet this summer, Jeremy didn't want to only hang with his boys. It was Gemma that he wanted to see. While at *The Collège International Antoinette de France*, which prepared students aged four to eighteen for the French Baccalaureate, Jeremy had often imagined being home on Karina Cay. He'd imagined seeing Gem. They wouldn't acknowledge each other with a nod like they had for the past few years. Nope. Jeremy couldn't wait because he wanted more. When summer arrived, his nerve would be up, and he would kiss Gemma.

While still in Canada at school, Jeremy promised himself, this was it. This summer, he'd be fifteen, practically a man, by his now-deceased grandfather's standards. And Jeremy had grown a few inches. He was five foot nine. He wasn't as tall as Jay, Lance, or Colin, and he never would be, but he could no longer be called shrimp. Now he was taller than the average man. He was just shorter than *une copine*, his girl.

Jeremy didn't know when he'd started thinking of Gemma that way, but that's who she was to him. She'd become that at *Printemps*. At the Academy, he'd watched her. While the beautiful brown girl had giggled with red-haired Heather, he'd composed odes to her. He had also drawn Gemma, long and rangy but with the innate grace enhanced by Ms. Spring's ballet class. Using mechanical pencils and charcoals, Jeremy had lovingly lingered over her hips. He wanted to do it now, but with his hands and his penis instead.

Although she'd been a girl and not even a pre-teen back then, Jeremy had seen promise. Perhaps because of what people called his old soul, Jeremy had known Gemma would blossom. Her slightly rounded hips had said so. Therefore, when he drew her naked, he enhanced her body parts. Many times, he'd drawn her lying spread-eagle—for him. He'd captured the sultry glance she'd often thrown over her shoulder in class.

He could not wait to get home! He thought of her in the air, on land, and riding the sea. He thought she was mostly unaware that he'd been infatuated with her since third grade. Jeremy was sure Gemma didn't know that he'd only gotten more into her when she'd knocked his books from his arms. When she'd taken the time to help him, he'd smelled her. Her scent had been soft. He'd noticed her skin, and gazing into her eyes, he'd become lost. Jeremy would swear she'd felt the same way. Back a few years, he'd tiptoed around Gemma until that afternoon at lunch.

He'd worked up the nerve to sit next to her. He hadn't cared that freckled-faced Heather was there or that it wasn't done. Boys hadn't sat with girls, but he'd had to be near Gem. Since she hadn't minded, that had become their norm. Jeremy sat with Gemma and Red; ah, he meant Heather. Jeremy's friend, blond Jay, a little older, had joined them. Then other boys and girls began to sit together, even in groups. Therefore, Jeremy and Gemma had started something.

Now they would do so again, the fifteen-year-old thought, because this was his year! He was definitely going to kiss Gemma, and more.

Jeremy did what he'd planned. He did it the first time he saw Gemma again. However, it didn't happen like he'd imagined.

She was in *Splendid Choco-Latte*. Jeremy entered the café that served the finest candy, lattes, and other confections, all laced with chocolate. Gemma was at the counter, with perky red-haired Heather, her bestie. Sun-bronzed, Gemma appeared leggy while sipping a creamy iced mocha, Jeremy's fave. Walking up, Jeremy intended to surprise Gem, but she surprised him. Gemma gave a little shout. She jumped up and threw her arms around him. "Jere—Harden, you're here!"

Feeling her buttery-soft boobs pressed to him, he knew it was now or never. With a chin jut for Heather, Jeremy grabbed Gemma's hand and pulled her from the café. In the alley beside it, he reached up. Taking her face in both hands, he kissed her like the flirtatious girls at school had taught him. Afterward, Jeremy was proud of himself for having done it.

Now, he and Gemma were an item. Sometimes he and she even forsook the cohorts—Heather, Jay, Colin, and summerhouse Lance—to be alone. Gemma had even shared a few profound things with him. She'd told Jeremy about her mother's husband. That clown, Lyle.

One Saturday, Gemma revealed how the man had seemingly hated her all of her life. Lyle had often taunted her. However, in recent years, his threats had become sexual. Gemma did not look at Jeremy when she softly admitted she felt like Lyle was gearing up to rape her. Gemma hugged herself although it wasn't cold out. "How can I tell my mom that about her husband? How would I say I'm scared of him—of what he might try? I can't tell her that he said I'm a hellion. He said my fathers let me run all over them, and that's why I'm a whore."

Hearing about that bigoted fool, Jeremy burned with fury.

"I haven't had sex yet, Jere. Oh, and Lyle said that as 'fags,' my Dad and Pops are gonna burn in hell, right along with me." Gemma sighed. "All of those are why I didn't go to New York this summer."

"But you always go. You see your mom and your brothers and sisters. You see your grandparents, too." Jeremy knew there were even others.

Gemma shook her head, and her huge crinkled chestnut ponytail bobbed behind her. "I just couldn't go, Jere, not this time."

Squeezing Gemma's hand, Jeremy said he understood. He revealed he really didn't want her going, not to wind up in a jeopardizing situation.

Seated in the rear, Gemma faced him on the stretch of beach between their homes. "Thanks, Jere, and for listening. I haven't even really told Heather. I mean, it's embarrassing." Undoing her scrunchie, the fifteen-year-old let her hair fly free.

Blowing in the summer breeze, Gemma's hair reminded Jeremy of a voluminous, soft, fragrant, sunlit cloud. It was one he wanted to touch.

Unaware, with closed eyes, she leaned back, lifting her face to the sun. Therefore, Gemma did not see Jeremy as her hair flew sexily about.

Yet he saw her, her halo, and more of her than he could stand. Then Jeremy's long shorts became too tight. Noticing Gemma's boobs, he ignored his bulge. It tried to burst from his khakis, just like her tits seemed about to burst from her tangerine bikini top. He noticed her thighs, shiny beneath her teensy denim skirt, and her impossibly long legs. They were crossed at the ankles on a yellow beach towel.

Jeremy wanted to touch Gemma like he had touched others. He wanted to begin with her string top that he would slip his fingers beneath. He would feel the nipples that made him ache and harden. He loved boobs; he loved staring at them in magazines or online. Gemma's he even wanted to taste. Enticed, he guessed they were the size of grapefruits under the fabric that barely covered them. Quickly, because she opened her eyes, he looked away.

"Jere, I can't tell my mom why I no longer want to spend summers at home in New York. I love her to death, but I wouldn't hurt her for the world. Anyway, my sister Belize is never there anymore, either."

Gemma explained that she and her sister had been close. "Still, now I feel like Leez and I grew apart. I think it happened the summer that my mom's ex got thrown out. Maybe Leez was upset about us getting grounded," for ditching security. "Maybe she feels it's my fault that her father's gone, even though I still have two."

"Then you need to speak with her," soft-spoken Jeremy suggested. His mind was on ravishing Gemma, if that was what she wanted, too.

She stared at him. Something about how Jeremy was looking at her... It made Gemma feel she was seeing him for the first time. Jere had once reminded her of a Dresden doll with pink lips, sun-gilded hair, and soft hands. Now though, he was more. He was muscular like he worked out. He was leaner, and for some reason, he made Gemma's heart go pitter-pat. Glancing away from his storm-colored eyes, she realized. He was a man, almost, and the notion excited her. "Jere, when I think certain things..." Gemma ventured, "I wonder if I really am what Lyle said."

"You are not. You're young and beautiful. He's old and asinine—and he's prejudiced, a real homophobic." Jeremy spoke over the hiss and growl of the ocean. "Just watch out for him; use your self-defense class stuff to kick his ass if you have to; remember how you felled big Andy?" Forgetting the class bully, and her mother's spouse, Jeremy told Gemma, "Speak with your sister and your mom. Tell them the truth. Then they might surprise you."

Gemma closed her tilt-tipped eyes and lay back on her towel. "I might," she volunteered. Suddenly she wanted Jeremy's touch. Although she did not say it, she wanted that badly, and she wanted him to want it too.

Lying there, Gemma had no idea that beneath the blazing sun, Jeremy would have done nearly anything she wished and so much more.

Chapter 8

Another fifteen-year-old had dreams that summer. In a town not far from Durham, North Carolina, Ursa stared at her big-boned friend, Biffi.

At fifteen, Ursa was a year younger than big-boned Biffi. Still, slender Ursa readily agreed when big Biffi suggested they get fake IDs.

"Then," Biffi said with a southern twang, "you 'n me'll git work." Big-boned Biffi said she knew a guy who would make the identification for them. "He will...if we blow him."

Sucking somebody *else's* dick? Slender Ursa didn't know.

Seeing the thinner girl's indecision, Biffi asked, "You wanna live with Mam-maw-'n-them yer whole laf [life] in that trailer?"

Ursa admitted she didn't, so she agreed. Another suck coming up.

Afterward, Biffi's friend handed over the fake IDs and social security cards. The two girls spiffed themselves up and went to the employment agency. It was a town over, and they were signing up for work.

However, slender Ursa didn't think she liked the idea of cleaning other people's houses. Still, she appeared when it was time to get in the van that took her and the other girls to the new sub-division. The suburbs were where the upper-middle class lived. Rich people, Ursa thought.

On the ride over, Ursa promised herself that things wouldn't be bad. At the very least, she would get paid, but she'd quit if she didn't like working. She'd go home and watch the soaps with Mam-maw. Then they'd just wait on her grandma's two monthly checks from the county.

But what if she did like working and having her own money? Slender Ursa with the long brown hair felt that would be great. She'd no longer have to take the change Mam-maw doled out. Ursa might even save and leave the Lawd-forsaken place where her people were destined to die.

The white van pulled into the manned gates of the sub-division. Ursa remembered she would clean other people's toilets. Ugh! She gazed out the window. Only on TV had she seen grass that manicured and green. The houses looked like those on the *Dallas* and *Dynasty* reruns that Mam-maw watched in the evenings. Wow. Ursa forgot cleaning and craned her neck, needing to see everything. Then she was inside the first home. Walking around, she trailed a hand over beautiful objects. Ursa wondered. What was living in a house like? What if the house could be like the one she was in and in the same kind of neighborhood?

Ursa jumped. She was told quit gawking and get a move on. With her mop and pail, she followed her lead into the *master* bedroom. There, her heart nearly stopped. It was so large, with its own bathroom! It was bigger than Mam-maw's trailer put together with crazy Uncle Jed's doublewide. Working, Ursa couldn't help but glance into the closet, another room unto itself. She wondered. What would it be like, knowing all those pretty clothes, purses, and shoes were hers?

That night, Ursa again dreamed of getting out. Then she woke. She patted the tears that streamed down her face. Reality was back, and it was a bitch; it was the cramped trailer and Mam-maw's loud snores. Ursa swung her legs over the side of her lumpy mattress. Might as well get up, even though it was still dark. Uncle Jed's crowing rooster felt the same, making all that racket. Ursa had to catch the van. She needed her pay. She splashed water. She'd see other homes and pretend they were hers. To get through each day, she imagined she cleaned her own home. But when she got her check, she scowled. Where the eff was the rest?!

Gazing at her pay, Biffi was happy as a pig in a pit. "Ain't it great?"

"Yeah," Ursa replied, feeling unbelievably disappointed. "Really."

"What's wrong?" big-boned Biffi inquired, her southern twang pronounced. "I thought yew wanted yer own mun-ney. I thought you'd lak gittin' paid. It'll help ya git out. If ya save. I know yew want thet."

Slender Ursa summoned a too-bright grin. "Ah am happy!"

Ursa didn't mention that with chump change like this, it would take *years* to get out. She'd never be able to afford a camping tent! She might purchase a cheap sleeping bag, if she never ate. She could see it now. She'd be old and on the ground between Mam-maw and crazy Uncle Jed's trailers. Folding her meager earnings, Ursa knew she and Biffi had to get back to work. Dang. Work blew, bigtime.

Heck, a dick suck paid more than work. Yep, and if Ursa did a few of them, she'd get more money. Sucking dicks took a lot less time, too—if a girl knew what she was doing. Sure, men tried to prolong things, but Ursa could suck them down; no one outlasted her. She just had a way when it came to that.

Suddenly, Ursa realized something. It would take a heck of a lot more than some measly job to change her life. Only, she didn't know what that more was yet, but she would find out because life had to change. She swore on grandpa's grave.

Chapter 9

Jeremy was so happy. This summer, Gemma wasn't going to New York! Therefore, he imagined all he and she could do when she wasn't off on modeling gigs. In the evenings, they could hang with their cohorts sometimes. Days, he had to work, at Home Wares, his dad's company. On weekends though, Jeremy and Gemma could swim or take his skiff out. His custom-built sleek chaser provided hours of fun. On the water, Gemma could show him her makeup ads in teen mags. They could drink, dance, smoke a little weed, or go to *Splendid Choco-Latte.*

At the café, they'd have iced mochas, and they could go to the movies. The island had no multiplex, but he and leggy Gemma could kiss at the darkened duplex. Jeremy really wanted that, among other things— where they'd get naked, maybe near a bonfire at the ocean's edge.

"Jere…" Jeremy's heard his mother, and her voice pulled him from his Saturday afternoon musings. "Jere," Giselle called. "Phone."

Unwilling to abandon his dreams, he sullenly asked, "Who is it?"

"Gemma."

Scrambling to lift the house phone receiver, Jeremy had no idea that his plans were about to change. With his heart crazily pounding, he said, "Hey." Then he noticed she sounded strange. "You congested, Gem?"

"No. Just come out back." Now she sounded worse. "Please, Jere?"

Jeremy didn't hesitate. Running downstairs, he yelled. "*Maman!*"

His mother, whose work was featured in *Vogue Living* magazine, nodded. Jere was going to Gemma, whom Giselle really liked. Giselle liked Gemma's Dad, for whom she'd decorated DeVeaux House, just up the beach. Actually, for Beau, Giselle had done many projects around the world. In some, she'd created beautiful rooms for Beau's headstrong, young daughter. Giselle's son was infatuated with her and had been since the petite ones were at the island academy. In the manse, puttering in her interior design office, filled with textiles, storyboard presentation kits, paint chips, and flooring samples, Giselle called out. "Everything okay?"

"I'll let you know!" Jeremy left Windsor Pines, one of the homes that both *grand-père* and *grand-mère* had left to their only daughter. Biking on Beach Road, the young man forgot his family. Minutes later, he skidded to a stop before a high, ornate, wrought-iron fence. Having seen it umpteen times, Jeremy didn't notice the imposing brick wall with the house name engraved on a sign affixed. Walking his bike to a hidden squeaky gate, he unlatched it. On foot, he took the far side shortcut.

Jeremy wound his way through a dark copse of sugar pines on a carpet of pine needles and moss. He pushed branches from his path until he wound up in the sunshine. At the rear of DeVeaux House, he remembered. Elderly islanders still called it the old Habersham place.

In the sun, Jeremy squinted and scanned the brick path out back. Through waving seagrass, that path led to the horizontal wooden boardwalk. Jeremy saw the DeVeaux's two-story covered pier. It resembled a gazebo. No Gemma. She had to be nearby, maybe on the porch. Past it were trees, cypress and rot-resistant tupelo, all dripping Spanish moss. Climbing a sand dune, Jeremy passed begonias in pots and flowering white gardenia. Then his heart skipped.

There she was. Her red nose and puffy eyes revealed she'd been crying. Climbing wide steps, Jeremy took a seat. He didn't see the inviting porch or outdoor furniture. Settling amongst African fabric-covered pillows, without a word, he ran a hand over Gemma's hair. Like Gemma, he remained silent, staring out at bricks. Laid through nearly a mile of wheat-colored sea oats, that path joined the horizontal, sun-bleached wooden boardwalk. The boardwalk and the beach were private, all up past the manse where Jeremy lived. Jeremy forgot their neighbor.

Buddy B was a man crazy enough to jog alongside two dogs in the blazing sun. Before Jeremy knew it, Gemma fell on his neck, sobbing.

Alarmed, Jeremy wanted to ask what was wrong, but he let Gemma cry. Feeling bad for her, he knew she would tell him, in time.

When she was spent, Gemma rested her head on Jeremy's shoulder. Her tears had wet his tee, but he didn't care. All he cared about was her.

Realizing she could cry no more, Gemma became cognizant of Jeremy's scent, warm and outdoorsy. He smelled like the sea, salt, and citrus. Inhaling, Gemma felt comforted. Jeremy was familiar when her world was giving way. She pressed her face to the skin on his neck. That she concentrated on and not what had made her cry. Now she only wanted to taste Jeremy, and she wanted his hands on her.

Jeremy's arm tightened around Gemma as he felt her tongue flick on his skin. Silent, he stared out to sea. And Gemma tongue-flicked again.

Bending slightly, Jeremy looked at her. She stared at his lush, pink lower lip. Then he knew. He had to do what he'd dreamed. Leaning in, he kissed Gemma. Beneath his, her sweet mouth opened. Then Jeremy really kissed her, plundering with his tongue. His hand rose, and he cupped a breast. When Gemma pressed into his palm, all he could think was *wow*.

Soon, the pair got up to walk down sunbaked bricks.

On the boardwalk, Gemma said she was leaving.

Jeremy felt like he'd been gut-punched. "Why?" he asked, nearly reeling from the unpleasant sensation.

Gemma descended to hot sand as she spoke. "My Nannie...died."

Jeremy's heart broke. He knew Gemma loved her grandmother. Every summer, Gemma's leaving was why he and she didn't spend much time together. This summer was supposed to be different; she hadn't been going to New York. Now Gemma said she'd leave the next day.

She turned away. "Ever since I heard, Jere, I keep feeling like I caused this." Gemma appeared anguished. "I feel like I should have gone weeks ago! I would've seen my Nannie one last time if I had."

Jeremy asked if Gemma's grandmother had been sick.

"No. That's the thing. She went to bed and never got up again."

Like Gemma, Jeremy was in turmoil, worse than last night when he'd been in bed replaying their café kiss. While masturbating, he'd imagined removing her bikini top and tiny denim skirt. Lying there, he'd imagined doing things with Gemma that he had only done with girls in Montreal.

Now Gemma stood before him, appearing forlorn. He hated that she had to go. What would he do every summer evening without her?

Gemma's eyes filled, and Jeremy's dropped. He wouldn't be able to stand it if she cried again. That was how he found himself pondering her tits. Damn, they were pretty. He saw them through her tee and bra, which was thin and light blue. Darker, her nipples were also visible.

Jeremy felt like he had the night before; he wanted Gemma. He wanted to touch and inhale her, to run his hands up until he could cup and fondle her. He wanted his cock in her, doing everything he'd dreamed of with her. Maybe if they did those things, she could forget her pain for a little while. But nope, she was leaving. Therefore, Jeremy stated, "I hate that this happened and that you're going."

"You and me both." Gemma looked at him like she was waiting.

He waited too, but he didn't want to waste precious time. So he leaned forward and pulled her in for a hug. Then they kissed. This time was different, he thought because he'd initiated it. This time he held

Gemma's head. He offered his tongue and eased it into her mouth. Just like he wanted to ease into her elsewhere.

Jeremy could feel his own pulse, throbbing in his penis. Kissing Gemma, he thought, man –she even made his palms sweat!

Gemma swayed, feeling overcome and better than she had since she'd heard the news. She nearly felt like she would fall; good thing young Jeremy put his strong arms around her. It was nice, being pressed to his hard masculine chest. Snuggling up, Gemma wanted more kissing.

Suddenly, down by the water's edge, she felt another part of him, the male, against her. Gemma tried not to move, but the receding ocean sneakily stole sand from beneath their feet. Still, she hoped Jeremy would remain where he was because she wanted to keep feeling him. She liked feeling the sensations that ping-ponged within.

The ocean playfully dashed their shins as the sun breathed warmly on the pair. Jeremy felt fireworks and Gemma's twin peaks. With them pressed against him, he was happy. He was sad too because she was leaving. Still, the truth was; if she wasn't going, he might not have had the nerve to do as he had. Still, there was so much more that he wanted. Oh, well, at least he'd kissed her. That was one good thing that had come out of this summer that was not to be.

Before she turned to go, Gemma hugged Jeremy.

When she turned away, he grabbed her and hungrily kissed a path from her mouth and her chin down her neck. Gemma shivered at the ocean's edge, standing in the blazing sun. Then slowly, she began to make her way back over hot sand toward the boardwalk. Gemma knew Jeremy watched as she trod the brick walk with seagrass on both sides. She walked on, the back of her home coming into view.

Standing alone, Jeremy gazed after Gemma. His eyes caressed her slender back, flared hips, long legs, and enticingly round bum. Ding-dang! In those frayed denim shorts, the curve of her bottom winked at him. Each time she took a step, the sight made him horny. Watching her, he wondered if she meant to leave without another word.

However, Gemma turned. Smoothing back her blowing sunlit hair, she called out, "I gotta pack, Jere." She didn't want to leave him, so she added, "Dream of me?"

Jeremy nodded because if Gemma hadn't asked, he would have.

Unbeknownst to her, he had been doing so ever since their third-year lessons.

Chapter 10

Ursa continued to work, but she still had to figure a way out because this work stuff was not for her. Then one day it hit her. While cleaning a bidet— a contraption that washed people's tails—she realized. In the houses where she worked, there were all sorts of things. There was stuff she'd never heard of, like the bidet. Some of the stuff Ursa could steal— and pawn! The homeowners wouldn't even miss it. This, Ursa told herself. It was only fair. They had so much, and she had so little.

Slender Ursa began to pilfer things, a watch, a string of pearls, and bric-a-brac. She told herself that there probably wasn't a pawn shop in the town where she worked. And if there was, going there would be risky. So she waited to get back to the holler. Then at the shop back home, she stood her ground, thirty dollars or more for each item.

One evening after work, the girls neared the holler. Slender Ursa asked Biffi to accompany her to Cain's trailer. "Ah need to see him," in the low-lying area shadowed by the mountains. Ursa said so because she knew the boy-man and the bigger girl were together, almost. Whatever that meant, in their little butt-crack of beyond.

Bigger Biffi declined. "I gotta check on Suster's kids 'n git dinner started, so I'll see yew tomorrah. Oh, and tell Cain to stop by me."

Ursa nodded. With darkness descending, she ran down the dusty trail. Cain's squat, metal camper came into view. When the blue-eyed boy-man came outside, his tin door slamming, Ursa gave him a chin jut.

"S'up, Ursa?" Cain wore no shoes. In a faded black tee with hacked-off sleeves, he stuck his hands in his jeans pockets.

Ursa wasted no time. "I need you to do something."

With a cigarette between his teeth, Cain looked her over. "Seems you done growed up some, Ursa..." She was still nearly flat-chested, he mused, but who cared. "So now you need me." Cain smirked. "Well, what if I need something too—fer doing yer something? Whatever it is."

Ursa knew what Cain was getting at, even though Biffi considered him *her* boyfriend. Slender Ursa felt the rise of anger because it seemed every man in the holler wanted the same thing, a slick dick. "I got yew," she snapped.

Cain appeared satisfied. "Now thet that's out the way, what yew want?"

"Ah need ID."

"You *got* ID, girl—jest gave it to you 'n Bif couple'a months back!"

"Ah need *new* I.D., Cain," Ursa whined, "with a new name."

Cain flicked away his diminishing cigarette. "Ain't asking why."

"I ain't telling," Ursa shot back. "I jest need it, so kin yew do it?"

The thin young man hated when his abilities were questioned. Thus, he sounded mean. "Ah can do anything—if I want to." He gave the skinny girl a once-over with his eyes. "Yew gonna make me want to?"

Ursa felt exasperation. "Said I would."

"Then what stupid name yew need, and what age?"

That was more like it, Ursa thought. Although her plan was far from stupid, unlike Cain. "I need age eighteen, and I'll gi' yew the name."

"What yew givin' me fer doing this? Mun-ney? This is..." Cain spoke slowly, using the large word for the first time, "a con-sul-tay-shun."

"Okay." Ursa played along since it wouldn't do to anger him. "It's a consultation." She didn't mention that on TV, the lawyer commercials said the first one was free. Cain would have thought she was trying to seem smarter than he –which she was. "I ain't got no money, Cain."

"Yew working!" Then he thought aloud. "Alright. My consul-tay-shun fee is..." Like a silly girl or The Joker, he giggled high-pitched, "Ass."

"No." Ursa decided. She was not going to bend over for another soul in the holler. She tapped her foot. "What else yew want?"

"Yew ain't got nuthin else! Ya got no titties, and yo' hole wore out."

"Look, Cain, I'll gi' yew a hand job."

"A frickin' haind job?" Cain tossed his head, "No. No good."

"It'll *be* good—good enough for a 'consultation' where yew ain't done shit fer me yet. Yew got baby oil, right?"

"Naw." Cain appeared sullen, "Got some used Crisco, though..."

Ugh. He was so trashy, Ursa thought. Well, they'd use lard. "Let's go. Don't take long, either," Ursa groused, "because Bif's expecting yew."

Cain pulled on his tin door. "Well, git on inside, girl 'n git to work."

Chapter 11

Jeremy wanted dinner to be over. Sure, he loved his dad, Michael Thomas Harden, and Jeremy even liked spending time with super busy M.T. Harden. However, the fifteen-year-old just didn't want to do it this evening, not when Gemma was leaving their little island in the morning.

Jeremy's dad ran Home Wares. The international empire had been founded by M.T. Harden's grandfather. Therefore, Jeremy's dad understood being busy. Still, Jeremy didn't think he could tell his dad that *he*, too, was busy. Yeah, with needing to rush out to see *une copine*, his girlfriend. So, Jeremy attempted to endure.

Giselle noticed her son, who seemed antsy. If teenage Jere left, she realized, she would get rare alone time with her husband. Therefore, Giselle regally suggested their young man be excused. Jeremy mouthed his thanks. He practically flew from the dining room, an exceptional, mahogany-paneled affair, and his mother winked.

In the quickly descending dark, Jeremy jumped on his bike. Racing like the wind, all he could think about was Gemma.

Back in the dining room at the manse, lean forty-something M.T. Harden did as Giselle instructed. The dark-haired man with the graying temples placed his chair before the ornate fireplace. Then he surprised his petite wife by quickly pulling her onto his lap. "Michael!" she gasped, liking the turn of events.

Pedaling in the dark, Jeremy remembered his grandfather. Island lore said his mixed-race *grand-père* had loved the Priestess, a brown woman who'd been as powerful as she was beautiful. Furiously pumping to get up an incline, Jeremy wondered if, in years to come, people would speak of him and Gemma the same way. He knew his mother already did, and *Maman* made weird little comparisons. When he'd been younger, she had even told him bedtime stories. Although he hadn't been aware then, Jeremy now knew; *Maman's* 'tales' had been couched in truth.

Petite blond Giselle admitted she didn't believe her father had ever loved her mother—well, not like he'd loved Priestess. Jeremy recalled *Maman* further stating, "That is just how it was. My father married *ma mere*," my mother, Gwendolyn Windsor. "Many people thought he did so because his family was simply well-off, while hers was unspeakably wealthy. *Ma mere*, your *grand-mère*, was an unmatched heiress. In those days, Jere, when she married, a wife's fortune became her husband's. That was why people whispered.

"Still, I happen to know differently," Giselle said her father, a French mulatto, married Gwendolyn Windsor—not for her wealth but to get an heir. Giselle further spoke of her father, who'd hated the term mulatto; in the American South during slavery it had been common. Gentry Baptiste considered the term that referred to those of mixed ancestry, offensive. These things Giselle had always told her son. She spoke of his grandfather, a black man who appeared Caucasian. "Your *grand-père* needed a spare to go along with his heir." He needed another son, too, "For the future of our family. For posterity." Giselle told little Jeremy that her father intended to build generational wealth, like white people.

Giselle shrugged and said still; the truth remained; long before her father ever met her mother, he had already met the woman he would love, his life-long. "By the time my parents married, my father had no room in his heart for anyone but the priestess."

Small Jeremy had asked, "*Grand-père* had no room for you?"

"He loved me, sure, as best he could." Her father taught her many things, petite golden-haired Giselle revealed. She tickled her small son, *but I was a girl*, she did not say, and *mère* died trying to get his heir.

Following playful shrieks, Jeremy again became the sober child. As such, he inquired about his grandfather's heir. "Was it you, *Maman*?"

"*Mais non, chouchou.*" Giselle no longer played, and she told the truth, "But no, pet. My father—your *grand-père's* heir…is *you*."

Slipping through the hidden gate, Jeremy dropped his bike. He forgot his family history and looming responsibilities. Jeremy wended through, knowing the layout of the now-black stand of sugar pines like he did the back of his hand. He raced down the brick path, bursting into the clearing behind DeVeaux House. Then with footsteps thudding on the unpopulated boardwalk, he pulled up short…

There was Gemma in the moonlight. Nude and rising from the silvery sea, she was a vision who stole young Jeremy's breath.

Unaware that he'd arrived, the female teenager had been swimming naked in the moonlight. As she surfaced, droplets of saltwater languorously slid down her bronzed body.

Jeremy wanted to do the same as he watched Gemma bend.

When she grasped her towel, her breasts hung enticingly. Unhurried, she stood then to squeeze water from her long hair. Afterward, she stepped into faded denim. With lunar light spilling over her, Gemma began to knot her white string bikini top.

Barely breathing, Jeremy could hardly move, yet he forced himself from the seagrass shadows. He told himself he could not waste a moment because, in the morning, Gemma would be gone.

Unaware of Jeremy, Gemma squinted. Recognition lit her eyes. As the dark ocean receded and rolled behind her, she waved. Thinking better, Gemma bounded toward Jeremy.

She was up and in his strong arms when he knew anything, her legs wrapping themselves around his torso. Holding Gemma close, Jeremy swung her around, nuzzling her neck, throat, and barely concealed orbs. Kissing her, he tasted the salt that lingered on her skin. To better support her, his capable hands slid beneath her plump rump. Gemma held Jeremy to her with arms around his neck, and her ankles crossed behind him. Just as she'd desired, ardently, he kissed her breasts.

When finally, she slid to the sand before him, she felt every inch of him, especially that all-male part. That, she wanted. Kissing Jeremy, fifteen-year-old Gemma divulged her feelings. "I couldn't go without seeing you Jere or giving you something to remember me by, but we have to hurry. My Dad or Ina," the DeVeaux's motherly Jewish housekeeper, "will look for me in an hour or so."

As Gemma stood in the hard-packed sand before him, Jeremy watched as her eyes slowly slid over him. He knew that through his much-laundered jeans, she saw *him*. In the moonlight, Gemma eyed his cock as, before her eyes, it grew. Yet Jeremy could not know that seeing the thickening made Gemma feel hungry with desire.

Sidling closer, she told him. Cupping Jeremy through his jeans, she whispered it in French. In English, Gemma pled, "Let me feel you…"

Wildly aroused, Jeremy pushed into her hand. As all around, the ocean roared and filled the night, Jeremy closed his blue-gray eyes. Opening them, together, he and Gemma quickly undid his zipper.

"Jere!" She sounded shocked. "You're not wearing underwear."

He said nothing, just wrapped his hand around hers. With them both holding his fevered log of flesh between them, he kissed her. Feeling his tongue in her mouth—like his cock would soon be in her body—sixteen-year-old Jeremy knew. *This was forever.*

As Gemma descended to her knees before him, she sensed it too. Holding Jeremy's penis with two hands, she said she just wanted to taste it. As though he were a lollipop, she licked. Then Gemma took him between her lips and realized that there'd been so many things that the young one had itched to see and do before her grandmother passed. There were places that she, a young woman, had wanted to go. Now she could only think of one thing she wanted more than those things. Jeremy.

He collapsed to his knees, and he and Gemma became all hands. She fought to remove Jeremy's shirt while he picked at the knots in her bikini top. With Jeremy fondling and ravenously kissing her, Gemma spoke. "If we do this tonight, Harden, and if I don't come back next week, or even the week after, can I count on you?"

He licked and lapped at her, having set her bounty free. Lifting each breast to better suck it, Jeremy exposed his heart. "If you never came back, *trésor*, I would still return to look for you." Jeremy said so because he had long thought of Gemma as his treasure.

In the moonlight, she lay on hard-packed sand. Widening her legs, she told Jeremy the truth. "I'm a little scared."

He shushed the girl who opened herself to him. With his heart racing, he positioned his nude body between her thighs. With her heart rapidly beating, Gemma babbled, "There are so experiences I want to have—"

Nudging his way inside, Jeremy interrupted her. "Then have them."

Drawing her knees up, Gemma breathed through momentary pain.

Trying not to groan, Jeremy felt he'd entered the gates of Heaven. He barely managed the words, "Dang, you feel good."

Withdrawing nearly all the way out, Jeremy eased back, as instinctively, Gemma met him.

They found a rhythm in the moonlight, with the roaring ocean as a backdrop.

The more experienced young man dropped down on Gemma to slow his pace. Within her, he momentarily held still. "Let everything," he rasped, beginning to move again, "lead you – back – to me, *cher*. Always."

As her body greedily clasped his, Gemma sighed and offered one word. "Always."

Chapter 12

One morning, Biffi and Ursa waited for the maid service van. However, the 'the agency lady' ordered them into her office. With stiff lacquered hair, she mentioned a few thefts. "An ormolu clock and a Fabergé egg," she concluded, "are also missing."

"A or-what?" Biffi asked. Appearing disgusted, she added, "And what fool steals aiggs? At Winn Dixie, they eighteen fer two dollars—"

"Enough!" Ms. Agency commanded. With eyes narrowed on slender Ursa, the woman asked if the girls knew about the thefts.

Both looked sufficiently shocked.

"If one of you did this," the woman glowered, "you'll be fired." She mentioned the jailhouse, too. Getting on Ursa's nerves, the woman declared 'her' agency hired people who didn't have records, "But that doesn't mean those people don't steal." Staring at Ursa, the woman griped, "It just means they haven't got caught—yet. Believe me, though, you will wind up in a cell, and in the afterlife, you'll burn in hell!"

The agency lady thought she'd allow that to sink in.

Disdainful, Ursa mused, This itch thinks she's threatening somebody. Heck, I already live in a cell—Mam-maw's hot trailer. That was hell.

Hearing the transport van, Ms. Agency shooed them. "Go, but trouble awaits. Remember that—if you're stealing from clients."

Big-boned Biffi just had to say she would never steal. In a hurry to leave, she added, "I lak this job. What's more, Ah need it."

"Very well." Lacquered hair gestured the two girls out.

Striding to their ride, Ursa couldn't believe Bif! Scraping 'n bowing; *I like this job.* That old crone had no power, not when she wasn't behind that metal desk. Climbing into the back of the van, Ursa added that scene to her list, Reasons for Wanting Out. No more lectures, ever.

"I hate that ol' bag," Biffi groused on hot, sticky, blue vinyl.

A black girl with gold teeth asked, "She ga'e y'all da speech, too?"

Ursa did not respond, but Biffi got drawn into a conversation about self-righteous old battleaxes. While the others commiserated, Ursa sat quietly aside, needing to adjust her timetable. She'd put her plan into action sooner than later, and she might even ask Bif to join her…

The next day at lunch, in a low voice, Ursa mentioned getting out.

Appearing amazed that the thinner girl had that much nerve, big-boned Biffi said, "Ya know, Mam-maw'll never forgi' yew for leaving."

Ursa shrugged. Sure, the old woman depended on her, but Ursa was tired of being a crutch. She might lose Mam-maw's forgiveness, but so be it. Mam-maw was old. Ursa's grandmother had a heart condition too, so, Ursa mused, her fat ass probably wasn't long for this world, anyway.

Also, Ursa didn't know if the big woman really cared for her. If Mam-maw did, she had a funny way of showing it. Ursa felt Mam-maw only needed a do-this-'n-that gal. The heavy woman had trouble walking, so Ursa was Mam-maw's white slave walking stick. Mam-maw was mean, too. Anyway, Ursa now had her new name documents. Silently, she voiced her new moniker. ASH-lee... *Ashlee*. To Ursa, the name sounded ritzy and not backwoods, which she would no longer be, soon. Ursa would leave the holler. She would become *Ashlee Caro Durham*.

Slender Ursa planned to get new breasts, which would go along with her new name. She even knew the right doctor. He'd performed abortions on her mother, but he was into plastic surgery as well.

Ursa shook herself from thoughts of her future. Slowly, she let the little smirk slide from her face. "So Bif, yew jest gonna stay here?" After asking, Ursa noticed tears in the thickset girl's eyes. Touching Biffi's hand, Ursa whispered. "Bif, what's wrong?"

"I'mo miss yew." Bigger Biffi shook her head, "And...I'm pregnant."

Ursa's eyes widened. "Cain. He the daddy, right?"

"Yep. He ain't much, but Ah figure me 'n him can make a go of it."

Ursa understood. "That's why yew cain't leave..."

"Un-huh; another reason is Ah take care of Suster's kids." Although she spoke to slender Ursa, bigger Biffi sounded more like she was trying to convince herself. "We don't know where Holly is half the time, and them lil' hooligans of hers need a mama."

Slender Ursa claimed she understood, but she didn't. She only knew she had to do *for herself*. Forget somebody's sister's smelly kids and a document-forging boy-man, Cain. He was a lot like The Joker from Mam-Maw's 1960s Batman re-runs. Remaining silent, slender Ursa promised herself one thing. *She* would not wind up like Bif; stuck, in No-Where-Ville, with a no-account like Cain. Still, slender Ursa hugged her friend and told the biggest lie. "Everything'll be okay, Bif."

Yep, Ursa cogitated, if not for Biffi, then for her. That, slender Ursa would see to, and very soon, because now she had a plan.

Chapter 13

Nannie's funeral was held at the family church in New York. It was sadder than Gemma had anticipated. It was painful for Gemma's mother, Kismet. It was the same for Gemma's Dad; Nannie had raised Beau, even though he was her nephew. Gemma's other father was saddened, too. Over the years, Pops had grown to love his short, outspoken in-law.

The night after Nannie had been laid to rest, Gemma lay in bed. With her head hurting and her eyes puffy from crying, she called, "Leez." In the dark, she repeated it, "Leez..."

From her bed, the twenty-one-year-old inquired, "What is it, Gem?"

"It's nothing," Gemma said, feeling as estranged from her sister as she ever had. It had begun when she'd been twelve, and stuff happened.

Suddenly Gemma wanted to be back on the island, at her full-time home. There, she could be with Jeremy. She didn't think she could ever feel uncomfortable with the young man she sometimes called Harden. Nor could she feel that way with her bestie, perky red-haired Heather. Red wanted to become a veterinarian. Come to think of it, Gemma couldn't see feeling strange with any of her cohorts. She wouldn't even mind hanging around motherly Ina. Round Ina was so much more than the DeVeaux House housekeeper. She was...everything. Gemma had never minded bossy JeRell either, the family chef had called her Girlie from the day she was born. He, who was Gemma's third doting father, made the most amazing meals, most of them designed just for her.

Then remembering what Jeremy had suggested, Gemma sat up in bed. Pleating the sheet, she spoke. In the dark, she said, "Leez, I miss you... I miss how we used to be." Gemma said she felt they'd grown so far apart after the Lyle fiasco. "Granted, I never felt that close to Déja," their oldest sister, "but I thought I'd have you. Now I don't, 'n I hate it."

"You shouldn't feel that way, Munch."

Gemma's heart fluttered because her pint-sized sister had just used the abbreviated form of her nickname. When Gemma had been smaller than everyone else, all of her siblings had called her Munchkin.

"I know," Gemma blurted, "but I only have four girls that are my real friends—and you're at the top of that list. You and Heather G. And Nannie... I've been talking to her, even though she passed on." Momma had said Nannie would forever be with them. "You think that's strange?"

"Nope, sweet Nannie will always be in our hearts. And you'll never have a lot of girlfriends because you're cute," short shapely Belize stated. Rising, she tweaked her younger sister's nose. Seating herself beside Gemma, Belize sighed. "I'm a tell you something, Munch. Girls are notorious haters. Oh, and my father," Lyle, "isn't why we've grown apart. We really haven't. I've just been busy. I'm in college now, and I graduate next semester—I busted my butt to do so. I've also been working on a business that I'll soon launch. That's why you think I haven't had time for you, or Mom. She moans, too."

Gemma smiled. Aware that her sister could not see her do so in the dark, she rested her head on Belize's shoulder. Leez's hair smelled comforting, like coconut. "You upset that your dad's out?"

"Munch, I'm glad he's gone," Belize spoke of the man with the long locs that he'd often pulled back into a ponytail., "I shouldn't say this, but I wouldn't want him here with Momma. Not while we're all out becoming adults. He'd try to fight her. Truthfully? I'on't know why she put up with him. For at least sixteen years, he's been wilding out."

Hearing it, Gemma realized. Belize and Bonaire's father had started cutting up the year that *she*, the family baby, had been conceived.

Hugging Gemma, Belize ordered the fifteen-year-old to lie down. "Go to sleep, Gem. I gotta get up early. On this summer internship, they don't believe in days off. Not for bereavement, anyway."

The following day, as she sat in the kitchen, watching her mother make coffee, Gemma again recalled what Jeremy had told her. She needed to have a conversation with both her sister and her mother.

Gemma watched silver-haired Kismet, who was visibly saddened. Kismet Staar was taking the loss of her mother pretty hard, and Gemma did not dare mention Nannie. Nevertheless, Gemma screwed up her courage to quickly ask, "Momma, did I ruin your marriage?"

Turning to face her youngest, Kismet sighed. "I knew you'd one day ask. So I guess now you're old enough to understand." Seating herself in the big pretty kitchen, Kismet truthfully stated, "You did not ruin anything. Gemma Janelle, I chose to have you. My first cousin really wanted a child." For Beau, his cousin, whom the fam called Kiss, had been able to make that happen. "I informed my husband," Lyle. "He didn't like it, but oh, well." Kismet shrugged.

Gemma's voice was small, "You did in vitro anyway…"

"I sure did," Kismet nodded. "As a woman, this is *my* body, and no man gets to tell me what to do with it. Therefore, since I was compelled to use my body to bring you into the world, I did. That decision I have *never* regretted. You hear me, baby? I have never regretted being your mom."

The mother of five shrugged. "It wasn't like I cheated on Lyle. I simply had the power to grant my cousin's wish, so I did."

"Then Lyle started drinking."

"No, no." Kismet shook her head. "My ex had already been drinking. He started after the twins were born," Belize and Bonaire. "Lyle thought he kept it a secret for a while, but when I got a huge promotion," at the IT company from which she'd just retired, "the man became threatened. Mind you now, he had his own thriving engineering firm. Still, Lyle started saying he wasn't enough for me. Then when you were conceived, things just went downhill, fast."

Gemma pleated a napkin. "Why didn't you two divorce?"

"It's never that easy." Kismet stared through the window. She seemed to view her life fifteen years back. "We had a family. Even without you, Lyle had adopted your oldest sister and brother, like I had before I'd met him. Then I wound up pregnant—with twins. Lyle and I married. It was good until it wasn't. Still, I tried; I wanted my kids to have their Dad."

"Then *I* came along," Gemma mewled, "and messed everything up."

Using manicured fingers, Kismet lifted her daughter's chin. "Get that out of your head. You came along and perhaps sped up the inevitable. Sure, my cousin and I had to figure out how to raise you. We did so through trial and error, but you did *not* break up my marriage. Lyle and I had been headed that way for a good while. The summer that everything came to a head, your brother Bonaire helped me see; it was time. Lyle and I had a divorce decree drawn up years earlier. So I was ready."

Afterward, glad to have had that chat, silver-haired Kismet hugged her youngest. "Remember this one thing, Gemma Janelle. In life, things are usually not as simple as they seem."

That night Gemma went to dinner with her fathers. Seated in a Long Island eatery, one of Beau's favorites, he informed his daughter. Soon they would head back to their little island.

Gemma was ecstatic; Karina Cay, here I come! She thought of Jeremy and could hardly wait. She would also catch up with Heather.

"Before we go back, though," Beau revealed, "Mireya asked if you'd stay a night with Arlise."

Gemma would gladly do so. It would help cheer up her friend who was bummed out. Arlise had broken her arm at the summer camp where she worked. It had been a freak accident. Gemma also didn't mind the sleepover because she would see her Dad's former bodyguard again. The fifteen-year-old had a thing for big bi-racial Boulder. It had begun when she'd was twelve. Gemma knew it was childish, but her crush had started during another visit with Arlise. At the time, Gemma had seen her Dad's former bodyguard *with* her friend's mother.

Gemma's Dad, and her friend's mother, had been friends back when they were kids. Now, 'Auntie' Mireya helmed a booming business that sold women's sex paraphernalia via the internet. Therefore, at her home, Mireya had many things that her daughter and Gemma loved to ogle.

Auntie Mireya had no idea that Gemma had seen too much at twelve. Back then, in the privacy of her own home, Beau's longtime friend had tried out one of her adult 'toys.' Mireya had done so one evening while her man, Beau's former bodyguard, watched. Gemma had watched too.

Seated in the eatery with her fathers, she recalled the humming. The sex machine's motor had drawn Gemma as Auntie Mireya lay before it, her legs splayed. Unaware of young Gemma peering into her bedroom, nude Mireya had gasped each time the mechanical penis entered her. Looking on, Beau's bodyguard had fondled his man-piece.

Twelve at the time, Gemma had been old enough to know gawking was a no-no. She should not have crept away from her friend toward the humming. Gemma should not have watched through the crack between Auntie Mireya's bedroom door and its frame. Still, Gemma had, and her young body tingled. She'd watched Boulder too, who'd watched Auntie Mireya. Then Gemma became smitten with the former bodyguard.

However, other things had also enthralled Gemma. One was the way Auntie Mireya embraced her inner siren. The woman had been so free; she'd reveled in her sexuality. Another enticing thing for young Gemma had been the idea of a man's part slipping inside a woman. Finally, she had been able to see how things fit!

A day later, caught giggling and poking about the machine, Mireya had candidly explained to both Gemma and her daughter. The device was an adult sex aid.

Now at fifteen, Gemma watched her Dad settle the restaurant bill. She was unaware that something else had happened on peeking night. That night, Gemma had embraced her own inner siren, her budding sexuality.

As Gemma and her dads left the Long Island eatery, she whispered to Nannie. Gemma wished she'd already spent time with her friend. Gemma loved Arlise, but Gemma wanted to get home. Back on the isle of Karina Cay, she wanted to eagerly try out a few things with Jeremy.

She couldn't stop remembering their last night on the beach. During her time away, she re-lived her and Jeremy's kisses, among *other* things.

However, by the time she and her fathers returned home, Gemma received a surprise.

Brooding, strawberry blond Jeremy was gone.

Upon finding out, Gemma wanted to scream and cry. Managing to bravely hold herself together, she thanked his mom for letting her know.

Feeling for the tall yet coltish girl who was visibly saddened, petite Giselle stood in the grand foyer at Windsor Pines. Watching Gemma, Giselle realized. When Beau's daughter had been little, she'd been cute, like other kids. However, Giselle quickly cogitated. The tall, slender, shapely teenager's true beauty was *just now* beginning to unfurl.

What lovely skin Gemma had! And such graceful hands, Giselle mused, along with that gorgeously free, unprocessed brown-gold mane. Knowing Gemma would one day appear most striking, Giselle realized one thing. She could not wait to see Beau's daughter as an adult.

With her mind quickly returning to her son, the interior designer explained. Jeremy had felt that there wasn't much reason to hang around, with Gemma gone. "You know, *ma belle*," my beautiful, "for Jere, classes start within weeks, so...he returned to Montreal."

Feeling dejected, Gemma admitted she knew. She bent to hug Jeremy's diminutive but queenly mother. Turning away, Gemma did not say that a few weeks was all she and Jeremy would have needed to try out all the things she'd had in mind. Those curiously naughty things.

Walking stiffly away, deflated, Gemma thought, now all she could do was go find Heather. To her bestie, she would moan about unfairness.

Chapter 14

Ashlee remembered being Ursa. Leaving her little town, she rode through Durham, North Carolina. In many ways, leaving home had been hard. Although she had not been fully healed, she'd needed to scram.

While riding the northbound bus, Ashlee knew that Dr. Len, with the terrible comb-over, could not have been a real doctor. Still, when Ursa had needed the operation, she hadn't cared. So what, the doctor might have gotten his degree from an internet buy-here-pay-here place? Ursa had only felt excitement while looking at his before-'n-after photos because finally, she had been able to see, in color, her new life.

Soon, she'd mused, she'd have the 'tools' for a new existence. Then she could stop imagining life far away from Dr. Len's small office. Hers would be a life far from the disreputable holler—the low-lying secluded area at the mountain base—where she'd subsisted since birth. Soon, she'd thought, she would live a new life, one where she'd never again fight off men she did not want. She would also be able to thwart the pangs of hunger. She'd no longer have to sit quietly aside while Mam-maw acted the pig.

All of those things had made Ursa willing to gamble with her life. Sure, she knew the phony doctor could have killed her. If so, she'd told herself, then she would no longer need dreams, or new boobies, not if she was dead. So, either way, Ursa had thought, her life would change.

Back while contemplating her new existence, dreams of being someone's plaything because she *wanted* that spurred her on. When she had her new 'life tools,' Ursa had promised herself, never again would she swallow for one of Mam-maw's fat stinky boyfriends. Never again would she do it for her wild brothers' friends either, because as Ashlee Caro Durham, she would be elsewhere. She would have choices.

When 'Dr.' Len pressed his dick to Ursa's knee as she'd sat on the white butcher's paper in his tiny exam room, it hadn't bothered her very much. She was getting out. She knew his wasn't the thinner roll of paper like at the hospital. She had been there before. As Ursa, she'd been trying to outrun crazy Uncle Jed when she'd tripped, fallen, and broken her arm. Big jiggle-y Mam-maw with the heart condition had not wanted to spend money for the hospital. Griping, she'd gassed up the old Bonneville. Hating its sun-faded hood, nearly immobile, obese, Mam-maw had driven along, grumbling. She'd carped a few times that a one-armed girl would be of no use to her.

Forgetting her gran and Dr. Len's bogus paper, Ashlee recalled that as Ursa, she had only wanted him to fix her. For that, she could have endured almost anything. Ursa hadn't even cared that with no nurse present, the unattractive man had fondled her tiny ta-tas more than he'd examined them. As he did, an idea struck. What the heck, Ursa thought. Moments later, she opened her legs. As Dr. Len surged into her—all hot and sweaty—she explained that 'this' was his bonus, and Ursa had 'paid it in advance' to ensure he would do a good job on her the next day.

Then before the surgery, Ursa told herself, while the seedy doctor wrote all over her chest, that nothing was worse than being flat-chested.

Staring into the grimy mirror in the bus station restroom, Ashlee reminded herself. Without the right' tools,' a girl could not get ahead. That was why she had done what she had. Lawd knew that she had wanted out of that life when she'd been Ursa Blank. Now that she was no longer Ursa, Ashlee could go anywhere! In the grimy bus station mirror, she eyed her new boobs. In her skimpy clothes, she really did look hot. Therefore, *as Ashlee*, she would shamelessly use her fake tits to gain entry. Gazing at her nips, visible beneath her top, Ashlee wanted to forget. She no longer had feeling in her chestal area. But that was where faking it came in. The important thing was she was on her way!

She had left the North Carolina mountains behind.

In the bus station mirror, Ashlee eyed her new blond hair. She'd colored and cut it at Biffi's as the bigger girl's raunchy little nephews ran around. When they'd given her a frigging headache, she'd yowled, "Bif, how do yew stand it? They scream like banshees, and they break shit."

Ashlee forgot the hooligans. In the grimy glass, she looked at her teeth, now white. Her eyes were blue too, now. Heck, she looked good enough to be on TV! Maybe she should head for Hollywood. Lawd knew she could act. She had done so all her life. She'd made people believe she was fine and that she hadn't wanted more. She deserved an Oscar.

Knowing she hadn't much time before the bus took off again, Ashlee gingerly pulled up her shirt. She winced while looking at her swollen chest. It was still black and blue from all the cutting and stitching.

Trying to pull her shirt down without further aggravating the soreness, Ashlee didn't want to think about Dr. Len, abortionist and plastic surgeon, to the poor. Yet she couldn't help it. Patting her shirt at her midsection, she tried not to think about Mam-maw.

Indeed, by now, the older woman knew she'd skipped town. By now, Mam-maw was cursing Ursa seven ways to Sunday. Biggums probably told anyone who would listen, "That dang Ursa sho is one ungrateful little wench —running off like thet."

But Ursa was no more. *Ursa was Ashlee*, now, and Ashlee was *new*.

Ashlee found herself in Baltimore, where nothing went right. She had more dead-end jobs than she could count, and months of meaningless sexual encounters. Some were for pay, while there were others where she literally got beat. Then Ashlee met a man.

She figured he was gay because he didn't even try to get any. Well, that was fine with her. He mentioned a woman who lived in the D.C. area. The man said this woman helped young girls get on their feet. The-probably-gay man claimed he'd help get Ashlee to the woman in the District of Columbia. Ashlee began to believe he was the one Good Samaritan in the world.

Later, she learned. The probably-gay man was a headhunter—for runaway girls like her. He was paid to bring them to Mallory.

Mallory turned out to be a second-rate Madame. The busty woman housed, fed, and protected girls, but they had to earn their keep.

Mallory and the man were sex traffickers, Ashlee realized, too late.

Ashlee often woke, remembering the night she'd been dropped off at Ms. Mallory's... She'd slept like she hadn't in all of her fifteen years that night. However, the next day, summoned by the woman of the house, she'd been roused early. In an office done up in red brocade and too much frou-frou, Ashlee wound up standing before Ms. Mallory. Present, too, was a beautifully made-up Asian girl. China Doll. A massive black man, wearing a tiny open vest, stood watching. His shiny biceps and chest were so muscular that he nearly frightened Ashlee.

Before this assembly of three, Ashlee was told to remove her clothing. Aware that this was her 'inspection', she did as bid.

Upon seeing her breasts, with their mismatched stitch scars, the trio of onlookers shrank back. Clearly etched on each person's face was revulsion.

Feeling so ashamed, Ashlee wanted to cover herself. Really, she wanted to tear out of the room and the house, *but* she had no place to go. That she remembered. Therefore, she stood before Ms. Mallory and thought about Mam-maw. The older obese woman's granddaughter had willingly left. That was tantamount to the unforgivable. Even if she could return home, as Ursa, she would wind up alone, like now. Back there, Ursa would wind up a poor whore. Here though, Ashlee considered; with the peignoir-wearing Ms. Mallory and mean-eyed China Doll, Ashlee just might get paid for tricking; *if* Madame chose to take her on.

Finally, Mallory spoke. "Well, it'll cost me too much to fix—that." Mallory wiggled blood-red fingertips in the general direction of Ashlee's chest. "So, let's see..." The woman in the high-heeled slippers appeared to think. "You'll need a gimmick and a name." Her hard cold eyes stared into Ashlee's. "What do you do?"

Ashlee knew what the woman was asking. "I can lap dance."

Balanced on six-inch stilettos, China Doll derisively snorted.

Ashlee ignored her because living at Mam-maw's had prepared her for this, although she would never give up her dream of a different life. It was why Ashlee spoke with no trace of the southern twang with which she'd grown up. "I can take it in the front and back. I suck, I swallow—"

Mallory, with the pointy red nails, was not impressed. "Ya talk dirty?"

"Yes."

"You toss the salad?"

Ashlee was momentarily stumped. "Come again?"

"Butt. Male behind. You eat it?"

Ashlee swallowed the lump in her throat. "I can."

It was harshly asked, "Do you, or not?"

"Shut up, China," Mallory ordered, flicking her wrist and managing to hit the girl in the face all at once.

Gathering her courage, Ashlee replied, "Yes, I toss the salad." If she had to, she would be better than that Asian cunt. That was a promise because Ashlee was tired of people looking down on her, especially those who weren't white. They were beneath her, Mam-maw said.

"Then China will teach you other techniques," Mallory decided, to the Asian girl's dismay; clearly, China Doll felt threatened.

"But whatcha gonna call her?" the too-muscular African-American man asked, staring at Ashlee's scars, courtesy of Dr. Len.

Mallory remained silent as her eyes narrowed. "I don't know, Black. Stitches? Tracks?" Mallory had asked no one in particular, but all the same, Ashlee blushed with shame from her torso to her temples.

"Why not," Mallory asked, thinking aloud, "dress her in white? We'll call her *Bride*, for some of our...uh, more discerning patrons."

At that moment, Ashlee could have screamed because Mallory could not have hurt her more if the woman had knifed her. Bravely hiding tears, Ashlee told herself to forget what the busty woman meant. Still, the very notion stung. Ashlee had seen Mam-Maw's old horror movies, so she knew. Due to her stitches and disfigurement, she would become the whorehouse's *Bride* of Frankenstein.

As anger choked hurt, Ashlee recalled Dr. Len. That probably wasn't even his real name! All those before-'n-after photos, she recalled, they were fakes! Indeed, the photos weren't that man's work. Suddenly, Ashlee hated the 'doctor' who had messed up her body.

She hated everyone else who had ever done her wrong, too.

Still, new Ashlee was determined to become the girl of choice for Mallory's clients, those with kinkier appetites. So Ashlee sucked it up and pressed the hurt down, deep inside her, just like always.

Shortly after that, Ashlee even made good on her vow.

When China Doll became aware that some customers were choosing 'The Bride' over her, China became enraged.

Aware of the other girl's feelings, Ashlee almost smiled. Maybe now Mallory's pet knew how her blond rival felt, every single day.

Ashlee's upset knew no end.

Chapter 15

Jeremy and Gemma didn't see one another again until the summer they were seventeen, and both felt they had grown apart. Gemma mentioned it to Heather while sitting in *Splendid Choco-Latte*, their favorite haunt.

The lean athletic redhead, with her long hair in a French braid, dismissively waved. "I've seen you and Jeremy together, so I know you two could never grow apart. Love like you guys' doesn't dwindle, no matter how much time you spend apart."

"You're basing that on what, Heather G? The fact that when we were kids, we were drawn to each other?" Gemma shook her head. "I think we've finally outgrown that."

"So you're saying you don't still think about him?" Heather leaned forward. "You don't dream about him or wish he were here?"

Gemma schooled her expression to mask the truth. She'd learned that in acting class. Her dad had insisted she go if she wanted to follow him into the business. "Can't have you unprepared," he'd stated. Forgetting him, Gemma glanced at her besie, who would soon leave the island.

At the summer's end, Heather would become a lay assistant and work at a pet clinic on the mainland. To become a veterinarian, Heather Garrahan had years of schooling ahead of her. She'd need to obtain a bachelor's degree, and a Doctor of Veterinary Medicine – a D.V.M. – degree from an accredited college.

Therefore, Gemma knew she and Heather would no longer see a lot of each other. Just thinking about it hurt because boy, would Gemma miss her childhood friend! About the same amount that she missed Jeremy.

Before Gemma knew it, she'd said as much.

"See?" Wrinkling her nose liberally sprinkled with freckles, Heather clapped. "I knew it! I'm going to wind up in you guys' wedding."

"Just because I'll miss you—the way I miss our other cohort," Gemma began, "doesn't mean there's more to it. That was puppy love. Now Jere's off, Lord knows where, and I'm off to New York." There Gemma would model and finish high school with a tutor. That had been her parents' stipulation since her modeling career was on the upswing.

"It's almost like we don't know each other the same way anymore."

"Well, don't look now," Heather spoke through her teeth. "Do *not* look, Gem, but Puppy Love just walked through the door."

Four evenings later, Gemma sat out back of DeVeaux House. In a journal, she listed all her tasks for the coming week. Glancing up, she saw Jeremy. Off in the distance, he was on the boardwalk. Opposite him, the sun's lingering rays were but a peach smear on the darkened ocean.

Gemma had watched Jeremy earlier. Out on the bay, he'd ridden waves. Then he'd strode about, like the son of Poseidon. She'd had to admit, Jeremy no longer appeared the cute little doll. Taller, he was about to pass her house. His hair was sun-bleached, and he was built, not too much, but he appeared nicely ripped.

Before Gemma knew it, she'd risen. On the brick path, she called out. Of course, Jeremy could not hear her over the ocean's roar. Yet, in the twilight, he had seen candles. They flickered on her father's cozy porch, so he slowed his pace. Returning from hanging out with blond Jay, surfer dude, who lived a few properties down, Jeremy thought of Gemma. He often did. On this evening, he also saw her. In his mind, she lay beneath him, moaning with pleasure, as he had his way with her.

She called his name. Jeremy squinted and turned. That sounded real. Oh, it was; she had been on the porch out back.

In swim shorts, Jeremy left the boardwalk that would have taken him past DeVeaux House. Veering right, he met Gemma on the still-warm sun-baked bricks. In the gloaming, that magical time when day turns to night, he noticed that she wore only a tank top and a pair of shorts.

Seeing his eyes roam her, Gemma recalled her lack of clothing. She and Jeremy exchanged greetings. Both barefoot, they headed up to her home. He asked why she had been sitting in the near dark, alone.

She didn't say she never felt alone, not since Nannie had transitioned. Gemma said her dads were at an eatery, and longtime housekeeper, Ina, was off. Thus, with the place to herself, Gemma was making a list.

Jeremy nodded, "You always would do that."

"You remember." She held back her billowing cloud of hair.

His voice was soft but no less compelling when he admitted, "There's not much about you, Gem, that I have forgotten."

Forcing herself to breathe, Gemma listened as Jeremy mentioned how he, Jay, and summerhouse Lance had been in the water moments before.

Climbing the steps to the porch, Gemma admitted having seen them. Forgetting the members of the next gen cohorts, she said she could smell the ocean on Jeremy. In her mind, she could almost taste the salt on his skin. In fact, she mused, she often thought of him as the son of the sea.

Seating himself in the DeVeaux's inviting outdoor room, Jeremy told Gemma the truth. "You're still in my dreams." In French, he acknowledged, "I still feel about you like *grand-père* felt about *her.*"

Gemma knew Jeremy meant his grandfather and the priestess.

In English, he added, "You bewitch me like she did him. The only difference is *I* don't have a problem with touching. I *want* to touch you. Here," his fingers skimmed her shoulder, her collarbone; "and here..." He found her pulse-point. Then beneath her breast, he cupped her rib cage. His eyes were fastened on her. "I want to touch you everywhere."

Jeremy's fingers curled around Gemma's back to bring her forward. He breathed words into her mouth. "I *ache* for you, Gemma. Kiss me."

Unable to speak, she could only obey, and he took over. Their lips meeting was so sweet that Gemma felt she would melt. Afterward, she admitted, "I hate that I couldn't really talk to you at the café."

"You were with Red." Jeremy brushed the apology aside. "Anyway, had you not been, perhaps I would have done this." He kissed her again.

"Then rumors would've started," Gemma knowingly stated.

"I care not." Jeremy stood. Pulling Gemma up, he splayed one hand over her abdomen. "I only want to be in you." He slid his hand down. "I want to be between your female lips, in your flowery parts."

She chuckled. "My flowery parts. Really, Jere?"

He silenced her with another delicious kiss. "*Oui.*" Jeremy slid his middle finger into her heat despite her shorts, which were more like panties. "I want you to open, for me, like a flower unfurls for the sun."

Remaining silent, Gemma loved when he spoke to her the same way he had often written about her, from his heart. Yet she played coy, telling Jeremy he wasn't supposed to say those things to her.

"Why –because now you too suffer from some type of misplaced American morality? The kind that says sexuality and wanting is wrong."

"You're so international, Jere." Gemma held his hand in place, "But no, I said that because you're making me want—you. Feel that?"

Indeed, he felt moisture through the cotton of her shorts, and hungrily he kissed her. "Then we shall have those things, *bébé*, and more."

Suddenly she needed to know. "Why didn't you come to me before now?" She knew there were women and girls on the island itching to get at him, and the thought that he preferred to spend time with them rankled.

Improbable

"Don't pout, *ange.*" Releasing his angel and looking away from her, Jeremy didn't know if he should tell or withhold the truth.

"Four evenings in a row," he began, deciding to apprise Gemma, "I passed your home. Each night, I thought of climbing in your window."

Gemma slowly rose. She bent to extinguish candles. Then she slid the kitchen's glass doors open. "Wait here," she said and slipped inside.

Jeremy eyed her long shapely legs and the hips that called to him. He wanted to touch the luscious bum that jiggled a bit when she walked. Suddenly, he hoped she hadn't gone to pull on more clothing.

Turning, Jeremy heard something. Scraping? Faintly, he also heard Gemma calling his name. Rising, he descended the porch steps while she called again. On a grassy path, he followed her voice.

Looking up, he saw her silhouetted in her open bedroom window. He could also feel the air conditioning, as in cozy lamplight, she beckoned.

Careful not to crush an azalea bush, Jeremy hoisted himself up. When he entered, Gemma reminded him. "You wanted to climb in my window, Harden." She baited him, "You're in. Now, what do you want?"

Jeremy blinked, and in the lamplight, his storm-colored eyes appeared confused. "I'm inside your house. Not you."

Staring at him, Gemma could barely breathe. All the air had been sucked from her room with Jeremy there. She took a seat. Facing Jeremy, Gemma again realized he was no longer a soft kid. He was attractive, tan, and muscular, with thick, sun-gilded wavy hair—that was a little too long but oh so sexy. About five-ten, he was nearly a man. The thought thrilled Gemma.

Jeremy stared and noticed Gemma's nipples. They'd become taut little peaks protruding through her tank top. He pulled her from her bed, realizing she was no longer a precocious kid. He ruminated that she was nearly a woman, and a most alluring one.

"You want me," he whispered. In Montreal, he had seen the look enough times to know. When Gemma didn't argue but clicked off her lamp, Jeremy wound up on his knees in the rising moon's light.

Aiding the removal of her top, he watched as Gemma lowered her arms. He could only stare at her creamy, full, café au lait breasts. He longed to taste her rosy nipples and have their sweetness against his lips.

"Where," he reverently inquired, running his hands up her sides, "did you get *these*?" He cupped Gemma's bounty, and with practiced fingertips, he encircled the distended tips.

Feeling most beautiful, Gemma shrugged as Jeremy hooked his large hands in the delicate sides of her shorts. "They came with the package."

He slipped her shorts down. Watching as Gemma stepped from them, Jeremy felt like he had never seen anything more erotic. Remaining on his knees, he slid his hands up her legs to the outsides of her thighs. "*Mon Dieu*," My God, "you're gorgeous," he breathed, squeezing her.

"You too," she replied and stunned him when she admitted on a sigh, "*How* I want you. I always have. Since the night that we…"

He winked. "Good, because it can't be any more than I want you."

She placed her hands over his, on her flared hips. Clasping his fingers, she tugged, and he stood. Gemma whispered, "I like it, Jere, that your head only comes to my chest." She placed her arms around him.

"Me too," he murmured, "because I can do this." He suckled first one sweet breast and then the other. With hands splayed on her back, he urged her forward and more into his mouth.

Reaching for one of his hands, Gemma placed it between them and angled his fingers downward, into wet and warmth.

In the moonlight, Jeremy's eyes became opaque, darkened by desire.

Gemma felt powerful and most womanly. Undoing Jeremy's shorts, she found him thick and ready beneath. "But you had on Speedos…"

He didn't respond, only placed her smaller hand about his length.

"I'll bet I got my tits the same place you got *this*." With her hand, she wrapped him more tightly. "Man, Harden," she exclaimed, barely waiting to sample him, "I never dreamed you'd get so big."

"I never dreamed *you'd* grow so, either." He fondled a plump breast with one hand before licking its tip. "—Or so beautiful."

Dipping her head, Gemma kissed Jeremy. The teenager murmured against his soft hot mouth that tasted of cream and secrets. "I'll ask you again. What would you do once you're in, Harden?"

He walked her backward to the en suite bathroom door. Then shifting slightly, he pressed his rod to her thigh while sliding his hands around to squeeze her bottom. Not letting go, he maneuvered to lave one areola, the cloud that surrounded a nipple. "I'll ask *you* again." He spoke between sucks, "If I was inside you, or your window?"

Gemma sounded breathless. "You're already in the window, Harden."

"But not inside you." Jeremy probed her from the rear with practiced fingertips while using his rod to poke her in front. "Not yet."

Forced to widen her stance, Gemma gasped as fingers opened her. Into Jeremy's mouth, she again gasped. What trickery? He used those same fingers to explore and arouse her even more.

Hoisting Gemma, Jeremy ordered, "Wrap me with your legs, *bébé*."

Gemma obeyed and held on. His lips covered hers, and Jeremy swallowed the mewls that meant she felt the nudge, then the push. He surged upward, and Gemma moaned, feeling his rigid invasion. Allowing her head to loll, she enjoyed Jeremy kissing the column of her neck.

Wiggling to receive more of him, Gemma licked lush lips, a provocative sight. "OK, Harden, you're inside—me." So excited that she could barely breathe, she inquired, "Now what?"

Gemma felt Jeremy's smile. "I'm going to rock your world."

"I hate to admit it," she gasped as he ignited more within her, "but you really are one hung son of a—"

"Shhh," Jeremy cautioned. "We'll find a better use for that pretty mouth."

"You sure?" Gemma asked, holding on as Jeremy pumped.

Moving within and increasingly causing Gemma to moan, Jeremy nodded. "Totally."

Enjoying his every thrust, teenaged Gemma sounded breathless when she murmured, "Cock sure, I'll bet."

Chapter 16

Ashlee had to service the boy again. Well, he really wasn't a boy. He had been, back when he'd initially been brought to Ms. Mallory's whorehouse. He'd been timid, too, so Ashlee wasn't chosen for him.

However, after becoming a regular, the young man wanted more. Therefore, he sought *The Bride*. He appeared once, sometimes twice a month. Sometimes, he actually talked to Ashlee. Sensing she was alone in the world, he told her he was, too. He told her his fantasies. It was her job to make them come true. He did not tell her he dreamed of having his own bride, one who wore what she wore. He liked her veil and transparent 'gowns' with the cut-out cups that showcased her scarred tits. Her garter belt, lace-top stockings, and heels made him horny. However, being a pimply-faced geek, he didn't divulge all of that. He didn't want her to laugh, although he didn't think Bride would. As he lay in the dimness, allowing her to pleasure him, the young man felt he was growing to love Bride. He wasn't supposed to; he was being fanciful and stupid; he'd been called that all his life. He knew she was a working girl, but he couldn't help himself, so he brought her a gift.

When she opened the little box, he held his breath.

Although Ashlee had an idea, as she parted tissue folds, she asked, "What is this?"

When she was told, she remembered. The pimple face worked at some gourmet coffee and fancy teashop on The Hill. Supposedly, it was where many lawmaker's assistants fetched them expensive tea leaves and such. Ashlee didn't care. She hated the rich. She wasn't one of them. It looked like she never would be because she had no plan. She hadn't yet thought of how to leave Ms. Mallory's and still move up in the world.

Nevertheless, she was sick and tired of the horizontal life. Ashlee knew though, that an idea would strike. Then she would be on her way. Until then, she would enjoy Pimple's gift.

Pleased to know she'd try it, he told her there was more.

Later Ashlee asked for more. "If you can get it," she slyly threw in. She asked questions, and Pimple was glad to answer. He grew things. Cannabis, he divulged, was not the only plant that could get people high. He said he had a vine from South Asia in his cramped apartment. His unique plant had 'Hawaiian' in the name, and the seeds had hallucinogenic properties. "Still, to extract the hallucinogen is considered illegal." Pimple was overjoyed upon hearing Bride's next question.

"Have you done it?" She averted her eyes. "The illegal part?"

He gazed at her scarred and stitched chest that made her special to him. "I have." Pimple got hard anticipating her next question.

"Does it work, the extraction stuff?"

"It does. Actually," he confided, "it's LSD's forerunner."

Ashlee's eyes actually glowed. "So it has *psychedelic* effects?" She asked because her brothers had stumbled upon something similar. They'd started growing it for manufacture just before she'd fled Mam-maw's. Remembering gave her an idea. It was why she said, "I'd like to try it."

"I don't know…" Pimple hesitated. "It's pretty potent."

"Please?" Ashlee whispered. She said she'd do 'that thing' he liked for free. "Just get me some of the Hawaiian LSD stuff. Okay?"

Pimple would have done it for no charge if she'd asked, but now *he* would get something. He knew there was a reason he liked Bride.

Each day, Ashlee grew sicker of China Doll's high-handedness and her snide remarks. Due to China's cattiness, nearly all the girls in the cathouse despised her. Nonetheless, Mallory didn't care, maybe because the mean little Asian girl was her pet.

Just before 'showtime,' for a moment away from China and her yammering, the girls smoked out behind the house of ill repute. Madame hated that. Mallory didn't want her girls doing drugs—other than those she provided. She didn't want them lacing their cigarettes with stuff they'd gotten elsewhere. Again, she'd given her speech, saying no one in the cathouse was to put foreign substances into their bodies.

"What a crock," Ashlee told another girl whose brain seemed nearly fried. "Dicks and semen are foreign substances if yew wanna get technical. Heck, we weren't born with those—or men's tongues—in our bodies." Ashlee expected a laugh, but the other girl just blankly stared.

Closing her eyes, Ashlee took a pull and let the heat from her cigarette cascade down her throat. Opening her eyes, she saw China Doll.

"Gimme some," the house pet commanded.

Ashlee's eyes narrowed, but she handed over her done-up cig.

After puffing, China appeared mellow. "That's good stuff, Bride."

Bride. Out came the claws. Ashlee hated that name, almost as much as she hated slanty-eyes who believed she was the top kitty. Ashlee thought, feeling the anger that never quite left her; she'd show China.

Unaware, China Doll greedily asked, "Yo, you got more of this?"

Inspiration struck, and Ashlee retracted her claws. "I can get it..."

The next time she saw Pimple from the fancy teashop, Ashlee asked him to fulfill a 'specialty' order. Then while Ashlee waited, China Doll—who was Vietnamese—spoke high-handedly. "Get me the stuff I asked for, and hurry it up. Bitch."

Ashlee smiled. It wasn't pretty, but for once, she felt something other than the anger that was her constant companion. "Okay, China."

The pimply-faced young man did as Ashlee asked. He threw in a little wormwood. Ashlee knew about it from home; it was a perennial, an herb, with pale yellow flowers. Mam-maw, the trailer park's continual gardener, said people used the flowers to make pain reliever. With all her useless knowledge, Mam-maw had said the plant was poisonous and could only be used in small doses. Mam-maw, who had a heart condition, knew about wormwood oil, a cardiac stimulant. She'd claimed 'illegals' often smoked wormwood. Mam-maw said those who weren't like her and Ashlee used the dried form, with weed, to get a higher high.

Suddenly, Ashlee's eyes widened because *that* was what her brothers had been growing before she'd left their raggedy little town. Now she, too, had a plan! Feeling darn good, Ashlee pretended to share new stuff with the other girls, but she kept the wormwood back. She reminded them of the cathouse rules; no foreign substances. She laughed, saying the girls had to keep it hush-hush. She knew word would get back to China Doll—who would want in. Then top kitty would get 'the special,' Ashlee's volatile mix of weed, Hawaiian whatever, *and* wormwood.

Ashlee would then see if the top kitty could handle it.

Mallory was furious! Despite her girls playing dumb, she *would* find out who'd dealt the coke-laced cigarettes. Those little stunts couldn't outwit her, and she would make them pay! With her, they had it good. If they were elsewhere, with a daddy or even one of them new little pimp-wannabes, her tricks would be dead or beaten, every day. If the cunts weren't with her, they'd get *more* beatings than those she sometimes had administered. A pimp would beat them at will when Mallory only had big Black do it to keep the girls in line.

Angered, Mallory told a different minion, "Go search those rooms." Mallory's employees knew why. Madame deemed it necessary because someone had lured China Doll out back, promising something new. Now she was upstairs, under doctor's care, which was friggin' expensive. Currently, China incoherently muttered about some 'good stuff.'

Downstairs, pacing her over-decorated red brocade office, Mallory couldn't believe China. How was China so stupid? Mallory couldn't believe the girl had such a weak constitution, too. How could a cigarette, sprinkled most likely with dandelions, cause China to lose her mind? The cunt was costing Mallory money, when she should have been making money. Upstairs, China was hot, then cold, and agitated. True, she had been on her back for a few days, but she wasn't making money!

In turn, Mallory was agitated. She pondered the stupid dream that China kept yammering about. How many times did Mallory have to say it? The kid-sellers were no longer after China; she was an adult now.

What in the world? The busty woman crossed the red carpet. Pulling back heavy drapes, she swore because it had sounded like a car hit something.

Hearing more commotion, Mallory whirled. With a hand on her drapes, she intended to reprimand whoever had burst into her office. Angry words died as big Black, and one of the girls jostled. Out of breath, both shouted, but Mallory had not heard right. There could not be an accident outside her brownstone—involving China Doll! China could not have run into the street thinking the kid-sellers were after her, again.

"Nooo!" Mallory howled. "This can *not* be happening!"

Standing just outside the Madame's office, Ashlee believed it was. She had one dispassionate thought. *Oops*, no more fake China fer us.

Chaos reigned as the cathouse front door stood wide. Outside, blue and red lights flashed. Neighbors huddled and gawked. In the descending dark, bottled blond Ashlee sauntered down the steps to join others.

They'd seen the house pet. Bleeding from every orifice, she was carried away, with an emergency medical sheet pulled up. It covered the face and head.

Without emotion, Ashlee blinked her new blue eyes. Guess China Doll had issues, Ashlee mused. Guess Chinka Bitch jest couldn't handle 'the special.' Oh, well, she asked for it. Ashlee shook her head, tsk-tsk.

Chapter 17

Jeremy was in his third-semester *à l'université* in France. There, he had an apartment in the 5th *arrondissement*. In The Latin Quarter, it was located in the *Rue Monge*. He liked taking the lift up to the second floor. The stately building was located in a residential neighborhood with narrow cobblestone streets, his being named after a French mathematician. Twenty-year-old Jeremy liked the area where many buildings were from the 19th century. He used shops and services needed by other Parisians, the *boulangeries* and *boucheries*, bakeries and butchers; he frequented wine stores and produce markets. Jeremy loved a short ride on the Metro. He'd visited the Pantheon. Built in 1757 it sat atop the *Montagne Sainte-Geneviève*—Saint Genevieve's mountain. A tourist attraction, even at present, it still functioned as a church. *Rue Mouffetard* was one of Paris' oldest and liveliest streets. Jeremy loved it, with its plethora of restaurants, shops, cafés, and regular open market.

Whenever he and Gemma got the chance, they explored other streets, searching for bars and boutiques. They whiled away the hours on restaurant terraces; other times, they people-watched. Jeremy liked that once when Gemma had been in Paris for a photoshoot, they'd stolen a day, just for themselves. In the dark of the morning, they'd made copious amounts of love, trying to make up for all the months spent apart.

While within *une copine's* body, Jeremy had whispered sexy suggestions, which they'd tried. Afterward, he'd dashed out of doors. Swiftly, returning, he'd offered large steaming cups of *café crème*, deliciously strong coffee laced with hot cream. Having no need for food, the couple drank as morning sunlight slanted over them. Trading kisses and caresses, the sight of their sleek young bodies aroused. Sighing and arching to meet each other, thrust for thrust, between sex sessions, they drowsed. Later that evening, Jeremy took Gemma to a tattered old collegiate haunt. There they listened to live jazz.

Seated on Jeremy's lap, Gemma eyed poster-covered walls. Sighing, she said she simply adored the freedom she always experienced while in Paris. "Here, I always feel waves of romantic intrigue." She asked didn't Jeremy feel the vibes of young people who'd visited or lived there decades ago, too. "I'll bet, Gemma whispered, "they enjoyed travel and *amour* as much as we do."

Jeremy, who seemed moodier than usual, acknowledged the feeling of freedom. "I like it here, instead of being back home," he revealed. "Here, I don't have to keep hearing about my responsibilities." Then squeezing Gemma's hand, Jeremy kissed her ferociously. In the dimness, his eyes appeared stormy, "*But* don't mistake *ange*; I do not want *us* to want freedom from each other."

Jeremy said so because it was becoming more noticeable; Gemma had a light that drew people. In the last couple of years, her modeling career had skyrocketed. Jeremy could not go anywhere, especially not in Paris, without seeing her likeness. When the couple managed to steal a few moments, Jeremy could not help but notice; men of all nationalities watched Gemma. They openly ogled her, while some even disregarded him in their efforts to gain her attention.

Because he had again mentioned such things, Gemma took Jeremy's hand. In the dimness, she guided it to the inviting flesh beneath her top. On Jeremy's lap, she sensually moved. Turning to place her lips on his, she murmured. "I like that you feel that way, Jere because I don't want freedom from 'us' either."

Although Gemma did not say it, it wasn't like she'd failed to notice. Fashionable women vied for Jeremy's attention, and French girl students sought his tempestuous gaze. Attempting to attract him, it was apparent that they longed to lie with the beautiful man with the mercurial moods.

Nobody's fool; Gemma knew some chic women got that chance. Sexy Jeremy wasn't a eunuch, and she wasn't often present. However, when she and he were together, it was common knowledge. Jeremy was hers, alone. Therefore, with her lips yet on his, Gemma reassured him. "I only want *you*, Jere—right now—as a matter of fact."

Weighing and fondling her beneath her top, Jeremy thought of spreading Gemma's beautiful brown thighs. He thought of parting her womanly curtain, as he had earlier.

Unaware of Jeremy's thoughts, Gemma reminded him of the morning when she would leave. Flying to Budapest, she would meet her glam squad and photographer.

Jeremy sighed because, for him, study called. Rising from the sofa where they'd been nestled, he knew such was their life right now. As budding adults, they were matriculating through school and starting careers. Therefore, Jeremy didn't want to waste time, not when he'd grown stiff with desire. Succulently kissing Gemma, he suggested going.

As the couple rushed back to *Rue Monge*, Jeremy told Gemma he wanted to suck her *seins*. Aware that she loved it when he talked dirty, he told her he would move down her body. He'd use his tongue to enter her, thereby getting her glistening and gloriously wet. He further said he would use his lengthy fat cock to enter her quivering, hot, juicy twat.

Unable to wait, the pair dipped into an alley. There, both excitedly tore at clothing. Quickly, they kissed and coupled like common street urchins. All of those things Jeremy remembered. And he almost smiled, thinking about *grand-père*. If that old man could have seen his *heir*, near-nude, screwing against a wall on a dark street.

Now, Jeremy recalled, whenever she had downtime, Gemma was back home. She returned to their little island. Like him, she carried a full college course load, so she crammed for exams. Then when it was time, she jetted away for another modeling gig.

That, Jeremy didn't mind, but he did mind the stories. He heard them all the way across the Atlantic and the English Channel. Nowadays, Gemma spent more and more time with Sheriff Macaw's son. Trip.

On Karina Cay, curly-haired Colin, Jeremy's closest cohort and a reliable source, saw Gemma and the sheriff, as did others.

Prowling his Parisian apartment, Jeremy knew. Being a student at one of the most prestigious *grande écoles* in France meant he should have been studying. But he could not get Gemma off his mind. Jeremy couldn't help but ponder the man who was a little older than she.

Trip was married, right? He'd been a cop in Houston. That was what Jeremy's sources claimed. Well, if so, why wasn't Trip still on the mainland? Why wasn't he running down criminals—in Texas? Why was the man back on the island where he, too, had grown up?

What Jeremy really wanted to know was…what was between Gemma and Trip? Why were they hanging out?

Why indeed.

Jeremy knew what Trip was after—because most men wanted the same thing from the international sexy lingerie model. Jeremy included.

Chapter 18

The day came when Ashlee wanted to leave D.C.

Mallory told her to go. The woman looked haggard, and worn.

Noticing, Ashlee guessed busty had loved China Doll, in a way. The woman sure didn't love any of the other girls, and she especially didn't seem to feel much more than contempt for Ashlee. However, the blonde couldn't dwell on that.

Ashlee thought of Pimple; he would miss her. She would forget him. She had not gone through all she had, to get tangled up with the likes of him. He was poor. Soon the woman who sat in her gaudy red office, tapping her red-tipped fingers, a habit Ashlee despised, would also be a distant memory.

Reminding Ashlee of what she told all her tricks, the amazon didn't deign to look up at the blue-eyed chick. "I won't chase you."

Mallory told her girls they had a good thing with her. She told them that most couldn't make it alone. She also promised them that some would return within months of leaving her, while others would wind up dead. If they didn't, Mallory promised, they'd wish they were.

Rolling her eyes, Ashlee turned to go. She mouthed Mallory's following sentence right along with her. "Black will accompany you to your room."

Mallory added, "He and Robin will make sure you take from my house only what you bought while here." Then the old crone scornfully added, "You'll be back."

Nope, Ashlee thought. She could make it on her own. She had already proved that. And never again would she be made into a freak.

Gemma's modeling career was still on the upswing, but, she explained to her sister, she had an upcoming *acting* gig. Gemma said that maybe she would make a friend or two in acting, unlike in the bitchy modeling business.

Founding her own scented candles business, pint-sized Belize said what she always did. "You're attractive, Munch. Rule one: expect hate."

During one of her and Heather's infrequent conversations about similar things, Gemma admitted to missing her redheaded friend.

"I miss you too, booby," porcelain-skinned Heather moaned.

"Then meet me at home soon. I've got the January blues—you know, now that the holidays are over." Gemma revealed that she'd have a three-day hiatus later in the month. "I'd love it if I could see you."

"No can do, Girlie—as Chef JerRell calls you." Heather reminded Gemma that she worked an internship. After class at veterinary college, she went to the pet clinic. "But if you really do go home, maybe you can get with Puppy Love..."

Thinking of Jeremy, who attended an elite academic institution, Gemma chuckled. "Highly improbable," she said. She and Jeremy were busy getting their budding careers off the ground. Their schedules rarely meshed. "Still Heath, I miss him like crazy."

"Sounding like that, Gem, I know what you miss."

Both young women yowled with laughter before redheaded Heather predicted, "You guys'll get it in at some point. Oh, and when you do, go easy on him, girl. —Ooh, I gotta run, but let me tell you this. I saw you and Puppy Love in online photos. You guys were at an HIV awareness event. You looked hot, girl! And he's always sexy...Mmm."

"Yeah, hang up," Gemma chided. "Be good to the kitties! Love you."

Heather made kissing noises, "Hugs, kisses, 'n love to you—byee!"

Disconnected, Gemma thought about calling Jeremy, who was always coming or going, or in one of his moods. Bah, she waved. She told Nannie that she'd let him text her. Then Trip Macaw crossed her mind.

The man was at least a decade older. Still, Gemma hoped to see him when she went to the island home that her fathers now infrequently visited, although sweet motherly Ina was still there. Gemma would love to see the lawman, even if Jeremy didn't make it home. The truth was, she liked flirting with the deputy. It was why she sometimes went into town. She was sure Trip liked seeing her. Sure, he had a wife, somewhere, but Mr. Virile and the Mrs. had to know, Trip had swag.

One day while seated in class at Pantheon-Sorbonne University, Jeremy realized why depression often plagued him. His dark moods stemmed from the fact that he resented primogeniture. It was the custom of families passing land, or an entire estate, down to the firstborn son.

Although he was the youngest, due to his primogenitor—*grand-père*—Jeremy would inherit. That had been the old man's wish. Since he'd been a boy, Jeremy had known that one day, he would oversee and grow his maternal family holdings, the Windsor-Baptiste fortune. Just because he had been born male, he would do so. Sure, Jeremy's parents,

Giselle and M. T. Harden had daughters. Jeremy's sisters were older than he, but tag, he—*the male*—was *it*. That Jeremy resented.

He had not minded that every summer, he'd worked in his father's business. Jeremy knew that he'd be expected to helm the Home Wares empire one day as well. But Michael T. Harden, his dad, enjoyed his work. Hopefully, the man could do so for years to come. Jeremy prayed for that while feeling as though he really had no choices in life. His friends could choose their own career paths, but he could not.

Still, like him, surfer Jay, summerhouse Lance, and curly-haired Colin did well in school. But they had chosen their fields of study.

Was he jealous of the young men he had known since they were boys? Jeremy didn't think so; they were his greatest friends. Since he had a hard time letting people in, they were his only true friends—them and Gemma and red-haired Heather. Jeremy loathed that once people found out who he was, they wanted something. He'd learned that most people's desires always won out, if he waited long enough. Still, his cohorts were different. Thinking about them caused Jeremy to call the fellas. Wearing a leather jacket and a muffler wound about his neck, he conferenced Colin and Jay. On his way back to *Rue Monge*, they added Lance.

Before anyone could ask about school, Jeremy said he didn't want to discuss it. He simply wanted to see about getting together.

Summerhouse Lance mentioned skiing in Vale. Surfer, Jay, mentioned riding waves, which caused everyone to sputter with laughter.

"Ah, mate," Lance called, "you will always mention surfing."

Curly-haired Colin said he had to go, so nothing was settled. However, they would all speak again, and Jeremy felt his dark cloud lift. A little bit. Plans, he knew, would be firmed up sooner rather than later.

On Karina Cay, Deputy Trip Macaw took the call. "Hey, girl." For the moment, he was glad to leave the office and paperwork.

Gemma said she just wanted to know how things were going at home.

"Well, I ride by your house. I even walk the grounds. Saw Ms. Ina, this week. She was out and about, and she insisted everything's fine."

Bundled in a waffle weave robe, Gemma tried not to wince as her hairdresser wielded a dryer. The woman simultaneously pulled a brush through Gemma's lengthy hair. At her makeup artist's command, Gemma looked downward, and she felt him sweep liner onto her top lid as she spoke. "Trip, thanks, but I meant, how are things with *you*?"

The caramel-brown bear of a man felt warmed inside. Gemma was a beautiful woman. Like his wife. However, unlike his estranged wife, who was a cold fish lately, Gemma cared about Trip, even though the lingerie model had blown up and was now internationally known.

Trip's wife had stopped caring when they left Houston. Back there, he'd been a celebrated law officer. Wifey had been well-known, too, a social butterfly. On the small island of Karina Cay, where her husband had grown up, wifey knew no one. Not wishing to know any Karinians, despite the deputy wanting her to feel at home, wifey hightailed it away.

Recalling that Gemma was yet on the line, Trip revealed, "Some people don't like that I've thrown my name in the hat to become sheriff."

Gemma knew he was referring to his spouse, among others.

"Some don't care that the job is mostly administrative and less dangerous, in a few cases, than prior positions I've held." Trip sighed. "Guess if I got the job, the wheels would finally fall off this thing."

Gemma did not allow her eyes to widen. Her makeup artist was transforming her. Wisely, too, Gemma said nothing about the deputy's currently missing spouse. Yet Gemma harked back to, "That's right, Trip. Your dad," the current sheriff, "will soon retire."

"Well, look at that," the deputy sounded surprised. "You remembered; big international sex goddess like you."

Gemma smiled and reminded Trip, "People remember those they love." And she truly did love him. She found the big, gruff, caramel-brown man easy to talk to; he was protective. He had been, ever since her teen years. Knowing they hadn't much time, Gemma mentioned being home soon. "I'd love to see you—in that sexy uniform," she teased. She liked the way Trip wore his utilitarian belt slung low on his hips." Mmm, she thought, she did so adore a man with swagger.

Trip said he would like to hang out if he could. He didn't mention it, but he appreciated that, unlike his wife, Gemma understood. Duty was his first love. His priority.

Ashlee, who had once been Ursa, got a job waiting tables at a British-type pub. In New Haven, Connecticut, the rotund manager had not wanted to hire her. For some reason, he'd disliked her on sight. Knowing it caused her to feel ever-present anger. However, during her interview, she tamped her anger down to mention blowing the man. Then open mouth, open sesame.

Ashlee worked at the dimly lit bar 'n grill, tricking on the side. Why not? The college kids from the nearby university—whose parents had money—drank there, and Ashlee deemed them little snots. Some groped the wait staff, so Ashlee supplemented her pitiful pay.

Ashlee even met a guy. Somewhat tall, he had dark hair. The young college man came in a few times a week. He always chose her table. Ashlee said nothing when he put a hand up her short skirt, part of her uniform. She only widened her stance, a clear invitation.

Accepting, the college man fondled Ashlee's naked buns, then he dipped fingers inside her. The next time, when his hand crept up under her skirt, Ashlee imprisoned it with her thighs. Then she took way too long getting his and the other guys' orders. She didn't even breathe hard when he impudently finger-effed her. Later, she met him out back. With trash all around, Ashlee bent, allowing the college man to bang her. She didn't care that afterward, he flung his soggy condom, flipped his dick, zipped his pants, and tossed bills at her before leaving, without a word.

He showed up later with a suggestion and his name, then he left.

Ashlee arrived at Lance's designated downtown spot. She turned tricks for him and a friend. Ashlee purposely didn't offer much skanky stuff, just enough to get Lance hooked. First, she thought, she had to get the fish on her line. Then she could reel him in. Pocketing her earnings from that episode, Ashlee was determined to move up in life, even if she had to lie down to do so.

One week later, Lance asked if Ashlee wanted to accompany him to Aspen. At least that was where she thought he'd said. She couldn't ski, but heck, she could look cute. After all, that was what college and successful men wanted, right? A cute woman.

Ashlee knew she could lose her pub job for taking time off; the greasy manager had angrily informed her. Yet she had already decided. She was *going to* become some rich man's wife. So she couldn't let a little server job stand in her way. Heck, her husband would have money, and she had favors, so they would trade. She just had to work her plan.

The way Ashlee saw it, she couldn't get a rich husband if she didn't put herself out there. That was why she'd bought new tits. Doing so had been one of her first steps. Now she just had to go where rich men went.

Sex-hunting Lance and his skiing offer were just one more rung on Ashlee's ladder. Each rung got her closer to the top. She reminded herself, there she would fetch her prize. Her new life.

Chapter 19

Ashlee had very little fun in Aspen, Colorado, for many reasons. First, she spent what was, for her, an exorbitant sum. She blew it on ski outfits, only to find they were not appealing or warm. Compared to the other young women present, Ashlee felt she looked cheap.

She knew her excuse for not skiing had been shoddy, too, at best. Still, she could never have admitted that she'd accepted the invitation knowing she couldn't hit the slopes. So she staged a little trip 'n fall up in the day. The scenario garnered her attention, but Lance vamoosed, saying he wasn't a babysitter. He'd asked if she'd be okay, although he didn't care. Then he took off with a bosomy bombshell.

Disgusted, Ashlee realized. She wouldn't be the only woman making the rounds at the exclusive villa, but she bet Bosomy wouldn't get paid.

When evening arrived, Ashlee received another shocker. Lance's black friend—Ashlee believed he was Colin— mentioned watching the sunset. Over the Elk Mountains. What was Colin, gay? Ashlee wondered, as the group spoke, too, of going night skiing, getting in a few more runs. She hadn't even known people did that.

The next evening wasn't any better. Ashlee was only grateful that a couple of the guys mentioned handling the dining excursion. If they hadn't, she would not have been able to afford one glass bottle of water. At the cozy tavern, everything was expensive and upmarket. It was not like the dim New Haven pub where she'd been employed. Yet everything was been-there-done-that for Lance, whose father was from England.

Watching Lance and his group of chummy friends, Ashlee felt like the odd duck out, especially when they ordered fondue. What was that? When it came, they enjoyed it, all melty. They drank expensive wine and spirits. They discussed meal choices, the names of which she had never before heard. And they called it casual dining. Please.

The close-knit group of four young men enjoyed themselves so much together until, half the time, Ashlee simply stared at the stone walls. She found nothing interesting about strategically located fireplaces. The sleek young women didn't seem to mind. Speaking amongst themselves, they even leaned over the guys to whisper to each other.

There was nothing that Ashlee could add to the conversation going on around her. Everyone seemly spoke a foreign language; places she didn't know about or had never been, they alluded to portfolios, degrees, and pedigrees. They discussed graduate studies, internships, fellowships, and Lawd knew what all else. Ugh.

Ashlee truly felt out of her depth, so much so that when Lance actually *told* her that she didn't mind if Bosomy shared their room, Ashlee nodded. Tearing her gaze away from trees festooned with miniature white lights, Ashlee gestured as if to say, 'Have at it.' Bastard.

One golden god kept hinting that things would have been better if they'd gone surfing. Perhaps his name was Jay, and he had said hello, but he was clearly caught up with twin brunettes. So no pay there for Ashlee.

The brunettes and the other females, high-class snobs, Ashlee felt, shunned her. It was as though she wore a sign that said *I do not belong*.

Only one of the young men had been halfway decent. Ashlee caught his name. *Jeremy*. He wasn't into all the cavorting and conviviality. He didn't often smile. He just alternated between listening and staring off into space. Yet Ashlee liked his look. His glutes were cute. His broad shoulders, toned midsection, and strong upper body and arms attested to daily workouts. The man had the stormiest eyes Ashlee had ever seen, and she found his brooding sexy.

Wearing a superbly fitting cable knit sweater and jeans, the man's jaw was shadowed by blond evening stubble that only added to his allure.

Listening to garner knowledge about him, Ashlee learned Jeremy was a martial arts buff. Sipping a full-bodied *Pauillac*, a wine from France's renowned Bordeaux region, Jeremy said precisely what was on his mind. That was most often someone named Gemma.

Ashlee wondered who she was. What was so special about this Gemma that caused strawberry blond waves to keep mentioning her?

Later in the evening, while hanging before a cozy fire, someone announced the trip would be cut short. Elated, Ashlee could have danced a jig. The golden young man spoke; the one that she thought would have been beautiful were he not so full of himself. "I'm going home."

Jeremy appeared to agree. "Great idea, Jay." He said he'd do the same and excused himself. Not long after, Jeremy returned, saying the plane was secured. He tossed out a departure time and started an exodus. Ashlee took it that all the guys were going with him. The young women calmly spoke amongst themselves, excluding her as usual. Ashlee felt at loose ends. She had no job to go back to because her fat greasy manager had said she should never return if she took one day.

Yet half an hour later, while zippering his designer duffle, playboy Lance glanced over and asked, "So, where you off to now, Luv?"

He'd sounded so British and non-committal that Ashlee's old companion, anger, rose. The bastard had invited her, but he'd ignored her half the time. The other half he'd turned to her in bed, condom in hand, not long after banging Bosomy. Ashlee hadn't cared, and the smell of another woman on him had only made her feel competitive.

However, Jeremy, the one person Ashlee felt had been decent, mentioned having only so much time off. As a result, he told dark-haired Lance to get a move on. Then headed away, presumably to gather his things, Jeremy spoke offhandedly, telling all to get themselves in gear.

Did that mean *she* was going? Her heart jumped at the idea that stormy eyes had invited her! It hadn't been the most concrete offer, but Ashlee would surely be in the Hummer when it arrived. She would take her first ride on a private plane, too, come hell or high water. She'd overheard that the luxury aircraft comfortably seated fourteen. Therefore, having no idea where she would wind up, Ashlee realized it couldn't be worse than where she'd been. So, like a cat, she would land on her feet.

Ashlee could not believe she was there, on a U.S. barrier island! She'd never heard of the quaint place with timeless beauty. Unlike Aspen, winter on the isle of Karina Cay was mild. The sky was blue, the sun was bright, and all was highlighted by the sight and smell of the sea.

They'd had to take a ferry, which had been more of a slow paddleboat ride. Then they clomped down a wooden ramp where several people driving golf carts had picked up their party. Ashlee heard that cars and their emissions weren't allowed on the island. The isle of Karina Cay.

In the golf carts, they passed an outdoor market, really an old-world shopping area. It was crammed with inviting shops, an ancient theatre, museums, and art galleries. Overflowing with charm, a Victorian district had people lounging amongst flowers on second-story black iron balconies. It was the way she had imagined Savannah. Amid stately architecture and a town green, Ashlee felt she had stepped back in time.

It felt strange because there were quite a few Negroes—well, black people—around, making Ashlee uncomfortable. Nevertheless, with them and others colorfully dressed, biking, and walking everywhere, the place seemed like one she could get used to. Then they arrived at a sprawling white house on a wide, palm tree-lined lane called Beach Road. It had the beach for a backyard! Ashlee walked around what Lance called the summerhouse. She believed she just might have hit the jackpot because who knew college boy had it like that!

Ashlee asked herself the question a second time when he showed her to a vast pretty room. Nonchalant, he told her to stow her things. Walking away, Lance called out that they would go to Jeremy's later.

He lived on the island, too? Ashlee pondered that as she walked around Lance's airy home. Noticing that it was open to the sea in the rear, she could only wonder what Stormy Eye's place was like.

Attempting to make a warm-ish weather outfit from the things she'd brought, Ashlee could only think her plans were paying off, already!

With beer bottles high, some raised wine and shot glasses as the group yelled, "House Party!" Corks were popped, and libation flowed.

Although no female said a word to her, Ashlee no longer cared. All she knew was the friend's place was better than Lance's summerhouse.

Jeremy's home was like something out of an old movie. It was huge. It sat haughtily up on a cliff, with a narrow stretch of beach miles below. Scary. Yet the outside of the house—the manse—looked like an oversized, expensive, antique dollhouse. Everything inside appeared costly. From the windows divided into myriad grids of glass, Ashlee knew they were mullioned; to the wide-planked dark wood floors. Each room was so pretty or masculine, depending on where she happened to be. Some things were vintage while others were newer, but everything seamlessly meshed to form an inviting home.

The only thing Ashlee did not care for was *her*...

The boisterous group and others had been congregated out of doors. People had stood around drinking, and a male, obviously the help, operated the grill. Others sat enjoying crusty buttered bread, crawfish, corn on the cob, and more island fare. It was supplied by others. The guys spoke about football. Then without a word, *she* appeared.

Yet it had been like they'd sensed her presence before they saw her. All noise had ceased, and Stormy Eyes turned. Seeing *her*, he moved swiftly, silently, through those congregated behind his colossal home.

She moved at the same time. The mystery person stepped from the doorway where she'd been silhouetted. Ashlee had not been able to see her well until *she* and Jeremy were running toward each other.

With her silky hair in a topknot, she jumped. Though slightly taller than he, Gemma launched herself at Jeremy as she long had.

Capably, Jeremy caught her. With one hand on her buttocks and the other beneath it, he lifted Gemma. Dressed like Audrey Hepburn, from Mam-maw's old movies, this beauty wrapped her leggings-clad calves around Jeremy and crossed her impossibly high heels behind him.

The guys cheered. Raising bottles, glasses, and voices, the cohorts drank, and her name floated in the air. *Gemma. Gemma.*

"*Lingerie lady.*" "Sexy Gem." "S'up, chica?"

That was the person on the brooding man's mind? That *black* chick?! Ashlee was stunned as another person appeared.

"Heather!" In tandem, the guys all leaned, as if taken aback, "Whoa!" They spoke at once. "How's vet college?" "S'up, girl?" "Hey, Red Hot." "Didn't think the Irish siren would make it."

So she was studying to be a pet doctor, huh? Ashlee took in the skinny jeans, cuffed to reveal wedge-heel boots. Ashlee saw green eyes, alabaster skin, and a lean athletic build. Ashlee glimpsed hair, long, full, and healthy. Incredible, it was a fiery natural red. For Ms. Wholesome, there were hugs, kisses, and the veiled innuendo of familiarity.

Ashlee even heard Colin say, "I miss you, girl." Ashlee wondered if Red suffered from coon love, jungle fever, too. Then the curly-haired black guy asked, "When am I gonna get my running buddy back?"

Okay, so maybe they weren't involved. The bottled blond dismissed Heather, who snorted. "Are the dawns too dark without me, Col?"

"Nah, Ma." He chucked her beneath the chin. "I just miss huffing wit'cha. You miss it too," Colin teased. "Looking a little soft there."

Then the party began in earnest, while Jeremy and the tall one kissed and murmured with their arms around each other. They were the only two in their world, and it hurt Ashlee to see what no one else paid attention to. The guys were drinking again, dancing and flirting with the snobby females. Yet among everyone, there had been a parting that allowed Red, Heather, to become part of the unit. Unlike Ashlee.

Noticing all, especially the couple who kissed as though they had long been parted, Ashlee told herself it was stupid for her to feel upset. She didn't know that guy, Jeremy, and she sure didn't know the slinky girl cradling his head and murmuring with her lips against his. Ashlee knew she'd seen that skank somewhere before, though… She just couldn't remember where. And it definitely wasn't like they ran in the same circles; Ashlee had spent most of her life on her knees or bent over.

Yet Ashlee noticed Jeremy's arms around Slinky. He was rubbing her back. Appearing utterly intoxicated, Jeremy had one hand beneath Gemma's cute cropped sweater. He squeezed her plump sexy rump with the other as though he couldn't get enough of her. Like they were just getting started, in back he slipped his hand into her black leggings. Down past her waistband, he visibly squeezed her fat ass, again.

Ashlee bitterly wondered, what was he *doing* with that wench? This *Gemma* was a *Negro*—well, a black, or an African-American. Ashlee didn't know what they called themselves nowadays. She didn't care. She only knew one thing... That *nigger* girl being with Jeremy was *wrong*!

Ashlee told herself she shouldn't care that the slinky, coffee-with-milk-colored chit had appeared. Still, Ashlee cared, too much. She told herself she wouldn't feel bad if Stormy Eyes had been with Red. She'd stood behind blackie. The one with the flaming halo and a supreme air of confidence would have been a more acceptable choice.

But who was Ashlee to judge? She didn't know these people. Still, she wanted to know *him*. Jeremy. She surreptitiously watched. Seeing how Jeremy was with Slinky, angered Ashlee. He couldn't do enough for Slinky, like he was the enslaved—when *Slinky* was slave material!

Ashlee pondered all the snippets of conversation she had overheard. On Jeremy's mother's side, his grandmother was white. Jeremy's rich grandfather, a French black judge—who'd looked white—had become riotously wealthy after marrying the heiress, the daughter of a shipping tycoon. That sneaky nigger, Ashlee thought. One of the female snobs had told another that on the other side, Jeremy's white father owned Home Wares, like his father before him. Ashlee's interest had piqued because she knew about that chain of superstores! They carried everything from coffee tables, hand-knotted rugs, scented candles, and patio umbrellas to fire pits and outdoor-living furniture. Therefore, for Ashlee, all of that meant one thing. Moneyed Jeremy had no business with a *black* chick!

Taking a huge gulp of beer, Ashlee realized something more. Slinky wasn't a girl. Sure, she and Ashlee were perhaps both nineteen or early twenties. Yet the tall, shapely black young woman looked...grander. Staring, Ashlee unconsciously touched her own face. Why did Slinky look like she had been pampered since birth? What kind of world was it when some mud-skank did better than a white girl?

Again, Ashlee felt the anger that never entirely left her. Leaping to life, it burned hotter. Anger prevented Ashlee from joining the football game, and she stepped back as players nimbly dashed about. She didn't notice that the islanders deftly avoided the cliff edge. Gemma and red-haired Heather, now barefoot, played and did the same. Ashlee did not see that if one of the female snobs perched precariously close, an islander would gently nudge the girl snob away from the cliff's edge. Ashlee was unaware that attuned to it, the next generation of cohorts and other islanders always heard the crumbling bedrock falling miles downward to the ominous Atlantic ocean below.

All Ashlee could do was watch Gemma, and Jeremy.

Within minutes, those two fled the others, dashing into a darkened, near-private space with white morning glories and huge, hanging yellow trumpet flowers. Ashlee had never seen that particular type of trumpet before, not with the flutes appearing blood red. They were so big they actually appeared spooky. Knowing so much about flowers from Mammaw, fake-blond Ashlee forgot plants and her grandmother.

What was back there? Creeping along, she thought the space was like a shrine for the dead.

When Slinky did not immediately return, nor did sexy Jeremy, Ashlee put one foot before the other. And the party went on. Hearing it caused Ashlee to feel her companion, anger, rise higher. She knew what those two were doing back in that eerily shrouded area. Skulking along, Ashlee figured Slinky was probably getting naked. She was probably lying down on a pillow of leaves with her arms wide and her legs spread.

Tiptoeing, Ashlee figured she would come upon the couple. Ashlee knew she would see Slinky welcome Jeremy into her plush, open body.

Ashlee would catch Jeremy between Slinky's thighs, pushing in and out. He'd be pumping away as greedily he sucked on light brown tits; Ashlee imagined how pretty they'd be. She would see Jeremy's beige buns moving up and down. She might even get to see his *parts*. He would give that girl all he had to give.

That much had been obvious when Jeremy had been back out where everyone else remained, still noisy and having fun.

Attempting to turn her mind off to such things, Ashlee absolutely despised that Jeremy could be back where she was going, doing evil... kissing, hunching, and hugging, partaking of ripe, juicy, inviting, *forbidden* flesh.

Chapter 20

Inside the manse, seated in one of many rooms expressly decorated for living, Ashlee curled up on a plush sofa. Across from *them.* Inconspicuously, she watched Jeremy—and slinky Gemma.

That *person* sat on a large luxe velvet sofa with her long legs crossed. Portions of her hair fell sexily from its topknot. Next to her, *he* sat amid a profusion of pillows. In one hand, Jeremy held a pilsner glass. Possessively, he slung the same arm about Gemma's shoulders. Every so often, pulling her close, he gulped lager. He even pressed a hard kiss to her cheek. On her forehead, he let his lips linger. Then on the mouth, he kissed Gemma several times in rapid succession. He gave her tongue, leaving no room for speculation; he was clearly enamored.

They sat so close, with her shoulder nearly beneath his arm. The curly-haired black guy sat on Gemma's other side. His skin was lighter than hers, but Ashlee wondered if the blacks were related. They seemed so easy with each other, and Jeremy didn't mind.

Jeremy and Gemma laughed together, and he called her *ange.* Ashlee figured it meant angel in French. Jeremy spoke the language to Gemma often. Calling him Jere, or sometimes even Harden, she spoke it back.

Ugh. Despising Gemma for no good reason, Ashlee tore her eyes away. She looked around the room. Everyone seemed so mellow. Jay, the surfer dude, was seated at the opposite end of Ashlee's sofa. He caught at some pretty young thing. Jay spoke as Pretty tried to pass him.

Ashlee noticed someone had started a welcome blaze in the mammoth fireplace. It was large enough for a good-sized child to stand in. Good thing, because out of doors, when night had quickly approached, so had a chill. Ashlee glanced at people playing cards. Seated at a small pedestal table before the fire, each one studied the hand they'd been dealt. In a cozy corner, others relaxed, puffing and passing a joint. Wind rattled the shutters and windowpanes of the enormous old house. However, a bevy of glowing lamps added to the general feeling of warmth.

Ashlee noticed Red; Heather was her name. She was perched on the arm of the plush upholstered chair where dark-haired Lance lounged. He had one loafer-clad foot on the comfy ottoman before him and one of his hands on Red's back. He genuinely laughed up at something she said.

Ashlee's eyes widened because Lance liked Red! He actually listened to her, forsaking all else. Ashlee dismissed those two. Forget fickle Lance.

Returning her attention to the couple before her, Ashlee hated that still seated too close to Jeremy, Slinky surely smelled his soft but inviting manly scent. Ashlee had gotten a glorious whiff when he'd excused himself, squeezing past her in the crush of his kitchen. She hadn't been obvious, but for a second Ashlee made sure they had full body contact. She'd acted as though it had been natural, and he'd probably thought someone behind had jostled her against him.

As the evening wore on, full stomachs, jet lag, and the spirits imbibed set in. People dispersed while those remaining discussed sleeping arrangements. Surfer Jay, the golden god, lived on the island, too. Therefore, he, the brunette twins, and the pretty young thing he had been bothering would bunk at his place. Curly-haired Colin lived nearby, so the cute brown girl, another of the snobs, would head off with him. Ashlee found out that she, and the bosomy bombshell, would be Lance's guests. No surprise there. Of course, Gemma would remain at the manse with Jeremy, and actually, those two had already disappeared.

Readying herself to go to her family's sprawling home, Heather turned. "We on for the morning, Col?"

"Ah, you sure you wanna run with the big dawg?" curly-haired Colin winked, "Yo, I mean, *I* haven't been slacking, like some people."

Heather waved. "Just be there, no lip, the regular spot, on time."

"Wait." Lance said he'd run Heather to her house and return.

Immediately, an idea struck. Aloud, Ashlee claimed she'd never make the short golf cart ride back to the summerhouse, "Not if I don't potty."

When she left the room, Colin frowned. "Potty? Is she three?"

Ashlee did not hear. She was busy poking about, trying to find Jeremy's bedroom. She didn't know why, but she just needed to see it.

In the *salle haute*, she found it and was about to enter. In the upper hall, she stopped short, though; someone was inside. Sidling up to the alcove outside half-open double doors, Ashlee saw *them*.

Both were across the spacious room done up in masculine shades of sumptuous brown and beige. On the far side of Jeremy's bed, the pair were down on their knees.

Ashlee saw clothing, strewn helter-skelter on the patterned carpet. It was as though they'd rushed into the room, disrobing as they'd entered. She could picture it and how they'd collapsed, falling naked to their knees. Thus their current position, where hurriedly, Jeremy had entered Gemma from behind.

Ashlee watched. The beauty, who only wore dangling earrings, was mightily ridden. Jeremy repeatedly bumped into her with raw sensuality and power, causing her tits to jiggle. Since her eyes were blissfully closed, and his were on Slinky, Ashlee looked her fill at the couple who were simply breathtaking together. Begrudgingly, she acknowledged it.

There was a luxurious faux mink coverlet on the bed before Gemma. Fisting it in both hands, she made throaty little erotic noises. Obviously enjoying her and Jeremy's activity, Gemma glided backward. Meeting him as he thrust into her, Gemma appeared unable to get enough of Jeremy. Watching himself slide in and out he couldn't touch her enough.

Ashlee felt like she was viewing porn, but with real live people! The sight and sound exhilarated as well as suffused her with escalating anger. Yet she noticed that behind Gemma, Jeremy slipped his arms around her. He squeezed her soft-looking breasts. Ashlee remembered her own, botched and scarred. She felt volcanic anger. Jeremy bit at the sides and nape of Gemma's neck. Then before Ashlee could turn to flee, despite preferring to watch, Jeremy whispered something in Gemma's ear.

The café au lait beauty quickly flipped over to lie on the bed, right before Ashlee's eyes! Nearly facing the doorway from which their voyeur watched, Gemma did not sense or see Ashlee. Unaware, too, Jeremy used one hand to grasp both of his partner's. Pinioning them above her head, he imprisoned Gemma with his hovering body. Nibbling her lips, he worked down to her breasts.

Man, were Gemma's tits beautiful. Just like she'd wanted hers to be, Ashlee thought; Gemma's were smooth, round, and so full, with near-mauve tips. In an envy-induced haze, Ashlee watched as Jeremy noisily laved and hungrily sucked on those tits while holding Gemma's ribcage with his free hand. Gazing at the man who used his teeth to tug on Slinky's nipples, Ashlee knew profound jealousy, especially when Gemma moaned in ecstasy.

Ashlee wanted to cry; she wanted tits like that! Even more, she wanted *feeling* in hers. Ignoring jealousy, she focused on Jeremy's taut abs. His hard body was nearly covered in sparse blond peach fuzz. She watched as he purposely dragged his lengthy cock, which looked to her like an enticing cylindrical pointer, over Gemma's fevered flesh.

Gemma raised her legs and widened her thighs, anticipating receipt of him, and Ashlee tingled. Jeremy shook his head. Visibly wanting, Gemma raised her body. With it, she tried to meet the slick, slit head of Jeremy's thick veiny cock, and he spoke softly in French.

He must have said 'not yet,' which made Ashlee wonder. What would it be like to have Jeremy talk to *her* that way? She imagined him pointing his handsome log of flesh at and then ultimately into *her*. The thought made Ashlee ache to open for him. Licking her lips as she watched the couple sensually play, Ashlee realized. She would take Jeremy in and receive all of him before giving him the ride of his life.

Jeremy hovered over Gemma, poking her every so often with the penis that Ashlee longed to slip into her mouth and suck dry. Jeremy kissed his way down Gemma's torso, and when he reached Gemma's navel, she made giggly noises. Watching, Ashlee burned with jealousy because the couple seemed so comfortable with each other. Ashlee had never had a man who'd made her feel that way—and she'd had plenty.

With her and men, it had always been a chore, or a means to an end. Most had been insensitive. Others had beat her. Ashlee had never felt as beautiful as Gemma looked, with Jeremy tightly grasping her hips. Gemma managed to sit up as Jeremy parted her thighs, and he gazed at her apex like he'd found gold. With hands cupping her own tits, Gemma watched Jeremy down before her. Gemma appeared so sexy until Ashlee knew that if offered the chance, she too would do Slinky.

It further shocked Ashlee to see enigmatically lean but muscular Jeremy rest his head on Gemma's thigh inside. His face was only millimeters from her core—which was as pretty as the rest of her. Keeping his head pillowed on her thigh, Jeremy appeared to savor the nearness of Gemma's shaved-clean hotbox. When he dipped his head, kissing her there, Gemma widened her legs and offered herself up. With the soles of her feet on the bed, she raised her pelvis and angled her core toward Jeremy's searching mouth.

Using tapered fingers, the man widened Gemma and his mouth, which he placed on her. Watching, Ashlee saw Gemma catch her breath. Ashlee saw Jeremy's tongue move slowly, tantalizingly, in...and out, teasing the exposed stamen of Gemma's flower. He did things to her quivering soft, moist flesh that Ashlee's own swollen nubbin and humid folds ached to experience. She wanted some! Now!

Snapping back to reality, Ashlee told herself she had seen enough. Yet she only wanted to trade places with Gemma when Jeremy licked from Gemma's stamen back to the exposed line of her lovely near-upturned buns. When Jeremy sucked on a finger and stuck it into the plush cleft, Ashlee craved that finger within her. She desperately wanted to feel the warmth of Jeremy's body on hers. She wanted him drinking from her as though she, too, were a cup. Forget Slinky. Ashlee wanted Jeremy licking and lapping at *her* like that.

Again coming to herself, Ashlee remembered—she had to go! Lance would be back. He and Bosomy would never wait for her if she continued to stand there watching what was supposed to be private.

But the beautiful couple hadn't closed the door, Ashlee petulantly recalled. She stood for another moment. Curiously, she peered at the man who slowly rose to pack Gemma full of his sexy, thick, ready rod.

Unseen, Ashlee slipped away, but not before erotic images were branded on her brain. *That* was what she wanted, she told herself. Sex, like that, with a man like that. No. Correction; she was unwilling to look any further. Now was her time.

Ashlee wanted *that man* that way.

At the end of the hallway, Colin, too, slipped into the shadows. Something had prompted him to go looking for the tag-along girl. When she'd disappeared with that stupid 'potty' excuse, he'd wanted to see what she'd get up to.

Jeremy's closest cohort narrowed his eyes because now he knew. That nosey pushy heifer.

Afterward, still unaware that they'd had a voyeur, Jeremy half lay beneath Gemma, who slept. With one hand, he brought her limp hand to his lips. Kissing the pads of each lovely finger, he only wished they could spend more time together. He knew she wanted the same thing. He wished he could live with her every day. He'd wanted that since they'd been relatively young.

He pulled his fluffy beige coverlet up and over Gemma's slender exposed back. Jeremy also brushed wisps of hair from *une copine's* forehead and realized. He liked things this way. Still, with them, peace never reigned. Hating to, he wondered. Who would be the next person to try to take her from him?

Chapter 21

The cohorts and friends dispersed. Jeremy was back in France at *université*, and Gemma had left the states on assignment. Curly-haired Colin returned to his studies, and Heather was at vet college. Summer-house Lance had returned to his New Haven University's School of Engineering and Applied Science. Only surfer Jay remained on island.

Karina Cay was the home base for the guy's lucrative business. A little older than the others, Jay, a software developer, designed and met clients' needs. Another Karinian was a ruddy-faced analyst. Dark-haired Lance had come aboard as their programmer. He converted designs into a series of instructions easily followed by computers. Colin, who studied journalism, was the firm's social media/advertising guru. And for the whole venture, Jeremy had supplied the initial capital.

Jay had wholeheartedly embraced the idea of both living and working on Karina Cay. Having grown up there, he was devoted to the picturesque place that enabled him to unwind by surfing, his passion.

The firm only had one problem, now. Ashlee. Everyone else had returned to their daily grind. Yet the tag-along girl—as Colin called her—had not. It seemed she had nothing to do, making the guys sick.

So he wanted her gone, huh? Lance had even suggested she go back to the mainland or wherever she'd come from, but Ashlee knew. There was nothing for her in the states, so she stubbornly decided to stay.

She had heard Lance, too; he wasn't aware because he had been on his cell phone. He'd said something about belonging. Ashlee's eyes had narrowed as she'd wondered, was he talking about her?

Ashlee had found out something more; Lance and the others truly were a tight-knit group. Although most spent a good deal of time elsewhere, they still believed living on the island made them exclusive. They thought it made them better than other people, especially Ashlee, she presumed. But she did belong, now. At least she told herself that because Jeremy Baptiste Harden had sort of invited her.

About him, Ashlee wanted to know more and about his girlfriend. Therefore, the bottled blond plagued Lance, who hadn't yet turned her out of the summerhouse, but it was coming. Lance arrived on island some weeks and went to class remotely on his laptop. And when spring vacay arrived, he'd be home for a while; so before then, Ashlee hoped she'd have other arrangements. She just didn't have a plan. Yet.

Stalking past her one evening, Lance inquired, "Why do you have so many questions about Gemma?" He really wanted to ask, 'Why are you still here?' Instead, he became derisive, "Quite obsessed, aren't you?"

"Nooo," Ashlee tried to sound nonchalant, but he'd hit the nail on the head. Ashlee recalled seeing Gemma in a few movies, and she knew that Gemma was considered one of the sexiest models in the world. *That* was where she had seen Gemma before! Slinky was one of the angelic vixens who wore bejeweled wings and lovely lingerie in advertisements.

Ashlee was so jealous! She had seen full-color photos of Gemma in a tastefully done British lingerie catalog. Then on the Internet, she'd viewed Slinky strutting down a catwalk—before celebrities. To them, Gemma was a star. And she had been majestic in high heels, a lace bra, and what could only be considered itty-bitty matching panties. The scrap of material had barely covered her bulbous behind.

Ashlee was aware that many women sought to duplicate Gemma's glutes via plastic surgery. What Ashlee really wanted to know was how that mud-bunny got that job. And where on the island was her house; Ashlee had heard that Slinky had a home somewhere up the beach. Still, Ashlee couldn't blurt out all her inquiries. She was smart. So again, she said, "Nooo, I'm not obsessed—with *her*?" Gemma? "Please."

With a beer in hand, Lance looked skeptical. He knew Ashlee thought she was slick. He'd met her kind, time and again. Now he actually regretted having shagged her, repeatedly. Thus, he spoke while looking as though through her. "I thought you were different."

"Different. How?"

Although he itched to tell her the truth, Lance assembled his thoughts. Initially, to him, it had seemed like Ashlee had been aware that she was another sort. "I thought you were your own person," Lance stated. He'd thought she knew she was of a lower class. There was nothing wrong with that. It was why he hadn't begrudged her plying her trade, selling sex. "I believed you were someone who marched to her own drumbeat." Yet here Ashlee was, attempting to force her way where she would never belong. Neatly summing things up, Lance shrugged. "You're nothing like I thought. You're really just," *pathetic*, he wanted to say. Instead, he verbally tossed out, "Like most outsiders, mate."

Stung, Ashlee tried to keep her voice neutral. "What do yew mean?"

Lance wished he had never met the trick-hick. Feeling protective, he said, "Most off-islanders are obsessed with the both of them." Ashlee knew he meant Gemma and Jeremy, "For obvious reasons."

Lance's face then took on a shuttered appearance.

Ashlee knew she was being shut out. She had seen that look quite a few times since she had been on Karina Cay. At an outdoor market, while fondling fruit, she'd attempted to slyly question a man about Gemma. Garnering the same look, the man had harshly asked, "Miss, do you mean to *buy* anything?" When prodded, the man coldly declared his stiffened stance. "We—Karinians—jest protect our own."

Ashlee felt like she'd been slapped, by a white man—'protecting' a nigger, from *her*. Shouldn't it have been the other way around? Forgetting that scene, she watched Lance enter his home office. He called, "Next week, I leave town. You're leaving too, off to…wherever."

Ashlee didn't need him to say she was out of there. She knew the summerhouse caretakers would see to it. Since they never spoke to her and seemed to hate cleaning up after her, she figured they'd be glad to toss her out. Snooty ol' servants, they weren't any better than she. Still, Ashlee knew she could return—if 'the master' called her back over wanting some ass. If Lance did, then she would make him pay, dearly.

In sunny California, Gemma could not believe she had stumbled into the role of Arma Geddon, Warrior Woman!

Some time back, she had tossed the script aside, saying it was B-movie shtick and unworthy of her or her talent. Although it was a period piece, she had seen how it could be tweaked. "It could be awe-inspiring," she'd said, "but chances of that happening are slim."

"Read for the role anyway," her agent begged. "Please, just to get the director and the C.S.A. to see you." He then became candid. "I want you on their minds. There's an upcoming Oscar-worthy role in the pipeline."

So Gemma made sure everyone who saw her would remember her.

For the reading, she donned a hooded cape. She wore patent leather knee-high boots. On those stilettos, she did her commanding catwalk stride. In the audition room, with a whip in hand, she quickly drew off her cape. Cracking her whip, she stood there in what appeared to be a fighter princess outfit, a twisted brass and leather bra, matching second-skin boyshorts, and brass and leather wrist pads. She'd had leather and beads woven into her lengthy braided hair, becomingly caught atop her head. Extensions cascaded from the high ponytail and hung enticingly down to her backside.

During her audition, Gemma wound up laughing aloud. She even shook her head while reciting the corny lines. Abruptly, she stopped to announce, "This is ridiculous." Swinging her cape back over her shoulders, she declared, "Enough. I've got someplace else to be."

The C.S.A. raised a brow. "Really," the rotund woman sarcastically droned, "dressed like *that*?"

Gemma was unfazed, "Yes, oh, highly sought after casting director."

"But you haven't been dismissed yet, and you're a..." Nancy, with the pig hands, nearly snarled. She made the word sound dirty, "*Model*—not an actor. As such, if you leave now, there'll be no coming back."

Gemma was congenial. "Oh, I know." Calmly she gathered her whip and designer tote. Gemma knew envy when she encountered it. Thus she remembered the words of her tiny older sister, Belize. *Rule one, Munch: expect hate.* Gemma caught the casting director's eye, knowing her sister would be proud of her; "Uh, and for the record, I'm a damn good model. And *I*, too, am highly sought after because," Gemma winked and gave the cinematographer a shimmy, "*the camera loves me.*"

Turning, Gemma stage-whispered, "I must be off now dahlings, dressed—as our casting director so aptly put it—like this."

Gemma guffawed while leaving because she'd sounded much like her actor/director dad. Hollywood insiders had often referred to Beau as a prima donna in his heyday. Still chuckling, in true DeVeaux fashion, with her cape swirling and her stiletto heels clicking on the polished floor, Beau's baby dramatically strode from the room.

Later, having heard about what some were calling 'the debacle,' one of the producers wanted to know why Gemma Janelle had thought his script ridiculous. He had his people contact hers to invite her to lunch.

She declined. Then recanting, Gemma wrangled his personal cell number from a handler and accepted, so she could tell the man the truth.

As a result, he and another producer met with her. To the writer's dismay, the screenplay was tweaked, and Gemma was offered the lead!

She made it plain. *The* Gemma Janelle would only accept if her wardrobe consisted of the same 'ridiculousness' that she had worn to the initial audition. The twenty-something explained to her dad and Jeremy—who both roared with laughter—that to do so would be her way of sticking it to nasty Nancy, the pig-faced casting director.

The producers of Warrior Woman thought Gemma was brazen and sassy. Still, she got her wish. After signed contracts, scene-shooting, and editing sequences, audiences felt the same. What audacity! Repeatedly they went, in droves, to see Arma Geddon. Most thought she was formidable and super sexy as she strode across Marloes Beach in Wales, where fight scenes had been recorded. On the screen, the warrior woman's braided hair and layered faux fur cape streamed out behind her as she parried with her war captain. Also, her lover, the character was played by scrumptious, mahogany-dark Nile Narcissi. With the war captain, Arma Geddon plotted revenge on all who'd decimated the ancient woodland and mythical home of her people.

Near the movie's end, viewers' hearts hammered as Warrior Woman vaulted up and onto her destrier. Collectively, they held their breath as fearlessly, she charged her sleek black Marwari into battle. Her battalion eagerly followed the majestic beast's galloping hooves. Beneath their furiously waving flag, Arma Geddon rode, intent to gain justice for her people. Her face streaked with soot and ash, she vowed to die fighting.

Bloggers and viewers alike often mentioned the prior scene, Arma Geddon rousing those who'd promised to follow her from this life into the next. With her leading, the would regain what was rightfully theirs. Bloggers quoted her famous rousing battle cry., "I'd rather *die* on bruised knees, brethren than spend my life groveling there! Now, let us ride— and recover all!" Said many, Gemma Janelle's performance was so compelling that by the time she recovered from aches, bruised ribs, and the fractured wrist garnered in a battle scene, the movie had obtained an occult following. Just like her father, Beau's films had, decades before.

Gemma was still amazed at the turn of events, beginning with that first wayward audition. Two-plus years later, aware that audiences were calling for a second movie, Gemma decided she wanted *producer* credit.

She let it be known: she was not like some Hollywood newcomers. She was like her dad, the great Beauregard DeVeaux. She understood; the job was both creative as well as financial. Gemma made it known. She was willing to work for the title, and she wouldn't just raise capital. With the backing of GemCo, her production company, she intended to do more than invest money. For her efforts, though, she wanted top billing.

Hers had been an uphill battle, but she had been mentored for it. She got to work. Engaged in the second WaWo—as the first was dubbed— Gemma wrangled her way into the hiring of writers and script development. The way she saw it, she needed to, since she'd put her name and her money on the line, *and* it would be her up on the screen. Win or fail, she kept reminding herself; it would be all on her.

Gemma even approached pigface. The wary casting director had feared this go-round she'd be out. However, working together, the women found their vision the same. For every part, they simply wanted the best actors. Amid discussions, Gemma and Nancy laughed together, and each uncovered mutual respect for the other.

Why was I ever jealous of her? Nancy wondered. Oh, because she's gorgeous, and talented, the C.S.A. remembered. Nancy amended the thought because Gemma really was knowledgeable; and there were times when even Gemma had self-doubt, like everyone. Still, Nancy marveled at Gemma's being genuinely nice, and not narcissistic, unlike *others*.

Nancy's eye fell on a photo of that dark, handsome, but totally self-absorbed, WaWo co-star. Nile. While he soaked up glory and praise for nothing, Gemma tirelessly worked. She pushed the project through the studio and marketing and distribution channels. Gemma even applied and became a Producer's Guild of America member.

Gemma recalled how quickly her life had changed following that first audition. And she could only think one thing; what sheer courage she'd had and how young and irrepressible she had been.

The full-blown special Hollywood screening quickly approached. For the sequel, Warrior Woman Crusade, Gemma was excited. People would get to see that a great portion of it was filmed on Quiraing, the Isle of Skye. In Scotland, there had been untold extras employed for war scenes.

To Gemma, this particular screening was more exciting than the first. One reason was because this screening would be held at Grauman's Chinese Theater. On the Hollywood walk of fame, it opened in the 1920s. Gemma's sequel screening also began the summer movie season.

Then the New York City premiere loomed. It was one of four. Gemma found it uncanny how the first movie had been so well received. Its reception was likened to Star Wars or Avatar, and now she and her team had done a follow-up!

Gemma and the sexy mahogany actor, Niles Narcissi, who played opposite her, were scheduled to make publicity rounds. They'd head to Japan. They would jet to London, too, amid the chatter that had labeled them an item.

Gemma longed to post her one wish, that her sweetheart, *Jeremy*, could be with her for the New York screening. However, she had been advised not to mention him. "Let this thing with Nile play out. He's A-list. Due to his last two blockbusters, he's hot. If the public thinks you're with him, it generates interest. That's what we want, and loads of it."

Still, Gemma informed Jeremy of how she really felt in late night and wee morning contacts. She told transitioned Nannie too. Rarely to Jeremy did Gemma ever mention her co-star Nile.

Although he despised paparazzi and any type of fanfare, Jeremy just could not see disappointing Gemma. She wanted him at her premiere, despite her handlers. Giselle, his mom, also said he might enjoy himself. Therefore, Gemma Janelle's man, the heir to the Baptiste and the Harden fortunes, agreed to escort the actress to New York.

The buzz on the island was about a movie. It would soon hit the duplex. Karinians gloated about the flick that starred their very own. Gemma Janelle! They spoke of the young woman whose relationship with 'the heir' mirrored his granddad and the priestess.

Sickened, Ashlee had heard that a dozen times. She'd also heard that for the first movie, Gemma had learned to fence and ride a charging horse bareback. The movie star had had months of grueling fight and strength training. She'd been taught rock climbing to nimbly navigate the crags on the icy beaches where fight scenes had been recorded. Afraid of heights, she'd conquered her fear. She'd scaled castle walls and raced up hundreds of stone steps with no railing to hang onto.

Hearing all the talk, Ashlee was as tired of it as she was of that bitch, but she could not dwell on such things. Instead, she focused on needing someone who could help her. There was the rub, though. The islanders seemed padlocked against her, and Lance had shut her out of the summerhouse. Surfer Jay was not an option either because the golden god had always made it clear; he didn't do skanks. That left Colin, whom Ashlee wouldn't approach because he was black.

Feeling out of her depth, Ashlee thought about home. No! She forgot her lil' crack of Carolina. There she would never return. Still, sometimes she recalled the trailer park and Mam-maw. Ashlee wondered if the old woman was still alive. She wondered about Bif, too. The thickset girl had been pregnant. Had Bif had a boy or a girl? Did Biffi now have other kids? It had been a few years. Was she still with document-forging Cain?

Thinking about Bif, whom she hadn't called once since she'd left, Ashlee realized. She needed a friend, but she never met women who wanted to befriend her. Most quickly eyed her hooker heels, skimpy clothes, fake yellow hair, and 'assets' and disliked her on sight.

However, on Karina Cay, Ashlee had met a man. Sure, she always met men, but they were usually wrong. She drew them the way trash drew flies. Still, this man seemed novel. Ashlee knew she had been fooled before, but there was something about this one... Ashlee believed he could be different. She felt she just might be able to trust him.

Big, scruffy, and blond, the man was the outdoorsy type. With sun-leathered skin, he had an open, craggy face that had immediately put her at ease. On Karina, in a coffee shop—the one that had chanced hiring her—the man stuck out a massive paw. Shaking his hand, Ashlee liked him. Yep, because, for her, the man just might become useful.

Supposed to continue working, instead, Ashlee pushed out of the coffee shop. As was her way, she attempted to poke her nose in. "Hey, Buddy B," she called. "What's the B stand for?"

Taking the leashes of his two dogs in hand, the man's faded blue eyes narrowed, just a fraction. Ashlee didn't notice as he nodded. "Tell you what, Chickadee," Buddy B stood back and mentally assessed her. "If we make it far enough along, I jest might confide in ya. Howzat?"

"Okay," Ashlee agreed while watching the man depart with his two canines. She shrugged because everybody had secrets. Lawd knew she had quite a few of her own. Heck, if things turned around, somehow—and started going her way—she just might acquire a few more.

Chapter 22

Never before had Jeremy paid attention to things like critics and movie screenings. He hadn't done so even when millions had first become conscious of Gemma's most prominent movie personality, Arma Geddon. In her skimpy outfits, the glamazon had burst onto the screen. Taking all captive, she'd seized the hearts of many.

Yet after appearing with Gemma Janelle at one of a few premieres for Warrior Woman Crusade, Jeremy realized. Not only do those who star in a movie show up for the special screening, but a bevy of other celebrities did too. Many did so in support of those in the movie. Others did it as a studio favor. Dimmer personalities appeared, hoping for some light.

"That's because," Gemma whispered, "their agents want it for them, if only for a few minutes."

Being hustled along, Jeremy noticed. The glittering event allowed the waiting public to scrutinize several big names all at once. He thought it was silly, the way people hung around outside the theater, just waiting to ogle celebrities arriving in expensive cars.

However, Jeremy liked that Gemma Janelle made it her business to interact with the crowds. She knew people had waited hours to see her. From erected bleachers, they screamed her name and waved posters. Others hyperventilated when she approached, looking regal with her lovely hair up. Hanging across barricades, teenagers just wanted to touch her. Adults photographed her in her beautiful backless silver column.

Girls wore glitter and feathers, and some had even affixed contraptions to their bras in back with wire and foil. Regardless of shape or size, many wore skimpy Arma Geddon-esque costumes. At the sight of a few, Jeremy inwardly shuddered. However, Gemma seemed happy to sign autographs and even people's skin. Nearby, security hovered, making sure she came to no harm. Then she was turned. Her personal assistant murmured away to her as they traversed the famed carpet.

Jeremy took note before they went inside where it was dim and air-conditioned. For crowd control, law enforcement had roped off many areas while they had erected barricades elsewhere.

With his head buzzing from all the flashbulbs, non-stop chatter, and screaming, Jeremy did not understand how Gemma stood it. People swarmed, like makeup and hair people, others darted in and out like busy bees. They dabbed and lifted. They brushed and appraised. For Jeremy, the experience felt disjointed and exhausting. He had an encroaching headache. Yet those types of appearances Gemma handled with aplomb.

The notion caused him to view her afresh. She really loved what she did. She loved people, too, evidenced by the fact that a while back, she had suggested a charity premiere. When she'd mentioned pitching the idea, Jeremy asked what a charity premiere was.

Gemma had explained. Regular radio, as well as satellite and online radio personalities and disc jockeys, promoted her event. To foster awareness, they gave away tickets as part of a contest. "Tickets can also be sold to raise money for my cause."

Jeremy hadn't had to ask what that was, he knew. Ever since she'd learned the legend of Hollow Well Lane, Gemma had been incensed. She'd hated the tales that claimed two men had murdered their wives and dumped them at Windsor Pines, long before the property had come into Jeremy's family. Gemma had railed at the notion that "*Domestic violence*—because that's what it was," she'd sputtered, "—has been elevated to legendary status!" She'd repeatedly asked, "Jere, don't you think something's wrong with that?" Therefore, she'd clapped back. At age twenty-one, Gemma Janelle used her model status. She'd become a spokesperson for the activist group Women Against Domestic Violence. She championed children of domestic violence, too. In the years since, she'd remained vigilant, using her platform to enlighten and encourage followers to join the fight. She said when women spoke out, they should not receive vitriol and anger—and especially not from other women.

As females, Gemma said, not one could afford to remain silent. As a result, many Arma Geddon memes were created, thus furthering Gemma's reach. She was like her dad, who had been in the moviemaking business long before. The model/actress used her fame, not to promote herself, but to shed light. She brought about real change, for real hurting people. At age twenty-three, Gemma graduated with a communications degree. She had also become a philanthropist. Along with other concerned citizens, she'd started a grassroots initiative. It informed women, young and older, about the dangers of domestic violence. Countless women and children were offered aid and lodging. They were educated or were taught a trade, and they were introduced to mental self-sufficiency. Gemma felt Nannie would have been proud. Gemma had even started a chapter back on the isle of Karina Cay. There, where she lived, many women knew and adored her.

Still, despite all the good she did, the tabloids just would not leave her alone. That bothered Jeremy and summerhouse Lance, too. Sometimes the men conversed, mentioning how people really did not know Gem.

Yet the twenty-something said she could care less about those rags. Jeremy knew that was because of her famous dad. He was married to another man. Growing up in the spotlight, Beau's baby had developed a hard shell. Despite that, Jeremy didn't know how Gemma stood it all. When he was with her, he loathed the shoving, the catcalls, and the constant camera clicks in establishments or on certain streets.

In The Big Apple, hurrying New Yorkers were self-engrossed, so things were often different. Only when she was about to premiere a movie would Gemma be accosted upon exiting their swanky Tribeca, New York apartment.

However, too many times in L.A. and in some places overseas, flashbulbs would cause momentary blindness. Jeremy said he hated being accosted at all hours, and Gemma tried to soothe him by reminding him. "It's not just me that people are interested in. They want to know about you, too." They called him *the heir*. Gemma was always honest, "As long as you're with me, Jere, you'll be poked and prodded. Perhaps you wouldn't mind becoming a recluse, but you spark interest too, bae— maybe more than I do." With a few words, she gave him a choice. "Right now, Jere, this is my life..." Jeremy refrained from further complaints, realizing he wanted Gem more than he despised parts of her existence. Still, he wondered, when would things be different? When would he stop seeing her in the *tabloids*? When would the tales end, those that kept questions ever before him. The lies and stories were emotionally roiling, but what got to Jeremy most was always being away from Gemma.

The twenty-seven-year-old had thought receiving his MBA and starting work at the Home Wares London offices would mean he would see *ange* more, but no. The man who was now called J. B. Harden had much to learn. M. T. Harden made that clear, but his son had a plan. Jeremy would endure about eight more months of separation, and then something had to change. Jeremy needed to see the girl –no, the woman—of his dreams more often. He wanted it to be just them two.

Needing to breathe Gemma, live, eat, and sleep with her every day, Jeremy swore to make that happen.

Chapter 23

Having remained on the isle of Karina Cay, Ashlee rented a room in a woman's house. The blond knew she should be grateful to frail, bent, old Mrs. Pigeon, but Ashlee hated the hag's rules. 'Wipe your feet; wash your dishes; don't stand with my Frigidaire door open; don't touch my washer...' Even more, Ashlee hated the pug dog that the gnarled little old widow treated like it was royalty, like a real, special, little person.

Sometimes Ashlee felt she was slipping down a rabbit hole instead of climbing her ladder of success. She felt she lived in darkness because she had never stopped tricking. Now, however, she did so for men who didn't want it known. They met her where they thought no one would see, mostly in shadowy bayou places. They were often rough with her and crude. Numerous times, she'd been assaulted. Patrons paid in cash, so that was okay—when they paid, but Ashlee wanted more. She wanted a different life. She wanted jewelry, nice clothes, a car, off-island, and her own home. Really, Ashlee wanted Jeremy's home, the manse, with him in it, and she wanted him to want her, too. Therefore, Ashlee guessed, what she really wanted was *Gemma's life*.

Ashlee just needed a plan. Then all her dreams would come true.

She often saw Buddy B around town. One day, in the coffee shop where she worked, they nodded. Letting curiosity get the best of her, she pried, asking, "Where yew live, Buddy B?"

The big man spoke offhandedly, "I'm down the beach." Running sausage-like fingers through his blond crew cut, Buddy B noticed the girl's eyes. For a second, they'd lit. "Mind you, I ain't in the ritzy section," he stated, disappointing her, "but where I stay is okay."

Ringing him up, Ashlee said, "Well, maybe one day I'll see."

The fifty-something ox of a man left. He thought about the girl with the raging spirit. He, whose father had long ago been the island sheriff, had ogled Ashlee's bare legs, visible beneath her work shorts. Out of doors, Buddy B spoke, as though to the girl with the parched hair. "Maybe one day you will see, lil Chickadee…maybe you will."

Staring at the full-color photos on his tablet, Jeremy felt a fire blaze within. Gemma was at an event with her Warrior Woman Crusade co-star, Nile Narcissi. That actor Jeremy was beginning to despise.

Jeremy tossed his tablet down and forgot what curly-haired Colin had goadingly texted regarding the photos.

Can't blame G for hanging out with that guy. U in London, now. Dude there with her. He tall dark n fine - so says half the female population. They know what women want — right?

Jeremy suspected Colin hadn't texted those things to rankle. The cohort that Jeremy felt closest to had a way of getting under his skin. Jeremy's greatest friend had done so since they'd been kids. Curly-hair also texted didn't Jeremy think it was time to lock Gemma down.

Not boys anymore, man. Put a ring on it. Knock her up. Don't; you'll keep being upset - n she'll keep seeming like she belongs to no one—but herself.

Jeremy didn't want people to see Gemma that way because she was his. Damn Colin! Then Jeremy amended his musings because his friend hadn't texted out of spite. Colin, now a columnist, had congratulated Jeremy on his new job at Home Wares. Then the curly-haired one had more to say.

Thought u was getn yo ass in gear Frenchie; thought u be home, wrkn the HW offices here.

Colin certainly hoped Jeremy would wake up. Anyone could see the businessman was sprung. Gemma Janelle was Jeremy's whole world, she had been, ever since the next gen cohorts had all been eight or nine.

Now twenty-six or twenty-seven, Gemma remained cool, Colin mused, when her celebrity status could have made her an ice princess. Moreover, Colin remembered, Gem was second-generation Hollywood. Still, after hanging with her again, Colin was impressed. Gem hadn't changed a bit. She still really cared about the cohorts. Why, just days ago, she'd sent *him* costly champagne. Her own handwritten note offered kudos on his syndicated column! He'd been surprised she even knew.

Colin recalled having met different seasonal people; a few had vacation homes on the island. While he'd free-lanced, Colin had met enough of that privileged class to know. Many of them really were idle. Some were lazy, spoiled roustabouts. They only wanted to get drunk or high and attend the latest parties. They'd show up, for a fee, then intentionally appear bored, while they waited to inherit.

Gemma was the exact opposite, and she always had been. That was why Colin felt his boy needed to get his head in the game. Right now.

That night, Jeremy still couldn't get his mind off those photos. There Gemma Janelle had been, laughing and partying it up with Nile Narcissi.

In his large four-poster bed, milky luminescence silvered Jeremy's nude skin. Brooding, one of his greatest pastimes, he kicked at tangled sheets. In the moonlight, Jeremy raised one knee while massaging his throbbing penis. Grasping his length, he pulled and imagined Gemma in London with him. She'd be wearing what she wore most often at home, swimwear, preferably a bikini; he loved her in those. Jeremy knew she loved to see him hard and ready. She'd likely have talked dirty to him and remained just beyond his reach, had she been present. He knew he would have strained to reach and enter her. It was a game they played.

In the eye of his mind, Jeremy could see Gemma's tits. Perfectly round and soft, her pretty nipples would scream, 'Taste me, lick me, suck me.' He knew she would have taken pity on him after a while. Then she would have straddled him. When she finally lowered her sexy body onto his, he thought while pumping himself, she would have done it slowly. She loved it when he agonized over her. He envisioned the tip of his cock just missing her heat. Then when *she* couldn't stand not having *him* anymore, she would allow her yawning cunt to descend and eat his cock whole. He loved that! As he stabbed himself into his lubricated hand, he could almost feel her. Handling his balls, Jeremy realized. This felt nothing like Gemma. Maybe he was too rough. Still, he pumped himself and recalled her hot mouth and the suction.

How Jeremy wanted her! He wanted to be inside Gemma, even in her plump sexy rear. He wanted to part her with his thumbs. He wanted her to take all of him, repeatedly. He loved her bent over and moaning. He could see it. Her slender back would be sheened with perspiration while she fisted the coverlet in her hands.

He imagined her sitting on his face, too; his tongue would be inside her. He wanted to tease her, lick her clit, and drink her nectar, and it would flow *only* for him. That Jeremy told himself as he erased images of that actor. Jeremy lay pulling on his pipe and trying to imagine Gemma atop him in the moonlight. All he could see was her co-star. The Nile. Jeremy prayed she hadn't lain with that guy. However, the man *was* tall, well taller than Jeremy. With gleaming mahogany skin, Nile had incredibly ripped abs. Then again, that actor was so full of himself that he could only play one character—himself.

Still, had Nile showed Gemma some kinky new stuff? Jeremy wondered; because of Nile, would she now feel Karina Cay was too déclassé, too provincial, for her? Jeremy shook questions from mind to simply imagine his palpitating man root inside his *ange*. He imagined looking up at Gemma while they became one.

Ah, but that wasn't going to happen; Jeremy cogitated and tugged again. It didn't matter what Colin or others said because Gemma didn't want oneness. She didn't want marriage. Truth be told; it was something they had never discussed, so Jeremy didn't want marriage either. That he told himself.

However, Jeremy did want exclusivity, even though he slept with others. He lied, justifying that he only laid with other women out of necessity. J. B. Harden reminded himself, he only did so when he and Gemma weren't in the same vicinity—like proximity mattered.

He pondered exclusivity. That was another thing Jeremy didn't believe Gemma wanted. Truthfully, he and she hadn't discussed it, not since they'd become adults. Nevertheless, exclusivity was one thing Jeremy didn't think the lingerie model could manage. Why just look at her, he mused; look at how many men chased her, and wasn't a loser in the bunch.

Yanking hard on himself, Jeremy imagined Gemma breathless and calling his name. Come to think of it... She called him one of two things, Jere, just like his mother, or when Gemma was upset or even enamored with him, she called him by his last name, Harden. The beauty would either scold or goad him into getting balls-deep in her, depending on how she felt.

Thinking on the latter, Jeremy decided. He would take dark-haired Lance's advice over Colin's; *put a ring on it.* Who was Colin channeling? Mega music mogul Beyonce? Please.

Like Lance advised, Jeremy would spirit Gemma off to Amsterdam or Germany, her choice, for nights she would never forget. Then perhaps the producer/actress would dismiss that co-star of hers, the man who really was a character. That narcissistic Nile.

Chapter 24

When Gemma arrived, no Jeremy. He'd been scheduled to be at the HW offices on the island for at least two days. He was transitioning there to use it as his home base. Gemma knew he would do so for the express purpose of one day helming his paternal family business. Still, he'd left for India to check on textiles. All of that, he had explained in a call.

Gemma claimed she understood. Then she added, "Harden, I just want you to know I'm pissed." In French, she cussed a blue streak. "I feel like we never get to see each other." She tossed in, "And I hate it!"

"I know, *chérie*. I feel the same way; call you soon!" He had yelled just before boarding his father's plane. "We'll discuss how to fix this!"

"Whatever." Gemma rang off. She stared at her phone before flinging it away. She told Nannie that Jeremy's not being around made her want to cry. For months, she'd dreamed of him! Now, who knew how long they would be apart, this time?

Maybe she needed a different man. But she wanted him.

Amid her longing, the new sheriff of Karina Cay called. He asked Gemma out to dinner. "To celebrate my promotion," he reminded her.

Gemma didn't want to accept; she'd have preferred to sit home and stew. She was much too cute for that though, and here was a man, she mused, who actually had time for her. She told Trip when to collect her.

Gemma showered and wished for Jeremy. If he'd been present, they would not have been going out. Tonight they'd have been going down, on each other. Gemma exited the shower and wanted to scream. No, she really wanted to make love with her man—who was presently across the ocean. The thought made her breath hitch. Bravely blinking back tears, she dressed.

At Ms. Nalonni's upscale restaurant, Gemma wore sexy hi-heeled sandals, a spaghetti-strap cream top, and a pencil skirt. Black, it boasted a cream starburst pattern in front. At The Constellation, Gemma had more fun than she'd thought, though her mind wandered back to Jeremy.

Following dinner, and dessert that she refused, Trip, the new sheriff, suggested a walk, "Maybe on the beach," in the moonlight.

Gemma declined but later wound up at the off-duty sheriff's home. She'd never been before because he'd had a wife, the woman who'd fled the island. In her wake, she'd left divorce papers—and talking Karinians.

"So," Gemma said, entering on terracotta tiled floors, "I finally get to see where you live, now, because I know where you grew up."

Trip's bungalow was cute, with stucco walls, archways, quietly paddling ceiling fans and dark wood. Island style, the floor plan was open and comfortable, in a not so bachelor way.

On the rear deck, warm winds blew, and Trip asked, "Want a drink?"

Why not, Gemma thought. She couldn't share one with Jeremy, and he was probably out, lunching. Most likely, he was seated with some female HW executive. Forgetting that, Gemma named her preference.

Trip nodded, heading indoors. "Coming right up."

With her face upturned in lunar light, Gemma made a wish.

Her hair blew crazily about, and the moon silvered her profile. Stepping back outside, Trip thought he had never seen a more beautiful woman. Handing over Gemma's drink, he told her so.

Gemma said he was sweet. In the looks department, he ran a close second, with his caramel-colored skin and liquid brown eyes. "Trip, your eyes remind me of cognac," Gemma revealed. With his large lush lips, closely barbered hair, and muscled body, the man was a walking fantasy. "You know," Gemma teased, "you could be a calendar's Mr. July."

Standing close, the big man pressed a kiss to her swanlike neck.

Feeling the warmth of his breath on her skin and his soft lips, Gemma didn't object, since Jeremy had hied off to India. Trip was present, and he smelled so deliciously male until she turned into his waiting arms.

Gemma liked the way his large frame surrounded her, and before she knew it, his lips descended to hers. Their kiss was magic—until she caught herself. Refraining, she rested her head on Trip's broad shoulder. Softly, she said she didn't kiss. Not elaborating, the truth really was: *that* she saved for Jeremy.

Trip understood. When Gemma remained in his arms, he allowed his big warm hands to slowly slip downward, to cup her buttocks. When they crept back up to fondle Gemma's breasts, he breathed her in. Trip admitted he'd dreamed of touching the lingerie model, "Just like this."

Gemma informed him that she'd had dreams of her own.

"About me?" Trip's eyes twinkled as his rod and his heart leaped.

Gemma nodded, and he placed a hand at the spaghetti strap on her shoulder. His eyes asked, 'May I?'

She nodded again because what the heck? People always talked or wrote about her. They said she did this and that, with this or that one, so why shouldn't she do *something*? Jeremy wasn't present, and she needed to feel a man's body on her own. She needed the contact.

Feeling Trip's lips on her fevered flesh, Gemma moaned and pressed her breast deeper into his mouth. As he drew her nipple further between his lips to encompass her areole, she held him to her. Trip's hands sought and slowly removed Gemma's clothing. They roamed her shapely body. When his clothes were gone, she saw his formidable package. Gemma could only think, wow, her evening was about to get a whole lot better.

Lifting a breast, she again placed it against the sheriff's mouth, and opening it, he suckled, causing sparks in her deep.

When she produced a condom, in the moonlight Trip's eyebrow rose. There was a chuckle in his voice when he said, "I like that; preparation."

Turning Gemma, Trip helped her ease down onto a cushioned outdoor sofa. Between kisses, Gemma said she just needed to feel him for a moment. With her beneath his massive body, Trip gladly slipped his brown log between her womanly folds. Not entering her, Trip felt Gemma's heat. Feeling the silk of his skin, she allowed him to feel her wet. Nearly breathless, she said, "Condom." Aching for the riding and the release, she added, "Now."

The evening took a turn...

Gemma knew Trip Macaw was not an alcoholic, although some in law enforcement were, due to the pressures of the job; yet her friend was not. So why did he seem impotent? With such great 'equipment,' why was he unable to use it? Perhaps he was nervous. *The* Gemma Janelle—her public persona—had that effect on men, sometimes. Still, Trip knew her, so...

Trip could see the beauty thinking. He heard her mental questions as loudly as if she'd asked them. Therefore, he refreshed her drink and turned crooning Luther down. Trip then lay facing her to tell his story.

Gemma had heard that as an HPD officer, he had been shot. Still, to see where the bullet lodged and where fragments remained just aside of his groin made Gemma's heart go out. Her hands did, too, as she saw the place on Trip's thigh where another bullet had entered, near the femoral artery. Her breath caught because, with each heartbeat, he could have bled away.

Trip told of lying wounded in a crime-ridden area of Houston. He'd lost so much blood that he hadn't been expected to survive. Now, however, psych evals said he was okay. "But subconsciously, I must still be freaked out," he ruefully admitted. "Maybe that was why my ex lost patience and left." She hadn't wanted to move to the island in the first place. Then on Karina Cay, she had been unable to see its beauty. The woman had only longed for the suburbs of Texas. "Maybe if I'd given it to her good after we got here..." Trip smirked, "She *was* used to me putting it on her." Holding Gemma in the moonlight, the sheriff suddenly frowned. "Then again, maybe she'd still be gone; you know city girls."

With all playing aside, Trip admitted he wanted children. "But if my shit ain't working right, or if it malfunctions at the wrong times..."

Suddenly, that struck him and Gemma as funny. Amid their diminishing laughter, Trip asked, "But really, how am I supposed to get kids—with this problem?" Sobering, he also divulged, "I wanna be a dad like my dad was with me. I wanna screw again too without anxiety."

Gemma's eyes found the man's cognac-colored ones. "Oh, Trip..." She touched his face, realizing, even big tough lawmen had dreams.

"So you see," he gestured, "I have the equipment, but sometimes when I need it to work, it might—or not. When it does, it's great."

"I'll bet." Gemma felt bad for her friend and for herself because she had so wanted a romp. She thought of Jeremy and reminded herself. Every man wasn't Jere, ride-able and ready. Still, she would bet he had never gotten caught up with a woman he couldn't do. Blast.

Again, she felt perturbed with him because, in a way, this was his fault. If he were around more, to satisfy, she'd have had her butt at home.

Aware that she needed to be sated, Trip told her that, despite things, he could please her. "I want to."

Gemma said it was okay, "No pressure here." She announced she would go on home. Getting up, she began to gather her things. She said she knew Trip was probably on call, so a driver could collect her.

Trip wouldn't hear of it. With hands on Gemma's shoulders, he turned her. Softly, with lips at her ear, he said, "Lie back, for a while?"

She did, knowing her friend felt bad enough about what he hadn't been able to do, so she wouldn't strip the man of all his pride. Thus, she relaxed. Having known Trip for most of her life, she knew he wouldn't hurt her. It was why she allowed him to push her legs apart.

With his big hands, the caramel-colored man grasped Gemma's thighs and pulled her to him. While she lay on the sofa, he put his face in her and did what he had no problem doing. Trip did what he never worried about doing. With his mouth and tongue, he gave Gemma incredible pleasure. He used his hands and body too. Then feeling they should take things inside, he carried her to his bedroom. There, massaging Gemma everywhere, he slicked her with oil and slid all over her. With warm hands, he pressed every coil of tension from her body. Using those same hands, he fondled and squeezed her bottom. "Ooh, girl," he whispered, his deep voice drizzling over her like warm honey. "You 'n this big-ass beautiful booty got me going *in*-freakin'-*sane*." Using his massive hair-spattered body, he generated heat and friction.

For Gemma, the experience was unlike any other.

The new sheriff made her quiver and want to beg out loud. Then manipulating his log, he caused her to shudder with release.

Nearly bursting with pride, Trip kissed her there, again. He also said, "Don't think about reciprocity. Tonight beautiful, it's all about you."

With his heart showcased in his eyes, he said if she didn't have to hurry home, he would love to simply lie with her. Trip didn't say it might be his only chance, but the truth was Gemma was often gone, all over the world. And she did have that man that news outlets called 'the heir.'

Taking her friend in her arms, Gemma cradled Trip against her breast. Hugging his powerful shoulders, one of which had a puckered but healed bullet hole, she held him tightly. With his head pillowed on what he viewed as Gemma's remarkable rack, he drew a nipple between his lips. Within moments, in the dark, Trip's hands began to creep. Gemma spoke when she felt his huge thumb slip inside her. "Well, isn't *your* bag full of tricks?" Aroused again, she could only ride the wave. As she did, she felt the man's equipment enlarge; then, the pair no longer just imagined him using it. Trip quickly produced the right-sized condom. He spread Gemma wide, loving the sight. Nudging and pushing, he worked his way into her plush warmth. In the moonlight, he watched her eyes go opaque. He knew Gemma felt herself stretching to receive the sheer size of him. Holding her knees apart, by degrees, he gave her as much of himself as she could stand. Then he gave her more.

Moaning in ecstasy, Gemma mentally harked back to what Trip had stated earlier; he really could put it on a woman. Amen, she thought.

The experience became a high that neither of them would soon forget.

Yet in time, trembling, satisfied Gemma came down. As Trip hugged her close, they both slept.

Before dawn, Trip prodded Gemma with his formidable log of flesh. Opening for him, she again took him in. Then feeling safe, languid, and like the cat that ate the cream, she drifted off once more. Then just as the sun rose; shower fresh and in uniform, Trip kissed Gemma's body until she woke. On her lower back, the feeling of his magic lips pulled her from erotic images of the night before. Shapely nude Gemma stretched.

Unable to watch or he'd need her again, Trip handed the sex goddess a mug of steaming coffee. Smelling sinfully good, he bent to place his cushiony lips on her forehead. "Thanks for not making me feel like half a man last night." It was what his ex had done, in the end.

"Oh, you're not half of anything," Gemma assured him. "You're whole, and what happened between us was—special. My God, Trip, once you get going! I wonder," she teased, "if I can even walk today..."

Facing the window, Trip chuckled. He felt a bit more love, as well as infatuation creep into his heart, because, what a lady. He then wondered, how many men could truthfully say they'd had her—*the* Gemma Janelle—in their beds, although he would never tell.

Turning back, Trip's big fingers caressed her cheek. Gemma could see love in his eyes as he told her, "You're as beautiful when you wake as you are all dolled up." She highly doubted that, and said so.

When it was time, Trip helped collect Gemma's things to take her back to DeVeaux house.

On his golf cart seat, she held her heels in one hand as they sped along wide Beach Road. It ran parallel to its namesake the beach. With her hair flying free, Gemma glimpsed the ocean. Despite the wrap over her top, in the crisp morning air she felt chilled. Still, she knew the sun would soon burn off the mist and the dew. The pristine beach and serene inland waterways would warm. Cranes would take flight and pelicans would dive for fish. Watching sea island scenery slip past, Gemma did not feel the same way she would have, had she spent the night with Jeremy. However, her evening with Trip had held candor, sensuality and sweetness. All of which cemented something more between her and the big gruff sheriff.

Turning for DeVeaux House, the uniformed man spoke. "You know Gem, I've said it before, if you ever need anything, I'm your man."

Squeezing his muscled arm she nodded. "I'll never forget it."

Then they passed Colin, the reporter, out for his daily dawn run.

Chapter 25

Jeremy arrived on Karina Cay to find no Gemma. However, at his home off Beach Road, another woman awaited him.

Wearing a swimsuit with the sides cut away, along with a snug pair of joggers, Ashlee stood outside the imposing gates of Windsor Pines. Looking inelegant, she could not convince the gatekeeper to allow her inside. She'd tried to glimpse the manse, hidden in the distance behind palm fronds and other island foliage.

As Jeremy turned onto Hollow Well Lane, some woman teetered over on chunky sandals. She looked vaguely familiar. Not pleased, he mentally tried to place her. When he did, he did not want to be bothered.

Why wasn't she with Lance? Jeremy had nothing against the tag-along girl—as Colin called her—but Jeremy was in one of his moods. Also, he did not take well to strangers. She didn't notice as she informed him she had a job. He wondered why she thought he should care that now she worked for Buddy B, the island's Jack-of-all-trades.

Then she hit him with, "I just need a place to stay..."

Jeremy knew he couldn't deal with her right then; he had two days at home, and the first had begun all wrong. With his blue-gray eyes stormy, he glanced at the harsh-looking blond girl. Could he leave her beside the road? Braking his golf cart, he *wished*. Reluctantly he said, "Get in."

On the cart seat beside him, she talked all the way up the crushed shell drive. Bumping along, he glanced at her sun-dappled face. Did she not notice? He wasn't interested. He should have left her on the road.

Jeremy's tall brown houseman appeared to greet him and take his bag. The fit older gent did not have a single word for the girl. Were Jeremy not thinking about finding Gemma, he would have wondered. What happened, or what had his houseman heard, in their tight-knit little community? Jeremy would have considered; there had to be a reason for Gerard to be so stiff with a young woman he most likely did not know.

Never would it have crossed Jeremy's mind that Gerard knew someone who'd paid for sex with Ashlee out in the bayou. Unaware, Jeremy entered his cool home. It seemed dark after the shining sun out of doors. He led Ashlee to a bright, comfortable parlor where sun-gold silk drapes were open to the sea. He gestured toward a sumptuous white sofa. On it were white silk pillows stamped with sun gold tulips. Jeremy gave the girl no more thought. Entering the office that petite Giselle used when she was in residence, he got on his mother's phone. He snarled, "Where are you?" Facing the restless ocean, sparkling in the sunlight, his back was to the door. He was unaware that Ashlee had crept up.

"Mmm. You picked up a gig," Jeremy repeated. "When will you return?" He listened. "I know about him. Him, who?" Seized with anger, Jeremy grabbed a pretty glass paperweight. Hurling it, he watched as it shattered against the stone fireplace. Through stormy eyes, he saw it rain shards on the floor. "Never mind what the noise was." Ominously, in French, he warned, "No games with me, *chère*." Suddenly he was partially glad she wasn't there. He would not have wanted to hurt her by accident. Incensed, he informed Gemma, "You were seen."

Jeremy hurled another glass piece he would need to replace before Giselle returned. Yet through his jealous haze, he couldn't think about that. "*Le shérif a été vu aussi*," the sheriff was seen too, with you.

Feeling enormous fury, Jeremy rumbled, "You know when." He lowered his voice. "You let him fuck you, *bé*?" In French, he asked, "You do it because I wasn't here—to do so? Or did you want to try something—or someone—new? Even though he is old." In French, Jeremy argued, "He's older than you. Now, will you tell me you've gone black and you're not coming back?" Listening, Jeremy growled in French, "I know better than anyone who, *and what*, I am. You don't reprimand me. Just tell me, Gem, you want him?"

Behind the homeowner, the bottled blond figured Jeremy must have been talking to her—Slinky. Ashlee hated that she'd only understood two murmured words. Sheriff, and Gem. Was that a sore spot, could it be probed? Ashlee wondered, as Jeremy's houseman soundlessly arrived.

Why, the nosey little chit! Gray-haired Gerard thought it as wordless; he grasped Ashlee's elbow, closing the office door simultaneously. Feeling contempt, the strong houseman towed the eavesdropper away.

On the opposite side of the door, Gerard's employer stood motionless. The disconnected phone remained at his ear. Jeremy stood that way interminably, his eyes on the sea. Then covering them, he called Gemma back. When her phone rang and rang, he knew.

He would need to apologize.

Later, to his houseman's dismay, Jeremy said 'that girl' would stay in the guesthouse for a short while. Tossing a few things in a carry-on, Jeremy told the man with the closely barbered hair, "I'm headed out."

"Back to work in London, sir?" the tall, fit houseman inquired.

"No, G, I'm off to Amsterdam," Jeremy said he wouldn't be home afterward, not for another month. From Amsterdam, he would return to Home Wares, London.

Smooth-skinned brown Gerard did not appear surprised. Yet he delicately inquired. "What is to be done, ahem—about *her*," the girl with the awful yellow hair, "for that length of time, sir?"

Jeremy was vague. With his mind elsewhere, he had actually forgotten Tag Along. "Pretty soon, she should have a place of her own."

His employer could only hope, Gerard thought, keeping his face neutral. But that girl securing a place? To Gerard it seemed improbable.

Jeremy didn't necessarily want to do it, but he had to. He hated that he'd let news, photos, and curly-haired Colin's texts get to him. Still, all those things had caused him to remember the trip that summerhouse Lance had advised him to take.

Therefore, Jeremy had apologized to Gemma, even though he was still upset with her. Despite it, he believed what he'd planned would be different. He hoped it would be a treat for her because he wanted her happy. Then maybe he would feel—not happy, but a bit more peaceful about leaving her on her own so much.

Now pondering what would soon occur, Jeremy's heart beat faster…

In the exclusive bathhouse, they had already removed their clothing by the light of dimly flickering wall sconces. Jeremy knew he would soon watch some young stud do Gemma. Jeremy was a new-age type of man. He repeatedly told himself that lie. Maybe he, too, would even get off. He sure hoped so.

Jeremy recalled being in the pool with Gemma. Their limbs had been intertwined. He'd felt like surging into her but using all his willpower, he had refrained. Jeremy had reminded himself that the purpose of the evening was to allow someone else to do Gemma, to try something new.

While in the pool with water covering their nudity, in Jeremy's arms, Gemma told the truth. With her face pressed to his neck, she sounded oddly childlike as she revealed, "I'm scared."

"*Bébé*, I am right here." Feeling protective, he squeezed her tightly. "I will not let anything happen that you do not want." Jeremy lifted Gemma's head to look into her eyes. "Trust me?"

She nodded because she did. Yet she wanted to tell him that she didn't want this. Still, *he* wanted it, for them, for some reason. He had flown them to the exclusive club, and Jeremy had wined and dined her. Now he would watch someone else screw her.

About that, Gemma felt... jumbled up inside. She wondered, how had wanting to be with Jere come to this? Yet she went along, not just for him, but because part of her wanted to know what it would be like. She wanted him there, watching and desiring her, as another man pleasured her. They passed more dimly lit alcoves housing beds surrounded by filmy curtains. They could just make out silhouettes. If someone was benched near the bed, others crawled all over them.

On their bed, Gemma rested. With her heart pounding, she was glad Jeremy had gotten her ready. However, in passing, she had seen another woman who probably felt as apprehensive as she did. That woman's stud had spit on her. Jeremy had squeezed Gemma's hand as the man used two fingers to spread his saliva all over the woman's nether region.

Gemma recalled turning her face into Jeremy's neck. "That," she'd whispered, clinging to him, "what he just did to her, I do not want."

Jeremy kissed Gemma. "Shhh-shh, pet." He sounded so French, "That is not for you. It is why I took you into the pool and why I used my own stiff cock and kisses, on your beautiful breasts even, to prepare you."

Now he only wished the nude women, appealing that they were, would stop prowling around him. In the dimness, he was trying to focus. He stared at the bed with four large carved wooden penises for posts. It was draped in filmy fabric. Jeremy did not care that the women believed the sight of Gemma with the stud for hire would arouse him. The consensus was: the sight should make him want to slake his need by using their bodies. The women would never know that there *was* no other for him. Sure, he used others, but Jeremy Baptiste Harden had realized one thing in the last year. There was only Gemma Janelle.

He thought about men he knew. Most would never pay to satisfy their woman, not like this. However, on this evening, he would do so; he'd repeat it, infrequently, if Gemma could be sated for a while. It would keep him from worrying about her with others—like that actor and the sheriff—for whom she might leave him. Using hired pricks would ensure there was no connection. It was a one-time thing that might allow Jeremy to get back to loving Gemma exclusively when he was around.

He forgot the future, where he and she could enter a similar club in a distant city. Next time it might be Germany. Currently, he paid attention because he knew it was coming. Seated astride the big Dutch stud,

Gemma was about to reach orgasm. Jeremy could tell by the way she rode the young buck. So, after being tentative, she'd gotten into it. Her back was thinly veiled with perspiration, but Jeremy did not like how the man's large hands bit into the flesh of her plump buttocks. The man's fingers pressed inward as he raised Gemma up and then down on his daunting muscle-corded pole. The Dutchman did so repeatedly. The sight both wildly aroused and infuriated Jeremy.

Suddenly, he wanted to fight because Gemma was his. Therefore, with fisted hands, he stood. Blindly pushing wanton nude women aside, he knew it was time to step in. He used his strong arms to gently lift Gemma off the stud in the near dark. Jeremy placed a knee on the decadently draped bed and aided *une copine* to face him. He lowered her to the satin coverlet as Dutch stepped away, removing his condom.

Softly, Gemma spoke. "Did you enjoy—*Ohhh…*"

Jeremy slipped his pulsing member into her. Gemma remembered what she'd been about to ask. "Watching; did you enjoy it?"

She felt shy with Jeremy now, for some reason, while he'd felt he couldn't enter her fast enough. Enraptured suddenly and about to tumble over the cliff edge because she was with the man she wanted, Gemma noticed large-chested women. From the shadows, they peered.

Forgetting them, Gemma felt warm, limber, and well lubricated. Panting slightly as Jeremy grasped her ankles, she let him push them up to widen her. Recanting, she realized she rather liked the idea of an audience. Yes, let the women watch her man love her.

Sensually rocking into Gemma, Jeremy tipped her over the top. It didn't take much because her whole body sang, thrived, hummed, and came alive beneath his hands whenever he touched her. Feeling her clench around him, Jeremy poured into her, loving that *he* was the one who'd caused it. Fervently he kissed her and held her. She could barely breathe, and neither could he, but they were them again.

Before they left the city, there was another stud with long chestnut hair. The second time, Gemma was not as hesitant.

In the dimness of the club, while watching, Jeremy fondled a woman's enormous breasts as on his lap, she incited him with movement. Wearing a condom, just in case he needed to plunge, intently he watched. Gemma lay on a filmily draped bed, not even four feet away. With the crown of her head toward him, her hair hung off the end of the bed. Jeremy could see that Chestnut was giving her his all. Suddenly seized with jealousy, Jeremy felt that should be him!

Forgetting his female companion, he rose. Discarding Companion and the rubber, Jeremy had his engorged rod in hand.

With the stud pumping away, Gemma raised her eyes to the man who stood over her. It was him she really wanted. She raised her arms, beckoning. When Jeremy bent, she clasped his head for an upside-down kiss. Against his lips, she spoke. "Stay with me." Then breaking Chestnut's stride, she backed Chestnut toward the headboard, although she and the stud never lost contact.

Chestnut resumed riding. As he did, Gemma fondled Jeremy's ballsac. Wrapping her arms around his thighs, she pulled, and he leaned forward. Realizing what she wanted, he placed a knee on the bed, on one side of her head. Halting Chestnut, Gemma turned and got on all fours. As the man entered her from behind, Jeremy braced himself. He also allowed Gemma to take his member into her mouth.

Jeremy's scent and taste rang familiar. Gemma became more aroused. Yet with Chestnut working behind her and Jeremy laboring over her, she tried to keep up with both men's insistent thrusts.

Gemma realized. Jeremy had never been that way before, not with her. He was nearly wild, and he almost seemed to want to punish her, the way he forcefully stabbed into her mouth while holding her head.

Trying not to gag, she sank into a sex-induced haze as Chestnut strove behind her. This was Jeremy's night, Gemma reminded herself. Since they spent so little time together, she was acquiescing to his will.

Ardently she sucked, and Jeremy tried to prolong the pleasure. Yet Jeremy felt himself slipping, as the stud plundering Gemma also brought her joy. Tightly she wrapped Jeremy's member. Gaining powerful release, Gemma knew she had given Jeremy the same.

They left Amsterdam. On the Gulfstream, he kissed her fingertips as she sat staring from the plane's window. With daylight dissipating, he watched her, loving her. Jeremy felt Gemma was so beautiful until he sometimes felt astounded. He also wondered if he'd made a mistake. Perhaps he should not have arranged this trip. He thought it because she was so silent, seated on supple tan leather. What was she thinking?

Lowering the volume on the passenger audio, he pondered what would happen now. Would she wind up hooked, addicted to the type of excitement they had recently experienced? What if she would now want to add clandestine establishments and places shrouded in mystery to those she already frequented? What if—going forward—she would always need more than one lover at a time? Would he be able to keep up and satisfy her? Would he even want to?

Amid the barrage of questions, Jeremy found himself telling Gemma the truth. "When I'm away from you, *Ange*, I can't get you off my mind." He shook a strawberry blond lock from his eye. "Sometimes though," he revealed, "I wish I could. Then I'd be free of you." He frowned. "I mean, I wouldn't always be plagued by inquiries and worry over you."

She turned to stare incredulously at him. Her voice was soft, and it was filled with dawning understanding and hurt. "You *believe* the things you read about me... Oh God, Jere."

He saw shimmering tears when she added, "You do."

"I do not believe *all* that I read. But you do things, pet, questionable things. You leave me in the dark many times." He shrugged. "You always say you can only tell me so much. You say some things are not your secrets to share." Jeremy steepled his fingers. "Those things, *chérie,* they cause me to wonder. I don't often know where I stand with you."

Gemma's eyes stung. "You don't know where you stand. Well," she hissed, "let me tell you. I *know* you sleep with other people, Harden—with your greedy self. Still, *despite* us being away from each other more than we're actually together, *I* usually don't. That's because in my heart, I belong to you."

Speaking as though to herself, she gazed from the window. "I get hit on all the time. I'll admit I do hook up occasionally, but I mostly save myself for you—even though I've *met* women you've screwed!" Gemma humorlessly laughed. "Those hyenas were only too happy to tell me they'd had my man —and *you* don't trust *me*," Gemma scoffed. "If I wanted to get technical," she spat, "I could ask how you knew about that place back there! I could ask who else have you taken there, but I won't. First, I don't want to know, and second, I'm aware that loving you doesn't mean I should try to possess you. I'll never cling so much that I'd wind up suffocating you. That's not my way."

Jeremy opened his mouth, but Gemma raised an elegant hand. "I'm speaking. You're not the only one who feels bad. Have you ever thought that maybe *I* might wish I didn't love *you*?" Gemma sounded mean, "Sometimes, I wish you'd been sent away before we ever met."

Jeremy appeared shocked. "Then we would not know each other..."

"Exactly." Gemma gazed out at eternal sky. "That way, my heart would belong to *me*, not you. Then I could give it to whomever I chose."

Leaning over, Jeremy's heart beat rapidly. Gemma's admissions were too much, and he feared what she would say next. Therefore, he attempted to kiss her wet cheek. "Shhh-shhh, *bébé*." The businessman no longer wanted to hear words that would pierce his heart. Hating tears, he lamely stated, "No crying, *sil vous plait*."

"Get off me," angry Gemma slapped at Jeremy. "—And I'll cry if I want to, Mr. Boss Man—who is not the boss of me!"

Although it tore him up to see her tears, he had to say, "I was simply telling you the truth, *chér*. In a relationship, that is what adults do."

"Do we even have an adult relationship?" Gemma inquired. "I wonder because this started when we were kids, and I've never known anything but you. I wonder if I'd be better off with somebody else, someone new, someone who I don't have so much history with..."

Jeremy's eyes became shuttered. "Someone like the sheriff."

Gemma nodded. "At least I would get to see Trip sometimes." Then to hurt Jeremy because she was hurt, Gemma blurted, "He and I discuss things; marriage, kids, real stuff that you and I never have time for. He wants kids. Do you? Two days ago, he said he'd be proud to have me as his wife, a woman making her way in the world."

Jeremy's eyes narrowed, and anger caused him to sound imperial. "I care not about him! Neither do I want to hear his idiotic blathering. We are discussing you. And me! If we cannot do that—with each other, then we turn to others now, yes? Is that what you desire?"

Gemma's eyes narrowed. "Sometimes you make me sick." She folded her arms because part of her wanted to scratch Jeremy's face to ribbons. "I ab-so-lute-ly – hate – it," she venomously whispered, "when you become imperious and arrogant, when you become 'the heir.' If you're gonna be that way, don't talk to me. I'm not one of your minions."

Jeremy humbled himself. He had to, or she would shut him out. That she was good at. "I was simply saying," he clarified, "that I go away. Yet you are there, in my dreams." He spoke French before repeating in accented English, "For me, you are everywhere, *ange*. I've found that I truly love you like *grand-père* loved *her*. Although it is sometimes scary and uncomfortable, I feel I can never get away from you, but I do not want to. I only feel like you bewitch me, like she did him."

Gemma knew Jeremy meant the priestess, the one that there was so much island lore about. Clasping Jeremy's hand that had inched over to hers, she said, "Jere, I don't want to be like them, your grandfather and the priestess. I don't like the relationship they had. I want *us* to be different. I want us to find a way of being together that doesn't hurt. *And* I want you to be sorry, for real."

Jeremy knew she was referring to their fight, sparked by the sheriff.

"Sure, you apologized, but you only did it to get me back." Gemma dropped her slightly tilted eyes. "You hurt me, badly. You don't get to talk to me any ol' kind of way. You're not supposed to hurt someone you love, not intentionally." She raised a hand. "Listen, Harden. You were malicious. I would never be that way with you." Seeing the confusion in his turbulent eyes, Gemma explained. "I need more, now. We're older, and it's necessary." Gemma sighed, feeling far beyond her twenty-seven years. It was due to all the living that she had already done. "I'm willing to make concessions—for us, Jere—if there'll be an us. I'll do what I need to make this work. And if you want us, you should, too."

Gemma looked down. "It's why I did *that*, back at the club."

Jeremy's heart skipped as he turned her to look at him. "*Chèr*, never say you didn't enjoy that. Please." He held his breath, "Because *bébé*, I did that for *you*." He stared at Gemma. "You did not want to do it?"

"No," she truthfully stated, "not really. I mean, who wants some big stranger trying to screw her in the rear?" Gemma raised her eyes. "Maybe if we'd known where we stood beforehand, we could've enjoyed it more. Or we could have just enjoyed each other because we barely spend any time together, but to be together, I did that, mostly for you."

Jeremy expelled a shaky breath. Impetuously, he kissed Gemma on her forehead, pert nose, and lips. "But *non bébé*," he sounded anguished, "I thought *I* was doing it for *you*." He told the truth. "Half those moments, I was enraged. It was torture! I wanted to kill someone because you are mine. Seeing you with those men, I hated it." He pressed his forehead to hers, speaking softly. "It was erotic, too. You were *formidable*, but I was filled with fire and angst." Slumping in the leather seat, he hated to admit, "I thought I was no longer enough."

"Oh, Jere." Gemma clasped both her hands in her lap with a tear cascading down her cheek. "Now you see; we have a problem. We're so busy that we don't really talk. Then by the time we see each other, we've been so starved for contact until we fall on each other—"

"*Oui*," he acknowledged, "like beasts in heat."

Gemma grimaced. "I think we did 'that' back there for all the wrong reasons." With a fingertip, she dabbed a falling tear. "That's reason enough for us to now communicate, like adults. Let's be willing to talk to each other, to say what's in our hearts, okay?" Gemma said she knew Jeremy wrote things down, "But sometimes, just tell me."

The businessman nodded, although spoken words, from the heart, were not his forte.

"I'll do so too, Jere. I'll even start by saying this. I'd have been happy with you alone. You're not perfect, but I love you, my not-perfect man."

Jeremy squeezed Gemma's hand, knowing that she wasn't perfect either. However, for him, he also knew she was.

Aloud, he wondered, "How did I get things so wrong?" Listening to other people. That was what had gotten him, and them, there. Well, no more paying attention to stupid summerhouse Lance or bigmouth Colin, Jeremy vowed. Heck, those two weren't even in real relationships!

Jeremy stood. On the swirl-patterned carpet, he turned toward a luxurious bedroom. "I am fatigued." He said so because his mind whirred with too much information and the knowledge of his colossal failure. "Please, let just us go to bed."

Gemma remained seated. "Jere, if I go in that room, you will *sleep*. Or we're going to talk because I really would like to know some of what's going on with you, and I want details on this new position, too."

That was the last thing he wanted to talk about. However, Jeremy wearily agreed, "Deal, *bébé*." Jeremy pulled Gemma up and words tumbled from his lips. "Can you forgive me, *bé*? I mean it because..." *You are my whole world.* "Well, you know."

At the threshold of the teak wood bedroom, Gemma nodded. "Jere, you're forgiven." She smirked, "And maybe one day we'll do that again."

"*Mais non*," for Jeremy, it had been too much. "Never again," he divulged. He admitted that for him, their starting over—as adults—was more than enough.

Chapter 26

Four weeks later, back on Karina Cay, Jeremy met the new face of a luxury French cosmetics house. *"Bébé!"* he whooped, striding into DeVeaux House and scooping Gemma up. "You got the contract!"

Swinging her around, Jeremy remembered. He and she had only two days. Therefore, on the first, they holed up together. However, famished, they went out for a casual dinner that night, and Colin, Jay, and Lance met them. At Ms. Nalonni's Fish Frying House, the cohorts acknowledged missing Heather. All knew Red would soon return.

Seated with a paper menu before him, although he knew the offerings by heart, Jeremy recalled why he loved the informal eatery. The bar & grill served tasty island fare. Yet he couldn't decide whether to have the fried catfish or the grilled ahi. Perhaps he would order the tuna, or both, because 'working out' with Gemma left him ravenous.

In a cute A-line top, denim shorts, and high-heeled booties, she pondered having a salad. The family-friendly place was crowded and loud, evidenced by music jumping from a jukebox. Therefore, none of the cohorts noticed they were being watched.

Yet in a corner, down on the deck's far end, Ashlee sat, alone, at a table for two. She did not notice that she, too, was being watched.

Buddy B lounged across from her, hidden by a group of Karinians attending a raucous family affair. His gaze tracked Ashlee's, traveling the length of the deck to where the surfer's party sat. He saw Jay' n them. They sat beneath king palms strung with twinkling lights. The jack of all trades smirked, turning his attention back to his employee, Ashlee.

Unaware, Jeremy looked up. Standing aside, a server enthusiastically asked, "Y'all ready for some good ol' bayou cuisine?"

"Yep, yep!" Raising glasses and beer bottles alike, the quintet called out what they would have, as was often done at that eatery. Sipping water with lime, Gemma heard the guys' orders. A muffuletta, a po'boy, and someone would have bourbon-battered shrimp, all with coleslaw and fries, one order with sweet potato fries. Gemma felt she shouldn't because she usually watched what she ate, but she had been *so* hungry lately; thus, forgetting salad, she ordered gumbo and a side of dirty rice. Later, she knew she would sleep like a log because lately, too, she had been unbelievably tired.

During the meal, Ashlee could not hear what was said at the gang's table, but she could see. Jeremy and Gemma were as cozy as ever. Ugh. Leaning forward, he said something. Looking like they'd stepped from a clothier's catalog, his male friends suddenly yelled, "Whoa!" "No shit, man!" "Yo, thass what I'm talkin' 'bout!"

There were toasts all around, and Jeremy gave Gemma a big lip smackeroo. Golden god, Jay, kissed her too, for the heck of it. Playfully she swatted him, and getting up, Colin wrapped her in his arms. Then Lance joined the embrace, and the friends, including the oft-reticent J. B. Harden, could be seen shaking with laughter.

With stars overhead and twinkling lights glowing on the eatery's deck, Ashlee's eyes narrowed. She wondered what Jeremy said. Ashlee fumed. He'd better not have announced he was marrying that cunt.

Things were getting interesting. Buddy B thought it as he recognized Ashlee's mottled red fury. He knew it to be a mask for jealousy. "So…" the big man murmured, as the family that hid him from view began to clap and sing, "that's how the wind blows." Now, Buddy B mused, he just had to figure out which youngster the Chickadee had in her sights.

Since they would ferry or fly out soon, Jeremy and Gemma hid in DeVeaux house on their last day. Still, like wildfire on the island, his news spread. Jeremy would soon be home to stay! The heir would return to the manse. He would come and go; of course he had offices and clients to visit and factories to tour, but he had stepped into a managerial role at Home Wares. It was his family's thriving organization. Jeremy even wore a signet ring, one that had been worn by Hardens before him.

In the coffee house, getting java for her new boss, Buddy B, Ashlee heard it all. She passed a man telling a woman. Ashlee realized that must have been what Jeremy had shared with his friends. Yeah, on the prior evening, when they'd been so jovial. In a way, Ashlee was happy. The news meant she'd get to see more of Mr. Brooding, but it also meant she might see more of…her. Slinky. As she pushed out of her former workplace, Ashlee guessed she would just have to fix that. Walking in the brilliant sunshine, she nodded. She needed to start planning.

Gemma didn't know how she felt about the news. The studio wanted a *third* Warrior Woman. Being a producer was a given; the position was hers if she wanted it. Of course, with her as a driving force behind it, the second WaWo had been a greater success than the first.

However, in the two years since, Gemma had forayed into solely dramatic roles. Those she loved. She ate, slept, and dreamt them, then she woke ready to immerse herself again. In dramatic roles, she could push herself to learn and do more. In the roles she used dialect and subtle facial expressions to convey more than her characters could ever say.

Recently, in an indie film she'd produced, Gemma played a multi-dimensional character. At overseas film festivals, the work had generated considerable buzz. At present, in the states, the movie was being shown on limited release but soon it would open in theaters everywhere.

Pondering Warrior Woman Onslaught, Gemma felt ambivalent. A third action flick? Really? She felt that way because she had a secret.

She was going to have a baby. She was knocked up and happy.

Two months along, Gemma didn't relish putting in the time or the effort required for such a physical role. She'd put in months of pure hell for the last two movies in the franchise. First, she'd furiously read to know her lines and be off-book by day two. Then there had been the physical work. It included cross-fit training, running, cardio, and fencing. Often she'd left workouts and practice fight scenes aching and bruised. Habitually, after filming she had felt the same way.

Gemma didn't even want to think about the downtime, when she'd sit idly in a trailer that never really got warm because it was so cold out. Did she want to stand for hours in Wales on a nearly isolated stretch of Marloes Sands Beach? Sure, she would wear a layered cape beneath a blanket, but one or both she would have to throw off when scenes were shot. She would then be wearing something skimpy, her own fault, while acting as though her buns weren't freezing off. And Gemma hated to be cold, perhaps because she had grown up where it was mostly warm.

Hanging out in Pembrokeshire in misty rain was not something she looked forward to either, not in her condition. She dreaded being doused by freezing sea spray. She no longer wanted to nimbly run along rocky outcrops in Norway. No more slippery peaks rising from an icy ocean for her. Gemma no longer wanted to ride or fall off a temperamental beast. She hated trying to avoid heavy hooves. Nor did she want to race up hundreds of stone steps in the remnant of an old castle. And vaulting into a wicked fight scene? No. In the best of times, she hated the hoists that bruised and strained her torso but made her appear to do superhuman leaps. Thus, Gemma told herself, if she would play Arma Geddon again, doing so would wait. The producer had more critical things to consider.

One of which was finding time with Jeremy. Perhaps they should do so at home, on Karina Cay. She felt her news was something he should receive face-to-face.

Then after she told him, Gemma happily mused, she could call her mom. Gemma would call Dad and Pops too, but Kismet's call would be first. It was a girl thing, which reminded Gemma; she could three-way Belize and tell her older pint-sized sister and Momma simultaneously.

Gemma suddenly recalled that during her youngest years, everything had been about Daddy and Pops, especially her dad. Then the shared female experience had caused her to gravitate toward her mom. As an adult, Gemma now realized how special her parents were. Neither of the three had ever coveted the time she spent with the other; they'd never made her feel like she had to choose. Smiling, she could hardly wait because all three of her parents would become grandparents! Giselle and Michael Harden, too, but this would be their fourth grandchild.

Gemma also had to tell her bestie, red-haired Heather. Gemma had to apprise her management team as well, and soon. Contracts, dates, and production schedules would need to be rearranged, or set, in the case of Warrior Woman Onslaught. *If* she would indeed do it...

Jeremy told Gemma he had something to discuss with her. She, too, had news to share, she'd said afterward. Now the couple just had to find time to spend together, alone, at home.

Ashlee knew people wanted her gone. Well, she wanted something too. Jeremy. It was why she couldn't leave the island, even though the reeve, the steward at the manse, had informed her. "You need to arrange to live elsewhere." But Ashlee didn't dare! She was too close.

She knew the man responsible for running everyday affairs was only acting for his employer. Still, sexy, brooding Jeremy really didn't know her. Not yet. With all his going and coming, he hadn't spent any time with her. He didn't know she would be the best wife he could ever have. She was the right color, too, unlike that other *thing* that he had been screwing. Well, that mess would soon stop, Ashlee vowed it.

She just had to make Jeremy see because if she didn't, who would?

Ashlee decided, no more waiting for the heir to throw her a bone. It was time for her to step up.

He was going to be a father! Jeremy could hardly believe it; Gemma was three months in. Yet he felt they actually should have been parents long before. He had never known Gem to use birth control, not with him, nor he with her, and they had been spooning and furiously forking since fifteen. Forgetting those things, he could only think, *wow*. Him. A dad!

Jeremy's mind kept wandering from his work back to Gemma. Hers was the best news. The only thing was…the tabloids were speculating.

That was his fault, though. He wanted to kick himself. Instead of meeting her in their small enclave, he'd suggested their swanky Tribeca apartment. At the time, he'd believed it would be easier to access.

That night, the couple went out to eat at Interludes, a trendy New York hot spot. There, Jeremy offered Gemma his news. He would need to spend six months, or more, in Paris, France. He and his dad, the Home Wares CEO, had had long talks about the trip and stay. They'd discussed other things, one of which was that in time, Jeremy would be made COO.

"Chief Operating Officer, Jere?" Gemma seemed overjoyed.

He'd explained that it was still a ways off, although he'd worked every summer, had done internships, and knew nearly every position in the company. Still, there were many organizational aspects to learn. Jeremy said he and M. T. Harden had discussed changes which would start with the French office. Jeremy explained how his stay in France would aid him to organize employees and systems for optimized results.

For Gemma, all the talk of transient resources, integration, artisans, and good ole American craftsmanship caused her to wonder. Where would *she* fit? She and the baby that she now carried. As Jeremy continued, Gemma hugged herself like Nannie would have hugged her.

Seated opposite her at a cozy table, Jeremy finally wound down. Then Gemma said she understood why he wanted no failures or cost overruns. "I wouldn't want your projects taking more time than foreseen, either, Jere. I mean, you'd hate to miss the birth of your son. Or daughter…"

Jeremy stared. "You said birth? And my son, or *la fille*?"

"I did." Unsure of Jeremy's reaction, Gemma held her breath. With all he had going on, he might feel now wasn't a good time.

But this baby was coming.

Launching up, Jeremy plunked down where his feet had been only moments prior. On the cushioned banquette bench beside Gemma, he fumbled with her layers. Beneath the table, he strove to touch her now-curved belly. In awe, he admitted, "I didn't notice, at the apartment."

"Well," Gemma teased, "you weren't exactly looking for changes."

Kissing her, he became a wellspring of murmured questions, "You are *enceinte*, with child? *My* child. Wow. *Oui, bien*, yes, good, but how, *bé*? Well, of course, I know how. Do you feel…half-half? *Moitié-moitié*?" Jeremy remembered laughter. Gemma squirmed somewhat, too, as he'd wriggled his hand from her belly into her jeans beneath the table. He recalled that between her parted legs, with his fingers he'd spread her. Feeling her desire, he had lost all ability to think. He remembered whispering, "We must go, *ange*. At once." He'd wanted her so badly.

Out of doors, with a hand before her, he'd helped her into his roadster with the black pearl coat. Flashbulbs had caused him to see white. Snap and click! Again. Those dreaded photogs had been hanging around!

The photos ran in multiple tabloids. One caption read, **Heir Apparent?**

After that, the relentless chasing and hounding ratcheted up. In the states, security had to be raised for both people. Now in France, at his desk, Jeremy tossed the latest tell-all aside. He wondered why he'd even bothered to look at what had been written.

Still, everybody he knew must have read that trash too. His boys had called with jokes and felicitations. Others reached out, including his sisters, one of whom lived in the UK. Dang, Jeremy thought, he had wanted to tell his peops *his* way, in time—after *he* had grown comfortable with the news. He hadn't wanted his affairs spread this way.

Feeling unaccountably moody, the man that business associates called J. B. Harden remembered. The only call that hadn't put his back up had been from Giselle. Speaking French and English, she'd said, "I saw *votre* photo, *chou-chou*. The one of you and *votre femme*."

His wife. Was *Maman* hinting? She said she liked the idea of a new grandchild too, although she did not think Gemma was at all safe. "I've never liked those photo hounds. I think Gem should be here, in France with you, and near us, until the furor dies down. You know, pet?"

"I know, *Maman*." Jeremy revealed that repeatedly, he had asked Gemma to think about joining him. He said the model/actress/producer had said she might. He did not consider that to do so would take enormous juggling on her part and on the part of her team.

He didn't mention that she'd said, "Jere, your mom'll be back here soon. A few weeks prior, Giselle told Gemma about a couple of resort projects she had on Karina. "When I asked, your mom said she'd like to fit me in—you know, to decorate the nursery at DeVeaux House. I think she even mentioned sprucing up the nursery wing at the manse."

Dammit. Forgetting those things, Jeremy did not tell Giselle that he and Gemma had not had a chance to firm up any plans of their own. Nor did he mention the only thing they'd realized. If Gemma had the baby in France, the small Baptiste Harden would have dual citizenship. That was because Jeremy, the father, possessed French and American citizenship.

Jeremy did admit what he despised. Knowing that his and Gemma's personal business was fodder for perfect strangers to chew on.

"With everything happening here," at Home Wares Paris, "I haven't even had time to get used to operations. Now I'm becoming a...*père*, a father. And the whole world knows. *Maman*, I feel like too many eyes are watching. I feel...judged."

Giselle was aware that people who worked in HW offices everywhere were talking. Michael, Jeremy's silver-haired father, had told her.

Aware of it, too, Giselle's son said the loss of privacy felt all wrong.

The petite one made sympathetic mother hen noises. "I understand, Jere. Remember, I told you, I was hugely *enceinte* with your sister, before Michael and I married. Back then, people like me weren't supposed to allow things like that to happen or be known. Still, the news got out."

Sagely Giselle advised, "What is done is done, my pet. Now you must do what I did. Move forward."

Jeremy knew his mother was right. Therefore, he kept the remainder of his thoughts to himself. Yet the truth was sometimes he hated how big his and Gemma's lives appeared. Sometimes he just wanted their moments, especially the small, special ones, to be theirs, alone.

Chapter 27

When Jeremy said he'd go to Home Wares Paris, she'd thought, okay, that's his job. Gemma had panicked when he said he'd be there six months, or more. She'd sat quietly in the Manhattan restaurant, but she'd felt like hurling—when before, she had experienced very little illness.

Still, Jeremy had been pleased upon hearing her news. Then after speaking with her mom and sister, Gemma decided. She'd jet to France. She couldn't see being away from Jeremy for months, and especially not while pregnant. Now, as adults, she felt they needed to be together.

To Jeremy's relief, Gemma apprised her team. She stated that while expecting, she really wouldn't work. Of course, while in Paris, she would do cosmetic headshots for print ads. Those weren't strenuous, and she'd be pampered. Gemma had other small jobs and charity events to which she was also committed, but this phase of her life she would enjoy.

In her fifth month, she boarded the Harden Gulfstream, greeting the chief pilot and staff. Then on the flight to France, the mother-to-be tried to relax. It was hard, though, because her mind raced in many directions.

Arriving at her destination, she was not met by Jeremy, but by Giselle instead. The petite one said her son was in meetings. Offering hugs and kisses, she exclaimed over Gemma's bump. Then she, who never seemed to age, revealed, "I have something to show you."

Riding in a hired car, Gemma noticed the 8th *arrondissement*, an area she well knew. Thinking aloud, she murmured that Giselle and silver-haired Michael's flat wasn't on the tree-lined *Rue de Tilsitt*.

"Shhh-sh, *ma belle*," Giselle advised, sounding like her son as the car stopped before a stately building. In the lift that took them up to the third floor, Giselle remained mysteriously silent as in a marbled hallway, she unlocked a door. Peering into a luxuriously furnished apartment, Gemma saw her luggage. But hadn't it been down in the car?

"As you can see," the impeccably dressed older woman stated, walking through, "this flat includes four bedrooms. There is a living room, a formal dining room, three full baths, and one with a separate shower stall. *Oui*, and here is your kitchen!" Giselle beamed. "Nearby," she indicated a window, "is the *Charles de Gaulle Étoile*."

Gemma laughed, aware that it was a station on the Paris Métro Line. Then remembering something, she asked, "*Maman* G, did I see Jere's clothes in one of those bedroom closets?"

"*Mais oui*," his mother nodded. "But of course; this is where he—and now you—live, for as long as you are in beautiful *Paris*."

Gemma squinted, "This isn't a company apartment, is it?"

"*But non*, it is not. My son picked this place exclusively for you."

"I know you helped," Gemma nodded because design was Giselle's life. Her portfolio included high-end commercial and residential spaces, beautifully designed, eco-friendly, and highly functional.

Jeremy's mother chuckled. "I helped, yes, but this is all him."

Turning in a semi-circle, Gemma said she loved the traditional appearance, the high ceilings, with walls the color of cream. She spoke of the architectural millwork, which was exquisite. Touching a crystal doorknob, she said she liked the gilded mirror over the dining room fireplace mantle. Giving Giselle's hand a quick squeeze, Gemma revealed, "I can tell that this was a labor of love on your part."

Walking, Gemma mentioned wall sconces and the sparkling chandelier. Running a hand over heavy drapes, she said she liked the large windows and natural light, "But you knew I would." She gushed over hand-knotted Aubusson rugs; some had fleur de lis patterns on the parquet floors. Gemma touched inviting furniture in shades of cream or taupe. "*Maman* G, thank you for choosing neutrals." Now Gemma could add any accent color desired.

Giselle's eyes twinkled. "You're sure that was my doing, *chèr*?"

Gemma chuckled because, in so many ways, Jeremy was just like his elegant mother. "I'm sure because only you would think of such things."

Giselle bobbed her blond head. "True. Only a woman can know what another needs to make her feel at home." Giselle raised a bejeweled hand. "You are nesting, so I make sure you have the best."

Hugging Gemma, decadently fragrant, Giselle glanced at her watch. "Oh. Oh!" Jeremy's mother crowed, "I must be off." She had errands, and then she would meet Michael and a client for cocktails. "There is prepared food—until later, *ma belle!*"

When alone, Gemma walked through her luxurious abode. Aloud, she spoke to her grandmother. "Nannie, isn't this wonderful?" Respectively, Gemma said Jeremy and Giselle had done fantastic. Rubbing her belly with one hand, Gemma used the other to text Jeremy and tell him so.

That evening, with his tie loosened, Jeremy had his jacket slung over a shoulder. Entering his home, he took one look at the love of his life. Lustily, he fell upon her.

As she tore at his clothing, he ran his hands over and over her. While kissing her and noticing the changes of just the past few months, Jeremy said he liked that Gemma was near naked.

"Now," she enthused just before he speared into her, "Let's get to this!"

Afterward, perspiring and satisfied, Jeremy stated, "See what you do to me *ange*? You stay away so long until you make a beast of me."

With a shapely leg tossed over his, Gemma lounged amid comfy down pillows. Had she been in a movie, she thought, she'd cap off their most recent sex session with a cigarette.

"I was quite beastly too, you know," she laughed. "I wanted you so badly, Jere, until I almost felt like a hungry bear. Man..." Gemma appeared to be thinking. "I sure hope our baby doesn't come here with whiskers and a little snout."

Jeremy covered his eyes. "Heaven forbid."

Chapter 28

Gemma's first week was spent adjusting to her new surroundings. Each day, she noticed that Jeremy rose early. On the premises, he worked out before showering and heading to Home Wares. Left at their luxury apartment, Gemma lazed about, eating like she never would have while on her grind. Yet, for her, the unhurried pace got old.

Aware, Jeremy suggested she take cooking lessons. "Not that you aren't already great in the kitchen *ange*, but why not—"

"Take French cuisine lessons!" Gemma excitedly finished for him.

Soon afterward, she enrolled in a morning class. The first day, she wore a tee partially covering her belly. Leggings covered her long shapely legs and derriere. Her lengthy unprocessed hair she wound into an up-knot. Grabbing a designer tote, in suede boots, she was off.

On other days, as lean, toned Jeremy dressed, he surreptitiously watched Gemma, realizing other things he loved about her. Often seeming blithe and carefree, she always appeared stylish. As she wound a cashmere scarf about her neck, she mentioned returning later than usual. She said her day would consist of cooking class, then multiple voiceovers, some for advertisements, while others were public service announcements. The PSAs, about battered women, she said, were short messages that would air on the internet, radio, and TV.

Out of the lift, Jeremy possessively pulled Gemma to him and kissed her thoroughly. Then hopping into a waiting car, he headed to the HW offices. On foot, with near-invisible security, Gemma set out for her class. She stopped, though, at a nearby café for *le petit déjeuner*, the small breakfast. Most days she enjoyed a croissant and *café crème*, something she'd never have done had she been back in the states or steadily working. Instead of the deliciously strong coffee with hot cream, she would have had hot water with lemon and an apple or plain yogurt.

However, she was having a baby! This was her time, she told herself, and she would enjoy it. "No sense depriving us," she said aloud while jaunting off to make roux and sauces. As she went, she recalled interviewers who'd been surprised to learn she cooked. Gemma always admitted that way back, she'd learned cuisine/presentation from her mom.

Within a week of making Paris home, Gemma even visited her highly recommended new doctor of obstetrics. Not long afterward, the mother-to-be posed for the cover of a notable women's magazine. Several non-featured, tasteful semi-nude shots she had framed. The gifts for Jeremy, he proudly displayed in their bedroom and private spaces.

Back on Karina Cay, bottled blond Ashlee was determined to wait Jeremy out. She didn't care that he'd gone overseas. She'd heard that tidbit through her own branch of the island grapevine. Hearing it had also made her glad, in a way, that she'd met outdoorsy Buddy B.

When she couldn't get info any other way, the ox of a man was a good source. The only thing was, sometimes, Ashlee felt like he knew too much about *her*. He'd once said that with his background, he could gain info on almost anybody. Yet when she'd probed, wanting to learn more about him, he'd shut her down. Still, she knew that being bonded and licensed, the jack-of-all-trades was the man Karinians called for odd jobs. This made Buddy B privy to much of what Ashlee could never have found out on her own. And sometimes in conversation, he shared.

Working in Buddy B's small office, answering phones, and doing dispatch, Ashlee had seen the huge outdoorsman gaze at her. When a man looked at her that way, she knew she could get what she wanted from him. Still, there wasn't much to gain from big Buddy B other than info. Wasn't a thing wrong with him, Ashlee mused. The man was in shape, but he was old, like fifty-something. When he didn't shave, his stubble was gray, ick—and most important, he wasn't rich at all.

What Ashlee wanted could only come from the younger, sexy Jeremy Baptiste Harden. Therefore, when he returned, she would get him to look at her the way Buddy B often did.

Evenings, when he arrived back at their Parisian flat, Jeremy might find Gemma in the kitchen. Once, he overheard her speaking with her dad as she prepared dinner. Gemma squealed following something Beau said. "I knew you'd tell Momma!"

Entering the kitchen from which delicious scents wafted, Jeremy noticed *une copine*, bending to tend her oven. Damn, if she didn't have the sexiest ass he'd ever seen. As lust punched him in the gut, Jeremy sidled up. He eyed the top that slipped down a pretty shoulder. Placing hands on Gemma's flared hips, he pulled her to him. With his groin to her derriere, he whispered. *"Bonsoir, bébé."* Then locking hands before her, one at a breast and the other over their belly, he kissed her neck. With a finger, he circled her clothed nipple.

"Okay, Dad, I gotta go." She said it as Jeremy turned her. "Mmm-hmm." Gemma sounded distracted. "I will. Love you, too."

Lifting her, the man who'd recently asked her to marry him set Gemma on a countertop, and she forgot the phone. Raising her shirt, Jeremy eyed cleavage before raining kisses downward. His lips traversed the vertical line that Gemma claimed bisected her 'beach ball' in half.

She splayed fingers through cropped strawberry blond hair. Jeremy had had it cut when he'd become an executive. "Hello, J.B. Harden, company man," Gemma whispered. She spoke, casting an eye over trousers and a button-front shirt currently open at the collar. "I love your professional look, sometimes. Other times, I love you...nude."

Within his clothes, Jeremy's rod jumped while he caressed Gemma.

Aware that things were heating up, she turned off the burners.

"Ah, now we're getting somewhere," he murmured, peeling away her top. Unhooking her bra, he exposed her heavy breasts. "Damn, you're gorgeous," he intoned, pushing each up to gently suckle; he recalled she was tender these days. Standing between her legs, suddenly, he pulled Gemma to the counter's edge. Fighting to release his length, the couple made love on multiple kitchen surfaces.

During intermission, as Gemma called it, she put the finishing touches on the meal that she would serve, at some point.

Evenings later, while watching Jeremy devour the *Tarte Vanille* that she'd purchased, Gemma realized. She loved living with Jeremy, despite them griping about keeping the commode lid down. She said it was only fair because they would both have to lift it when needed.

Forgetting small things, she realized she liked hearing Jeremy outlay his work plans. She offered ideas, and they talked, sometimes, until nearly sunrise. Noticing, they would try to rest, aware that soon the day would begin. Gemma even liked that she and Jeremy could have what they'd never before had as adults when days were done. Uninterrupted time. They used it to get lost in one another. Sometimes there was no sex. They simply walked, hand in hand, around Paris, the city of lights. They sat in or outside small cafés. When Jeremy put reports and his glasses aside, they played cards on other evenings. He even filled the air with music. He loved the song '*Home*' by Phillip Phillips. One line grew on Gemma, the one about making this place her home.

Back on Karina Cay, anger-driven Ashlee realized. She had skulked around Windsor Pines so much until she knew the help's schedule. When each person was elsewhere, she came out of hiding. Some days after working with Buddy B, she entered the manse, instead of going to the guesthouse that she had been advised to vacate.

Since she lived on the property, entering the main house was not hard. Ashlee had to be careful, though, not to be seen slipping into Jeremy's home, or she'd be gone. Yet she did so through the maid's door when it was left slightly ajar. The older, longtime cleaning woman, Mrs. O'Shea, was good for doing that. She beat rugs or swept and was generally occupied with domestic chores. Therefore, Ashlee bypassed the alarm, ensuring the first-floor cameras didn't record her image.

Once inside, with house personnel moving about downstairs, she would climb upward to enter Jeremy's quarters. There, the fire of her envy and rage burned hotter each time. Ashlee told herself it kept her focused because she *would* become Mrs. Harden—not that black chick.

Ashlee reminded herself to control her anger. She couldn't smash framed photos of her intended and Slinky. Doing so would leave a trail. That was why she hid the image she'd damaged. Despite hating Gemma, Ashlee helped herself to the other woman's things. Why not? That black cunt had so much. It wasn't right when Ashlee, a white girl, had so little. Another thing. Why did Slinky need to have her stuff at Jeremy's house? She supposedly had her own home, somewhere up the beach.

Ashlee was careful not to take any of the lingerie with tags on it, even though Slinky had oodles of beautiful things; perks, probably, for being the company model. But Ashlee did strip before Jeremy's massive wood-framed mirror right there in Jeremy's large masculine bedroom. As Ashlee disrobed, she pretended Jeremy was there, watching her. Then she stepped into whatever beautiful lace undergarment she knew Gemma had worn. Ashlee knew because the fabric smelled faintly of perfume. So that was what a lingerie model smelled like. Ashlee thought it the first time. The fragrance reminded her of the expensive scents available at the resort boutique. Soon she, too, would have authentic perfume.

Ashlee often held undergarment crotches to her nose, and she inhaled the faint scent of her rival. She'd even licked the cotton panel a couple of times to see if she could taste Gemma, but no such luck.

Before the huge mirror, standing on its animal legs, Ashlee arranged herself on Jeremy's bed. Thinking of when he would belong to her, she spread her legs. Via the mirror, she watched herself masturbate. Breathing hard, she climaxed. She made sure she got her fingers good and wet. Then all over Jeremy's pillowcases, she smeared, marking her territory. Yep, Ashlee thought, when her man came home, he'd feel overcome with *her* scent. Then he would want only her. This Ashlee believed. Footsteps! Oh, no! She remembered where she was, and she could not be caught! Damn. No good could come of that, so she hastened to escape. Under cover of falling darkness, she snickered as she ran. Passing saw palmetto, white oleander, and potted pink begonias, Ashlee felt so alive. Sprinting across the crushed shell drive, she felt exhilarated!

Slamming into the lovely guesthouse, she laughed. Feeling unaccountably high, she removed her clothes. Beneath them, she wore Gemma's racy undergarment, and she removed it, adding it to her pile.

Ashlee ignored her crisscrossed, scarred body. She again felt aroused, just thinking of the heap of her own worn underthings. She'd left them in the manse, in the closet that was obviously Gemma's. Ha!

Ashlee plopped down on the cushy floral sofa with Jeremy on her mind. Picturing the heir to two fortunes, she used her fingers and a dildo to work herself into a sex-induced lather.

One day *she* would have pretty tits. Ahhh. Jeremy Baptiste Harden was going to splurge for them—among other things.

Ashlee slapped her vagina with one hand, while with the other, she worked herself. Soon she heavily panted. This time when she crested, she let loose a blood-curdling scream.

Unbeknownst to her, in the night, others heard.

When she was in her eighth month, Gemma spoke to Heather Garrahan, D.V.M. Gemma's red-haired friend spoke of her purchase back on Karina Cay. Said the Irish siren, "I like being a homeowner, Gem, but I sure do miss my mom's cooking."

She and Gemma laughed. "I know my little chalet is nothing like yours or Jeremy's," Heather teased, "but I'm happy with it. Oh, and Colin and I are back to running again."

Aware that her friends did so every dawn, Gemma acknowledged, "It must feel so good to be home, Heath—and as a doctor, too!"

"It does," Heather agreed. She admitted she loved working full-time at the vet's office, whom she would one day succeed. "Got a couple of dogs now, too; they're rescues. Sometimes I take them to meet Colin.

But on another note, I feel bad, Gem, because I wanna throw your baby shower. It'd be co-ed and catered, the biggest ever, if you were home!"

"Aww, Heather G, that's sweet," Gemma cooed. "You sound like my mom and Leez. They're bummed about the same thing."

Into the phone, Belize had said, "If you were in New York, Munch, me 'n Momma would throw you a big blingy baby shower."

"I don't need all that," Gemma had assured Belize. "Jere and I will get stuff. His parents are helping. Guinee," his sister, Guinevere, "sent all sorts of things already, and Giselle is an absolute angel."

"Do not tell Momma that," Belize had advised. "She'll feel like her place as grandma is being usurped. She wants you with her, now."

"Gotta remember that," Gemma chuckled. "Thanks, Leez."

Momentarily forgetting her sister while still on the phone, Gemma spoke. "Heath, a few of the angels," the lingerie models, "were here," in Paris, "and we met. They all had baby gifts for me—I was so surprised!"

Heather pouted. "They did what I want to, and you're *my* best friend. You don't really know them; you just work with them."

"I know, Heath," Gemma soothed. "Tell you what. You can be my baby's Godmother; how about that?" She held the phone away as. Happily, Heather squealed, just like when they'd been girls.

"Doctor Heather G," Gemma called, "I gotta go—assistant's on the other line. I'll call you soon. Love you."

"Hugs, kisses, 'n love to you—byee!"

After the calls, Gemma realized she felt like a tortoise. Every day. She told Nannie that she was so ready to have her body back. She even imagined her grandmother chuckling. Although Gemma lumbered along, she was reluctant to give up one activity. Shopping. There was one Parisian market she adored, the city's *marché biologique*, and the organic market on the *Boulevard Raspail*. On market day, Gemma was up and out early, even in November, late in her pregnancy.

She couldn't wait to get to the place that was chock full of enticing produce, fresh fish, and a bevy of other products. She loved gawking at wares, bottled wines, balsamic vinegar, and oils; prime cuts of meat, trays of olives and peppers, lovely browning rotisserie chickens, and the vast assortment of sausage and cheeses.

Sometimes Gemma went on Tuesday or Friday. It was now a struggle to get there early. Thus, one day, late, she found out. When vendors were packing up, they called potential customers. "You. Come!" They were quite bossy.

"*Belle fille*! Come!" The fishmonger ordered, and feeling ungainly, Gemma obeyed. "For you, beautiful girl," he offered, "a great deal for *vingt*—twenty euros!"

Beaming at her good fortune, Gemma watched the aproned round man with the congenial face. With efficient hands, he swiftly cleaned, filleted, and wrapped her purchases. The fishmonger then dispensed advice. "Now I tell you how to cook my beautiful fish..."

Back at the apartment, Gemma rubbed the fish with olive oil and added garlic cloves, sea salt, and ground pepper. She added fresh thyme and roasted it in the hot oven. She even halved a lemon inside, just as she'd been told. *Délicieux.*

Gemma loved perusing the *patisseries*, too. The pastry shops smelled divine, and try as she might, she couldn't stay out of the *boulangeries*. The French bakeries just called to her. She purchased baguettes, flaky croissants, and her favorite, *pains au chocolat.* Classic, rich, flaky pastry dough baked with dark chocolate.

Gemma even sent her pint-sized sister Belize, Heather, motherly Ina, her assistant, and others, decadent chocolate treats.

From *Le Bon Marche*, the department store, she sent many items that the ladies would love. Gemma did so for the same reason she had when she and her next gen cohorts had been little. Like her dad, Beau, Gemma derived great pleasure from giving.

Chapter 29

In early December, Jeremy made good on his promise to take Gemma to the *Champs Elysees* holiday market. That evening, she planned to buy last-minute Christmas gifts. Walking among lights and decorations, her step slowed. She unwound her scarf, trying to breathe.

Sipping *vin chaud*, Jeremy noticed, Gemma had fallen behind. He turned—and froze. In the busy, brilliantly decorated aisle, *bébé* was doubled over. Her coat was at her feet. Two maternal-looking women stepped toward her. Jeremy's cup of hot mulled wine fell from his hand. Dashing to Gemma, he knew; *ce moment magique* was upon them.

For both, it was frightening. Gemma seemed to be in so much pain, despite attempts to concentrate on her breathing. Feeling powerless to aid her, Jeremy got her home. Then he thanked God that her mom was at the apartment because Gemma's water broke…

A few days before, Kismet Staar had called. After greetings, she told her daughter, "I need you to open your door."

With the phone in hand, Gemma waddled to the apartment foyer. She asked, "Mom, what are you up to?"

"Just making sure you get your gift."

Cautiously, Gemma opened the door. And screamed. "Momma!" In Kismet's arms, Gemma broke down and cried. She literally boohooed.

"I know, Munchkin." Hugging Gemma, Kismet understood. "That's why Momma's here." Silver-haired stylish Kismet took her daughter's face in manicured hands, "You didn't think you'd do this without me…"

Unable to speak, Gemma nestled further into her mother's fragrant embrace. Inside, when she could string words together, Gemma managed to say, "I love you, Mommee," before she burst into tears again.

Chuckling, Kismet revealed, "I was once right where you are. I was emotional, too. Your Nannie was there for me. God rest her sweet soul."

Both women dabbed tears, recalling Gemma's lovely grandma.

At *un hôpital* in Paris, Jeremy forgot his mother-in-law—well, Ms. Kismet. He needed to focus. He didn't like how Gemma seemed to be struggling to bring their baby forth. However, the hospital staff did not appear worried. Yet Jeremy agonized with Gemma, partially because her grip ever tightened on his hand.

Then she screamed, and began to laugh—through tears.

The doctor spoke, and Jeremy heard a small cry. He felt weird and like time had leapt forward as he heard the words, 'You have a daughter.' With his heart beating double time, Jeremy turned. A nurse did something to a tiny being on the far side of the room. *His* tiny being.

Then Jeremy was able to see. *His daughter.* Gazing down, he thought, boy, was she tiny! Her skin was reddish; he'd read the color would fade. The infant lay on her mother, moving in slow motion. Jeremy noticed Gemma, who didn't seem to mind, at all. Seeing the love on her face, he realized he felt it too. Gemma was perspiring. Sprigs of hair were plastered to her face and neck. Clutching the baby, she cried. Her bulbous parts were exposed but to Jeremy, she'd never looked so lovely and all he could think was: his Gem had given him that tiny *person.*

Using a fingertip, he touched the pudgy, doughy-looking cheek. He stared at the pink pout, so like his. Warmth rushed over him, and it was incredible. That tiny, almost fairytale-ish creature was *his.* She moved, making teensy noises. Hearing them, Jeremy felt suffused with love, and it was so different from the kind he felt for the baby's mother.

Jeremy felt pride too, and a twinge of fear—because would he be any good at fatherhood? He wanted to be, and for the baby, with the slightly pointed ears, he suddenly felt protective. Feeling profoundly and inexplicably different, Jeremy bent. Feeling conflicted, he straightened. His movements were jerky as again he leaned down. This time he made himself kiss the tiny hand, and it was so soft. Feeling emboldened, he kissed the head that brought to mind a peach.

Touching his lips to Gemma's, Jeremy realized. *This* was what his bi-racial *grand-père* had always wanted for him. Posterity. Family. Jeremy had not fully understood, until now. *He* was the keeper of family.

Grand-père had deemed it so all those decades ago.

Soaked with perspiration, tears trickled from Gemma's eyes. However, she told concerned Jeremy that she only felt joy. Sure, she ached, but he no longer wanted to wince in pain when she squeezed his hand. With a blink, he remembered the grandparents—all five of them! He needed to go announce that he had a daughter.

Appearing before them, he called out, "We have a girl." He laughed when they congratulated him. Unaware that he'd been holding his breath, he released it. Jeremy nodded when his dad and Beau simultaneously asked, "Scared you, didn't it?" They both knew birth was an experience.

Jeremy told the truth since they'd been through it, his dad several times. "Man, I wanted to faint—like a girl. For a while, I even prayed I would because then I could have legitimately opted out."

The older men uproariously guffawed, aware of just what he meant.

When she could see her daughter, Kismet kissed Gemma. Gently, Kismet held her granddaughter. Gemma's voice was reedy when she admitted, "Mom, I wish one thing…that my Nannie was here."

Kismet's eyes shimmered. "Baby," her voice shook. "I sure wish that too. And I'll tell you, it really doesn't matter how old I get; there are just some things that I will always want to share with my mama."

Gemma whispered, reaching for her mother's hand, "I know. I talk to her all the time, though, Mom…"

"You and me both, baby."

A knock sounded, and the door opened a bit. Glancing over, Gemma saw winsome older Beau. She held out an unsteady hand. "Daddy…"

Later, Gemma's oldest brother, Chance, offered congrats via phone. Bonaire, Belize's twin, even asked, "Munch, did it hurt much?"

"It hurts *now*," she winced, "wit' you making me laugh; asking dumb questions. It was hell—like a lemon squeezing out a watermelon."

It was her brother's turn to laugh.

Déja called too. "Munchkin, I hear you're a momma now."

"I am." Gemma leaned into her pillows, "Just like my big sister."

"Munch!" pint-sized Belize yowled via phone. "Who told you to have that baby?" Then quieter, Belize asked, "Is she cute? And little, like me?"

The new mother smiled. "She is, Leez. She's just perfect, like you."

Heather called, "Pops just told me! I can't wait to see our baby!"

Brett and Auntie Mireya, Daddy's friends, sent beautiful gift baskets. Momma's longtime friend Valeria René, and her daughters, did too.

Before her maternity ward release, GemCo, Gemma's production company, and the studio sent substantial floral arrangements. Her Warrior Woman co-star, Nile Narcissi, did too. Casting director Nancy even wired a gift certificate from a Parisian couture boutique for babies.

Having had the news passed along by the cohorts, Trip wanted to text. Yet he called from Karina Cay. The sheriff's smooth low voice was sexy when he said, "Congrats, girl. You did it. I'm proud of you, mama."

While they briefly conversed, Trip sounded jovial, but Gemma knew. He was a bit saddened. Therefore, after telling him her baby's name,

Gemma propositioned Trip. "I'd love it if you'd agree…to become her Godfather." Gemma knew how much the sheriff wanted a child, so softly she said, "This way, we can share the joy."

The huge caramel-brown man was touched. Swallowing emotion, he admitted, "Gem, girl, I'd be honored." He really would.

On Karina Cay, Ashlee heard about the birth of Jeremy and Slinky's baby. Their stupid friends were celebrating. The guys were sickening, that red-haired veterinarian, too. The four of them were telling people. Lance acted as though the Duchess of York had just given birth instead of plain ole Slinky. He passed out cigars. But Gemma was just some black monkey lucky enough to have gotten knocked up by the heir to two fortunes. Although Ashlee was majorly hating, she liked one thing. On the island, nothing was secret. She almost liked that people talked too much. This way, she always knew what was going on. With all the talk, Jeremy wasn't even aware. Still, she was keeping tabs on him. Her man.

Blond Buddy B with the crew cut heard, too. The ox of a man had gone to patch up some fencing behind the animal hospital. Inside, he had needed a signature, which was when cute Red told him.

He knew he would need to keep a close eye on his employee. At his small office, Ashlee opened the mail and answered the phone. For the other fellows working for him, she played dispatcher. Nevertheless, to Buddy B, the brittle blond never seemed quite right or stable.

Jeremy's desire to return to his apartment grew each day following work. He could hardly wait to see his baby. Sure, he wanted to see her mom, but he couldn't help but marvel at how their daughter grew.

At nearly two months old, Twyla Cher now appeared real. Her ears finally looked normal and not like an elf's. Boy, was she cute and round. She had her mother's slightly tilted eyes and Jeremy's bow mouth. Jeremy said Twyla even had the most beautiful brown skin.

"You used to say that about *me*," Gemma reminded him, grateful for the break he provided. "Gee, thanks," she teased, "guess I should be ok with you tossing me aside for a plump, sandy-haired girl. The so-called new and improved version of me."

The couple laughed, but in PJs, Gemma really was grateful that Jeremy wasn't jealous of the baby as some fathers were. She was pleased that he experienced a similar type of love for their daughter.

Turning, Jeremy saw Gemma place booties and bibs in a nursery drawer. Although he hadn't voiced it aloud, he wondered if the woman he now thought of as *sa femme*—his wife, knew. His love for her had grown exponentially. He watched her leave the soothing, pretty room. He walked the baby, in her onesie, over to the window. With baby in his arms, Jeremy could finally assimilate what he'd felt after her birth.

He was now aware that he had to make Home Wares work, *for her*.

As he rocked, many things that his Afro-French *grand-père* had done were now clear. Jeremy now understood why the old man had made him 'the heir.' Now, Jeremy no longer felt resentment. He didn't feel like he had been robbed of the right to choose his own path. This was his path.

He'd previously thought *grand-père's* methods of handling family and business had been outdated. Not anymore. Jeremy understood; his primogenitor had groomed him to become the keeper of hearth and home. Continuing to rock, Jeremy acknowledged the truth. He was not just the keeper of his little family—the one that consisted of himself, Gemma, and Twyla—but Jeremy would one day be the executor for all.

He didn't know when it had descended, but now Jeremy experienced peace. He embraced his custodial role. Minding family holdings no longer felt like such a burden. He now accepted the mantle that had befallen him. Now he could do what he did for his parents, sisters, and even their offspring. Now he could do all that he had to—with grace.

Planting a kiss on his daughter's nose, he spoke. "My little *cher*, if I am blessed to have a son, too, I will do as *grand-père* did." Jeremy would do as his father, Michael T. Harden, was yet doing with him. "I will make sure your brother has the same understanding I always had.

"As the male in the family, my boy will become the keeper of holdings and home. He'll be like me" –and those gone before– "or *you* will, my love."

While Gemma was pregnant, Jeremy took innumerable photos of her. She had expected him to tire of doing so after she gave birth. Yet the man with the blue-gray eyes had not. He, whose hair was slowly silvering at his temples, had morphed into a photo documenter. It should not have been a surprise. While growing up, Jeremy had done the same, but he'd used pens, pencils, and charcoal back then.

When he wasn't working, Jeremy's favorite photos to shoot were those of Gemma breastfeeding their daughter, Twyla.

The new mom had come up with the name because she believed they'd conceived at twilight. "Remember, Jere?" She pestered him, "Remember the plane ride back from Amsterdam?"

"*Oui.* Yes, when you said you would not give me any."

"But obviously, I broke down." Gemma became smug. "Now, look what you got."

Jeremy reflected that the couple had chosen the middle name *Cher* because he often called Gemma *chère*, which meant dear.

With her thoughts returning to Jeremy, Gemma recalled that before her milk had come in, patiently, he had given the baby bottles of water. Then one evening, he'd entered the apartment and heard his daughter's cries. He'd called out, "Everything ok, *bé*?" Gemma had streaked past.

Jeremy had noticed her wet shirt. "Ahhh," he said, removing his tie, "Must be nursing time." He made frustrated Gemma chuckle when he appeared, leaning on the doorjamb, saying, "I wish *I* were your baby."

"You are," she reminded him, attempting to get Twyla to latch on.

Aware that Gemma had been trying to get the hang of the mom thing, Jeremy got up in the wee hours to change the baby. He had known Gemma was exhausted, feeding every few hours, so he brought the baby to her. Although he was tired and had to rise early, he struggled to stay awake, but sleep inevitably claimed him.

Gemma felt she never slept. With nursing, trying to keep up the cooking, and straightening up while listening out for the baby, she hardly ever got restful sleep, even when Aimee was present.

"You have help, *ma belle*," Giselle reminded her. "You simply must let people do their jobs. No more housework for you."

Yet Gemma couldn't stop tidying up before the cleaning woman came. Back home with sweet motherly Ina, Gemma would not have. This she admitted, via phone, to both Heather and Belize. She even revealed she had darkness beneath her eyes, a no-no in her line of work.

Gemma spoke of Jeremy's business term in Paris with her bestie and pint-sized sister. It would soon conclude. "Even if that wasn't the case, I'd still have to return to the states for work." Gemma announced that she'd even gotten in some yoga since Twyla's birth.

"But don't you need to get serious?" Lean athletic Heather Garrahan inquired. "Don't you need your trainer?"

Gemma admitted that the workout aspect worried her, especially since she had looming Warrior Woman III.

"You've got other obligations," Belize pointed out. "Some to charities, and you've got modeling gigs that you can't keep putting off."

"You sound like my assistant, Leez, but yes, ladies, that sums it up."

Feeling restless, Gemma just wanted to be back in the grind again. She admitted more to her mother. "Due to upcoming appearances, I feel overwhelmed, and I don't know if I'll be ready." Gemma said one tiny baby was work! Had she known, she'd not have refused help in the beginning. "Although now I thank God for Twyla's nanny," a caring French woman named Aimee.

Understanding, Kismet vowed to help too, "But you've got to decide, Gem. What is most important to you? Do those things." Via phone, Kismet recounted how she had been a new mom who'd worked. "I was panicked, stressed, and depressed, but your Nannie was there for me. Many times, she reminded me to let the surplus go. She helped in other ways, too. My mama—that little woman—was as good as gold.

"So..." Kismet Staar sighed. "I said that to say what she said to me. Call me anytime, honey. I'm retired, and I don't know much about what you do, but I can listen. And I can keep our new little Munchkin."

Gemma was grateful. Yet during alone time, questions plagued her. How would she and Jere peacefully transition back to Karina Cay? When back home, how would they do things? Now they were really a family, but how could they be together? He couldn't leave the manse, and she couldn't leave DeVeaux House; both were entailed, heir properties.

With a sigh, Gemma told herself to cross those bridges when she got to them. As Aimee cared for Gemma's baby, the new mom supervised packing all that would be taken home. Other things would remain in Paris because Jeremy would be back and forth for business.

One evening after showering and eating, Jeremy gazed at Gemma while she nursed Twyla. With his eyes filled with adoration, he decided to try out Gemma's idea of saying what was in his heart, instead of writing it down. Thus, with eyes on his bare feet, he began.

"Gem, I know you're ready to go, but I'm grateful that...you weren't in such a hurry to get back to work that you neglected the baby." Jeremy sheepishly added, "You haven't neglected me, either."

He admitted more, not feeling half as silly as he'd initially thought. He loved that Gemma hadn't seemed desperate to lose weight, although he knew she soon would. As he had in the recent past, he said he had never seen her sexier.

He didn't divulge that he often felt like a drooling fool while watching her tend the baby, especially at feeding time. Seated in the rocker, Gemma would have Twyla's little body pillowed on her awesome bazooms. To Jeremy, the sight was so sexy, even when Twyla was clearly content. He imagined how the infant felt, just happy to lie with Gemma's teat—as *grand-père* would have called it—in her mouth.

"But what makes me love you more," Jeremy said because his heart had opened as never before, "is how you've embraced being a mom."

Seated on the floor with his camera, Jeremy focused and clicked. "And *Bébé*, I love it when you nurse...*sans* clothing," without clothes. "Or when you wear something transparent," like her current filmy robe that hid nothing. He took another photo. Lowering the camera, he allowed his eyes to roam Gemma's creamy, café au lait body, visible through the oyster gray silk. Again, Jeremy pointed and clicked.

Rocking the baby, Gemma felt like she could literally feel her man's eyes linger on her enlargements, which included her no longer flat belly. Yet beneath his amorous gaze, she felt beautiful.

"You *bébé*," Jeremy softly articulated, "have never been more enticing, or womanly, to me." Placing the camera on the Aubusson, he rose. On his knees, before his woman, the one he had asked to marry, he forgot that the timing had been wrong. Seeing all that beautiful skin, Jeremy only felt himself swell. In French he whispered, while parting Gemma's thighs, that he loved caressing her while the baby nursed. He admitted he was freaky that way.

Nude, Gemma had even sat on Jeremy once while nursing.

Excited, he recalled that they had been ravenous for each other. It had made them unable to abstain for the requisite amount of weeks. Yet Gemma's doctor confirmed that her lochia, the post-partum discharge, had tapered off. Nicely she had healed. "Remember the other times?" Jeremy asked, helping Mom scoot to the edge of her modern rocker.

The producer's heartrate sped as she cradled her near sleeping baby at one breast while Jeremy laved the other. She placed her free hand on his nape and held him to her fragrant body. With long fingers splayed in his hair, she breathed rapidly as he made her feel things that only he could.

"Let me take her." Wanting nothing between them, he stood and lifted the baby away. For him, Twyla indeed was a love child. Every time Jeremy saw her, he thought of the love he'd made to Gemma before and after Twyla's conception. Bending, he kissed the small closed eyelids. Then he placed the tiny one in her crib.

Swiftly removing his jog pants and tee, he turned. "Where was I?"

Looking up, Gemma pointed down between her parted legs. Sometimes to her, Jeremy appeared so lean and sexy, with his body rigid and chiseled; she loved his evening shadow too. On his jaw, it was blond, yet his wanna-be goatee was white, and at times the sight of him took her breath away. This was one of those times.

You were here," she whispered. She'd read that women who breastfed delayed intercourse because their estrogen levels had fallen. At the same time, the hormone levels of prolactin and oxytocin rose. Gemma had read that hormones had different impacts on women's bodies, even interfering with their sex drive. She'd read that the latter hormones sometimes caused women to derive a type of pleasure from nursing that negated the need for adult intimacy. However, Gemma had read the exact opposite happened to other women, those like her. Increased hormones, sensual gazes, and touching had increased her desire, especially when Jeremy touched her breasts, her erogenous zone.

Disrobing, Gemma forgot articles and the internet.

Noticing the voluptuous woman wriggling from her robe, Jeremy ordered, "Keep it on." Beneath the filmy fabric, he slid his poet's hands. Appreciatively, he fondled and weighed Gemma. On his knees, he whispered, "*Bébé*, your *seins* are *magnifique*." Sliding hands beneath her, he squeezed her plump buttocks and slid his fingers into warm crevices.

Arching toward Jeremy, greedy Gemma met his hot, searching mouth before it seared a pathway from her neck downward. Open, his mouth traversed the mountain of her breasts to their tender undersides.

Using his lips, Jeremy ravished Gemma everywhere. Widening her and hungrily lapping at her, he also unintentionally tickled her with his evening stubble. As the first wave slammed her, Gemma shuddered.

Then rising just enough, Jeremy guided his erection inward. Closing his eyes, he enjoyed the seductive clasp of Gemma's sheath.

The parents bit at one another and traded whispered obscenities, as was their way. With a sultry chuckle, Gemma wrapped Jeremy in her arms. Locking her legs behind him, she anticipated the sensual storm he was creating. The one that would soon overtake her.

Nevertheless, Jeremy untangled himself to again lick Gemma's orbs. Pulling her down to the nursery floor, he fit himself between her thighs. Gazing at her, Dad proceeded to give Mom what *she* needed.

Then when repositioned atop Jeremy, Gemma attempted to prolong the pleasure by rising up off him, but he held her there. With hands inching up her back to her shoulders, he pressed her downward. Pushing up with his pelvis, he met her, sensuously whispering, "Take it...*bébé*."

Doing as bid, she sighed as a thin ribbon of milk dribbled down between their bodies. Not caring, the carnal act left both people languorous and sated.

Days before they crossed the Atlantic, the fellas mentioned having heard about nursing sex.

Not one to kiss and tell, all Jeremy said was, "If a man's lucky enough to get it, he just might go into cardiac arrest."

Colin, Jay, and Lance all sputtered with laughter. Then the foursome agreed. If a man had to, it would be one heckuva way to go.

On one of her popover visits, Giselle asked about the mousy woman in her mid-forties, "Aimee, right?"

"She is divine," Gemma espoused. The nanny, recommended, came to life whenever she held tiny Twyla in her arms. "*Maman G*, I am grateful for Aims because now I get to do the needful, like speaking freely with my assistant and others, without worry."

"So..." Giselle did not relish bringing up the subject. "You are going back to work. Soon?"

"I am; full-time. I start in about two months."

Giselle nodded, aware that her son dreaded the prospect. However, it was not her affair. Therefore, she asked, "Will Aimee travel with you?"

Although the nanny had friends, she had no family, so Gemma had broached the subject, asking if Aimee would consider the move to America. Aimee had said she would ponder it. Days later, she'd agreed, saying she loved her little charge, and Aimee also wanted a change.

Remembering, Gemma's eyes lit up, and Giselle was glad; her youngest granddaughter would be well cared for.

Having Jeremy near one evening, Gemma forgot all that needed to be done. She vowed to live in the moment. Not caring that his eyes were on her, she felt sexy and powerful in her role as a mom.

It was amazing, she thought; the way the feelings that she and Jeremy shared for each other had created a little person. Looking down at the baby, who grew sweetly rounder by the day, Gemma became suffused with love. Now she knew why her mom had often, unequivocally quipped, "Because *I am The Momma*!" Gemma now believed there was something so right about being that person.

It was one of the roles for which she had been born.

Jeremy had said he wanted other children during her first trimester, and Gemma had not known whether she wanted that, too. Now, though, she wanted siblings for Twyla, and Gemma knew why.

She'd loved the whole experience, the getting of Jeremy's baby—the heated, sweaty, sometimes even primal sex and lovemaking part. She'd loved the miracle of that baby growing inside her, while outside, changes were visible. Gemma hadn't minded the fatigue or her hormones being agog. Giving birth had even been extraordinary, too. It had been super scary and exhilarating all at the same time. That last push had bedeviled her, but she would definitely do it again.

Willing herself not to cry—Gemma couldn't believe she was so darn hormonal these days—she now saw why her mom had brought her into the world, despite the odds. Now Gemma understood why her mom said that at forty-something, she had been *compelled* to carry 'that last baby' for her cousin.

Standing over her own precious baby, Gemma recalled how she'd tried to thank her mom. The younger woman used words and gifts. However, no way was lavish enough, although sweet sage Momma claimed thanks were unnecessary.

Just thinking about Kismet Staar made Gemma dab tears. For the woman who was in her seventies, Gemma was supremely grateful.

She only wished for one thing. That her Nannie—whom she often spoke to—could be physically present, not just in spirit.

Chapter 30

For weeks, Gemma had readied her little family to go back to the states. She had even had her unprocessed brown hair cut. She'd had it blown out and straightened. Now she had a sleek, sun-kissed, chin-length bob. On the Gulfstream, headed back to Karina Cay, Jeremy ran a hand over it. Gemma couldn't help but think things were yet up in the air as he did. She told Nannie that Jeremy wanted to go to Windsor Pines, his home. Yet she didn't want to, although she had agreed.

Again Gemma had explained. "Jere, I need to be in my own surroundings for once out of these months. I need to take back the reins of my life." Seeing that he still did not understand, she faced him. "Jere, I've made concessions for you, and us, because I was pregnant. I changed my whole life." She looked out the plane window. "Now I need to do something for me."

Gemma had spoken in earnest. "As a man, you didn't give birth; your body didn't undergo changes. Your hormones aren't everywhere. You're you. You've also lived in France for most of your adult life. I traveled there for you, and us, but I've been out of my depth."

Staring, Jeremy realized those things had not occurred to him.

"I just want some normalcy now, Jere. I want *my* home. As it is, I keep asking myself how normal things will be when I get there with a baby—when I've never had one before."

Jeremy did not fully understand, but he did know that he had asked things of Gemma, and she'd complied, and so he said. She had rearranged her whole life to do so for him. Therefore, he said he, too, could compromise if she wanted to take his daughter back to DeVeaux House. After all, he mused while falling silent, he *had* asked her to marry him. Wasn't that the most significant compromise of all?

Jeremy knew that at DeVeaux House, Ina and others would push in to help Aimee, who sat in the plane's kitchen. Occasionally chuckling at a rom-com, the nanny ate popcorn while eyeing his sleeping baby nearby.

"At home, I've got heaps to do." Gemma said, placing a hand over his. "Jere, this was wonderful." She revealed she would miss the time spent together in their beautiful Parisian apartment. Gemma would miss the routine they'd created. "But Jere, for me, it was a lovely holiday.

Reality," she reminded him, "is me getting back to work—just like you. It's me finding a way to do so without neglecting Twyla."

Listening, Jeremy felt what he had on many days prior. His old familiar cloud. As Gemma had readied them to depart, the shadow scooted back into place over his head. Then, one day in his office, he acknowledged the truth.

All of his life, he had been fighting depression.

He knew that certain things triggered it. He also knew that as long as there was no talk of leaving, he felt okay. Now the storm cloud was back.

Gemma had noticed Jeremy's brooding, too, minor that it had been. Busy, she'd told herself it couldn't be helped. Then her stance changed.

One day while at the elegant *Le Meurice* for lunch, she waited for the *sommelier* to pour the wine. When he walked away, she spoke. While pleating her linen napkin beneath the table, she informed Jeremy and Giselle that she wanted Jeremy to see a doctor. As he moodily stared at one of many magnificent chandeliers, Gemma articulated that perhaps what he suffered was clinical. "Most likely, a prescription can help."

The twenty-eight-year-old hadn't wanted to hear any of it because his mother had often suggested the same thing many times prior. Still, after that lunch, Giselle got her husband on board. Both older people urged their son to see a physician.

Now, days later, having kissed lovely Gemma and her sweet grandbaby, the powerhouse designer said she would return to Karina Cay when she could. Teary-eyed, she'd kissed her son. That morning, she'd watched him climb the steps of their private plane. On the isle of Karina Cay and in Manhattan, she knew he would work in the Home Wares executive offices. She knew he yet had lots to learn. As Giselle bid her children Godspeed, she knew they would need it.

On the luxurious ride back to the states, Jeremy had tried not to feel apprehensive. Seated aside, Gemma's mind raced, and she wondered if she'd done everything she needed to. Earlier, she had called home, alerting them to keep an eye out for her little family. On the phone with sweet motherly Ina, Gemma admitted she wouldn't immediately return to DeVeaux House. Gemma divulged that she and Jeremy would likely spend the night at the manse. "We'll get in late, Ina, and you need your beauty sleep."

"Sleep-schmeep," the housekeeper had scoffed. "Now, I won't rest. How can I? When I have to wait even longer to hold that baby. Oy vey!"

Ina was so excited. "I can't wait to see my new little Bubbe!"

Thinking about that call, Gemma reached for Jeremy's hand. She didn't know what all she and he might now face. Their lives had changed so much, but they would do so together.

When they got to Windsor Pines, Jeremy stretched out on his bed. He was grateful for those who kept the place running. He liked that the longtime housekeeper changed his sheets every week, whether or not he was home. Whenever he returned, his linens were crisp and fresh, the way he liked them. God bless Mrs. O'Shea.

Jeremy had no idea that the woman of Irish descent had found a pile of dirty women's underthings in the closet that Gemma used. Nor did he know that the housekeeper had informed Gerard, the head houseman.

Mrs. O'Shea hadn't wanted to, but finding those things had been...strange. She'd pointed out that Ms. Gemma had been gone, for months, yet the things kept turning up. The housekeeper also told gray-haired Gerard that dropping clothing was most unlike Ms. Gemma.

Mrs. O'Shea reminded him that she'd known the beautiful one since Gemma was a kid. That sunshiney-faced one was clean. Mrs. O'Shea repeated it. The one she now called 'Ms. Gemma' was a neat nick.

Gerard asked the housekeeper to let him know if anything occurred again. Yet he did not plan on it as he went to see the reeve. In confidence, Gerard told the man of affairs. There was a security breach.

They both had an idea of what had transpired. They took steps so it would not happen again. If so, they would wind up seeking work elsewhere. This both men understood.

Gemma got feisty four-month-old Twyla ready for bed in the manse nursery wing as Aimee looked on. The new mom also said she had to give it to Jeremy's mother. Giselle was the best at what she did.

Gemma explained to Aimee how Giselle had had the crib refurbished; as an infant, Giselle had slept in it, and her daughters and Jeremy had, too. To the nanny, Gemma had admitted loving the sense of continuity.

Petite blond Giselle also had a canopy set up. She'd explained that hundreds of years ago, they were used to keep babies warm in drafty old houses. "It will come in handy here, *ma belle*, during the cooler months."

Aimee agreed, saying it added a touch of panache. "*Madame,* I think it's darling."

The canopy draping the crib had amber vertical lines hand-painted on cream and resembled a charming little circus tent. Going with that theme, Giselle had added a stuffed giraffe and elephant. Cute buttercream-colored bears, soft lighting, papered walls in hues of amber, and a luxurious rug on buttery pinewood added to the ambiance.

Aimee touched the crib, a glossy eggshell. Appreciating the antique bedding, she glanced over. There were monogrammed hooded bath towels and soft blankets, some hand-knit. "All is so lovely."

Gemma agreed. "Twyla got the works, but that's because one of her grannies is a designer. You did too, Aims. I'm glad you like your suite."

The sumptuous area was one door away.

"But I think," the new mom teased, "maybe I'm jealous."

In the wee hours of the morning, barefoot, Gemma hurried down the *salle haute*. More than a century old, the upper hall was long and drafty, causing her to tighten the belt on her robe. Quickly she entered the nursery. Receiving small fussing Twyla from Aimee, Gemma shushed the baby as she returned to Jeremy's quarters.

There she removed her robe and got comfortable. Waking, he noticed that she lay with the baby on the bed before her, suckling. Behind Gemma, Jeremy slung a possessive arm over her.

He enjoyed drowsily lying there in those pre-dawn moments, wrapped around his woman as she nursed. With his man-piece nestled in the cleft of her buttocks, his fingers played over her hip. Not only was he warm and content, but Jeremy realized he felt wildly aroused. Glancing at the clock, he knew he'd soon need to rise. He mused that there'd be no time for sex, not with the way he felt because that could take all day, so he pledged to simply carry the euphoric feeling with him.

Rising, Gemma met Aimee in the hallway, where the nanny took the baby. Back in the bedroom, Jeremy mentioned forgoing his morning workout—if Gemma wanted a massage. Knowing where warming oil and Jeremy's searching hands would lead, Gemma welcomed all.

When she sufficiently gleamed, Jeremy fondled and laved her everywhere, paying more attention to some parts than others. He alternated between lovingly and wickedly whispering. Hovering, he did so until he could stand it no longer. Then anticipating ecstasy, he bent her over to deftly glide into her supple depths. Amid their moans and sensual strokes, Gemma reminded him of work. With few words, he said he'd be late. Kissing the long line of her back, he made Gemma

April Alisa Marquette
143

unbelievably happy, not with sex. Jeremy managed to say he knew she couldn't wait to get to DeVeaux House. Therefore, he would escort her.

Pleased, Gemma rose up, a glistening goddess. Pushing restrictive bedclothes aside, she straddled Jeremy. Cradling her bottom, he sighed as clamped between her thighs, *sa femme* took him to new heights.

Mid-morning, DeVeaux house erupted in pleasant chaos. Ina and the staff converged on Gemma. She had finally arrived, carrying her precious bundle! Each person, save for surly chef JeRell, oohed and aahed. He simply ordered Gemma to come eat, "If they'll let you breathe a minute." She was back in his care now. "Girlie, I know you hungry."

Those at DeVeaux house exclaimed over Gemma's chin-length hair. Some old-timers even said, "You look so grown up!"

Finally able to hold Twyla close, sweet Ina sighed. She announced she was in Heaven. She also divulged that Gemma hadn't been much older, "Back when I started work for the Kennings-DeVeaux family."

Gazing down into the baby's precious pudgy face aloud, Ina remembered New York. There, she had been proud to work for a big star. Beau DeVeaux, a lovely man, had known that as a thirty-something, Ina Goldberg cared for her ailing mother. However, the winters had become too much for Babba, so Beau used her nickname, asking if I, Ina, would move. Believing Beau was dismissing her, Ina had burst into tears.

Then concerned, as well as amused, Beau clarified. 'I—my doll—you and Babba should move *with* us.' Realizing Beau wanted her and her elderly mom with him, his husband, and tiny daughter, Ina cried harder.

"*Babba*..." Gemma remembered Ina's mother. "I loved her."

"Yes," Ina blinked back tears, "and how she loved you! She sang to you—in Yiddish. Remember, Bubbe?" Resuming her story, Ina told all present, "Babba was my mother, and back when we moved here, Gemma was maybe a month older than this little Bubbe is right now."

Released from the reverie, Ina looked up at Jeremy and said, "This angel looks like her mother, but see that pink lip? That's all yours."

The older woman caused his face to further flame when she announced, "Mr. Jeremy, you sure made a beautiful baby." Then in her brisk New York Jewish accent, she ordered, "Now we need another one."

Aware that all the attention made Jeremy uncomfortable, Gemma laughingly excused them, citing his work. Outside, she kissed him. In his arms, she recalled their sensual morning and promised more later.

His face pinked up. "Careful, *ange*, we might get Ina's other baby."

Inside, Ina followed the new mom to the nursery. There Ina laid sleeping beauty in the bassinet, a carved white swan. It rested on its own wooden pond of glossy blue 'water.' Trailing a hand over a white crocheted throw, Ina said Giselle was a decorating wiz. Gazing at a topiary amid the white-on-white, Ina admitted, "I didn't understand Bubbe when you said you didn't want a lot of color in here. Now I do."

Both women loved the small pair of frosted lamps shaped like tulips. There were silver photo frames, and the carpet was plush white. "In here," Ina remarked, turning in the serene space where sunlight streamed, "our Bubbe will feel peace and love."

Resting her head on the older woman's shoulder, Gemma whispered. "Wait till you go to the manse. The nursery there is awesome, too."

Switching tracks, Gemma mentioned that earlier she'd seen a blond girl. "She looked familiar... That girl was leaving the guesthouse. In the bustle of us coming here," Gemma divulged, "I forgot to ask Gerard," the houseman at the manse. "Ina, you know who she is?"

"I hear she's someone who came to party with our Lance," the older woman remarked. "It was a while back, when you and Heather came."

Gemma's eyes widened. "I vaguely remember her, but why's she at Jere's if she's Lance's friend?"

"She is no friend." Ina stared at the woman she loved like a daughter. Ina made air quotes, "Word is she fell on 'hard times.'" Ina's New York accent hardened. "She's been there long enough. All while you and Mr. Jere were away. To me, that is schlocky—cheap. It's not right. I don't like it; I say she needs to go." Ina pointed a chubby finger, "Now!"

Ina was telling her so much more, in not so many words. Of that, Gemma was sure. "Okay. Alright, Ina; I will speak to Jeremy about it."

Ina batted her eyes. "You'd better, Bubbe—for the family's sake."

Days later, seated in her aesthetician's chair, Gemma wondered how she and Jeremy would manage their two households now that they were a family. She wondered because she was crazy about her home, especially her chic farmhouse kitchen. At DeVeaux House, that had been the most significant change she'd hired petite Giselle to make. Gemma did so when her fathers moved back to their New York abode.

Gemma really didn't know how she could willingly leave the home that was as comforting as the womb to her. In it, she felt safe, like she often did with Jeremy. Gemma adored the sofa upon which she and Giselle had agreed; kidney-shaped, it sat in her large kitchen, in a curved trio of windows. With a table before it and upholstered chairs opposite, there Gemma fed her baby.

When she had the luxury of being at home, she'd often sat there chatting with her mother or sister. She and her bestie gabbed there. With her assistant, Gemma often worked there instead of in her office.

Yet the manse was Jeremy's home. It was drafty at present, but it would be cool and comfortable in the warmer months. So maybe they'd alternate, but they did have to do one thing. They had to discuss getting that blond girl out of Jeremy's guesthouse.

Since returning, Gemma had heard from too many people that to do otherwise would not be prudent, to say the least.

When Ashlee heard Gemma was back, she felt rage. Why had Slinky returned? Wearing frayed denim, clear heels, and too much dime store body spray, Ashlee fumed. She considered Karina Cay hers, now. Sure, Karinians had not changed toward her, but she believed she'd spent more time on the island, so it should be hers!

Ashlee's envy and rage burned a little hotter when she heard that Gemma's mother had arrived, and her sister soon would, too. Islanders were twittering about it like the Queen Mum had come to town.

Ashlee thought it was stupid when unexpectedly, she wound up face to face with Gemma and her mother.

The two women were going into *Splendid Choco-Latte*, the fine candy, lattes, and other confections café.

Pushing rudely past while tourists stared after her, Ashlee felt shaken. She only wanted to get hurriedly back to Buddy B's small office. Once there, she wondered. Why had seeing that duo been like suffering a jolt of lightning; because Gemma looked like her mother?

Ashlee booted up the dispatch computer while thinking. Slinky's mother's hair was white. Sure, the model was younger and thinner, but it was apparent. She would even look great in the years to come.

Somehow, that was most upsetting to Ashlee, and she made mental comparisons. The difference between her, her mother, and Gemma and her mother was stark. For one thing, Ashlee had not seen Betsy, whom she had long ago called Maw, since Ashlee's youngest brother was born. Even back then, Maw had looked beaten by life.

Swiping at tears, Ashlee told herself to forget Maw. Ashlee would soon have a new mother. Jeremy's mother. She would have that woman when she and Jeremy married—after Ashlee got rid of Slinky, for good.

Seated in the pleasantly decorated sweet treat café, Gemma mentioned the blond who'd so rudely shoved past. "Mom, she's the one staying in Jere's guest house."

Placing a manicured hand to her head, Kismet appeared to have a headache. As she closed her eyes, Gemma knew. A vision formed. Occasionally, her mom saw things, and they were usually warnings. Kismet had received those for most of her life, and so had Nannie.

Today's vision was no different. Opening her eyes, Gemma's mother spoke. "I saw a woman. I'm not sure if it was that one we saw or another. Although she shoved me, I didn't actually see her face. Still, the woman in my vision looked...hard. Gem, you were there too. I saw one of you fall, from a great height. Lord, there was frantic pin-wheeling in the air— it was horrible! I can't explain, but this person... She's a bad seed."

Kismet shook away the vision. She bit into a chocolate chunk brownie. "Mmm. Heaven." Dabbing her mouth with a napkin, she advised, "Be careful of that woman, Gem, whoever she is."

The model/actress wanted to say she hated how unclear her mom's visions were. Instead, she asked, "How can I know who 'that woman' is? You described most of the women in both the industries where I work."

That night while tossing in bed, Ashlee dreamed about Betsy Blank. Then right before her eyes, Maw disintegrated into thin air. In her dream, Ashlee became the scrawny girl she had once been, Ursa Blank. In the dream, Ursa felt hurt. Yet the years scrolled forward, enabling her to see all the petty thefts, prostitution, and other infractions.

Clearly, re-lived was the day that Maw had finally gone to live in the meth trailer. Then Maw was taken to jail, right along with her dealer. Maw was led away in shackles, and she went through a courtroom door.

In the dream, while watching, young Ursa uncontrollably sobbed.

In real life, Ashlee woke. Her cheeks were wet with tears of sorrow.

Days later, at DeVeaux House, Gemma showered. She wondered if her trainer had been trying to maim her with that strenuous workout. After donning a long peach and gold halter dress, barefoot, she appeared in her home's lovely rear outdoor room. Happily, Gemma greeted the vet who had appeared for an al fresco lunch with her and her sister.

Bearing baby gifts, Heather put them down to embrace Gemma. Heather gushed, wearing a lime green sheath, "I couldn't wait to see our baby. Wow, look at your hair! It's fabulous." She turned. "Hugs, Leez!"

They sat, and Heather asked, "Gem, when can I see the baby? I'm so excited!"

"Lemme check." Gemma laughingly excused herself. Recalling her full house, she went to peep at her little bundle. Poking her head into the nursery, she saw her dad. Beau had no doubt waved the nanny away.

How Gemma loved to watch Beau with Twyla. He'd sit for hours just holding her, even while she slept. He said the baby brought him a deep abiding joy. When he played with her, Beau emitted full belly laughs.

Aware that she had to get back to the ladies, Gemma remembered something her father had said the night before. He was amazed that not only did he have the most wonderful daughter, but a granddaughter too.

"Me," he'd said, sounding choked up. He'd dabbed an eye. "The man who was once the strange gay kid. The kid that not even his own mother could love... Now, look at me. Now look who loves me."

Moved to tears, Gemma squeezed his hand, reminding him. "My Nannie loved you too." Adopting him, Nell had raised Beau as her own. "Dad, this is strange, but sometimes I feel like she's here, with me..."

Beau looked up at his daughter. "I do too, baby girl. I really do."

As she quietly headed back toward the sunshine, it hit Gemma. *That* was one of the reasons she loved Jeremy! He, too, had once been a 'strange' kid. Back then, she had known her dad's story. As a little girl, Gemma had also known. There was often good in people, even the person that most people shunned. For her, that person had been little Jere.

Shading her eyes, Gemma sat on a black rattan chair, its cushion crisp white. Raising her phone, she angled it for a photo of Heather. Gemma would cherish that photo with lush island greenery behind, and with Red's striking hair gently blowing in the breeze. Just like the one in her sitting room. In it, she, the beautiful brown teenager, giggled with the other teen with the peaches and cream complexion.

Chef JeRell appeared with a clear bowl of grapes, a wedge of gruyere, and an oven-fresh grain loaf. On the black lacquered table, Gemma poured chardonnay for her guests.

"This is for you, Girlie," the chef said and produced lime water.

"Thanks, JerRell. Heather G, after lunch, I'll bring Twyla out."

"Great! And speaking of her, four months later, you look amazing."

"Stop, Heath. I still need to lose more weight."

"I know, for work, but you'd still look hot if you never did."

Gemma reached for shopping bags full of couture fragrances, blinged-out bikinis, sexy lingerie, and upmarket makeup items. "All from the job," she admitted. She enjoyed the ensuing squeals and hugs.

"You know, Heather, she'll soon be on the catwalk again."

"No, Leez. I wasn't told." Heather popped icy grapes into her mouth.

"I'm thinking," Gemma revealed, "this'll be my last year…"

Both other women's heads swiveled. "Why?" "What's wrong?"

"Nothing's wrong. I'm just over it. It was a job. I want a new one now. Anyway," Gemma sighed, "It's work to look that way nude."

"Nearly nude," Belize corrected. "Munch, just because you had a—"

"Baby's not it, Leez. I want to be like you for once in my adult life. I want to be real. So I'm making major changes."

The other women softly replied, "Oh." "Okay." "That makes sense."

"This year, I've got three looks in the show, one petal outfit—flowers, and I think there are two with wings."

"Any diamond-studded bras?" Gemma's sister asked.

"Actually, there will be, on someone else." The younger new star.

Discussing the annual event that was more than a showcase, Belize opined. "You know, Munch, because people see you on those shows, they think they know you."

"They do, Leez." Gemma shivered, "And it's become scary when I go out with Twyla. Before, it was *de rigueur*, but now…"

"The truth is, you being on TV and in catalogs—both of which are in people's homes—gives them a warped sense of familiarity."

"They feel they know her, Heather,' Belize interjected. "And some of them are nuts." Belize turned to her sister. "Gem, some of your fans don't realize you take on a persona to do runway and other things."

"Ohhh," Heather gasped, understanding. "Some people have no idea that you're not always the vixen or the sex kitten. Ooh," she waved as JeRell brought out delectable fresh snapper with fruit chutney. "Not to change topics, but aren't you gearing up for Warrior Woman III?"

"I am, but to tell the truth, that's presented a problem, so to speak."

"How so?" Pint-sized Belize inquired.

"Well, I'll have to live away from home for thirteen months—"

"Thirteen months!" both other women gawped. "But you just got back!" "J. B. Harden won't like that." "You taking Twyla with you?"

"Night and day, I've pondered those questions," Gemma admitted. So you know there had to be compensation talks. Then I had to ask myself if I really want to play a part I've already played."

"Twice," Heather reminded her friend.

"Right, but," Gemma's eyes danced, "this one will be shot in 3D."

"How does that work, Munch?"

"With his technical mind, Jere asked that same question." Leaning forward, Gemma explained. "Movies are usually shot in 24 frames per second, when human eyes see 60 frames. So 3D movies are shot in 48."

"12 frames lower than what our eyes naturally see," Heather calculated. "Cool. I have to say, Gem, you're great as Arma Geddon."

"That's a compliment, coming from you, Heather," Gemma's older sister pointed out, "because you've known each other your whole lives."

"I know, but when Gem takes on a role," Heather nodded, eating, "Gem diminishes. All you see is the character, unlike some *other* actors."

"I can hear you two." The ladies chuckled as the new mother said, "Thank y'all for the votes of confidence, but... I've got a secret."

"You're pregnant!"

"Again!" Heather chimed, fist-bumping Belize. "We figured it out."

"No, stupids," Gemma laughed. "GemCo has two tales in the works."

"Really!"

"Yes, and I'll be directing. I'm stepping *behind* the camera."

"Good deal!" Heather enthused, drizzling vinaigrette on her colorful salad. "So what kinds of projects?"

"Things I believe in, those that will best allow me to continue in my largest role—as Twyla's mom. Besides, I'm tired of haggling and nudity clauses."

"Sounds like you really are changing," Belize acknowledged.

"I am. Now enough about my life." Mischievously Gemma winked. "So... what's happening with you, Dr. Red Hot—as Lancelot calls you?"

"Oh no, you're not getting in *my* business," Heather quipped.

"I sure am," Gemma laughed. "You 'n Leez are all up in mine. So, Hot Tamale, you 'n Lance still tiptoeing around each other?"

Chapter 31

Gemma readied herself for dinner out with Jeremy and her visiting family members. Affixing an earring, the new mother also mentioned the girl in his guesthouse before asking, "Who is she, really?"

In her cozily lit boudoir, Jeremy, sprawled in a slipper chair, did not want to discuss it. He didn't want to go to dinner either, and he didn't want to make nice. He would only do so because Gemma had done it countless times for him while in France.

Glancing over, Gemma knew Jeremy was in one of his moods. She sighed; Nannie, he can be so trying sometimes. Reaching for her other earring, she thought, perhaps, for him, she should make an appointment with the island physician. *No. That is something he has to do.*

Forgetting brooding, again, she mentioned his yellow-haired guest.

With a sigh, Jeremy mumbled. "Lance met that girl someplace."

"Please. He screwed her somewhere," Gemma tossed back. "But—"

Jeremy attempted to circumvent questions for which he had no answers. He said what he knew his woman wanted to hear. "She'll be gone soon." He said so because he really wanted to get into Gemma, but that wasn't going to happen, at least not right now. Jeremy remembered they had a dinner to attend. Then they'd tromp back to DeVeaux House, where there would be another of her family members at every turn. Yet he would suck it up, Jeremy told himself, for his wife and daughter.

Oh, he remembered. Gem wasn't his wife. She didn't want marriage. The notion sent Jeremy spiraling further downward into melancholy.

Gemma noticed Jeremy's dismal mood at dinner, but what to do? Nothing. She simply vowed to enjoy her family's last night on the island.

When they all returned to DeVeaux House, she entered her bedroom. Engaging in her nightly ritual, she did not allude to Jeremy's abysmal behavior. Gemma did again remark on the blond girl. Gemma hadn't missed that earlier; Jeremy had been vague.

Removing his socks, he said the blond had nowhere else to go.

Yet Gemma didn't believe that. Although she didn't know the other person, Gemma knew something else. Blondie was no more a girl than she. Actually, fake blondie looked like she'd done a whole lot of living, hard living. Gemma knew women, too. They could be conniving. This one was probably trying to play Jeremy. The model had seen enough connivers to know. It was why Gemma said, "Jere, I don't see how this person having no place to go is your problem. Give her back to Lance, or have the reeve move her on. Real soon."

Jeremy said nothing, but he didn't like Gemma telling him what to do—like she was his wife when she wasn't. He hadn't forgotten. Before their daughter was born, he had asked her to marry him. Gemma claimed she wanted *a wedding* where their family and friends could attend and witness their vows. She said she wanted tons of photos. Yet they'd been back on the island for nearly two months. He'd watched her with her assistant; he'd watched her arranging things in the DeVeaux House nursery, which his mother had decorated. *Maman* had done so while she completed work at the island resort. Jeremy had found himself wondering, was Gemma making excuses? Perhaps, he'd told himself, Gem wasn't that into him. Still, his conscience said he should have presented *grand-mère's* unparalleled diamond ring. Then Gemma would have had to answer, and there'd be no foggy stuff.

Jeremy glanced over. Gemma readied herself to nurse his baby in her fully lined, Turkish cotton robe. *Sans* makeup; she was gorgeous. Naked-faced, hastily, she'd pulled her hair up, and through her open robe snatches of skin were visible. Unable to take his eyes off her as she sat and removed an arm, he realized. For the past few weeks, it had seemed like everything was more important than him. Watching Gemma put the baby to her breast, the businessman hated to think it. Still, there were times when he even felt displaced by his tiny beautiful daughter. Maybe that was because he just wanted Gemma all for himself most of the time.

Unbuttoning his dress shirt, Jeremy knew he should see Doc Dear, the island physician. Lately, Jeremy existed in a perpetual state of upset.

At the end of the week, Gemma had to go into town. She gave Aimee the afternoon off, saying she would take her baby with her.

While out, Gemma stopped by the sheriff's office. In the open area of the municipal building, she removed her shades. She introduced Twyla to interested deputies and Miz Miriam, who handled clerical work.

"You're looking good, Gemma." The middle-aged woman assessed the young mother's mid-thigh dress and her ankle-strap sandals. "You just take that lil cutie on back," Miz Miriam advised. "The sheriff's here, and I already let him know you're on your way."

In the private space, Gemma took the bonnet from her daughter's head. Smoothing the tiny matching dress, she told Trip, "I want you to meet your Goddaughter." Proudly beaming, Gemma admitted, "Twyla's feisty personality is emerging, and she's gonna be fire."

"Like her mama," Trip grinned before expertly taking the baby. He cradled her head, which appeared about the size of an orange, in his huge hand. With the other, he soothingly rubbed her back.

"Wow, Trip... You seem like an old pro. I'm impressed."

"Nieces and nephews," he grinned. He also marveled at the baby not being afraid of him, although she had never before seen him.

"Ah, but she heard your voice while I was carrying her." Gemma winked, "Sometimes you were on speakerphone."

Trip laughed as Twyla squirmed to face her mother. The baby gurgled excitedly, and he said, "Well, look at that." Planting a kiss atop the small cap of sunlit curls, he sounded sober. "Gem, you know I tried to holla, but..." Trip pursed his lips. "Now I've gotta let you down easy."

"Is that so?" the mom chuckled. "Next, you'll say it's not me; it's you, your fickle heart. Guess you fell in love with someone younger."

The sheriff kept the game going. "I didn't want it to happen." He feigned shame, "I was powerless to fight it." Loving the scent and weight of her, he held Twyla close. "It was first-sight love. Right, baby?"

"Guess I'll get over it." Gemma shrugged, watching the man make faces for her daughter. "But seems I've been getting a lot of that lately."

She and the sheriff chuckled. He enjoyed hearing that the baby's tiny hands were becoming dexterous. "And everything goes in her mouth.Oh, she's even learning to roll herself over."

"She sleeping through the night yet?"

"She does. I wind up waking her, though. I kiss her and dress her up at inopportune times. I've just never felt this kind of love before."

Noticing that Gemma actually glowed, Trip said, "I can see." Aware that she'd put on weight and that Gemma appeared all the more attractive, he had to tell her, "Motherhood agrees with you."

When Gemma was prepared to go, she turned to the door and trip caught her elbow. Staring down at the woman he'd always love, although she belonged to another, he admonished her to be careful overseas. He bent to kiss her cheek. On her skin, his large soft lips lingered. Holding Gemma's arm, Trip said, "I'll walk you out."

Outdoors, escorted by ever-present security, Gemma shielded her baby's little face from harsh sunshine, as well as onlookers. Mom smiled, forgetting those who snapped photos as she passed. She recalled what the big gruff sheriff had admitted. "Seeing you two made my day."

After work, Jeremy picked up the tiny girl he adored. Repeatedly, he kissed her chubby cheeks and cooed, just to see her smile.

Watching him, Gemma noted that Twyla was laid-back like her dad, when the baby was sated. Other times, she let it be known; she wanted her way! Gemma was aware that she and her daughter would butt heads in the not too distant future, just as she had with her own mother.

The actress/producer noted something else; Jeremy didn't seem depressed when interacting with his daughter. He carried her around and sang French songs to her. Gemma recalled she'd captured candid photos of the blond man and his brown-skinned baby a few times.

Careful not to look at the woman who was not his wife, Jeremy tried to sound casual. "So, what did you do today?"

"The usual. Oh, and I went into town."

He kept his eyes averted. "For any special reason? Where'd you go?"

Gemma's eyes narrowed because she knew he was probing. "Out with it, Harden," she commanded. "Ask your real question."

Gem was angry, Jeremy thought. She'd called him by his last name. Well, maybe that meant she had something to hide. Jeremy had yet to look at Gemma as he kept rocking his daughter, who fought sleep. "You sound upset, *cher*," he taunted. "Are you?"

"I may be—if you're trying to accuse me of something."

He knew he should have left it alone, yet jealousy spurred Jeremy on. "Could be you're upset due to guilt, *mais oui*?"

But yes, her foot! Oh, this was going to be good, Gemma thought. Saucily, she asked the executive, "What have I got to be guilty about?"

With his back to her, he said, "You went to see the sheriff."

"Yes. Your spies told you—and?"

Jeremy sounded angry. "You took my baby with you."

Gemma scoffed. "I did. I was out, and I had her with me. Big deal. I had security; she was covered. I introduced her to her Godfather."

"She has not yet been christened, Gemma! And I told you; I'm not crazy about that idea."

"Well, I – like – it."

Jeremy sighed. "Okay. Until we work this out, do me a favor. Do not take my baby by there anymore."

"Or what, Harden?" Gemma asked because this was so like him lately, imperial and hard to deal with. "What'll you do? No, a better question is, why would you begrudge your daughter having a man in her life that will love and protect her?"

Jeremy exploded. "That is *my* job!" He growled and startled the baby, who woke with a loud cry, "*I* am her *père*—her father!"

"Well, *he* will be her Godfather." Gemma walked over to quiet the squalling, but Jeremy refused to relinquish. "Godfathers love and protect, too, Jere. They aid parents with children and provide Godly guidance. Your daughter needs to know him because—Heaven Forbid—should anything happen to us, he and Heather will look after her."

"Shut up with that!" Jeremy spat. "I don't want to hear it."

"Shut...up?" Gemma's eyes narrowed. "Jeremy Baptiste Harden! You have been out of hand lately! There is no cause to be rude. Don't speak to me that way again—and give her to me. Oh, and for future reference, do not – ever – speak to my daughter that way, either."

Rocking then, the lioness shushed her cub. The one who felt all of her parents' tension.

"Well, don't you tell me what to do," Jeremy verbally clapped back.

"That's all you got? You sound like a child, Harden."

"You act like a child, running here and there, never settling down."

"Is that so?" Gemma kept rocking, "Hush Twy-baby. Well, you, Harden, won't be sleeping in *this child's* bed, tonight. No ass for you."

Jeremy shrugged into his suit jacket and left. On the darkened cart ride to the manse he knew one thing. Beneath the moon's silvery light, Jeremy mentally admitted *he had been wrong*, on so many levels.

Back at DeVeaux House, Gemma tried to calm down while nursing. She reminded herself that time was winding down that she would soon begin work on III, Warrior Woman Onslaught. She would be away for a good while. That was what had Jeremy so upset. Gemma knew it. Yet, she mused, he needed to get it together. Just because things didn't go his way didn't mean he should lash out at will.

While packing for her trip to New York, Gemma's breath caught. Again, she told herself, as she had before, she would not cry. Yet she hated to leave her baby—the little one, as well as the big one—but this time, she had meetings and conferences. She needed to be fresh and focused, and she couldn't do so if Twyla were near.

Gemma recalled the discussion she'd had with Jeremy. They'd both acknowledged the astonishing pushiness of the paparazzi. They'd agreed; no exterior photos for the first year of Twyla's life. It did not matter what exorbitant sum they were offered, not even for an exclusive.

Jeremy said the offers made him feel like they'd be pimping his princess. Therefore he was adamant. Not one photo. That was why this time, Gemma would leave her baby. She reminded herself that Twyla would be in capable hands, allowing mom to focus on work. Heck, Gemma realized while gathering toiletries, that even with Twyla ensconced safely at home, the baby would still be on her mind.

The one thing Gemma was grateful for was darling Aimee. The nanny would care for Twyla in the daytime, and motherly Ina would also be part of the equation. In the evening, the baby's father would take over.

Jeremy. Thinking of him, Gemma realized. For some reason, lately, all they seemed to do was fight. They had even had words because he'd said he didn't need the nanny's help. Not at night. "If any woman will be with my daughter and me then, it should be her *mother*."

Gemma pursed her lips because the man was so stubborn. Thank God for Mrs. O'Shea. At the manse, the housekeeper lived on the premises, and she had assured Gemma that with babies, she was an old pro.

Continuing to pack, the new mom forced herself to think about New York. There she'd see her Warrior Woman co-star, Nile Narcissi. Nile had suggested going out, and she had agreed, but only after meetings.

Gemma would set the next phase of her life in motion at those.

When she entered the hazily lit Manhattan eatery, Nile noticed right away. Gemma was different. It wasn't only her hair, shorter now, or because she appeared svelte in a sexy, belted, navy shantung skirt suit. She wore impossibly high heels. At well over six feet and wickedly curvaceous, Gemma looked...more confident than ever.

Now she appeared to truly live in her own skin. She was a *woman* who had taken possession of and owned all of her power.

Watching her sashay toward him, Nile did not fail to miss the stares, the whispers, or the poised phones. Grasping the elegant bejeweled hands that she offered, Nile chuckled. This chica had some kind of shine, and it beamed right out from within. "I'll say this, MaMa, you sure know how to make an entrance." And he'd thought *he* was the diva.

Nile aided Gemma to be seated. He ignored the flash of several camera phones. After pleasantries and a bit of banter about her baby,

Nile got right to the point. "I asked you to come because I wanted to speak about," he nearly snarled, "the new kid."

Oh. The young Australian actor. He was slated to appear alongside them in III, Warrior Woman Onslaught.

Nile leaned frontward, ensuring that no one nearby heard. "I don't like that he was written in as your rescued half-brother."

Nile said he wanted the new actor's part lessened.

Gemma stared. Working with Nile, she was aware that he could be pretty temperamental. Still, this was new, even for him, and she said it.

"It's not," Nile visibly pouted. "It's how I feel. A few weeks ago, you mentioned that even you wondered if you wanted to play A G again."

Gemma appeared unruffled as Nile alluded to the grueling hours, the strength training, and the fight scenes. Over the clink of glassware, he reminded her that she had said she didn't look forward to the aches or the bruising from mechanical hoists.

Calmly she admitted, "I did mention those things. I may have even said a younger actress might now be better for the role. I'm a mom, one who's nearing thirty. So?"

Nile leaned even closer. He hissed, "Then what d'you think about me? I have a few years on you, but in the interim, at least you did other things; you have causes; *I* don't have shit else."

Well, whose fault was that? Gemma wanted to ask the narcissistic actor. If he wasn't so in love with himself and his body, he could have accepted guest star roles or committed to charities.

Intruding on Gemma's thoughts, Nile moaned, "Now I'm typecast."

So he was, but he'd said that to say what?

"Come on, Gem. I need you. Go to bat for me, one last time. Please? You and I both know that whether or not that kid has facetime, the studio will still pay him untold sums. And unlike him, *I* need this."

Gemma placed an elbow on the table and rested her forehead on her palm. "Why me, Nile? Why aren't you speaking with Cecil?"

"Because you have clout. Like him, you're a producer. People listen to you." Nile grabbed her hand, wanting her to look at him. "You don't think I pay attention, but I do. I know this is your last hurrah. I know you've gotten into dramatic roles. I know audiences take you seriously, now. You're believable as the latest Bond villain and that hard-nosed detective—an ode to the character your dad played back in the day. I even saw your GemCo production. You starred as the mother who'd do anything for the ailing child that her angry ex kidnapped. Diva, you were explosive!" Nile looked down at the white linen tablecloth between them, "You've got options. *I* don't. So give me this, please... *Please*?"

When she didn't immediately answer, Nile mentioned having entered the business doing advertisements for shave gel. "Don't make me go back to that. As it stands, I still do a few, but overseas, I could never do those types of things again in America. What would my public think?"

That you're working, Gemma thought, as Nile dramatically continued. "I'd rather kill myself or accept a part on a nighttime soap. Gem, I'm telling you this because...I need this payday. I gotta set myself up. I know you think I should've done it years ago—and I should have."

Staring at the actor who always managed to remind her that he was self-centered, Gemma knew she would need to make publicity rounds with Nile. And now with the 'new kid.' There would be photos and production stills for promotional purposes. None of it did she look forward to because often she and Nile had to hold one another or gaze into each other's eyes. He'd kiss her whenever he thought a camera was turned on them. Most times, she made sure Nile got a cheek or her neck. Yet he was a frigging sham. With him, Mr. Narcissi, all was an act.

Sure, Gemma knew Nile loved her. Still, he didn't love her the way the public thought. He was on the DL, and as a down-low brother, she was his greatest cover girl, ever. Whether on or off-screen, acting alongside her made him appear to be the quintessential ladies' man. Yet every – single – day, he lived in fear. He worried that one of his multiple male conquests might uncover him, for money or a little limelight.

Nile loved to slum with ravenous, angry boy-men. To those greedy, forever-grasping slim twenty-somethings off the street, a few thousand dollars and fifteen minutes of fame seemed appealing; they would gladly rat Nile out to the tabloids. Therefore, the actor paid off his street urchins before *The Enquirer* could. The skinny devils who sexed him were bleeding him dry—and Nile allowed it. Aware of the sordid details of the actor's life, as few others were, Gemma asked a burning question.

"Nile, why not wrench open the closet door and live free?" That would put a stop to the implied threats and the outright harassment.

Taking his hand off hers, handsome groused. "Everybody can't be your dad; they don't have that luxury. *I* especially don't because..." something about Gem always compelled Nile to tell the truth. "I'm not as strong." The actor sighed, "Anyway, I can't come out—now. I started my career with female hotness, like you. I can't shed my lover man persona. It would be career suicide. Don't you see?"

He could, Gemma mused; Nile preferred shadows and shadow men.

Feeling burdened, he revealed, "My persona took years—no decades—to cultivate. Minus it, do you know where I'd be? Dead in the water." Nile appeared devastated, "Coming out would finish me."

Watching him, Gemma knew. For once, the actor wasn't acting. She knew Nile felt as trapped as he'd implied. Soothingly, Gemma patted Nile's hand like Nannie had often done hers. "Nile, I really can't promise anything, but I'll see what I can do." Gemma would give her friend one more run if she could. "We'll make it a good one, and then I'm done."

Feeling boneless with gratitude, Nile slid to his knees. Down before his co-star, he whispered, "Bless you, Gem." Nile kissed her elegant hands nestled in her lap. He looked up, too, just as a camera clicked. "Although there are times when I really hate this life," he said through his teeth; "all the pretense, there are times when I love it." He squeezed her hand before re-taking his seat, "And always, I love you."

Gemma smiled, aware that a grainy likeness of Nile—down on his knees before her—would show up on the internet or on the pages of some tabloid. Most likely on the following day. She could only guess what the headline would read. Jeremy would see it and become upset. Again. If only he knew. If only he would believe Gemma had never slept with Nile Narcissi; if *only* she could tell Jeremy the real reason.

Yet some secrets weren't hers to tell. So again, she would say what she had said in the past, that never would she sleep with Nile. Gemma wouldn't say the actor wasn't interested in her, which was true, or that she would decline even if he was. She couldn't say that a romp with Nile would put her at risk. That, she could never tell, or another harsh truth.

Nile lived beneath the veil of HIV.

Often, Nile refused to take his meds. "They make me feel so unlike me," he'd griped a time or two.

Therefore, were she to sleep with him, Gemma would be putting both herself and her beloved Jeremy at risk. That Gemma would never do.

She was Jere's protector, and he hers.

Uh-oh, the mahogany-skinned actor spoke, so she tuned back in.

"Gem, I know you think I only love me, but I do love you, too."

Sounding sage, she said, "I'm aware, and know what, Nile? I love you. I want the best for you." It was more than he wanted for himself.

Gemma conceded that Nile wasn't a bad person. He was just a prisoner of fame, and for him, the end was nearing. The studio had made that clear by bringing in the young actor from Australia. The kid was definitely a go for the third flick. Nile knew, as did she that most of the jobs that Nile had been getting would now go to Aussie. Or to someone young and hot like him, like Nile had once been. It was the business. Nonetheless, unlike Gemma, Nile did not have a life outside the movies.

What Nile had was clandestine. He had actively cultivated a life of secrecy and shade. His life, unlike Gemma's, was one he could not live out loud or in the light. That she thought about as they parted ways.

When she returned to her opulent hotel, Gemma readied herself for her short morning flight. Still she cogitated on Nile. Long after she would step behind the camera, to tell stories from that perspective, the mahogany-skinned man would remain. Although his star was dimming, he would cling to the chatter and the hype. Nile would stay on the carousel until the amusement park closed, for him. That was a shame.

Upon leaving his office, Jeremy dropped by DeVeaux House. His plan was to feed and bathe his daughter. He would also put her to bed.

"Oh, you're not interested in seeing me," Gemma teased. She was happy to see him and happy to be back home with her little family.

In his woman's kitchen, Jeremy lifted pretty baby from her high chair. He did not look at her mom. "I saw you," he tersely quipped. "So did half the world. That 'meeting' of yours *chère*, with that actor…it looked mighty cozy."

Gemma felt like she'd been slapped. "You know what, Jere," she said, noticing that Ina and Aimee were quickly making themselves scarce. "I can't do this. Not anymore." Gemma sounded broken as she headed for her office with her voice floating over a shoulder.

"Maybe it really was for the best that we didn't get married before or right after Twyla was born."

Now Gemma had Jeremy's attention, and he turned with his daughter in his arms. "Why would you say that?"

"It's true." Gemma's shoulders fell, but her voice rose. "You keep doing shit—stupid stuff—that makes me feel we're already estranged."

In the hallway, Gemma's back was to Jeremy. With his heart churning, he stared as *sa femme* spoke.

"Maybe, Harden…this—what was once between us—has run its course. Maybe we're done. And I'll be okay with that."

Chapter 32

Twyla was nine-months-old, and Gemma had almost gotten used to leaving her when for work; she occasionally headed to the mainland or overseas. Gemma tried to do so infrequently and never longer than two nights. If she were gone longer, her assistant made arrangements for Aimee, the nanny, and the baby to travel with Gemma.

Of course, Jeremy didn't like any of it, but he had Home Wares to run. Of that, Gemma reminded him. "Got milk?" she sardonically asked. "No," she pointed out, "that would be me. Therefore, she goes with me." The mom said it although she'd begun the weaning process.

Thinking about her daughter's age, Gemma realized. She and Jeremy had been apart for nearly three months, and he mainly stayed at the manse while DeVeaux House, her home, was a hive of activity. Sometimes, however, Gemma was the one who gave in and went to stay a night with Twyla's dad.

Ina had prodded Gemma. Mothering and bossy, the woman who was so much more than a housekeeper said, "You need to be with that man, so does little Bubbe. Don't be a putz." Ina used chubby fingers, "Go."

Gemma had taken Ina's advice. Those times her little family was all together. Often then, Jeremy wasn't consumed by foul moods. Still, things weren't exactly right between them. To Gemma, it seemed he held back or he held something against her, something he would not say.

Now Gemma couldn't forget one conversation they'd had. Their last really, on a Saturday. She had been in the bright, comfortable parlor at the manse, seated on the plush white sofa. The gold silk drapes had been open, revealing the sunny sea and gulls wheeling in the air.

Jeremy had stood with his back to her while nervously, her heart had hammered. With narrowed eyes, she'd slowly said, "Surely, you're not giving me an ultimatum…"

Jeremy ignored her, "We're a family with a daughter."

"We are a family."

"Then why try to break us up?" he'd asked. He realized he was angry about many things, especially the fact that he and Gemma weren't married. Sure, his daughter had his name, Twyla Cher Baptiste Harden. He, and his parents, had created trusts for her, but Jeremy wanted much more. He wanted his daughter, her mother, and him to legally be a family.

He reminded himself that they already were fam. Still, Jeremy knew he wouldn't feel that way when his girls were gone, he'd feel bereft. Heck, he wished he didn't love Gemma, then he wouldn't feel angst.

Oh, dash it all, as his mother sometimes said, Jeremy wondered who he was fooling. He'd been angsty and brooding ever since he could remember. Long before he'd met Gemma. But he didn't want to love her. That Jeremy told himself. Doing so was too much work. With her, there were too many highs and devastating lows when he just wanted peace.

He was lying. He wouldn't want things any other way, and he said so, using his sadly twisted and abbreviated mode of communication.

"I just want you to remain here, letting us stay a family."

"Ooh, Jere..." Gemma felt a cauldron of emotions. They included fear, hurt, anger, and more. "That is so unfair. You're always flying off somewhere. You've been going since we were kids. Yet I've flown around the world to see you and be with you. I did so whenever I could. Now you can't do that for me?" Gemma said he wouldn't be working 24/7; he had a team and assistants. "You can get updates."

Jeremy shook his head. She wasn't saying what he wanted to hear. "I've got to run this company, and my responsibilities are in the states."

Suddenly Gemma felt numb. She was so tired of the same old fight. It was why she sounded monotone. "You're telling me that your work is more important than mine. You're saying your stuff is more important to you than I am, and it's more important than Twyla."

"Gemma, be rational." See? There she went, he thought, doing that woman thing. Twisting his words. "People depend on me."

"Be rational," she echoed. "I hate when you say that. Like I'm some dim-witted, hysterical *female*." Gemma stood. "Sometimes you're so provincial—and chauvinistic." She waved. "Lemme finish, you caveman, because in case you didn't know, people depend on me, too.

"There are *tons* of people who wouldn't work, Mr. Harden, if I decided to stay home because my husband wants that. Did you ever think about the key grips, the dolly, the gaffers, the storyboard editors, and the costumers? Then there are caterers, the hoteliers, and stunt people. There are assistants and the camera crew—thousands of people —*who depend on me!*" she yelled. "And I depend on you, Jeremy Harden!" There were tears in Gemma's eyes when she stated, "*I* know who *you* are. Yet you don't know that the wardrobe mistress, costume buyers, cutters, mould supervisors, painters, carpenters, location coordinators, payroll clerks, cashiers, and accountants, depend on *me*.

"To you, I may just be a sex thing, no, let – me – finish! But FX artists, digital artists, motion capture people, the chief pilot and his crew, concept 'n lighting artists, the medieval advisor, compositors, the best boy, props people, crowd coordinators, stand-ins, the IT administrator, electricians, the matte painter, the period music consultant, orchestra, the special effects crew, music editors, the sound mixer, the scoring crew, sound editors, pre-lighters, and animators, they all depend on *me*.

"I'm so deep into this that," Gemma used fingers to pontificate, "the bureaus, like the National Park Authority, the Countryside Council, jewelry providers, and faux fur providers, would all lose. If I decided to sit around waiting for my husband to come home and diddle with me."

Jeremy blinked because had she just called him...her *husband*? Twice. Had that been a Freudian slip? Wow. Maybe they could—

Do nothing. He had to hear the lioness out.

She attempted not to cry, but her heart was breaking. Thus, Gemma divulged, "I don't begrudge *you* that people—your whole family included—need you, Jere. They depend on you and what you do. Still, you don't understand that about me. You think my stuff is all frivolity and fun." Gemma shook her head because, out of all the years of loving and fighting with Jeremy, she never thought it would come to this.

Saddened, Gemma offered, "I'm sorry you think I can just blow off my career and my responsibilities any time to suit you. But I will not."

Like he hadn't heard a word, Jeremy murmured, "But you'll be running off for over a year." That was what had him so ticked. "How am I gonna be away from my baby for a fucking year?! She won't even know who I am."

"We discussed this." Gemma sounded calm, although she was anything but, "It won't be a year. You can fly out to see me, and I said I'd bring Twyla home, too, when I can. You know this is my work, and I've never tried to take you from yours."

He didn't want to hear it. To make her hear his point of view, Jeremy said, "You're acting like what you do is important."

Her eyes widened. Gemma was astonished and highly disturbed that Jeremy would say such a thing! Yet she managed to sound calm. "To some people, my work has value. Oh, and if I wanted to get technical, I could say the same thing to you. 'You're acting like what *you* do is important' because some people don't think *patio furniture* is important. But I understand that however people feed their families is paramount."

"Home Wares is about more than patio furniture," Jeremy groused, "You know it. We create jobs, in turn, those jobs aid the economy. We use sustainable materials, and small and women-owned cooperatives."

Gemma spoke softly. "My work does all of that as well."

"But *I* depend on you!" There, he had said it.

"So I'm supposed to hole up here, Harden, or at my house, because you don't want me out of your sight. How narrow-minded is that?"

"I didn't say that." Frustrated, Jeremy ran his hands through his hair. "I just ask why so long? I thought we were in a different place now."

"We are, but this deal was made before we had the baby." Gemma felt a latent headache. "I told you—I don't know how often—that in my work, I've implemented change but those changes have nothing to do with this. What is so hard to understand about that?"

Seeing that her face was becoming blotchy and her nose red, Jeremy knew Gemma was upset. Thus, he tried to take her in his arms. Jeremy tried to say things were out of hand, when all he'd wanted was for her to see; he couldn't be away from her for more than a year. He definitely could *not* be away from her his daughter for that long. When his girls were gone for just a night or two, Jeremy felt like he couldn't breathe.

However, instead of apprising Gemma of that, Jeremy said, "I wanted to ask you to marry me. Again." Still, he was not putting a ring on it.

Gemma shook his hand off. Although her voice was soft, Jeremy knew she was serious. She said what she had never had before. "Don't touch me." Bending to lift her baby, she kissed the small sleeping face, the one that often took on expressions that reminded her so of Jeremy.

Usually, Gemma allowed him to say *au revoir* to his daughter, but this time she didn't. With her designer diaper bag slung over a shoulder, she toted heavy sleeping Twyla toward the foyer, and her voice carried.

"Since we no longer have anything—because I *am going*, Jeremy—someone will contact you...about this baby." Gemma swallowed acrid tears and unbelievable hurt. "Hopefully," she made herself say, "your stubborn ass will find a way to at least see *her* because I am done."

Staring after Gemma, Jeremy stood in the manse's open, front double doors. Pressing her golf cart pedal, Gemma bumped along. Beneath the leafy overhead canopy, she traversed the long, sun-dappled, crushed shell drive. Watching her get farther away, Jeremy could hardly think. He felt as though some man had punched all the air from his chest. Through hurt and confusion, one thought penetrated.

Gemma could not mean they were done.

They could *not* be finished, not just like that. This was something they could find a way to resolve. Wasn't it? And she could not be taking his baby away. Oh, but she was, he remembered because she was the one who nursed. She was the parent that his daughter cried for and needed most. He worked days and many nights, so what could he do?

Jeremy wanted a do-over! He wanted Gemma back! He wanted to say he loved her and that they could work things out. He wanted to make love to her. That, they always got right. Yet one thing would not let him call out. His stubborn pride.

Nearly three weeks later, she wound up at Trip's bungalow. Since he had the rare afternoon off, Trip had invited her up. Gemma knew that if anyone in their tight-knit little enclave saw her going to the sheriff's home, the news would be all over the island by sundown. Then Jeremy would be angry. He was always angry, and he hadn't tried to see her either, only their daughter. Well, if that was how he wanted it.

Who was she kidding? Gemma asked herself as she sat beneath the whirring ceiling fan on terracotta tiles in the sheriff's comfortable den.

Sliding the glass door back, he stepped outside.

Watching Trip grill vegetables for her and a steak and potatoes for himself, Gemma's mind wandered back to Jeremy. Anybody else would have thought he was arrogant, but she knew him. She knew he was used to getting what he wanted because he was 'the heir.' She also knew he meant no harm. She knew she meant everything to him. The baby, too.

Suddenly she recalled how sexy he was and how she used to climb all over him. She ached for that.

Trip came back inside, and they picked up where they'd left off, speaking about her busy life. Seated in his home, Gemma felt so comfortable until, after a while, she nearly forgot Jeremy. Then Twyla began to whine. Gemma had fed her, but the little girl who stood, wobbling at Gemma's knee, wanted to nurse.

Both adults could tell the baby meant now, not later, when she was on her mother's lap. "I'm weaning her," Gemma explained.

"But that's a process, right?" Trip asked. "And you've gotta do it anyway, right?" He said Gemma could go in the bedroom, "But why not do it right there? For my Goddaughter's sake, *and* mine." Trip grinned, "Man, I want to watch. Then I could pretend —Nah." He clammed up.

"You could pretend what, Trip?" Gemma really wanted to know.

Might as well say it, the big caramel-colored man mused. "Then I could pretend, for a while, that that crying child in your arms is...mine, because heck if I don't sometimes wish she was."

Seated in Trip's home, Gemma realized that their time would have to be cut short if she didn't nurse. Therefore, while Trip was operating the grill, she unfastened her clothing and put Twyla to her breast.

When the sheriff returned, he stood, staring at the blanket covering Gemma's shoulder and the top half of her baby. With his voice sounding hoarse, he uttered four words. "Remove the blanket...please?"

Before Gemma could do a thing, Twyla shifted, and her chubby little hand rose on the outside of the pastel fabric. As though she were hot, the baby clasped her blanket and yanked, and it fell to the floor.

Trip shook his head with his eyes on the baby, who suckled while looking up at him. Resting his eyes on Gemma's beautiful breast, he bent. "Well," he said, retrieving the blanket, "you did say our girl was fire."

On her way home, Gemma realized what she had not told Trip. She sometimes wanted a baby with him, too.

At his house, she'd let him hold her. She'd loved the feeling of being pressed body to body. That had calmed her, so had his hands roaming her back.

"Please, Trip," she'd wanted to beg, "just do me."

Silent, he'd massaged her, easing her tension away. Beneath his hands, she'd thought about becoming a mother for the second time.

She'd love the getting of Trip's baby. His hard body and his big brown pecs would be underneath her hands. Nude, she would sensuously slide over him while his muscular thighs would be beneath hers. His big hands on her bottom would have kept her impaled. His male member was massive, just like the rest of him. She thought of the hardness encased in silken skin and his big balls. Oh, Gemma fantasized, would she have fun with the sheriff! She would take him in, let him slip out, and... Oh, the joy, especially now that she and Jeremy were estranged.

Still, Gemma told Nannie, that was just a fantasy. It was one to make her feel better about her current weird space.

Chapter 33

At the going-away party that the cohorts goaded Jeremy into throwing for Gemma, he noticed. She had slipped away. He went looking and found her in the parlor with the gold drapes. With her back to him, she stared at the night sea silvered by the moon.

Closing the door behind him, he tentatively inquired, "You're not having fun?" Jeremy knew there was so much more he needed to say; he didn't know how to stand being away from her for over a year! Yet he didn't think he could start their heart-to-heart with that. Therefore, closing his eyes, he wished he had a notepad or his tablet. Then on paper or electronically, he could articulate his feelings.

The curvaceous woman in the lengthy, indigo halter dress had always told him one thing. Opening his eyes, he longed to caress her beautiful slender back as he recalled her words. 'Speak what's in your heart.'

Jeremy opened his mouth. *Mon Dieu*! My God, from where had those words come? "So I hear you were up at the sheriff's place."

Whirling to face him, Gemma hissed, "You are so foul, Jeremy! I was thinking about you, but here you are, plotting how to pick fights."

"I wasn't," he said, "not really." He allowed his eyes to voraciously slide over her. "I wasn't thinking about you up there screwing him, with my baby nearby." Suddenly with one hand, he covered his face. "Well, now you know where my mind is," Jeremy sheepishly admitted.

Instead of feeling angry, as expected, Gemma surprised him with curiosity. "Where exactly is your mind, Jere? What were you thinking?"

"That I want to have his ass hauled away from here, so you'll never see him again," he softly admitted. "But," Jeremy said louder, dashing to stand before her. He couldn't let her turn away or leave, "That is only because I don't want you involved with him. I want you with me, alone."

Gemma hated him speaking like he was king of the domain and she and others were his servants. Yet, she touched his face since his voice had been achingly soft and since he was slowly but thirstily ingesting her with his eyes. "Forget threats, Jere." Touching the hair that had begun to silver, although he was just shy of thirty, she enveloped him in her arms and the soft cloud of her perfume. "Just stop."

"Or what?" He asked, allowing his arms to slip around her.

"Or..." she near-teasingly quipped, "you'll be sorry."

"Hurt me, then," he said with his pleading heart in his eyes.

"You'd like that," she whispered, pressing his face to her neck. Aroused, she sounded breathless as his lips streaked quiet fire over her skin. "Then we wouldn't have to talk, and you could just whip it on me 'n we wouldn't have to deal with 'us' or this thing coming between us."

"*This* thing?" he asked, pressing his flagrant erection to her.

She moaned before initiating a kiss. "I see," she managed when he allowed her up for air, "somebody misses me."

Roughly, he ran his hands over her. He blocked out music, voices, and laughter streaming from other areas of his home. He skimmed her torso. With his palms, he covered the thin shimmery fabric that accentuated the enticing shape of her breasts. Those beautiful bulbous breasts nourished his baby, and they gave him such pleasure, too.

"Am I wrong?" she asked, not kissing him back. "You do miss me." She inquired while he semi-struggled with clothing, "Right?

"Do you miss *me*?" he asked with a hand at her nape. Undoing the bow at her neck, he wrenched her halter down. Bunching the dress at her waist, he couldn't get his mouth on her breasts fast enough or touch her enough. Lapping at one, with seeking hands, he felt her all he could.

Holding him to her, she shimmied from the garment. Yet she couldn't keep up with his mouth as it burned a pathway down her belly. At her *mons*, he inhaled, and on his knees before her, with his thumbs, he opened her. "Go back," he ordered, maneuvering them toward the sofa. He quirked a brow when she fell on it. He positioned himself between her thighs. This was the body that had housed his baby. It had cradled Twyla before her entrance into the world. On his knees, Jeremy slid hands beneath Gemma's buttocks. Squeezing supple flesh, he pulled her forward. Bending, he kissed her, there. Then, manipulating her thong, he fit his palpitating erection into her snug channel.

Provocatively undulating to receive him, she breathed, "I'm not kidding, Jere. No more threats."

"Okay." He growled repeatedly plunging into moist heat, "But don't think... you'll ever ... free, of me. I'll never... you go...to anyone."

Feeling a wealth of tenderness for him, she cradled his head against her. "Baybeee..." She bent to kiss strawberry blond waves as tears pooled in her eyes. Large and fat, they fell into his hair. "Jere, my love, I have never really wanted to be free of you."

Holding her tightly, he pillowed his head on a breast. Inhaling her, he softly queried, "Then why do you need *him*?"

She knew he meant the sheriff and grinned. "It's you I want, Jeremy. Trip's a friend, a good one. He's somebody I talk to—but I *need* you."

"You do?" Jeremy asked, still clasping Gemma's buttocks. He asked because she was so independent and outgoing until he didn't really know; maybe she could actually get along without him.

"Oh, Jere. I need you...like I need air." With her elegant hands beneath his strong jaw, she raised his head. Looking into his stormy blue-gray eyes, she asked, "Do you need me?" She wanted to know because sometimes he was so introverted. Often he retreated to his interior world, causing her to wonder if she was just a fixture and not fundamental. The desire to know caused her to ask again, "Is it *me*—not just the sex?" The incredible sex, and then there were the fights. It was the dance they did. "Or is this all because of Twyla? You trying to keep me to keep her?"

Jeremy kissed Gemma's chest and neck. He made her squirm and giggle while he remained hard and ready within her. He nibbled her chin. Then slowly, he said exactly what he would have written or typed.

"*Bébé*, before she ever was, it was *you* that I needed."

Having said it, he withdrew his pulsing member from her body, only to glide back in and take them higher.

Gemma was gone, and Jeremy felt bad that he hadn't ridden with his girls. He didn't know why he'd listened to Gemma. She'd suggested he go to work like it was any other day. She'd said 'this' wasn't goodbye. She said she was simply going to her job the same way he would. Yet he felt different because he would go home from his job each evening, and each evening she would not.

As he paced his office, he remembered standing over his baby. In sleep, her spiky lashes had swept her rosy cheeks. Every so often, she profusely sucked on her pacifier. So in love, he'd gently run a hand over her cap of delicate brown curls. In his office, he almost smiled as he recalled that his chubby kid was trying to walk at ten months. Just thinking about her caused a squeezing around his heart. Everything about that kid was like her mother, from her hair to her creamy skin, to her pretty little feet and hands. How he would miss those two!

At the window, Jeremy realized he'd wasted a ton of time. While Gemma had been present, he'd held onto indignation like a drowning man clasped a raft. Now he didn't recall what had caused the upset. He saw that he could have spent so much more time with his girls if he hadn't been so blasted stupid. Jeremy hated that they were gone, but the truth was, he and Gemma had work. They had both been blessed to have employment they loved. Well, he would do better. This Jeremy promised, because heck if he would miss his baby's first birthday. In two months, she would be a year old. It was a sobering thought.

Forgetting recriminations, he chose to remember Gemma's last night at the manse. She'd called Aimee to tell the nanny that she would return to DeVeaux house in the morning. "How is she?" Gemma had asked.

In bed with her, Jeremy had said it was weird listening to *ange* check in with someone other than him.

"Well, that's how things are now, Jere." Climbing atop him, she'd reminded him, "We have a daughter, and I check on her often."

Gemma had also mentioned that Jeremy should check on why that blond girl wasn't out of his guesthouse.

As Gemma began to ride, he'd moodily mumbled, "Don't know why you care. *You* don't want to live here."

Using his body, she'd ignored him.

Now scrubbing his face with a hand, Jeremy realized. He could be a surly bastard. He told himself the truth. It was time he sought help.

The first table read went great. There had been a rhythm, and most everyone's lines had flowed, but a few flaws in a scene's timing had been exposed. Yet to Gemma, it seemed like most of the actors had chemistry, a good thing. The only sour note was Nile, who made it known to anyone who would listen; he wasn't crazy about Chase Upstart. The young soap opera alum who joined the cast.

Oh well, Gemma thought as she memorized lines with her sleeping daughter in her arms. Right now, the only thing she wanted to ponder was being off-book. Still, thoughts of Jeremy attempted to intrude.

When she finally climbed into bed, Gemma had only a few hours, at best, for sleep. She let thoughts of Jere flood her mind. She recalled that he'd been in a mood; she had been aware as she'd ridden him. She hadn't allowed surliness to mar the fact that she would miss him and their delicious sexing. He really had been tender, showing her all that he could not say aloud. Then he'd offered turbulence.

Vowing to sleep, Gemma turned over and realized with a jolt. Sex was often the only thing she and Jeremy managed to get right.

Some evenings, Jeremy could be found on the beach back on Karina Cay. To an observer, he looked like any other man out for a stroll. In a way, he was different. He was searching for treasure. Hadn't Jeremy told

Gemma all those years ago that he would return to the beach, repeatedly, to find her, his *trésor*? Other evenings he unwound by hanging out with the fellas. Jeremy and Lance would lounge behind ay's place while Jay surfed, his passion. Sometimes curly-haired Colin joined them, when he wasn't researching an article or romancing island girls.

Through the visceral pain of missing Gemma and his baby, Jeremy noticed Lance. Dark-Hair seemed equally perturbed. Usually, while Jeremy sprawled, brooding, Lance sat with phone in hand and his thumb hovering. Lance admitted his desire to call the Irish siren, "But I fear getting shut down." He said Red Hot might do so because they'd all been friends forever. Dr. Heather might bolt if she knew his true feelings.

The guys said he wouldn't know until he tried. Lance argued, "Women are strange. All I understand about them is when they need a little trim." He made the guys laugh, "And the good doc never asks me to work on her bush," even though he would do anything for her.

That statement sent Jeremy back to his interior world, where thoughts and images of Gemma abounded. Recently, she'd told him she was fed up with his foolishness. She'd said so when he claimed he was too busy to travel at the moment. She'd also said he kept breaking her heart.

The truth was, she'd broken his, too, innumerable times.

Recalling those things, he wondered, would they ever get it right? Given their track record, he could only think it was highly improbable.

When she was in her trailer, with or without her baby, Gemma found herself playing Gavin DeGraw. His songs conjured images of her man.

One evening between takes, she rested her head on the sofa back. Listening, she willed tears not to fall. She tried to forget that although weeks had passed, she couldn't get the memory of Jeremy holding their baby out of her mind. Before she'd left their island, he'd accompanied her. In the dark of the morning they'd left the manse and headed to her home. There, he'd stood over Twyla, who'd slept. On impulse, Jeremy picked her up. That hadn't sat well with Ms. Chubby, who had only wanted sleep. She'd made upset noises. Jeremy held her tightly. Repeatedly, he'd kissed her pudgy cheeks. Over her grunts and squirms, he'd whispered in French that daddy loved her.

Seated on her sofa, Gemma remembered boarding the luxury powerboat that had whisked her away from the man she had known for most of her life. At the time, she'd had one thought. 'You can't leave him without a kiss goodbye...' With Twyla in her arms, she'd forgotten all that lay unresolved between them. Turning, Gemma reached out. Without reservation, Jeremy walked into her familiar embrace. Kissing, they'd clung, then she'd pivoted. She'd carried her precious bundle to the galley below deck with a heart heavy. Gemma had not looked back.

She had not called Jeremy either.

Still, they'd had wooden conversations on the few occasions he'd called. Those times, however, they mostly spoke about Twyla.

Harking back to leaving day, Gemma sighed and whispered, "Oh, Jere. Like Gavin's song says, I am so '*Not Over You.*'"

With his girls gone, Jeremy hated that he had ever wished he didn't love Gemma. He'd lied too, telling himself that he'd have peace without her. Now that she was gone, things were quiet. At Home Wares, things rolled smoothly, yet he had no peace. He felt strangely unhappy.

Therefore, from an area not far from the manse, Jeremy descended a precarious cliff-side stone staircase. Often as kids, he and the cohorts had used it to quickly access the beach. Back then, like now, most people deemed it unsafe. When he gained the boardwalk, Jeremy strolled along, headed in the direction of DeVeaux house.

With the sun's rays dissipating, and just a smidgen of peach on the ocean, his footsteps echoed on the sun-bleached wood. Jeremy saw Gemma's house. When he was about to pass it, he remembered another twilight... The evening he'd seen flickering candles on her porch. That had been the second night he'd made love to her. It seemed a lifetime ago. Jeremy recalled that he'd entered her bedroom window and her body, both at Gemma's insistence. He felt at peace. It had taken him all these years to realize. Wherever she was, that was where he wanted to be because wherever she was, that was his home.

Jeremy's eyes smarted, but he attributed it to the salty spray in the air and not to tears. In truth, he loved Gemma, and it was why he needed to get his derriere in gear and get overseas. He told himself so because it had been on this beach that he'd promised he would always seek her.

The first time had been when he'd made love to her. That time she'd risen like a nymph from the sea. He'd said he would always find her because she was his *trésor*.

Pulled from his musings, Jeremy thought he heard someone yelling. Turning, he looked back the way he'd come. Then he looked out to sea.

A woman in a black bikini top and yoga pants ran between two dogs. In the waning evening light, she waved.

Heather. Hey! Jeremy waved. Of course, they couldn't converse, not over the ocean's roar, not with him up on the boardwalk and she down on the sand. Still, comically they motioned. Red jogged on, and he thought about her. He hadn't known she ran in the evenings. He'd only thought she did so in the mornings with Colin. Ah, well. Jeremy sighed as he walked on. He wondered if, perhaps like him, Red was on this part of the beach because she missed Gemma.

Jeremy's stomach growled, and he realized he sure missed her *tartines*. Gemma's open-faced sandwiches were so French. They were thin and loaded with items like hot fresh fish, plump organic tomatoes, crunchy lettuce, and herbed cheese, all bubbly from the broiler. With a squeeze of lemon and a dash of cracked pepper, the bread would be warm, and the whole thing satisfied. Nearly salivating, an idea struck. He didn't *have* to miss Gemma. Jeremy could boat or fly out.

It could be a surprise.

Jeremy was tired, but he also felt excited because soon he would see Gemma—and his kid! He wondered if he should have alerted his baby momma; let her know he was coming. Maybe he should have waited a couple of weeks and arrived for Twyla's first birthday.

Jeremy shook those thoughts from mind as he approached. He'd had no trouble because Gemma had him listed as family. Fam was welcome in the cold makeshift movie town.

He zipped up his leather bomber jacket and shoved his hands deep into his pockets as he approached the set. The wind was no joke. Jeremy found himself walking slower over hard-packed sand as he scanned those congregated for a glimpse of Gemma. He didn't see her, but he noticed the crew. As they often did, they stood around while the director appeared to discuss something with 'the new kid.' Jeremy allowed his gaze to travel on. Ah, there she was, beneath a large open tent.

Wrapped in layers of real-looking fur, Gemma wore gloves and had a couple of scarves draped about her neck. Unaware of him, she vigorously stamped her kidskin-booted feet while standing before an electric heater.

Jeremy very nearly laughed, knowing she was cold. He swore she had the most frigid feet, too, didn't matter what time of year it was. Suddenly, he stopped short because he saw mahogany-dark Nile...

The actor wore a bulky wool hat pulled down to his brow. His clothing, including a greatcoat—his costume—was from a prior century.

Unnoticed, Jeremy watched as the tall, handsome actor stepped behind Gemma. Using gloved hands, Nile vigorously rubbed her fur-clad arms. Then locking his arms, Nile rocked. Jeremy stood, stunned, as his Gemma closed her eyes, obviously relaxing against that actor.

With his heartbeat suspended, Jeremy knew that *sa femme* had not seen him. The better, he thought, for him to see all. Feeling suffused with anger, he hated that Gemma and Nile looked cozy.

Feeling betrayed and angry, Jeremy wanted to surge forward and pummel Nile. The man had no business with his arms around Gemma! Jeremy also wanted to whirl her around. Then in her eyes, he would see the shock and the realization that she had been caught doing wrong.

Jeremy wanted his kid. Where were Twyla and Aimee? With his heart pounding, he sought them, then he realized. The smart thing would be for the nanny to be in a warm trailer or for her to have his kid back at the hotel. Keeping to the shadows, with a racing heart, Jeremy could only think, 'So this is what goes on…' Walking along the perimeter, he went unnoticed because most people's backs were to him. Irate, he eyed Gemma's co-star, who moved to the tent forefront to take a seat. Jeremy watched Gemma bend. She stretched her gloved hands toward the heater. She remained that way until someone handed her a steaming mug. Clutching it, she didn't drink. Jeremy knew she was simply using it to warm her hands and face.

He watched as moments later, she was about to pass Nile. Stiffening, Jeremy saw the actor reach for and catch at Gemma's layered cape. Turning, she walked back and stood next to Nile. Unable to hear them, Jeremy watched their jovial exchange before Gemma sat on Nile's knee!

He saw that there wasn't another unoccupied chair in the vicinity, yet Jeremy felt volatile. He tried to focus on other people, some holding clipboards, those adjusting props; while shivering, others waited to spring into action. A parka-clad young woman scurried to and fro. Yet all Jeremy could think was that Gemma and Nile seemed close.

Jeremy could not see what others present saw, that theirs was a friendship based solely on trust. With anger fogging the lens of his mind, Jeremy saw only what he wanted to see. Yet had he been close enough to hear their words, he'd have regretted his turbulent mood.

"Gemma, dahling." Nile tapped her shoulder. "You've got to get up."

"Or what?" she teased.

"My leg's gonna go to sleep. You don't look it, but you're heavy."

"Heavy?" She stood. "I'm insulted. She kept her gloved hands around the mug that rapidly cooled.

"Ah, so no one's told you the truth," Nile quipped. "Not even your man—what is he anyway? A prince? A king or something?"

She waved and did not say articles often referred to him as 'the heir' when he was so much more to her. Catching her breath, Gemma blinked away tears because it hurt to think about Jeremy. She could not ponder all that lay unresolved between them, for little or no reason.

Nile spoke on, unaware that his co-star fought to keep from bawling right out in the open. "See, that's another reason I prefer men." Nile whispered now, "Less drama. I can tell them the truth. I don't have to be so careful—you know, about what I say or how it's said. I hear," Nile became dramatic, "that with women, it's different. Men must not hurt their 'tender sensibilities.' With a man," Nile boasted, "I can just be me *and* bang the stuffing outta him!"

Forgetting hurt, Gemma sputtered with laughter at Nile's candor. He squalled right along with her.

Seeing them do so, Jeremy angrily stalked away. Without his longed-for reunion, he left. He was headed for home.

Back on the sands of Pembrokeshire, the actress was informed that J. B. Harden had come and gone, and he hadn't taken the time to see her or Twyla.

He hadn't had to rush back to work. This Gemma knew because Jeremy didn't work in a trauma unit. So why travel so far, only to fly back out—and without a word? What sense did that make? Assailed by questions, Gemma suddenly remembered Jeremy's irrational fears. They involved two men; Trip, the sheriff, and Nile, her co-star.

Although the Home Wares heir's actions baffled her, they also felt like a stab through her heart. To Gemma, the hurtful feeling was nothing new.

Chapter 34

On Karina Cay, Jeremy plunged into work, and Ashlee... Lance had told him of the girl's side hustle. Therefore, Jeremy left the manse under cover of darkness, and he appeared at the guesthouse.

The young woman with the damaged hair knew not to ask one question. She simply allowed the man to fall on her and have his way with her. She felt triumphant. Still, she was perceptive enough to know. The brooding businessman had shown up on her doorstep, essentially his doorstep because something had happened...with Slinky. Why else had a man ever sought her? Because of problems with other women.

Ashlee told herself she didn't care. She only cared that Jeremy came.

As he stabbed his condom-clad member into the blond, he imagined being with Gemma. Behind his closed lids, he saw her lovely tilt-tipped eyes and her expanse of creamy, café au lait skin. Making the mistake of looking down at the woman beneath him, Jeremy became enraged.

Gemma wasn't the one he was coupling with, and he couldn't pretend as he tried to forget the orange-ish tan. It was sprayed over puckered skin that silently suggested old wounds. Jeremy looked away from the fake blue eyes that stared eagerly up at him. He felt further enraged at the thought that Gemma was probably getting her freak on, at that moment, with that tall devil, that actor! Thinking murderous thoughts, Jeremy pounded into Ashlee. Feeling like she rode a mountainous wave, she loved every moment. Of course, as she hung on, Ashlee knew that Jeremy was most likely thinking of *her*—Slinky, but Ashlee didn't care. Slinky was not present. The way Ashlee saw it, she was. Now Ashlee had Slinky's man, and she would hang on to him. Ha-ha bitch!

When daylight arrived, Ashlee noticed two things. Jeremy was gone, again. Yet he had left money. This was the fourth time in four months that he'd done so. He didn't often seek her, but those were exciting times when he did. She could not know that Jeremy left the crisp bills to assuage his guilt for so wickedly using her.

Unaware of exactly why he sought her, and only in darkness, Ashlee liked feeling as though Jeremy could turn to her. She just didn't like him leaving cash. Ashlee could always use it, but she would have preferred it if he had offered to take her out. She wanted to go to dinner, maybe at a surf 'n turf seaside place. She wanted to get dressed and walk in beside Jeremy. She wanted people to see them together, out and about.

As she pondered their time spent alone, Ashlee fought the notion that she was being used. If anybody was using anybody, it was she who was using Jeremy. Ashlee refused to believe she was a stand-in for some black...cunt. However, the fact that Jeremy did not talk to her or even invite her to the big house, the manse, set off warning bells.

He had never gone down on her either, and she had seen him lick Gemma, so she knew he did that kind of thing; some men didn't. Come to think of it, Ashlee mused, Jeremy never called—she'd put her number in his pocket. He'd never bought her trinkets, nor had he offered one friendly gesture. Ashlee's heart pounded. All of that meant one thing.

Jeremy only saw her as a hooker.

She was trying to get away from that life! She'd never wanted it. She had only sold herself to make money. She'd had to live, but she was not a trick, in her mind. Working as the dispatcher for Buddy B's small business, she tried not to let her upset show. Ashlee didn't want him or the guys questioning her. They saw too much, and she knew Buddy B liked her. She didn't like him, though, not that way. Sometimes she wished he and the others working for him would pay attention elsewhere. Ashlee didn't mind them hitting on her occasionally, but flirtation could go no further. The truth was, she did not want a measly worker-man.

She wanted a billionaire, a man who had power, in the boardroom and the bedroom. She wanted a man who wore Brooks Brothers, Armani, and Brioni, all names she had recently come to know. She wanted a man who owned a Maserati, in addition to other pricey automobiles, a man who owned homes in various lovely locales, a man who had yachts and belonged to country clubs. She wanted a man who had been in magazines like Bloomberg Markets, Forbes, and Money. She needed a man whose name conjured up images of a superior lifestyle. She wanted a man like J.F.K., Jr. She wanted the man the New York Times and the tabloids referred to as J.B. Harden.

Fielding calls for Buddy B; Ashlee forgot hurt. She vowed to simply be there, for Jeremy, without question. Then when he saw that she was, while Slinky wasn't, Jeremy would change his mind. Ashlee knew it.

Giselle was going to be on island for a few days. She hadn't said she would stay at the resort, as she sometimes did. Giselle didn't mention her in-town chateau. *Grand-père* had moved into the elegant space back when his daughter had come of age. Maybe *Maman* would stay at the manse. Indeed, it had been her mother's property, one of many that Giselle had inherited, but Jeremy didn't know. In the last few years, Giselle said the manse was her adult son's home, and she respected it as such. Still, the Home Wares executive thought, if *Maman* wanted to visit, he was game. That meant Ashlee needed to vacate the guesthouse. It was time. He would never be able to explain her presence to his mother; he hadn't been able to justify it to Gemma. Thinking about it made Jeremy uncomfortable. Another reason he needed Ashlee gone was because she was unpredictable, now. Guess he should never have slept with her. It hadn't meant anything, although, with the way she was acting, to her, it had. Forgetting his now unwanted guest, Jeremy's mind returned to Gemma, causing him to recall a conversation with his mother...

"*Chouchou, si vouz avez un problème,*" my pet, if you have a problem," Giselle had said, "then you two stay apart. If not, *n'hésitez pas,*" don't hesitate "to make things right with *votre femme,*" your wife.

His mother had been referring to Gemma as his wife for a while now. Jeremy recalled it while wearily scrubbing a hand over his eyes. "Jere, only you can make it so that you share moments of *magique* with Gemma. My pet," Giselle's voice hardened, "find a solution." His mother had further revealed that she could not wait to see her little *chérie.* "Now that," Giselle was referring to her granddaughter, "is a tiny heartbreaker—if ever there was one," like her mom.

Knowing her son as she did, Giselle quickly parted. If not, he might have griped that what was between him and Gemma was just that. Disconnecting, the petite one had left no room for argument.

Ah well, Jeremy sighed as thoughts of Ashlee again intruded...

On the evening prior, Jeremy recalled, *Ashlee had appeared at the back door of the manse.* Having just returned from work, Jeremy had not been happy to see her. He hadn't even shed his suit jacket, and there that girl had been, knocking on his multi-paned kitchen door.

"I told you; I'd come to you when I want to see you..." he slowly reminded her. He knew he sounded haughty, but she made him angry.

Ashlee knew he meant for her never to darken his doorway, but things had to change. Jeremy needed to get used to her being there since Slinky was not. However, Ashlee knew she and Jeremy had to start slowly. Therefore, she said, "I didn't mean any harm, Jere. I just wanted to—"

"My name," he spat with clenched jaw, "is Jeremy. You know that. "

Ashlee felt hurt because she'd thought they were on friendlier terms since they sometimes had 'relations.' Before she knew it, Ashlee blurted, "But *she* calls you Jere. "

Jeremy stared, knowing the blond was doing the comparison thing. Why did it seem like she believed she was competing with Gemma, whom she really did not know? Jeremy wondered as the harsh blond girl whined like a little girl. "She's not even here. She's always gone, and yew think she cares about yew. She's off, who-knows-where, doing who knows whut, and Um here. Did yew forget thet? "

Grinding his teeth, Jeremy knew it was time. Facing Ashlee, who stood in his kitchen, he knew they had to get a few things straight. She needed to comprehend that just because he got his rocks off with her didn't mean there was more to it. She was a whore, who had been paid.

Tamping down ire, Jeremy realized. This chick had gotten to the point that other women had. She didn't understand, but she was trying to; thus, he would have to kick her to the curb. Loosening his tie, he wondered. Why weren't women more like men? Forgetting Ashlee's layers of makeup, he internally asked why'd women always try to put the pieces together, like his and Gemma's love life was some kind of puzzle.

He knew the girl with the fake baked-on tan did so because she was trying to see where she could fit. Therefore, the businessman figured it was time. He had to tell her. She didn't fit, and she wouldn't, ever.

Without preamble, Jeremy let Ashlee know that even though they'd hooked up, spent moments together at different intervals, there was nothing more for them. "We're not that kind of fit. "

"Oh." Ashlee felt like the wind had been knocked from her. "Really."

"Really." When he actually didn't have to, Jeremy explained that he wasn't trying to be cruel, but it just wasn't that kind of party.

The bottled blond asked questions like, "Why? Whut kind of unnatural hold does that—" she bit her tongue, that...*actress* have over yew? I mean," Ashlee huffed, "what's so different 'bout her?"

Before he could answer, Ashlee continued, her face becoming a dull red beneath her makeup. "I know she got mun-ney, but what else she got that I ain't got? You could let me in, Jeremy, if yew wanna. We're more alak—yew 'n me—than yew 'n she. "

Jeremy abhorred begging and pleading. He hated thinking about why he couldn't allow any other woman fully into his life. He despised that although Ashlee, with her brittle hair and bitten down fingernails, was getting on his nerves, his most prominent reason for dismissing her would crush her. He just wished she would stop trying to press him for answers, answers that would surely hurt her.

Yet Ashlee attempted to goad Jeremy into feeling like a total bastard. She thought she could shame him into doing what she wanted. As she got louder and more irrational by the moment, he held up a hand. Without words, he told his houseman, tall gray-haired Gerard, to hang on a sec. His burly security men understood, too. Jeremy saw his housekeeper. On the peripheral, Mrs. O'Shea nervously hovered in the mudroom.

Wanting to remove the remainder of his clothes and his Italian leather shoes, Jeremy tried to remember that Ashlee was basically an OK kid. Sure, he knew she was about his and Gemma's age, early 30s, but she wasn't as worldly, so he thought of her as younger. Due to circumstances, she hadn't traveled much. She had once said that although she loved magazines, she had not read many books. He knew she had been dealt a lousy hand by life early on. Ashlee didn't think he was aware, but Jeremy knew about her. Her having dragged herself up from nothing was not the point. For him, there just was not room.

Jeremy had no place in his heart for anyone who wasn't already there. Gemma took up most of the space. She always had, and his kid took up the rest. If he and Gemma made another baby Harden, although they were estranged, that would be it. Jeremy would have nothing left for anyone else. Like his Afro-French *grand-père* with Priestess. That was the way Jeremy wanted it. He managed to say it all concisely.

"Well, I don't believe yew," Ashlee sullenly persisted. "I think yew think you should be with her becuz...yew have black in yew. " Mammaw said if one had a *drop* of black blood in them, they were a nigger. Still, for Jeremy, Ashlee could overlook that flaw. Thus she told him, "You think that makes you not good enough fer a white girl lak me."

What the—? Jeremy did not allow his eyes to widen, but was this *cinglé* trying to psychoanalyze him? With a southern twang? Guess she really was as crazy as Lance and Colin said. "Yo, I am only going to say this once," Jeremy growled. "Lay off her."

Ashlee knew Jeremy meant Gemma as he added, "Subject closed."

Ashlee crossed her arms. "All Um saying is Ah kin be all yew need. I mean, you'd look respectable with me... Um the right color—"

"Enough!" Jeremy had had it. "*You* will – never – be – what I need." He did not say it, but he absolutely hated it when racists started their 'superior' shit. Doing so, Ashlee had invoked J. B. Harden's ire. She didn't know that because Jeremy appeared as he did, he often heard more racist propaganda than he could stomach. And often, he said so.

Feeling like he'd sucker-punched her, Ashlee turned. Grabbing her arm, Jeremy turned her back. "Look at me, so we are clear."

She stared, attempting to focus, despite stinging angry tears.

"You are not to mention my kid's mom. Ever. We," he gestured between them, "you and I, do not discuss her."

"Why?" Ashlee cried, "What's so sacred 'bout her?"

Jeremy could see this was futile. Thus, he advised Ashlee to leave.

"No!" She lunged, nearly tackling the man she felt should have wanted her. He should have loved her and wanted to marry *her*.

"I git it…" she cried as the houseman and security held her off. "I know what yew saying. Jeremy!" Twisting to see him calmly stroll through his home, which she was supposed to share with him, Ashlee nearly choked on the words, "She's off-limits—to me." The crying noises, emitting, against her will, mortified proud Ashlee.

Jeremy had not looked at Gerard, but the houseman knew. Without a word, tall Gerard and security escorted the troubled young woman to the rear exit, even as in his study, the homeowner slammed the door.

While being hustled from his kitchen, Jeremy had not known that Ashlee flinched at the door slam. As she was herded across the crushed shell drive, she felt like she would explode from the rage inside her.

A golf cart rolled up, humming before the owner shut it off, Ashlee glared. When that ape Colin trotted to the rear of the manse, Ashlee's eyes narrowed. They all thought that bitch was so special. Well, a few changes would be made—and she, Ashlee, would make them!

Watching her in the evening light, curly-haired Colin didn't say a word. Yet he noticed the mottled red, furious face. With a nod for Gerard, he glanced at barefoot Jeremy, who had again appeared. "I know one thing," Colin said. "That girl needs help—serious mental help."

Jeremy also remembered that his closest friend had said, "I ain't trying to be all up in your business, bro. But you need to cut the extracurricular; need to get yo' shit togetha with Gem." Colin shook his head. "You gonna lose her, J... Betta recognize. You know a sista will only take so much; then yo' ass'll be out. The sheriff, or that actor, will be *in*, banging *bébé*—the big one," Colin clarified. He shuddered at his next thought. "I'd kill somebody if they touched my 'niece.' "

Forgetting curly-haired Colin and his ominous predictions, Jeremy picked up his phone. Without contact, he tossed it back down. Instead, he chose to go for a walk, out back of DeVeaux House, of all places.

That night, Ashlee tried to drink a whole gallon of five-dollar wine. As she swigged from the heavy plastic jug, she acknowledged that just sometimes, she hated this new world. It wasn't the one she'd dreamed of, all those scorching nights back with Mam-maw while watching *Gone With the Wind*. Back then, Ashlee had not known she'd wind up contending with those who thought they were better than she. Blacks, and other white folks! Hell, on this stupid island, didn't matter what color they were— even the fricking help thought she was beneath them!

Oh, but she would get to planning because she had come too far. She had lost too much. Well, she had given up too much; her family and her friends—well, her only friend, Biffi. Ashlee felt she had put up with too much; crazy Uncle Jed, Mam-maw, her smelly boyfriends, stupid Maw. There were Ashlee's brothers and their nasty friends, document-forging Cain and Dr. Len. Ms. Laquered Hair back at the cleaning agency; she'd threatened jail for stealing. Ashlee had put up with that headhunter and China Doll—until 'the accident.' There'd been all those Johns, and Mallory, the Madame, and her minions. Ashlee had put up with Lance and other snots like him. Now there was Slinky, her stupid friends, and other island idiots. Well, no more. It was time for payback!

Ashlee knew Jeremy's dense houseman thought she might try to steal the silver or a few trinkets, but she didn't want any of that crap. She'd stolen enough of that stuff back in Carolina while cleaning toilets! Now she had no use for frippery. What Ashlee wanted was flesh and blood...a *man* whose last name happened to be Harden, and she would have him!

He was going to commit to her. Just wait, she promised herself.

The next day she woke with a terrible headache and the driest mouth. Ashlee had had the worst night, where she'd been plagued by dreams. They had really been nightmares of how things used to be.

When she woke, she reminded herself, was no longer that nothing girl, Ursa Blank. She was new, Ashlee Caro Durham. As such, she got what she wanted. Ashlee reminded herself that her plans had paid off.

Un-crumpling herself, she limped out of the storage room at work. Late, Ashlee felt like Buddy B spoke excessively loud. The ring of the phone seemed shrill, too. But between taking calls, Ashlee thought her boss mentioned the arrival of Jeremy's mother. "Did'ja hear?" Buddy B seemed to yell.

Oh, so *that* was why Jeremy had those men throw me off the manse grounds, Ashlee cogitated. Last night, after being removed, Jeremy's men let her have half an hour to herself. Then the reeve pounded on the door. He informed her, she had only minutes to find other lodgings.

Before Buddy B left to start his rounds, he told his employee they were going out after work. He didn't say it was because Ashlee looked bleary-eyed and beaten. He didn't say he knew something had happened. He only advised, "I won't take any excuses. Tonight, out, you and me."

Forgetting her boss, Ashlee spent the remainder of the day thinking and alternately fuming. Good thing she'd had the office key, or she'd have had to sleep on the street. Although she didn't want to, Ashlee couldn't help but feel Jeremy had used her, like a whore. He never kissed her or touched her breasts, not after that tentative first time.

She could not know that he had never liked the feel of bought breasts on any woman. All she knew was that sometimes he'd been rough with her, and he'd seemed angry. That she didn't mind. Actually, she'd liked those times. Still, she didn't like knowing he had used her, her body, and that he had taken out frustrations caused by Gemma on her.

And never would Ashlee forget the morning he'd woken stiff and ready. She had been so happy that he'd slept in the dark morning hours because that had meant she would wake up to him, for once. She knew he'd dreamed of Gemma, and Ashlee hadn't cared because she was present, Slinky wasn't. More than ready for a romp, Ashlee wrapped his member with a hand. She'd seductively purred, "I kin help with thet."

Jeremy had held her off. In the morning light, he had not allowed her to swing her leg over his or straddle him. He'd upped and left. What sense had that made? She'd bitterly wondered, feeling hurt.

Then the fire of her envy and rage had burned a few notches hotter.

In the small office where she marked file folders and routed calls, unbidden, memories of Mam-maw drifted to Ashlee. Boy, did she miss that old woman, sometimes. There were even times when she hated that she couldn't just pick up the phone. She wanted to have a conversation with her grandmother, or just anyone from her old life. Oh. She had cut all ties to them. Now she had no one but herself—to blame.

Forgetting her family, memories of 'Dr. Len' rose and memories of how she had only wanted him to fix her. Back then, Ashlee had been prepared to endure almost anything. At her desk, she recalled the awful scars she still bore. Before the surgery, she'd told herself that nothing was worse than being flat-chested. Now she knew. After all she had given up, and all she had been through to get to this point, *nothing would be worse* than losing the man she loved…to an uppity *nigger*.

That evening at Ms. Nalonni's Fish Frying House, Ashlee sat with her boss at an umbrella table out on the deck. Waving palm fronds surrounded them as the sun began to set. Singing creatures tuned up for their nightly song. Sympathetically, Buddy B looked over. Gulping beer, he told Ashlee some things could not be changed. He did so because she'd moaned about injustices during the short cart ride over.

"Lil girl," the outdoorsman wisely opined, "no one can *make* another person love them." Buddy B said so because he well knew.

Drinking, Ashlee almost hated that Buddy B seemed to know all her business. She was so upset, though, and she didn't have a girlfriend to spill her beans to; she'd left Bif back in the holler. So Ashlee had to talk to someone, and Buddy was sometimes that person. She didn't see that he had asked her out or that he'd walked into the eatery with her as she'd wanted; she only saw that the leathery man was not Jeremy.

Having had a couple of drinks, which loosened her tongue, Ashlee continued to yowl about having had to vacate the Manse guesthouse.

As her boss listened, she said she couldn't shake the feeling she was being pawned off because Jeremy's mother was coming. "Ah think he didn't want her to know I was there—because of Gemma." Ashlee did not admit she loathed the actress/producer. Still, Buddy B read between the lines. It wasn't hard to do so with Ashlee adamantly claiming that 'Slinky' would never love Jeremy the way she did.

Indeed, Buddy B had wanted to know which of the surfer's crew his employee had set her cap for; now he knew. He thought it almost comical. Blondie could not have wanted a man more out of her reach if that man had been on the moon! And she wanted the unattainable with a desperation that was unhealthy. Boy, was this chickadee interesting.

Unaware of her employer's thoughts, Ashlee admitted, "I cain't stand seeing her photo in every café 'n boutique." Glossies of Gemma were everywhere, some with the proprietors. "Why's her father up there?"

"Uh," Buddy B chuckled, "because he's a famous philanthropist. And because everybody loves a winner, even us lil ole Karinians."

"Well, Ah hate thet," Ashlee moaned. "Ah hate hearing 'bout Jeremy's gran'pa Baptiste and some black priestess. The gran'pa was supposed to have been in love with her. I hate hearing thet Jere's love for that—actress is the same. An' I really hate hearin' stupid stuff like 'He's our own,' or 'she's our very own,' lak they national treasures." Ashlee swirled her drink, "People even speak of Jeremy's mama that way."

Her voice softened as she admitted, "I don't hate hearing 'bout her…"

Buddy B just had to say, "Miz Giselle is not the type of woman you would call mama. She's…" he gestured, "royal, more like a tiny queen."

"You *know* her?" curiosity rounded Ashlee's eyes.

"Know ever'body 'round here. Lived here near 'bout my whole life."

That was right, Ashlee thought. Buddy B had mentioned his father. The man had been the sheriff, years back. She needed to remember that Buddy was a fount of information. He might wind up useful.

"So what is Jeremy's mama—I mean, his mother—lak?" Ashlee did not look at Buddy B. She did not want him to see her avid interest.

Deliver me from questions, the man thought as their server showed up at that moment. Accepting his order, grateful, the boss got to eating.

Yet Ashlee would not let things go. She wanted to meet Jeremy's mother and be liked by her. Perhaps Mom would convince her son it was time to marry. Ashlee knew it was wishful thinking. Someone like Giselle Windsor Baptiste-Harden would never encourage her only son, the heir to both the Baptiste and the Harden fortunes, to pursue a non-pure breed. Still, Ashlee figured, for Jeremy, it would be better to take up with her than with that—actress. At least Ashlee was white; that lounge act girl was… wrong for Jeremy in every way. "Heh-yull," Ashlee groaned, hell, "why do that wench need him? She already got everything. Cain't she let somebody else have something?"

Accepting another beer, Buddy B recalled why he'd invited his employee out. He had wanted to take her mind off things. Still, she couldn't concentrate on him, for brooding over a man she could not have. Go figure. "You do know," the huge outdoorsman said, intently watching lil blondie, "you have more than you think, right?"

"Yeah, and you're special, like Pokemon."

Ouch, Buddy B thought, that hurt. His little kitty had claws.

Chapter 35

Gemma decided she would call. There would be no more hastily hanging up. What would she say? She asked Nannie. It seemed like forever since she'd spoken to the man who had sent a bunch of stuff for his daughter's birthday. Jeremy was the same man who face-timed with his kid, only when the nanny, not the baby momma, would be present.

Suddenly, Gemma didn't know if she should call. All she knew was Jeremy had been there. For some reason, he'd left. *Poof.* She vowed to stop torturing herself. She may never know why that man did anything he did. Tossing the phone, Gemma decided to do what she had with her baby. Wean. She would get Jeremy off her mind. She had work. Sure, she put her angst into her role as Arma Geddon, but she felt like she was sinking in the sands of Wales all the time. It was like she never climbed from the dark spaces for which the role sometimes called. Sure, the director said she was doing some of her best work, but she was tired of slogging through emotions. This Gemma told her best friend. Heather was as sympathetic as always. Heather even said she hated men. Right now. The longtime friends chuckled.

Then Gemma spoke with her mom and Belize, who said she sounded tired. Gemma let her family believe that since they adored Jeremy. Gemma's mind slid back to the man she'd once believed was the love of her life. Truth be told, she still felt that way, even knowing his adult flaws. Yet sometimes, she felt like the man who had been groomed for authority—the one who wore power like a priestly robe— wasn't ready for the adult her. She had matured, but Gemma sometimes felt Jeremy didn't respect her as a woman or a professional. Gemma felt they were both too stubborn to stop hurting each other. It was why *she* had to stop the madness. She needed to call it quits. Although the very notion burned, she just wanted to breathe again. She wanted to do so fully and without pain. Gemma wanted to laugh and not feel hollow inside. She wanted the same joy her small daughter felt when she saw snow, sloshed through a puddle. The only thing was Gemma didn't know how to rid herself of the man who had seemingly always been a part of her.

In the morning, Ashlee watched Jeremy leave the manse—and she saw red. Hiding on Beach Road, she hated that her few belongings were in the office storage room. Ashlee believed that Jeremy would never correctly see her as long as he was brooding over Gemma. How could a man ignore the woman who truly loved him? Ashlee knew she had to do something to change Jeremy's mind. She needed him to stop seeing her as a ho and start seeing her as his mate.

Damn that bigmouth Lance! Ashlee seethed because Lance must have told Jeremy about their early encounters, how he'd banged her in alleys, and how she'd tricked for him and others. That must have been why Jeremy had initially sought her and left money. Oh well, Ashlee mused; she would simply make Jeremy see. He needed a wife, but he needed one of his race. Ashlee would do that because he was whom she wanted. She didn't care that currently, things weren't right between them. They'd had a tiff, as Mam-maw called it. Black pussy had come between them. Ashlee told herself she really couldn't blame Jeremy because Gemma was hot. Ashlee wouldn't mind a taste of Slinky, too; she could see herself down between Gemma's legs... Ashlee shook herself. Back to reality. She had plans to make, and quickly. She hated thinking about maybe moving back into the rented room at old Mrs. Pigeon's. She hated the woman's pug dog. Ashlee needed to go home to the manse, where she belonged—with her man, Jeremy.

On her phone, Gemma saw that Jeremy had called. He hadn't left a message, but her heart pounded. Were they now on speaking terms? She couldn't remember the last time she'd heard his voice. Ah well, even if they did speak, she still had to go on. She couldn't be with a man who perceived her work the way he did. It was better this way.

No. This was hell. She wanted her man back. Gemma couldn't hide from that fact. She loved that man with her whole heart. It would always belong to him. Passing a thumb over his number, Gemma acknowledged the truth. Some days she felt like she was slowly dying. Some days when she cried on set, she did so for real. She'd brought the whole cast and even the crew to tears just yesterday. There had been silence at the scene's end. Then moments later, there was an eruption. It had been thunderous applause. She'd been congratulated; superb delivery!

Nonetheless, Gemma had only been able to wonder one thing. Was Jere okay? She'd wondered since they were kids, and she probably always would. However, now Gemma had to ask another question. What if he had gotten over her? God forbid, but was he seeing someone else?

Six days straight. She'd wrangled, and now she was off. Sure, they were many months into filming, but she'd had to get away. That Gemma made clear. She'd talked the director into shooting around her. She was going home. Packing a few things for her baby, who was now walking and saying 'Da-ee' Daddy, of all things, she and Aimee vamoosed.

Back on Karina Cay, Gemma fell into Ina's motherly arms. Without a word, the older woman held the younger as she cried.

Then both Ina and Aimee just let Gemma be. On the island, the young mom didn't get dressed, not even when Heather stopped by to see her goddaughter. Gemma simply sat out back of DeVeaux house in the lovely outdoor room Giselle furnished from Home Wares. Lean Heather mentioned how she had implemented vet house calls. "Us going to see about pets has become a big hit," Heather explained.

"I'll bet." Gemma sounded tired, "Especially with older Karinians."

The redhead said nothing. She beckoned Aimee, who gathered her little charge and the child's toys. Then Heather Garrahan quietly sat with her friend, whom she knew was depressed. Before returning to work, Heather kissed Gemma's forehead. "Well, bestie, *I* still love you."

On her third day at home, Gemma sat in her kitchen wearing a short silk nightie. She listened to sappy songs. *If You Don't Know Me By Now* was on repeat as she fed Twyla, who wore only a pullup and a tee.

"You, little girl," Gemma teased, feeding her baby mashed banana, "have bedhead." Gemma sighed. "I should get you dressed, but soon it'll be nap time, and booby, your mom just does not have the energy."

Feeling a presence, Gemma saw a shadow fall over the table where she sat. Looking up, her heart leapt. There was Jeremy!

Resting a shoulder against the doorframe, he appeared so sinewy, gorgeous, and angry, all at the same time. He wore a crisp, sky-blue dress shirt with a white collar and cuffs and an eye-catching tie.

His strawberry waves had grown out. Gemma longed to run her fingers through that hair. She ached to kiss that sexy mouth and feel Jeremy's hard body on hers. In a nutshell, she wanted to devour him.

As he stood watching *sa femme*, Jeremy loosened his silk tie. She sat in brilliant sun rays. They streamed in through the fanlight over the kitchen door. He noted the prism effect. The kaleidoscope of color played on Gemma's upswept kinky hair. Light and color caressed her creamy shoulders like he wanted to. It cascaded over her shapely legs and frosty pink toenails. Why did she look so tired? And there was his beautiful baby, smacking on banana while bathed in sunshine. *Hi, Cutie.*

"I hear you got in a few days ago," Jeremy said without preamble. "Sunday, to be exact. I hear Heather and the sheriff both stopped by."

Gemma's good feeling dissolved because who was Jeremy to keep tabs on her? It wasn't like they were together anymore. His fault.

"Funny," he said, "they both knew you were in town, but I didn't."

Gemma didn't look up when wearily she quipped, "If you came here to fight, I can't help you." She just didn't have it in her.

It seemed he ignored that statement as he reminded her, "It's Tuesday. So how much longer will you be here?"

"I leave Saturday." Gemma forced herself to sound calm, although she was not. She added, "And for the remainder of my time here, I'm gonna need you to call before you stop by." She gave Twyla the last spoonful. "Good girl," Gemma cooed. She revealed to the man in the room, "You can't walk in here unannounced."

"Why? What'll you be doing that you don't want me to see?"

When he had first appeared, she'd been worried about how she looked. She'd wished she had dressed, combed her hair, and applied lip goo. Well, so much for that, Gemma thought without responding.

She told her Nannie, no longer present, that she'd take care of things, just like mom had all those years ago. Yep, when Gemma showed Jeremy the door, she would get off the carousel once and for all. She'd begin by informing her staff; Twyla's father was no longer welcome at DeVeaux House. Then Gemma would have the locks changed.

Suddenly it seemed Nannie poked her. *You don't want to go down that road.* Oh. That was right, that had been Momma's path—with Lyle.

Jeremy advanced, speaking softly to the toddler who didn't appear to know him. Watching, Gemma had heard that Momma and Lyle had a good marriage. Then stuff happened, including that last baby; afterward, everything had gone south. Gemma had been that baby. Now she and Jeremy had their own baby, and it seemed everything was swirling down the drain for them too. Gemma didn't want that.

Furthermore, she didn't want Twyla amid an uncomfortable situation. Gemma had been the kid in the middle. What to do, though? Gemma asked Nannie, especially if Jeremy wanted to continue to act ugly.

Well, that would be on him. Imperceptibly, Gemma nodded as he crouched beside their daughter's high chair. Gemma wanted her girl to know her father, and she wanted them to have a good relationship. So what, Jere could be moody and angry? He was still a great dad who had set up a trust for his child before she'd been born. He had done it so that Twyla would always be taken care of; he'd said Gemma would not have to fight for a thing. Twyla would even go to university, courtesy of her dad. All that was his would become hers.

Unaware of Gemma's thoughts, Jeremy longingly stared down at his brown baby. She had grown so much in just the last few months.

Seeing his gaze, Gemma needlessly offered, "Her hair's growing."

"I see. She's beautiful," he reverently added, "like her *mère*."

"Oh Jere…" Gemma's eyes filled. He had always been able to throw her off balance whenever he spoke, seemingly from left field.

Within seconds, Jeremy was down beside Gemma's chair, hugging her. He placed a hand on Twyla. With Gemma's tilted eyes, the little one stared. On his knees, he kissed the baby's hand. He did the same to the exposed swell of Gemma's breast before working his way up to her lips.

"I've missed you," he murmured, silencing her with a kiss. Softly he revealed, "I want us to fix things, *bébé*."

Gemma tearfully admitted she wanted the same. Sniffling, she took their daughter's small hand and placed it in her father's larger one. "Twy-baby, this is Daddy. You know him. Say hi, Daddy."

The baby stared. Slowly, her little face crinkled. Her lower lip, Jeremy's pink lip, in miniature, quavered. Twyla began to cry.

Gemma lifted her. "Whoo! So heavy now," she huffed. Pressing the toddler to her shoulder, the mom rocked. Seated, she placed a hand over her own eyes. Wearily she admitted, "Your daughter needs to spend time with you, Jere. For her, facetime is like Sesame Street. It's not real."

His thigh muscles began to cramp, so Jeremy rose, but not before noticing more tears. These flowed from beneath his wife's unadorned, elegant hand. Jeremy refocused, not wanting to become emotional. He also knew he shouldn't feel absurd jealousy. Still, envy caused him to despise that in his wife's arms, and not his, Twyla's cries diminished.

Ah, he'd forgotten, as he often did, that his baby momma was just that, not his wife. —But how he loved this woman. He always had, and he always would. She was everything to him, that he could not flee.

Jeremy wondered if his kid cried because she'd sensed his initial anger. Had she sensed that often he acted like an ogre? It would be awful for her or her mom to know that those in his suite of offices typically steered clear of him unless they had been summoned. The only person who seemed indifferent to his moods was his personal assistant.

Middle-aged Donna had worked for his father. Jeremy sure hoped his kid couldn't sense what he couldn't forget; he had been unfaithful.

But Gemma had too, Jeremy rationalized. At least he thought she had. Now he had crazy Ashlee sending him letters proclaiming love. He'd told Colin, and the curly-haired man had shaken his head.

"Sound like she tryin'ta level up. Mess sounds like obsession, too."

"I figure if I ignore her long enough," Jeremy offered, "she'll quit."

"That girl, quit?" Colin refused the notion. "Improbable."

Standing in Gemma's kitchen, with late morning sunlight slanting over his little family, Jeremy forgot entanglements. Though it was hard, he humbled himself to say, "Gem. I am sorry for everything." He revealed he wanted to be bigger than he had been, and better. He recalled how she had always said she couldn't read his mind, so he spoke his thoughts aloud. He said the months without her had shown him that there was no one else for him. Jeremy knelt again beside Gemma's chair. With emotion clogging his throat, he sounded hoarse as he admitted, "I've been an ass, but I do love you, *bébé*; I never stopped. I never will."

Jeremy told Gemma the rest because she needed to know. "I am no good without you." Wryly, he smirked. "I am not that good with you, but *chére*, you make me a better man." Jeremy had to tell Gemma one of the biggest things. "I do *not* think your work is frivolous. I know it is fabulous, like you. You care about people, *ange*. You want them to eat and be warm and educated. You have grown into a good woman."

Gemma couldn't help it. She laughed.

Gently then, Jeremy attempted to pull her arms away so that he might hold his daughter. "Hey…" he whispered. "Twyla Cher, you know me."

He sang a lullaby. The *berceuse* they'd often sang while clapping.

Still feeling decidedly shy, the toddler hid her face. With grasping chubby hands, she pressed her nose and mouth to her mom's chest.

Jeremy saw the dimpled hand bunch a portion of Gemma's nightie. He hated that Twyla did not care who he was in the flesh. Some of that had been his fault. He could have flown out to see her, and her mom. As her dad, he wanted Twyla to know him and be excited to see him. Mentally, Jeremy rebuked himself.

Unaware, Gemma surprised Jeremy by opening her arms. She embraced him in colorful prisms of sunlight, with the toddler between them. "Jere," she blubbered, "I'm sorry too."

Then before either of them knew it, their lips were fused. "I love you and like you," Gemma whispered, engaged in kiss, "I want to fix this."

"I want *you*," Jeremy revealed, one hand on her, the other on Twyla.

With the baby between them, starved for each other, the adults ravenously kissed. Twyla squeaked, causing them to laughingly part.

"That's your daddy," Gemma spoke as she stood and easily settled the toddler on her hip. "You see photos of him all the time, booby."

Jeremy couldn't keep his eyes from straying to where Twyla's small fist rested, in the valley of her mom's near-exposed breasts.

"She's sleepy," Gemma informed him, attempting to right her skimpy garment. Then with a hand cradling the small curly head, she murmured, "It's sleepy time, *chére*." Turning toward the hallway, Gemma said, "Gimme a few minutes, Jere. I'll put her down, and then—" *We'll talk.*

He closed the distance, taking Gemma in his arms. He said, "We will put her down together." He needed to sing *Frère Jacques* to his kid as he rocked her. "Then *jeune maman*, I'll go down, on *you*."

The young mom's pulse quickened; that she'd missed, lying open before him. She'd missed them being together, talking, and sometimes doing nothing. Still, she asked, "You're not going back to the office?"

He answered by taking out his phone. He pressed, listened, then spoke. "Donna, I need you to clear my schedule. Yes, the rest of the day. For the next two days—matter of fact. Personal business." He listened. "Offer apologies. Send wine." He waved, "A fruit basket. If I've got time, get us on late next week." He nodded, satisfied. "*Merci*, Donna."

At Gemma's startled look, Jeremy embraced his woman. He held her tightly against his starched shirt. "There is something, *bébé*, that I need to clarify." Pocketing his phone, he kissed Gemma, and Twyla, who— miraculously—grinned.

Feeling his heart soar, Jeremy really smiled for the first time in months. He tweaked Twyla's pert nose before nuzzling her mom's neck.

"Gemma Janelle, you asked me for a few minutes. Now, I ask *you* for a lifetime… Give me that, with you and my kid."

Then the businessman presented the ring that *grand-père* had bestowed upon Gwendolyn Windsor. *Grand-mère's* ring slid perfectly on Gemma's finger. Seeing that, Jeremy thought one thing. The emerald cut diamond, surrounded by others, in its antique white gold setting, appeared incomparable, as did the woman to whom Jeremy would commit.

Chapter 36

At the old courthouse on Main, they and two friends walked up the curved outdoor steps. It was Wednesday, the next day.

Inside, in a quiet alcove with Heather, Gemma smoothed her long gossamer dress. Lovely pale yellow, it fit then flared. On bejeweled heels, Gemma turned, allowing Heather to see. The dress straps sexily crisscrossed in the back. "I wore this sundress instead of something more formal, so we wouldn't arouse too much suspicion."

The redhead nodded, "Because we know Karinians love to talk."

Gesturing to where the dress dipped low, revealing the small of her back, Gemma asked, "How does my butt look?"

Noting the way the wispy fabric hugged the well-rounded bottom, Heather told the truth. "Sundress or not, Gem, you look beautiful."

"Thanks Heath, and let's go." Gemma gathered her bouquet of yellow snapdragons, the delicate white bells of Lily of the Valley, mixed greens, and trailing ribbon. For courage, she grabbed Heather's hand.

"Yes, let's get you married!" the other woman squeezed. Wearing a short, moss green creation that set off her eyes, Heather added, "I still can't believe how quickly your names make things happen around here."

"In this case," Gemma stated. "It was Giselle's name that did it. The justice and the judge both knew her father," Jeremy's *grand-père*.

Gemma could barely breathe when she saw him. Wearing an impeccably tailored summer suit, he stood in the sunlight that turned his hair to gold. As she slowly walked toward Jeremy, Gemma had one thought. The man was all hers, at last! After more than twenty years.

Half an hour later, amazingly happy, Gemma laughed and cried when the justice said she could kiss her husband. Afterward, with her hand clasped in Jeremy's, she managed to hug Lance and teary-eyed Heather.

Dark-haired Lance, basically in business for himself, made his own hours. Therefore, he and the vet, two of the generation next cohorts, had been witnesses. Curly-haired Colin had wanted to be present, but he was on assignment, and on the mainland, surfer Jay wooed potential clients.

Grateful that her longtime sister-friend had taken the afternoon to be with her, Gemma whispered it into Heather's flaming curls.

Squeezing Jeremy's hand, Gemma felt a pang of regret as she thought about Momma and Ina. Hearing about her nuptials would upset them. Giselle wouldn't be pleased, either. Jeremy's mom would feel excluded, and Belize might feel the same. Thus, thinking about the women, Gemma realized. She could appease them all—by having a ceremony! She and Jeremy could do so shortly after filming wrapped; he'd just wanted them to be legal. Both her fathers could walk her down the aisle. Jeremy's dad, Michael, could also be there. Perhaps Jere's sisters and families would attend. Oh! And Gemma had seen just the dress for Twyla, her flower girl. The bride clearly saw it all, the sunny day, fam and friends, flowers, and food. It would be a beach setting, with Brazilian music, acoustic guitar, and timbales, while *Summer Samba* played.

However, for now, things were as they were and Gemma was happy. She was married, at last, to the male she'd loved since she'd been eight.

Following the nuptials, the foursome went to lunch. They walked on marble. Beneath the domed ceiling displaying the daytime sky, Gemma recalled it was so different at night. The ornate indigo 'sky' would fill with celestial light, seemingly from all of the stars and constellations in the galaxy; thus, the upscale refectory's name, The Constellation.

Gemma spoke in the powder room of that garden restaurant. "I can't wait to get to the resort." She gazed at *grand-mère's* heirloom diamond.

Chuckling, Heather slid onto a large, round, button-tufted hassock. "Anxious to jump your guy 'n do the boudoir boogie?"

Peering in the massive mirror, the bride nodded. "It's cray, seeing we've been together so long, but I can never seem to get enough of him."

Heather dreamily sighed. "We should all have such problems." Leaning forward with twinkling eyes, Heather caught Gemma's gaze.

"Gem, you just might want to go easy on Frenchie later."

"And why is that?" the new Mrs. Harden saucily inquired.

"Because…nursing mothers are often ve-e-ry fertile."

Gemma chuckled. "I'm not new. Twyla eats big-people food now."

"Okay," Heather smirked. "Just remember, I told you."

Gemma bent to sniff a lovely floral spray in the stunning silver and white suite, open to the sea. Artfully arranged, it stood on a twisted metal table. Exiting pocket doors, she walked out onto a wrap-around balcony.

Watching her, Jeremy's heart bumped. Lithe and feline, she was his wife, at last! With curls blowing in gentle trade winds, she leaned against the stone balustrade. Jeremy could only feel that the glittering ocean beyond was not nearly as stunning as *sa femme*.

Standing with the sea spread before her and the luxurious suite and her gorgeous new husband aside, Gemma actually felt nervous. Yet on bare feet and cool tiles, she pivoted.

Sometime later, having finished a sumptuous bath, she watched Jeremy pop a cork. With his mouth he tried to catch bubbling champagne, compliments of the resort. Gemma hurriedly held one flute and then another beneath spouting bubbles. Laughing, she recalled the prior evening at DeVeaux House. She and her man had talked way over into the night, vowing to work together to get through anything.

Jeremy had advised, "I know what that work looks like." He said Giselle and Michael Harden had done it for nearly fifty years. Then asking where Gemma would like to mini-moon, Jeremy reminded her. "You only have two days, so it won't be an actual honeymoon."

She remembered her reply. "I just want to be with you, wherever."

Later, he'd released pent breaths, saying, "All set." After their vows, they would go to The Canopus Arms. Jeremy shared why he'd picked the resort. It was on Karina; no travel needed, thus, no wasted time...

Now in the sumptuous bridal suite, Gemma and her husband clinked glasses. As she sipped, she recalled standing before the judge. Even then, she had anticipated standing naked before Jeremy. At the time, nearly trembling with anticipation, Gemma had just wanted finished vows. During the luncheon afterward, she'd thought of bathing, with scent and candles, a woman's rite. She'd anticipated slathering her skin with fragrant body butter. Then she'd imagined slipping into the whisper-light, sea-green gown and matching peignoir that she currently wore. Gemma knew Jeremy would not allow her to wear it for long.

Setting set her flute aside, she let him remove her silken robe. Quietly, she spoke, "I imagined taking you into my body." The lustful darkening of Jeremy's stormy eyes was gratifying. Easing down a gown strap, she watched him while exposing a plump breast. "When I take you in, Jere," she purred, "we'll finally be joined, fully, in matrimony."

Feeling his man-root swell, Jeremy kissed *his wife*—at last! Between soul-stealing kisses, he asked her to promise him one thing. "That tonight, nothing is off-limits," because this was their new start.

Bathed in the golden glow of muted sunlight, Gemma agreed with fingers splayed in Jeremy's hair. Holding his head while he ravished her, she and he promised to leave inhibitions and accusations behind.

Nude, Gemma positioned herself on the circular bed. Amid strewn flower petals, she lay on her stomach and spread her shapely legs. Tantalizing Jeremy, she raised her fat bottom. Aware that her sheath invitingly glistened, over a shoulder Gemma offered a sultry grin.

Seeing her that way made Jeremy's pulse crazily pound and he felt an unbridled urge to quickly mount. Yet as he approached, naked and sexy, with his throbbing erection in hand, he paced himself. Quietly, he chanted; they had two days, two days in which to savor every moment.

However, with his wife shamelessly taunting him and opening herself, he didn't know how slow he'd go. Jeremy took several deep breaths before he did scandalous things to Gemma. Using fingertips, lips, teeth, and tongue, he voraciously used her until she quivered.

Then all but out of his mind with desire, Jeremy hovered. At last he gave in to Gemma's pleas and employed his rod. Beneath him, Gemma sensually moaned. For him, the sight of her beautiful body, as repeatedly it engulfed his veiny thickness, became too much. Jeremy held himself stock-still. Yet he saw his tapered fingers bite into the plump flesh of her derriere. He saw his engorged pole erotically lodged within her, and the sensual sight nearly tipped him over the edge. Gentling his hands, he remembered not to bruise the skin that was part and parcel of her fame.

Breathing deeply, Jeremy steadied himself. With strong, tanned hands at Gemma's hips, he raised her. Then he withdrew, only to drive back in. "Receive me *bébe*," he breathed. He loved the little gasps she made as positioned behind her, he worked her. A few times he leaned forward. Adoring her so much, he kissed her nape and the lovely line of her back. With a hand before her, he held Gemma, being mindful to stroke and stir.

Jeremy gained momentum and Gemma trembled with ecstasy. She fisted the sheet. Inwardly clasping him, she flew—and took him, too.

Later, aware that her man was spent, Gemma found that she was not. Despite knowing he had given all, she was ready for round two.

Admitting she could never get enough of him, she rolled Jeremy onto his back. Straddling him, she offered sweet torture. She worked his nether region, grinding and sliding her moist core over his sexy pole. Reveling in his feel, all hard planes and jutting manhood beneath her, she gripped the headboard, and biting her lower lip, she bore down.

Jeremy lay there. With closed eyes, his was the smile of the satisfied. He enjoyed Gemma, enjoying him, until she shuddered and shook.

Then slowly, she slid down to rest with him, on top of him.

Unaware that he had drifted off to sleep, Jeremy woke. Opening his eyes, he stretched. "You know what I just realized, *bè*?"

"What, my love?" Gemma lay aside.

"For months, I haven't slept well—not until now."

Gemma noticed the sun. It had nearly slipped from the sky. Seeing it fade fast, she admitted that she'd not fared well without Jeremy.

With hands intertwined, the couple kissed and acknowledged that they had both always wanted to simply be together.

"So you're saying you can deal with my job?" Gemma asked, watching their suite darken by degrees.

Notoriously reticent, the man sighed. *"Oui."* He caused *sa femme's* toes to curl when, greedily again, he probed her sweet mouth.

Afterward, he quietly revealed, "I've got a thing for you, *ange*, I always have." Jeremy reminded her, "That is why I will deal with anything. And to answer your other question, we'll live wherever." He said they just had to be together. "And," Jeremy offered, "I am even saying I will deal with the tabloids and their tales about my wife."

Wrapped in a portion of the luxurious sheet, Gemma pushed herself up. On an elbow, she began, "Uh, about those things, Jere… Since we're married, I'd better tell you something—*but* do not think I'll become one of those wives who'll always spill the tea."

Puzzled, he asked what she meant.

"Jere, you've met them, married women. You tell them a secret, and they can't keep it. I won't be that woman whose husband shows up, saying, *Bummer. It sure sucks that you've got chlamydia.*"

Jeremy burst out laughing. "Ah, because *sa femme* spilled the beans."

"Right. I won't be that wife. I will keep most secrets told to me— although *this* you need to know." Gemma kissed Jeremy's palm. "My co-star is…gay. Yes, the Nile, as you call him." Gemma hit Jeremy. "Quit sputtering. Listen. He and I have never been involved. He's a good friend. Jere, that's twice in two minutes that you've asked why I didn't tell you. What have I always said? It's not my place to tell. I'm only blabbing now so you'll relax when I go back to work. I have never slept with Nile, nor would I. You mean too much to me to put you at risk, and *I* mean too much to me, too. Anyway, he is for damn sure not interested in me." She didn't have a penis.

Jeremy covered his eyes. "Ah, dash it! Now I must share something." He explained how he had flown overseas to visit her. Jeremy admitted he had become enraged when he'd seen *sa femme* with 'the Nile.'

Gemma was stunned and her eyes filled as she softly spoke. "I wondered what happened. That really hurt me, Jere. Then you wouldn't even speak to me. I was bewildered, then angry. I could have slapped the shit out of you." She looked away, feeling remnants of anger. "I still can. I felt like regardless of our mess, you should have at least seen Twyla." An angry tear seeped from beneath the young mom's lashes.

"I wasn't aware you knew," Jeremy admitted, feeling like a cad. "Back then, I only thought of myself, of how you'd wronged me." He kissed Gemma's fingertips. "Forgive me? *S'il vous plait?*" Please?

She begrudgingly said, "You're forgiven, but do not do that again."

Before she could take a breath, his magic hands were on her. Beneath Mr. Toned and Sexy, Gemma forgot hurt and anger. Skilled in seduction, Jeremy made it so that his wife could only focus on one thing. Him.

Mon Dieu, the husband thought moments later. She was so slick and swollen, he was about to erupt.

Following the fireworks, the couple dozed again. Gemma woke when the evening sky had gone to plum. Nearly black, tiny dots of starlight pierced it. Tearing her gaze away, she asked Jeremy, "You wanna eat?"

"You," he winked. "Then later," he advised, "we'll order in."

Whenever she had a moment to herself when back at work, Gemma remembered her mini-moon. The second night, Jeremy had taken her to an elegant restaurant. The décor was chic, the mood pleasant, and there was tinkling piano music. Amid conversation and the clink of cutlery against china, the sommelier appeared.

Jeremy gestured that he should pour for Gemma. Starched and stiff, the man changed. With a flourish, he said, "For the lady." He waited for her to taste. When she sipped, her smile was dazzling. "Perfection."

The man's icy persona thawed even more. "*Bien sur, belle dame.*" Offering the beautiful woman a bow, he topped her up while saying, "If I may be of service, you have only to glance over." With another bow, the raven-haired man turned and seemingly glided away.

Thinking back, Gemma recalled sexy Jeremy's amused remark. "My *bébé*, you have always had the same effect on men, all over the world." Thinking even further back, she could almost hear other words of his. *A lifetime… give me that, with you and my kid.*

Gemma thought of her Nannie, too, who'd passed at ninety. Never had the woman looked old. True, Nannie's hair had been white, but her smooth brown face had been minimally lined. Nannie's fragrant neck had sagged only a fraction more than when Gemma had been a child.

Gemma took a deep breath because never would she not miss that gracious lady. Softly, Gemma spoke to Nannie, as she often did, feeling less like Miz Nellie was really gone. "Nannie, Jeremy and I finally tied the knot. I only wish *you* could have been there, physically."

With butterflies in her stomach, Gemma recalled what she and her husband had done; the way he'd touched her and made her sigh. She remembered the morning she'd left. Waking early, she knelt before him, offering nirvana. Until she'd abruptly stopped.

Unfulfilled, Jeremy's eyes popped open. He reached out, but she'd already been halfway across their suite. "Got a boat 'n flights to catch."

"What kind of game—" the man swore. Sounding agonized, he pled, "Do not leave me like this. Gem. Gemma Janelle! Come, *bébé*. Please?"

Yet she'd smiled and called out, "You'll dream of me."

He caught her in the shower.

When she was back at work, her 'dream of me' statement was evidenced by her new husband's plethora of texts. To the latest, she rapidly shot back. **Hw r u getn any work done?**

Don't know, he replied. **Can't stop thinkn bout u -n that mouth.**

Feeling tingly, she heard the director mention her, so she was quick. **Gotta go But phn sex 2nite! M already juicy --4 u. Open 2. X O**

Damn! Hard -Thanks Want u bad -Can't wait -Xs 2 u

Smothering a smile, Gemma rose and slipped back into character.

Seething, Ashlee found herself talking to Buddy B. She didn't say why she'd been in the office slamming things and enraged for the past few days. Still, he had an idea. Heck, wasn't a thing that stayed secret for long on the little isle of Karina Cay. He'd mentioned that a worker down at municipal had seen Ms. Gemma, her rich beau too, and a few friends who'd joined them in the judge's quarters. Buddy B said that meant one thing. Somebody had gotten hitched. He claimed it couldn't have been the summerhouse playboy and the new vet—although summer boy had been tentatively sniffing 'round Red for years. Soothing Ashlee's ruffled feathers, Buddy B told her, again, some things could not be changed.

Still, the bottled-blond could not get the picture of *her* man and that black tramp out of her mind. Ashlee would bet he'd screwed that wench like he'd never done her. It wasn't right! Ashlee's rage burned hotter, reddening both her face and enflaming the tips of her ears.

Seeing lil blondie's fury before he left, Buddy B reminded her of what someone should have told her. "Ash, honey, you can't *make* people have feelin's fer yuh. 'Member that ol' song by Bonnie Rait?

Ashlee was sullen. "Ah know it. *Cain't make ya love me if ya don't.*"

"Then darlin' remember it." Headed to Krogan Hill, Buddy B told himself the same thing. *He* couldn't make Ashlee love *him.*

Jeremy could not wait. He'd left Gemma a message because he had news. When she called, he announced it. He had seen the physician!

Gemma was surprised. "You saw Doc Dear—voluntarily?"

Jeremy felt something akin to pride. "I did after you left, and I even had the prescription filled. Now I take a pill a day. At the time, though, *ange*, I was silent because… Well, you know."

"You wanted to try it out," Gemma supplied. "So, how do you feel?"

Jeremy was glad he could tell his wife the simplest of things. "I feel…normal." Then he clarified, "Not normal for *me*, but what is perhaps normal for someone who is not depressed. It's weird."

Gemma laughed. "If weird is good, I'm glad. I'm proud of you, bae."

After a few moments of chatter about Twyla, the pair parted.

Disconnected, suddenly Gemma missed Jeremy so much that her heart hurt. Wanting nothing more than to be with him, she fought not to lay her head on the table before her and bawl. She wondered what was wrong with her? Sure, she'd wanted to cry, and while they'd been apart, she had. But they'd coupled for life, and still, she felt like crying.

Aloud, she asked, "Nannie, how do you figure that?" Gemma liked her comforting 'conversations' with her gran. Silly; still, they were what she did. Gemma remembered that when Jeremy had been a boy, she and Nannie had discussed him—while Nannie lived. Gemma's gran hadn't seen Jeremy become a man, but in dreams, Nannie had always coaxed Gemma to marry that boy. Now it seemed the woman coaxed again. *Patience, my love.* However, Gemma didn't want to be patient. She wanted to be with Jeremy, day in and day out, for better or worse.

From Karina Cay, he took the powerboat to the mainland. Since he was gone, Jeremy's assistant had her instructions. That man; Donna, who'd worked for his father, smiled; her new boss was indeed a mover.

Gemma thought her eyes deceived her. She looked again, and she fought to do things right for the next hour. Finally, scene end and her time was her own. Overjoyed, she found Jeremy and gazed into his blue-gray eyes. "How'd you know I longed to see you?"

Engaged in kiss, his breath was sweet, "Because I felt the same way, *ange*. I ached for you, *my wife*, to touch, breathe, and love..."

Rushing, they couldn't remove clothing fast enough. Afterward, she hurriedly got back into her costume, just as someone knocked on her trailer door. They called out that she was needed on set. She apprised Jeremy that for her, there'd be no night filming. Then she held her breath. "Will you be here when I get back?"

Solemnly, he nodded. "I will, always, when you return."

That evening they couldn't kiss, touch, or love enough.

The following day Jeremy flew out to inspect commercial property.

Thinking about him that morning, Gemma sat in her male makeup artist's chair.

Like talk show host Wendy Williams, Mr. Makeup asked, "Hi yoo dooin' today, hon?"

Then he stared and dramatically asked, "How the heck am I supposed to cover *teeth* marks—and whisker burns?" The flamboyant cosmetics prodigy leaned in. "Don't say these hickies all over your body, gurl..."

Gemma spoke while laughing, "Then I'll keep my mouth shut."

"Bet yoo din do dat last night." The slim young man sucked his teeth. "Ooh, I'm so jealous! I got one question, though. He got bruvahs?"

Gemma and Mr. Makeup cackled with laughter before she admitted, "No brothers, sorry, boo. Still, I thought having more than twenty years in would diminish desire, but it hasn't, Royce. I'd do last night again in a heartbeat."

"It wuz dat good, huh?" The makeup artist waved a potion. "Well, this is my miracle erase, so only you 'n I will know about dis mess. Oh, and your man, of course. He da one who put all these marks on you. Look like he tried to eat you up, gurl."

Gemma smirked, "Those on my neck are nothing. If you saw my ta-tas and my na na..." She doubled over amid a good chortle.

"Shet yo' mouf!" Guffawing, Mr. Makeup threw up his hands. "Gurl, I thought I couldn't get any more jealous! Now we got to find *me* one, jest like him."

Chapter 37

She had been in the supermarket, buying what Mam-maw called rabbit food. At the checkout, a newsstand rag caught her eye. Ashlee stared at the photo that nearly sent her into a wrathful tailspin. Just in time, she caught herself. She didn't need people seeing her scowl at the pic of her archrival. Therefore, the blond purchased the tabloid. Rushing from the store, the fire of her envy burned hotter. She got into Buddy B's work cart. In the heat, she stared at photos of Gemma—and Jeremy.

With narrowed eyes, Ashlee knew that skeezer thought she was something. Furious, Ashlee scrutinized Gemma's long unblemished legs. Ashlee thought of the curvaceous body she'd once seen; it bore no scars. Well, none like hers, anyway. Ashlee wondered, again, when in tarnation had black girls become better than white ones?

Unaware that she had been taught to hate, Ashlee felt like Mam-maw did. Darker people were supposed to serve her. Racist, but unaware that she was, Ashlee believed other-color people should please her—or not exist! Gemma was supposed to be fanning Ashlee on a porch somewhere. –But instead of living the long-past good life, Ashlee fumed; she was wilting in a hot golf cart. Perspiration pooled between Ashlee's fake boobs and she just bet, Gemma was most likely somewhere cool and fashionable. The idea was infuriating!

Staring at the tabloid, Ashlee hated that the affair appeared to be one where Gemma had been made on over. Like she was special—when she wasn't! Ogling photos taken at night, Ashlee told herself they meant nothing. Still, there had been a wrap party—whatever that was—and Gemma wore a short black dress and a leather shrug. Hers were designer booties with sexy metal heels. She'd carried an expensive, soft-looking red leather purse. Her kinky hair, parted in the middle, was secured behind her ears with the back free. Dang, did it look pretty, and nearly wild. Her manicured nails were fashionably dark, and her skin glowed.

And there was Jeremy—with her! Ashlee positively seethed. He looked like an in-the-prime-of-life male model. Scrutinizing his black jeans, Ashlee noticed that casually elegant, he wore a dark, silky tee beneath black leather. Wait. Was that a masculine diamond eternity band on his *left* hand?

In the photo, he appeared tense, but Ashlee could hardly breathe because he and Gemma were holding hands! Actually, Gemma's hand was tightly gripped in his larger one, and Jeremy looked ready to pounce. In another nighttime photo, Jeremy held Gemma tightly. His free arm was out like he attempted to shield her from the paparazzi. Ashlee saw a wall of burly men surrounding the couple; they did the same. Ashlee figured they were security. *She* wanted security.

She glanced at candid but glamorous photos of famous women. One was an oil heiress. In another shot, the brown heiress stood with Gemma and a woman in a red dress. Red dress had gleaming dark skin. She was truly attractive. Mam-maw had said 'all them' were ugly. She'd lied.

Seeing the women, Ashlee fumed. Ogling photos taken on an old-world cobblestone street, some people stood around while others danced or sat at tables lit by candles in hurricane lamps. A few made out while the camera caught others laughing it up. There was a photo of a female DJ, and a well-known older actor wolfishly eyed her. A trio of white men of indeterminate ages posed, and a pink balding man raised a gold-label bottle. In each photo, people appeared to have a great time. Although nighttime, it looked glowy, like from a movie set. Why'd Slinky get to go to exotic locales, Ashlee wondered, while she had to stay put?

Then Ashlee wanted to scream bloody murder! The sight of that huge *rock* hurt her. Vintage and stunning, no doubt it had once belonged to Jeremy's grandmother. There was also a fiery diamond eternity band on the same finger. It was a smaller version of Jeremy's. Both rings should have belonged to Ashley! She swore it.

It hurt more to see the caption that referenced Gemma's circled rings. Speculative, it read, '**Arma Geddon - Queen of a NEW empire?**'

Bristling with rage, Ashlee told herself, *now* she had to confront Jeremy! She was no dog, and all he'd tossed her was bones. She wanted the whole kit 'n caboodle, as Mam-maw would say! Ah, but the best way to get it, Ashlee amended, would be to confront Slinky—send that heifer packing! Suddenly Ashlee would have loved to enter Jeremy's home, despite it being off-limits. She'd have destroyed many things there, including every photo of him and his black whore!

Ashlee hated that she no longer lived at the manse, in the pretty guesthouse. She was now a renter in old Mrs. Pigeon's much smaller home up on Krogan Hill. The picturesque neighborhood had once housed parishioners of the Methodist church. Thus, the area wasn't far from the manse. However, unlike Jeremy's home, Mrs. Pigeon's, and other pricey older homes like it, were shielded from the cliff-side by forestry. Those homes didn't have their backs to the beach.

Mrs. Pigeon's home was nice but old-fashioned. Ashlee could easily take it over, but it wasn't a place she wanted. She knew the former florist sought money to supplement a fixed income. The hag made it clear, too, she appreciated her dog way more than she did her paying tenant. How Ashlee wanted to kick that mean mutt, or better yet, kill it. But she couldn't. Not if she wanted to maintain her current shelter. So she'd suck it up for a while longer. She sighed. This was not supposed to be her life. When she'd left Mam-maw 'n the holler all them years ago, it had been to go to better. Why'd it seem like she'd traded one old woman for another, and one set of unwanted men and problems for another?

Ashlee felt depressed, and like she was no closer to her goals than she had been back in the day. She felt volatile, and despite people passing on the sidewalk, she screamed. Startled, some stared, while others shook their heads. Not caring, Ashlee told herself she *was* closer. She just had to flesh out her slowly forming plan. Wiping sweat from her brow, she knew it was nearly time. Ashlee felt like she had back when she'd given China Doll her just desserts at the cathouse. When the time came, Ashlee would reach out and take all that she wanted. When *she* became the lady of the manor, she would never again sneak into Windsor Pines.

She would do things, too. First, she'd stroll through the *front* door, wearing fur—eff those PETA people—and she would get rid of all things Slinky. Ashlee would fire the butler or whoever Gerard was. She didn't like him, nor he, her. *However,* when they'd met, in the growing dark, pushing their way through marsh grass, he hadn't disliked her too much… Had that been a year ago? Ashlee only knew that tall gray hair had paid her handsomely. Jeremy's slave had wanted her to turn all sorts of tricks, too. Gerard had said he'd heard she would do anything.

He had been right, Ashlee thought. She *would,* "So look out, Gerard," she sing-sang. "Your head is going to roll;" the head of the reeve, too. For messing with her, that monkey would lose his job. All everybody had to do was wait. As the lady of the manse, Ashlee Caro Durham-*Harden* would definitely make stuff happen.

Assailed by anger and consumed by inescapable jealousy, Ashlee wound up sleeping with Buddy B—and she hadn't even charged him!

Fool, her! How stupid. He was a business owner; it wasn't like he couldn't afford her, and she was a company owner, too. She was the CEO – the Chief Erotic Official – of Puss in Boots, her own one-woman operation, for which she had no papers.

So how had she *not* gotten paid? How had she gotten falling-down drunk, again, too? Ashlee couldn't execute any plan if she was super-sloshed. Shaking her aching head, she felt semi-ashamed, but only because she hadn't gotten her money. Next time, moolah first!

Heck, she hoped she wouldn't have to leave her job. Well, not before she married Jeremy. She also hoped Buddy B wouldn't think more of them getting horizontal than she did. She didn't want him hooked—on her 'product.' If that happened, his big self would be hard to get rid of, and she already had enough problems.

Suddenly Ashlee remembered everything when she didn't care to; she'd gone to Ms. Nalonni's Fish Frying House. After work, islanders often did. Ashlee was an islander now, so, like others, she'd popped over to the bar & grill. Out on the deck of the casual eatery, music had played, and she had been well on her way to getting lit.

Buddy B appeared. Was he stalking her? He'd suggested going someplace private. "Don't need ever'body in yer business—ya know?"

At his beach bungalow, miles from the manse, Ashlee spilled out that she had a plan. Hoisting herself up and onto his woodblock kitchen island, she'd slurred that she just needed to get rid of Slinky.

Perhaps he would not have known whom she meant, but Ashlee had kept talking. Fawning all over Buddy B, she'd pulled his tee, with the work logo on it, from his pants. She'd giggled while running her hands through the coarse blond fur on his massive chest. She'd further announced, "I…am going to become Mis-shis Baptiste Harr-den!"

Buddy B had laughed; it hadn't been pleasant. He'd suggested trading places. Then seated on his island, he'd pulled her onto his barrel of a knee. Tugging on her brittle hair, he'd nearly shoved his tongue down her throat. He'd felt her up, and she'd let him. Then she found herself wearing only a tank top while skewered on his meaty male member.

Now that the wild experience was over, Ashlee hoped she had imagined the little red light near a cabinet. Still, if Buddy B had recorded their animalistic acts involving vegetables and beer bottles, she didn't care. Ashlee bet she now had a customer for life. Whenever Buddy watched the replay, he'd get horny for her, and she'd take his money.

April Alisa Marquette
205

Forgetting her boss and their night of debauchery, Ashlee stumbled into Mrs. Pigeon's old-timey bathroom. She hated the linoleum, and the floral skirt that the hag had glued to the pedestal sink. Guess Grumpy Granny wanted to hide things underneath. Dismissing the floral fabric, Ashlee touched her face. She looked puffy and busted in the mirror—probably why Buddy B had said, "Come in this afternoon." Earlier that morning, he'd driven her from his bungalow. In the near-empty fish house parking lot, he'd handed her back the golf cart key she'd dropped.

Forgetting her bloodshot eyes, Ashlee pondered her proverbial loose lips. She had told Buddy B entirely too much, but it was his fault. He was like a big ole pal when she'd never had one. Oh, her bad; back in the day, she'd had Biffi. Then she'd left Bif 'n them behind. Ashlee pondered the massive ox of a man. He and she had energetically romped.

He really was a good listener, and surprisingly, he was a good kisser, and he had the hugest dick. It was the biggest she'd ever ridden, and ride 'em cowgirl, she had. Maybe she'd do it again. She'd have to see.

Slowly, Ashlee opened Mrs. Pigeon's medicine cabinet, careful not to let anything come crashing out. The old sea hag thought she was slick, placing tiny bottles on shelf edges as a booby trap. Karina Cay's former florist wanted to hear when someone opened her little mirrored door.

Searching for headache pills, Ashlee licked parched lips. She wouldn't mind climbing up on that ox Buddy again. Next time he'd pay her, though; her shit wasn't free. She couldn't just give away pussy. She wasn't married to money—not yet, but she wouldn't just *give* Jeremy hot and wet when she was.

He would pay her, too, in cars, jewels, and furs.

Oh yeah, and she wanted smooth, tan, new tits, just like Gemma's. Jeremy would pay for those, too; Ashlee swore it.

Chapter 38

Gemma knew something was up, and she told Nannie. Then when pint-sized Belize called, Gemma admitted what she'd told their grandmother, no longer physically present. "I think I may be pregnant. Again."

"That's great, Munch! If you're happy."

"Well, Leez, I'm not unhappy."

The elder sister asked, "Does the hubby know?"

"Not yet, but once I've seen my doctor, I'll tell him."

Months later, on the isle of Karina Cay, another woman was coming to a conclusion of her own.

Ashlee left Buddy B's small office. Headed for the coffee shop to purchase lunch, again she noticed her boobs were tender. Typically, they had nearly no feeling, and today, again, she felt ill.

Beneath beaming sunshine, Ashlee walked. She recalled slathering on her outdoor face, her Crayoleen—the super cheap version of Maybelline. These days she looked haggard before doing so. A while back, too, she'd noticed feeling fatigued. Ashlee had assumed there was a bug going around. Still, the illness had lasted weeks and then a month. She'd wondered, had she contracted malaria? To her, on the island, surrounded by so many darkies, that would not have been a surprise. Dadgummit, everybody knew the blacks were filthy and lazy. Forgetting them, Ashlee allowed herself to ponder the truth... *She* was pregnant.

Her secret made her feel smug, sort of, because this was big. Now, she could force Jeremy's hand. Thinking about how she'd tell him made her feel life was good... Until she saw Gemma. Why was she back? That long, lean redhead was with her. Unaware of Ashlee, the cozy pair stopped before *Splendid Choco-Latte*, a place Ashlee never patronized. The confection house was too expensive, with its snooty wait staff and unpronounceable treat names.

Yet what made Ashlee gape was Slinky. She wore cheerful capris beneath a sleeveless coral-colored top. The sight of her small yet clearly protruding *belly* nearly stopped Ashlee's heart. A *baby* bump! Ashlee became enraged as the tall thick-bodied sheriff appeared. If she liked black men, Ashlee mused, she'd have wanted to climb his mountain.

Forgetting that, she watched, unseen, as the big sheriff chatted with the women who smiled and twittered up at him. Ashlee's hatred and envy knew no bounds. She told herself that now she *had to* act because *that* was supposed to be *her*.

Oh, it *was* her, she realized with astonishing clarity.

No longer feeling smug, Ashlee promised herself one thing. Gemma would not steal her dream. She, Ashlee Caro Durham, would have Jeremy's baby—not Gemma! Ashlee didn't care that her own pregnancy had *not* been fostered by Jeremy. So what? She wasn't the woman he adored so much until there was no mistaking it, even in photos.

Ashlee did not care! As far as she was concerned, *no one had to know* she wasn't ballooning with Jeremy Baptiste Harden's baby. Not even the big oaf who was responsible for her predicament.

Thinking about her current situation, Ashlee wanted to rant 'n rave or cut herself. No. She wanted to cut the little invader out, just like Maw had when she'd gone to Doctor Len back in the holler. Maw had let that quack vacuum away rapidly multiplying cells. Maw had done so before the cells formed another kid that would fight its way out of her. Forgetting Maw, Ashlee realized. In the four months that Jeremy had messed with her, and in the months to follow, she'd had her womanly courses right on schedule. Now...hell! A month after romping with big-ass Buddy B, Ashlee was starting a miniature ox!

Ashlee hated kids. The brats took everything a person had, then left them high and dry—just like she'd left Mam-maw, and after all Mam-Maw had tried to instill in her. Ashlee pushed her grandmother aside to ponder her predicament. Ashlee nearly hated it. No. She hated Buddy B! Why hadn't he used a condom? Still, something inside her asked, how could she blame him when she'd slid down his pole repeatedly?

She had let him get it in the office, too. That had been exciting. Ashlee had liked that anyone could have come upon them, viciously biting and fighting in the storage closet. Then there'd been that time in the hallway. While sweatily humping and pumping, her clear heels had been overturned on the floor beside his big booted feet.

Ashlee had even told Buddy B about her sliding pay scale. Laughing, he'd obliged. Thinking the other guys didn't see, biggums had tossed bills onto her desk.

Not in her wildest dreams had Ashlee envisioned something like *this* happening! Well, she would make this mess work. She surely wouldn't let that black cunt have everything—while she had nothing. So what, she didn't want a kid? She sure could *use* one. The plan that had made Ashlee nearly feel smug was still in effect. She just had to tweak it.

That evening after work, Ashlee let Buddy B talk her into going to the fish fry house. However, at Ms. Nalonni's, Ashlee tried sweet tea. No more liquor for her. She couldn't afford to get drunk or even tipsy. She wasn't doing it for the baby. She didn't give a flying fart about it. Neither did she care that Buddy B was speaking. She heard him jawing on about the well at Windsor Pines. She wanted to scream 'you already told me the stupid legend." She'd heard that hollow well mess a hundred times!

Unaware, Buddy B guzzled beer. He said the same thing had happened in New York. All Ashlee could think was New York was where Gemma often went. If lingerie girl was smart, she'd have stayed there. Ashlee stared at Buddy B. He was yammering about the case he called the 'Manhattan Well Murder.' Ashlee turned her head, but she still heard about 1799, centuries ago. A man named Weeks was supposed to have eloped with a woman. Instead, people thought he killed her.

Buddy B continued, "Weeks' woman had told friends that she and he would marry in secret. Still, he was seen measuring the well. Look it up."

Using his fork and knife, Buddy B scooped up catfish and coleslaw.

Watching him, Ashlee hated the way he shoveled way too much food into his pie hole, all at once.

Unaware, with a full mouth, Buddy B spoke on. "The woman's body was found." Food particles flew, "In a marsh now called Soho Village."

In New York, Ashlee thought, where Gemma should have stayed.

"This guy, Weeks," Buddy B stated, in the know-it-all manner that annoyed Ashlee, "was acquitted after only five minutes of jury deliberation. The public violently disagreed and the citizens of New York ran Weeks off. He wound up in Mississippi." Buddy B wiped his mouth. "It's on the internet. Anyway, in a case like thet, based on circumstantial evidence, public sentiment can get real ugly. The accused might as well be convicted because people won't allow 'em any peace." Buddy B shrugged. "In the court of public opinion, a person can wind up dog meat..." Somberly, he said he knew. Past experience, he did not say.

Buddy B sat quietly for a bit. Then looking like he'd returned from afar, he nodded. "I'll tell you where all them accused guys went wrong. It was in them not making the murders look like suicides." Mr. Know It All claimed, "If they'd done thet, they'd have gotten away, Scot-free."

Buddy B mentioned his father, Karina Cay's former sheriff. However, Ashlee did not hear another word. She pondered what she had already heard...about the legend of Hollow Well Lane.

Up there was where Jeremy lived.

When she was alone in her little rented room on Krogan Hill, in pale, frail, old Mrs. Pigeon's house, Ashlee's heart excitedly pounded. Her mind returned to the fact that a century or so back, Jeremy's property had belonged to the Methodist church. At the time, a male parishioner had murdered his wife. Strangled her. Ashlee shook her head. Too messy. The man hadn't been smart, strangulation left marks. No jury would believe a person would or could do that to themselves.

Ashley could see why the man had done it, though. He'd been angry, like she was. The man believed his woman had been having another man's baby—like she knew another woman was having her man's baby.

The offensive woman had been found in the well. Great idea.

Decades later, another victim was found, this one with head trauma. Again, messy and visible. The body was dumped in Jeremy's well. The stupid legend said now, beneath every full moon, the murdered women howled. Improbable, Ashlee scoffed. The noise was most likely the wind.

But... an idea began to form... Ashlee didn't have a problem with the dumping of the bodies. Too excited to sleep, she pondered the well, a great place to hide evidence. However, she had a problem with the two men not doing as Buddy B had said. They should have staged '*suicides.*'

Were the murderers smart, they'd have made it look that way. Turning over in her small bed, Ashlee grinned. Maybe those men weren't smart, but *she* was. Matter of fact, she was the smartest person she knew! That was the reason she remained up, almost all night. She scratched out her plan, under the heading, The Way To Do This.

Surely, now, she could find a way to lure *Slinky* to the well...

After work one evening, Ashlee couldn't wait to get home—well, back to ancient Mrs. Pigeon's pad. Ashlee thought about mornings and how the old crone often sat in her backyard. Before the little concrete fountain, Pigeon watched birds splash, and never had she asked her tenant to join her. Ashlee didn't care about that. Her focus was the angel's trumpets. They grew behind Pigeon's house, just like those behind the manse. Granted, the widow's flowers were all white, not yellow with blood-red flutes like Jeremy's, but no matter.

Ashlee remembered Mam-maw. Of course, her grandmother, the continual gardener, had spoken of trumpet flowers. She'd said some were pretty, but they could prove deadly—in the wrong hands. Mam-maw had proclaimed all parts of those plants poisonous. That Ashlee counted on.

Since her landlady was out walking Pug, her mean little dog, Ashlee intended to try something. While out, the elderly woman would get to yakking with any neighbor she saw. Therefore, knowing she had time, Ashlee grabbed scissors. Humming, she sauntered through Pigeon's back door. In the evening light, Ashlee approached the dramatic, funnel-shaped flowers. Hanging from vines, they really seemed to be the trumpets of angels. Stepping over other island flora, Ashlee cut a few forbidden flowers. In the fading light of dusk, the white trumpets fairly glowed. Noticeable was their seductive scent. Exquisitely perfumed, their lemony top-note wafted on the evening air. It was intoxicating.

Back in the kitchen, with sap-sticky hands, Ashlee nearly felt giddy as she set a pot on to boil. When the old flower lady returned, Ashlee managed to smile. "Would yew lak a cup of tea? Jest made it."

Birdlike, Mrs. Pigeon cocked her head, thinking. She had never known the blond girl to be friendly. However, she wouldn't shoot down the child's efforts to turn over a new leaf. Karina's former florist nodded, "Don't mind if I do." Mrs. Pigeon said it, despite not really wanting tea.

Feeling unbelievably mellow, Ashlee hummed as she poured.

When her landlady sat to drink, the blond gestured, asking if she could join Mrs. Pigeon. Permission granted, Ashlee closely watched.

"My, that's fragrant," Mrs. Pigeon stated. Moments later, she removed her sweater, believing the tea was beginning to make her hot. Aside, Ashlee lifted her own cup as though to drink. Feeling unsteady, Mrs. Pigeon felt a floating sensation. Saying nothing, she simply tried to focus. Before the widow, her Formica tabletop seemingly wavered. Whatever the discomfort was, the elderly woman hoped it would pass.

Suddenly feeling as though something large and hairy crept up into her throat, the widow gagged. The china cup fell from her shaking hand.

It shattered, and Ashlee appeared concerned upon hearing a gasp.

"I – can't – breathe!" Frantic, due to the loss of air, Mrs. Pigeon struggled. She wanted to stand. However, her knees didn't get the message from her mind. She thought about running, but she hadn't done so in decades. Flailing but severely imbalanced, the widow keeled over.

April Alisa Marquette
211

Dispassionately, Ashlee watched the old crone crumple to the floor. Feeling as though everything happened in slow motion, Ashlee hazily thought, this is good. Those flowers really *work*.

Little Pug sniffed about his mistress' head. Bent over, Ashlee sounded worried. "Oh Lawd, Mrs. Pigeon, I'm gonna put something under yer neck." Ashlee slowly wadded up a dishtowel while asking, "Kin you tell me how yew feel?" The younger woman really needed to understand. Then she would put it in her plan, The way To preseed.

The older woman could barely speak. Her veiny little hands, now rigid, resembled claws as frantically she clutched at air. She felt like she was about to suffocate. Using all her strength, she moaned, "Help—me!"

Freaking out was good, Ashlee mused as she said, "Ah am." Then slowly, she dashed to and fro for effect, which she found most amusing.

"I think...I'm—dy –ying!" Mrs. Pigeon gasped. Then she shuddered.

Feeling smoothed out, like she'd smoked a joint, Ashlee laughed.

Dismayed, sickly little Mrs. Pigeon remained on the kitchen floor. The wadded-up dish towel was beneath her neck. Clutching her torso, the elderly widow curled into a small ball. Feeling alone, she began to cry.

Bending to better see the woman, although Ashlee's own vision crazily swam, the blond slapped Pug aside. "Move it, mutt."

The dog growled, then whined and licked his owner's face.

Seeing what appeared to be a villain before her, standing in the very flames of hell, Mrs. Pigeon shrieked, "You're –burn—ing! Get away!" Hallucinating, the elderly woman sobbed as her frail body convulsed.

Ashlee didn't know what the old relic saw, but the pensioner's reaction was great. Ashlee clapped her hands, aware that hallucinations had been triggered by the flowers' poisonous high. Still, Ashlee condescendingly ordered, "Ree-lax... I'll call 911." *Not.*

Instead, the bottled blond stood with her back pressed to the lip of the sink. Unaware that she had been affected by the flowers, Ashlee dispassionately watched. She figured that the old woman would pass out in a moment, so there was no need to call anyone. If Ashlee was stupid enough to dial, emergency workers would think the hag had been given LSD, and they'd swear that Ashlee, the tenant, had done it.

Therefore, Ashlee shrugged. If the old dame survived, with no help, okay. If she didn't, what could a girl do? Pigeon was a fossil. She was going to croak anyway, and it might as well be sooner rather than later.

Curiously, Ashlee watched sickly little Mrs. Pigeon writhe, snot, and cry in agony. Ashlee felt nothing, no alarm, no compassion, or sympathy.

Forgetting her landlady's distress, she remembered what heavy Mam-maw had said years back. 'People ought to always think twice before experimenting with plants.' Mam-maw mentioned kids who'd fooled with angel's trumpets. They'd gone to the hospital. Some had been in pain, some had suffered mental distress, while others had died.

On this evening, the heavy older woman's granddaughter had needed to see, firsthand, what those flowers could do. Now Ashlee knew.

Feeling light as air, Ashlee loved that Mrs. Pigeon just happened to be around. Although she was a pest, Pigeon had become invaluable, such a big help, and all in the name of research. What a great little guinea pig. Shuddering, moaning, and lying on the linoleum in a fetal position, Mrs. Pigeon clutched her stomach as foam dribbled from her mouth.

That told Ashlee a bit more. There was the loss of breath, delusions, and, best of all, there was pain.

Now came the wait—to see if there would be death...

Ashlee left the little dog to worriedly whine, paw, and pace. On her tippy toes, she danced to her room. If the old troll died, Ashlee told herself, she would starve the mutt. Then he could join his owner.

Ashlee clasped her hands together. What smelled so nice? Unlocking her hands, she placed them near her nose. Wow, her fingers, with their unkempt nails, smelled divine. She sniffed and sluggishly remembered. Ah. The scent of the flowers, but why were her fingertips—yellowed from smoking—sticky? Maybe flower juice had oozed onto them when she'd cut the trumpets. Oh, who knew? Who cared?

With a smile, Ashlee did not realize. She no longer felt her constant companion. Rage. On this evening, she felt mellow and as though one portion of her plan was complete. Handling her notepad, stolen from Buddy B's office, she scribbled, The Testing fayz.

She'd fill that part in later. Flopping onto her twin bed, Ashlee closed her eyes. When she could, she would write things down.

Then she would move on to her plan's Nex stage...

April Alisa Marquette
213

Chapter 39

It was Heather's day off, but she worked anyway because the office was short-staffed. She had planned to get prettied up and go to The Constellation. Now she wouldn't. She'd wanted to walk under the retractable domed ceiling with the stupendous heaven view. Now she would have to see Kismet Staar later, and she adored Gemma's mom.

Heather recalled how happy she'd been when Gem had finally returned after filming wrapped. They'd squealed like girls while realizing they could settle in. There was no more school for the vet and no more Warrior Woman for Mrs. Married. They had discussed this latest phase of their adult lives. "We can see each other every day if we want to!" They'd yelled, "Just like old times!" Seated in *Splendid Choco-Latte*, they'd vowed to relax. Sipping Irish Coffee, Heather had learned things.

Gemma's parents—all three—would soon visit. Her dad, Beau, said it had been too long since he'd seen his granddaughter. Gem's mom wanted to see toddling Twyla, too. Now Heather would miss all the action. Sure, she would hear everything. Secondhand. What a drag. She would even see Jeremy's mom, but later. As the new vet, Heather was on call. What she hated most was that she would miss the day's luncheon. Gemma was sure to spring some surprise on the ladies she'd invited. Dang, did Heather want to be there. Forgetting the fun she wouldn't have, the redhead sighed and re-checked her electronic pad.

Now Mrs. Pigeon's address showed up. Darn, if that little woman didn't call every week. Heather didn't know about the senior vet, but Mrs. P was about to make her re-think the house-call-thing. Grabbing her gear, Heather's plan was to get out to The Cascades, then over to Sea Scape. She'd head to Krogan Hill last, where Pug was likely fine.

Yeah, yeah, the log said his owner called claiming the little dog had pain. That was probably just a ruse whereby Mrs. Pigeon could get company. Heather didn't fault the sickly older woman, though. Heather knew what it was like to live alone. Her Grandma Garrahan did, too. Still, as the vet on-call, Heather could do without riding all over creation.

Ashlee fairly thrummed with excitement. She had put her plan into action! Early that morning, she'd called the vet's office. If she said so herself, she had been brilliant. She could have been like a trained actor!

Pretending to be Mrs. Pigeon, while using the woman's kitchen phone, Ashlee had asked for help for Pug. She'd made herself sound feeble without a hint of her Carolina twang.

The stupid receptionist had bought her act! The dumb girl said she'd put Pug down for an in-home visit. Then like the last time Mrs. Pigeon had called, Ashlee insisted. She wanted 'that nice redhead vet,' only.

"Pug likes her, you know," Ashlee announced as her voice had quivered with laughter. She'd tried to smother it. Then at the end of the exchange, she had been assured. Krogan Hill was on the schedule.

Time to go fishing, Ashlee mused when she hung up. Triumphantly pumping a fist, she thought one thing. She had baited her hook!

She wrote down, now all I have to do is wait fer a bite.

At the table in her inviting outdoor room, Gemma tore her eyes from DeVeaux House's rear brick walk. With a sigh, she again thought of how great it was to be home. Sure, she knew she was blessed to work at what she loved, but returning to Karina Cay was always special. It was a treat to have her mom on island for a visit, too. Her fathers would arrive later. Gemma glanced at her seventy-something mother, who wore a silk caftan. It was artfully splashed with tangerine and orange. "You know we're meeting Jere's mom for lunch today."

Statuesque Kismet nodded, enjoying birdsong and the breeze stirred by the ceiling fan. "I know. It'll be her, us, Ina, and Aimee for a ladies' lunch. I still can't believe we're leaving my Munchkin. Why not let me dress her up and take her with us?"

"Another time, Momma. Mrs. O'Shea," at the manse, "is glad to babysit. I'll drop Twy off on the way." Gemma caressed her growing belly. Thinking of Jere's glee that they might get a son, she watched the ocean repeatedly race inland. It licked at sand before it quickly receded.

In a one-piece swimsuit, Gemma had a sarong knotted at her disappearing waist. She thought about crossing bricks and the boardwalk. While sitting with her mom, Gemma imagined taking a refreshing swim.

Glancing at her daughter, whose kinky hair was caught up in a fashionably messy topknot, Kismet spoke. "Tell me again why I won't see my darling Heather today."

"She's gotta work—Ah," Gemma sounded preoccupied as her phone vibrated. She glanced at it on the glass tabletop. "Speak of the devil…"

The cherished photo she had taken of Heather the last time they'd lunched in the same outdoor room appeared on the screen. Gemma picked up. "Hey, Heath, what's up?"

Believing she had not heard correctly, Gemma's heart began to race. Slowly, she pushed her chair back as she stood. "Wait. Wait, baby— Heath. Heather G. I can't understand you..."

Hearing the distress in her daughter's voice, Kismet looked up. A square of cantaloupe remained on her fork tines. Hearing babbling through her daughter's phone, The Momma set the utensil down.

"What?!" Gemma asked. "Red, slow down. Breathe. Say that again. Heath?" Gemma spoke louder, "Heather G! Heather! Hello? Oh, God!"

"What's happening?" Kismet asked, feeling the makings of worry.

Gemma had been greatly upset by the tears in her friend's voice. Hastily, she placed her phone on the tabletop and turned. She absently knocked over her black wicker chair. Rapidly, she sidestepped the pristine white cushion. On cool Mexican tiles, she raced into her sunny kitchen. She speedily stepped into flip-flops, grabbing her golf cart key.

Pushing an electric sweeper, Ina looked up, and Chef JeRell stopped talking. As Gemma bolted, he called after her, "What's going on, Girlie?"

With a manicured hand at her throat, Kismet stood. Frowning, she watched her daughter hurry down the back porch steps, her footwear slapping against her heels. Again, Kismet queried. "Where you going, Munchkin—and in such haste? What did Heather say?"

Gemma hadn't the time to explain. She'd been summoned to old Mrs. Pigeon's home up on Krogan Hill. She wanted to tell, but Heather had specifically begged her not to, and Heather begged her to arrive alone.

"Don't mention this to anybody," the veterinarian had sobbed, "or... they'll hurt me. And Gem?" She whispered, "Hurry. *Please.*"

Then there had been silence.

"Gemma?" Her mom's voice pulled her from the recollection. The Momma called out as the golf cart was started. "Gem-ma Ja-Nelle."

Aware that the silver-haired woman was demanding her attention, the younger threw up a hand. Distracted, she shouted, "Give Aimee a break if she needs it, ok, Momma? I'll be back!"

"But Munchkin," Kismet Staar took a few steps. "You forgot—"

With the key in the ignition, Gemma zipped backward. Glancing forward, she saw worry and puzzlement on Ina and JeRell's faces. Her mom frowned as they all stood on the shady side of DeVeaux House. Trying as best she could to console them and herself, Gemma hollered, "I'll be back. I will, in just a bit!"

Kismet glanced at the housekeeper. Motherly Ina appeared as puzzled as she. Ever so slowly, Gemma's mom shook her head.

"See what I go through?" Ina tried to tease, despite her stomach pitching. "That girl is always dashing off somewhere."

"Yes, and she has always thought she knew what I would say," Kismet murmured. "This time, I wanted to say she left this..." The silver fox raised her hand, palm up.

Ina's breath caught, "Her phone." The women's eyes met; both knew it was most important to Gemma. "Bubbe goes nowhere without it."

"Well, today Girlie did," Chef JeRell chimed, his crusty manner belying the fact that he felt an inkling of dread. "Now, how the hell is anybody gonna call her?" Noisily he snapped his dishtowel. "I can't wait on her, even though she and I were supposed to finalize tonight's menu."

Watching him pivot, Ina tried to shake the feeling of foreboding. "Well, despite Gem not telling us where she's going," like she usually did, "she said she'd be back." Twisting chubby fingers, Ina watched the burly chef right Gemma's heavy overturned chair. As Kismet replaced its cushion, Ina mumbled. "Bubbe will be back. Soon. She said so."

On Beach Road, Gemma again realized. That choppy conversation with Heather hadn't sounded right, especially the 'come alone' part. And who was this mysterious 'they' that Heather thought might hurt her?

Tightening her hands on the steering wheel, the expectant mother felt one thing. Nothing that Red had said sounded right. Gemma acknowledged that she'd have told her peops what was going on, but Heather begged her not to; maybe this was best. Gemma clenched the wheel. No need to upset Ina when Mrs. Pigeon had been the first person to embrace her and Babba. That had been soon after the family had relocated to the isle of Karina Cay.

Back then, Gemma had been younger than Twyla was now. Gemma wondered, what was Heather doing at Mrs. Pigeon's, at this hour? Sure, the vet made house calls. Still, on weekdays, Mrs. Pigeon rode to the senior center with others. She ate a late breakfast there. Then she dawdled over crafts until lunch, after which she was driven home.

While passing through a stretch of wide, cooler, shady, tree-lined road, Gemma reminded herself. The frail woman who had long ago been the in-town florist did think her little dog was human. Maybe something had happened to him, which was why Heather had cried. Red loved all God's creatures. But why not call the senior vet? Gemma pressed harder on the go pedal. Bursting into brilliant sunshine, she continued to create mental scenarios designed to keep worry at bay.

Perhaps her friend had given the little dog too much dope-pin-nef-freen. Oh, stop making up stuff, Gemma scolded herself. Maybe though, Heather dreaded a reprimand from Dr. Percival. He was the senior vet from whom she was gaining invaluable hands-on knowledge. Gemma wrinkled her nose. Nah, not Heather G. She was way too conscientious. That scenario was highly improbable.

On Beach Road, Gemma flew past her second home. She glanced at the foliage hiding the vast house. She heard the ocean's distant roar. As she sailed past Hollow Well Lane and the manse's imposing gates, she felt tingly, thinking of Jeremy. Her sexy husband would be home in two days. She couldn't wait! She liked that his disposition had improved since he'd gone to the island physician. Jere would always be reticent, but now he wasn't nearly as surly as he had been for most of his life.

Suddenly an ugly thought intruded. What if this was some type of ploy *for ransom*? Anyone who knew her, or Jeremy, knew that either of them would pay nearly any sum to get Heather or their next gen cohorts safely back if taken.

With sickly cold perspiration skipping down between her shoulder blades, despite the bright, hot, mid-morning sunshine, Gemma turned. Pressing the pedal, she chugged up Krogan Hill. She gunned it when she leveled out in the cute little neighborhood, praying not to hit anyone. She swerved and bumped onto Mrs. Pigeon's driveway. All of her mental chatter fled. Then Gemma felt both fear and trepidation.

Hastily unfolding herself from her cart, Gemma ran around the side of the house as she had been instructed. As birds merrily twittered, she heard the slip-slap of her flip-flops, but what she didn't hear was the little dog barking. Pug. Gemma again pondered all that could be wrong.

Then pain! Oh, Lord, and more pain! Bursting bright, it clouded her vision because the back of her skull had been slammed. Gemma thought it as viciously she was felled. She felt an additional spasm of pain. This time in her knees, as they hit the ground, and her world went...*dark*.

At DeVeaux House, Kismet Staar took her bright, inquisitive small granddaughter from Aimee. Kissing the happily babbling child, she looked over at Ina, whom she addressed. Despite worry over where her daughter was and how Heather was doing, Kismet also spoke to the nanny. "I wonder if we shouldn't all just go ahead and get dressed."

"Well," Ina uttered, attempting to pretend things were normal, "Bubbe did promise to take us to the restaurant."

Aware that most people never expected her to speak up, Aimee did. With her French accent apparent, the nanny suggested that someone call Jeremy's mom; tell Giselle what was happening. Not appearing mousy, Aimee recommended that they say the family would be late. Clamping her lips, Aimee didn't dare add, 'Or we may not arrive today at all.'

"You're right, Aimee." Gemma's mom sighed as she accepted the house phone. "I'll call Jeremy's mother now."

"You can just talk," Ina said, "Jeremy's mom is on speed dial."

"Giselle? Hello to you, too. Yes, this is Kismet. It is a beautiful day for an outing. Hmmm, that's why I'm calling." The grandmother handed Twyla back to the nanny. "It seems we've got a little situation here..."

Slowly, Gemma came to. She winced. The pain in her head was unbelievable, as was the scene before her. Aware that she lay on Mrs. Pigeon's small rear patio, Gemma blinked against the now invasive brightness of the sun. Barely able to move because her hands and feet were bound, with hard plastic zip ties, Gemma saw Heather. Red was blindfolded and lay on the ground too. She was on her side, a foot away.

Gemma tried to whisper but realized someone had duct-taped her mouth. They had done the same to her friend who lay across from her, bound as well. Gemma's shoulder hurt from being pressed to the concrete. It was nothing compared to the throbbing in her head. She deduced she'd been hit, but by whom? She knew elderly Mrs. Pigeon didn't have enough strength to swat a fly. 'So someone else slammed me,' Gemma concluded, 'but why?' Her eyes darted to and fro because where was the former florist anyway? And her devoted little dog.

Gemma instantly wondered, was Mrs. P all right? Why no barking Pug? Gemma's heart beat faster, making the base of her head ache even more. Gemma's knees hurt from where she'd fallen after that vicious blow to her head. Attempting to manage pain, she made herself take deep breaths. At least she knew where she was and that Heather was alive, perhaps. Although her red hair was mussed, Heather didn't look dead, but she lay very still. Maybe Heather was unconscious. Gemma knew she had been herself. Gemma had been out for a while. She judged by how the sunlight glinted off the trees in the backyard. She could tell because the rear of Mrs. Pigeon's home faced the same way DeVeaux House did. Now Gemma decided she just had to figure a way out of this mess—before this 'they' that Heather had spoken of returned.

Silver-haired Kismet sat at the kitchen table. Surrounded by windows, she thought about what she'd had to tell Giselle. When Jeremy's mother asked if anyone had called Heather, Kismet admitted, "Indeed, we did." Each time, the redhead's phone had gone straight to voicemail, and her mailbox was full. On Gemma's kitchen sofa, Kismet divulged, "From one mother to another, I don't want to alarm you, Giselle. Still, if things don't change shortly, I will take other measures."

A while later, her vision—the one seen in *Splendid Choco-Latte*—returned. Some woman, or her daughter, fell from a great height.

The woman who had conceived Gemma suddenly pondered that she still hadn't heard from lil momma. And the producer had really looked forward to the luncheon they had now missed. Therefore, as big momma, Kismet needed to make a move. Toward that end, she dialed. Then she did what she didn't often do; she 'threw her weight around.' Mentioning she was Gemma Janelle's mother, she said, "I need the sheriff. Now."

"Ms. Kiss, right?" his admin surmised.

Big momma was brisk. "Yes, Ma'am."

"I'm ringing his office right now; how are you today?"

Kismet could always be courteous. "That you, Miriam? How're you?"

A grandmother too, Miz Miriam said, "It is, dear; I'm good—hang on. The sheriff just walked by. Hold please. I'll put you through."

The brawny man with skin the color of caramel answered. "Macaw here." Then becoming less formal, he warmed up, "Hey, Ms. Kiss."

"Hello, honey. I do hope you can help me."

"At your service, Ma'am. Heard you were in town. What can I do?"

"Mmm, I'm trying not to panic, but Trip, I need your expertise."

Knowing Ms. Kiss, suddenly the sheriff felt she sounded strange.

"Trip, I know it's not twenty-four hours, but I – am – seriously worried – about my daughter. Call it mother's intuition…"

Suddenly, beneath his uniform collar, the hackles on Trip's neck stood because he knew. The only reason Ms. Kiss was calling was because something had happened to the woman he loved. Gemma. He instantly felt his gut knot up as tersely Trip advised, "Go on."

"Well, I haven't seen or heard from my child all afternoon. Now it's going into the evening, and Gem was called away this morning."

And you're just now calling me?! Trip hung onto his temper to ask, "What time was this call? And do you know who the caller was?"

Kismet apprised the sheriff of how Heather had called, sounding upset. As Kismet relayed how Gemma became alarmed and went haring off, Aimee paced. While Kismet mentioned how they'd been calling around and how Gemma would never just blow off the ladies' luncheon that she'd set up, the nanny bit her nails. It was something Aimee hadn't done since she'd started work for the DeVeaux-Harden family. The family that now felt like her own. Aimee stopped gnawing and realized. Anxiety over her employer had caused her to slip back into a bad habit.

Kismet told the sheriff that Gemma would have called by now, from somewhere, because she had unwittingly left her phone.

Trip knew Ms. Kiss was right. Like any good mother, Gemma often checked on her baby. His goddaughter.

Not really listening, Aimee thought of how she really liked Gemma. In Paris, Aimee and the younger woman had become fast friends. Gemma was caring, sweet, easy-going, and she mothered everyone, not just her small daughter. Gemma had recently even treated her tiny daughter's caregiver to a mani-pedi, part of which Aimee had now ruined. Forgetting her nails, the nanny realized Gemma's mothering wasn't an act. Before Ina had said so, Aimee had sensed that Gemma had always been that way. Aimee thought it because she'd seen Gemma's friends, her siblings, her personal assistant, and Hollywood insiders. All deferred to the beauty and all sought her advice. Mr. Jeremy, too.

Gemma wasn't controlling or a micromanager either, like other mothers for whom Aimee had worked. However, Gemma took take an active role in rearing her small daughter. As a result, Twyla's bright, quirky little personality had emerged like a burst of sunshine.

Twyla was a joy. Although she didn't want to, Parisian Aimee wondered. How would that sweet baby get along—without her *maman*? If Gemma didn't return, what would happen to the baby? Aimee wondered. What will happen to *me*? Aimee liked it in America, especially at DeVeaux House.

Sacré bleu, what would happen to everyone who loved and depended on the pretty woman that Aimee now knew as a friend? Through scary thoughts, Aimee heard silver-haired Kismet adamantly speak.

"Trip, my youngest may be many things. She may also do many things, but the *one thing* she would *never* do…is leave this baby."

The grandmother patted the toddler who had crawled up into her arms. Kismet rocked and tried not to notice that it would be evening soon. Her daughter was still out there; who knew where? It was a terrible thought, one that Kismet tried not to entertain.

Nearby, Ina watched the little girl who focused on her grandmother's beads. "Um, Ms. Kiss, one of us needs to call Mr. Jeremy." Ina said it when Gemma's mom and the sheriff disconnected.

"Oh, God." Kismet hugged her grandchild as she asked, "How are we gonna tell your daddy *this*?" He loves the very ground your momma walks on. *Oh my Jesus.* Silently The Momma prayed, *bring my girl back, Lord. Please return her to me—to us, safely, before her fathers get home.*

Kismet did not want to tell her cousin that 'his baby' appeared to be missing, along with her beloved friend. Beau and Saavion had gone on a 3-day excursion. It was for a documentary on the coastal isles. That much Kismet remembered as she saw Ina reach for the phone.

"Since I spoke to him when he called earlier," the motherly housekeeper said, "I suppose I will be the one to tell him she's not back."

Tell him, who—what? Kismet battled fear but clued in. Oh. Jeremy. Kismet recalled that her son-in-law had called earlier, asking why his wife wasn't answering her cell, and motherly Ina had told him the truth.

Now the sturdy, longtime housekeeper dreaded having to call him again to further explain. That man was testy at the best of times. Heaven only knew how he would react when he received the news that the light of his life could really be missing. And while he was away on business.

Thinking nearly the same thing, Aimee saw Kismet reach for her phone. Shortly afterward, she announced, "The sheriff's on his way."

Amid tearing off a thumbnail edge with her teeth, Aimee again thought of Mr. Jeremy. She could see why in-town women thought he was sexy, but he could also be very *formidable*. That those women did not know. Tonight he would be even more so. Aimee figured he would have every right to be because it was apparent. The man believed the sun rose and set on his wife.

Gathering Twyla in her arms, the nanny headed toward the suite of rooms that would be peaceful. While giving her little charge a lamp-lit bath, Aimee would try to pretend that all was as it should be. In the princess' powder room, Aimee would run water, gather toys, and use baby shampoo and lavender lotion. In soft golden light, she'd again ponder the story, which, to her, was tantamount to a fairy tale. It was the tale of two beloved children. They had grown into a beautiful couple who'd married. Thirty-something at present, both were yet young, but they had loved each other for nearly a lifetime, already.

Those in Gemma's kitchen heard the doorbell. At the front of the house, it rang. In high heels, petite Giselle teetered into the hub of things. Making a beeline for the taller Kismet, the mothers embraced. Then Giselle announced she had spoken with her son.

Ina sighed. Now *she* didn't have to call. Whew! Someone knocked, and nearest the kitchen door, Ina opened it. "Evening, Sheriff."

Trip nodded, removing his Stetson. "Miz Ina." In the room buzzing with activity and people, he made the rounds. "Queen Giselle." He nodded. When he got to Gemma's mother, he embraced her. "Ms. Kiss," He looked down at her, "I sure wish I was here for another reason."

The sheriff got right to it, tapping notes into his PDA. "As you all know, it hasn't been twenty-four hours, but... special circumstances. I will need each of you to answer a few questions separately."

Another knock on the kitchen door. Everyone glanced over while Chef JeRell muttered, "Can't cook with so many people underfoot."

Dark-haired Lance entered. After greeting everyone, he broadcast his reason for stopping by. He had been unable to reach Heather. "I couldn't get Gemma, either," he thought aloud. "So I stopped in, thinking maybe they were holed up here with the baby." He wondered why no one seemed surprised he was seeking Dr. Red Hot. Dark-haired Lance hoped they didn't know that he and Red had an on-again, off-again thing. Forgetting it, Lance said, "I called the vet's office. They've been looking for her, too. I even called Heather's parents. They seemed most antsy."

Trip nodded. "Well, it's no secret, now. The Garrahans, Heather's folk, called and asked me to look into...this alleged disappearance."

In a different home on another part of the beach, big Buddy B got a bad feeling. His little blond employee hadn't been at work earlier in the day. She had been a no-call/no-show when she knew. That was grounds for immediate dismissal. She knew that when it came to business, he didn't play. He doubted she cared because she had been very strange for the last few days. Actually, the boss opined, blondie had to be mentally ill. Things she did gave Buddy B pause, but for him, Ashlee was perfect.

In fact, his little chickadee had been in a snit ever since realizing that rich feller was married. She hated that there was another bun in the oven. Richie Rich had knocked up that hot lil piece, the one who was always in them panty magazines. Those mags Buddy B had hidden in his office. In fact, he had beaten off to the beauty's likeness a dozen times. That had been good, so he knew Richie –Jeremy—had thoroughly enjoyed the real thing. Buddy B thought again about his overtly sexy lil Chickadee. He often fantasized about her. Now he wondered, what the devil had she gotten up to? Suddenly he knew. It could not be anything good.

In the air, on his way home, Jeremy could do nothing but worry. Shed of his elegant suit jacket, he'd folded back his shirtsleeves. He'd discarded his tie. Continually, he paced, making his staff nervous. As they pretended not to notice, he remembered

Maman called, saying she didn't want to alarm him. That had alarmed him. She told him about *le crise*, the crisis on Karina Cay. She said, "*Chou-chou*, it involves *votre femme enceinte*," your pregnant wife. He had literally been unable to breathe. Not Gemma! He'd thought it as his heart stuttered. He'd wanted to— Jeremy had not known what he wanted to do other than be at home to take Gemma in his arms. Then he could have known that she was safe and where she belonged.

Hells bells, he wanted off this plane! Better yet, he wanted his wife. He wanted her with him, their daughter, and those who loved them.

Thinking about Gemma, Jeremy had a hard time breathing. Ever since the news, he'd texted, made calls, and…whatever. He'd cut his business trip short. Still, he could barely think, utterly consumed with *le crise*. The crisis was the only clear thought he had. That and the fact that somebody had better fix this situation. For him, someone had better find *sa femme*.

Uncomfortably, Jeremy's stomach clenched. It churned because he needed to search for his wife! *Mon Dieu*, he couldn't! My God! He was stuck in the air when she was on the ground, somewhere. That woman was his whole world—she always had been.

Merde! Gemma just had to be found. Shit! Someone had better do so soon. Jeremy wanted *Maman* or anyone to call him and tell him Gemma

Janelle was safe. J. B. Harden wanted that before he arrived home. Or there would be hell to pay. That, the businessman swore.

Chapter 40

Someone was coming! Whoever it was tromped through the woods behind Mrs. Pigeon's property. Unaware of what to expect, Gemma focused on the concrete fountain. Still, she violently trembled.

Wearing all black, one person burst through the foliage, and Gemma couldn't tell who it was. The face was cleverly hidden behind a hooded 'Scream' mask. Staring at the elongated, ghoulish white plastic, like in the movie, Gemma thought, 'What in the world?'

When the masked person spoke, it was through an electronic voice changer. "So you're awake. Well, now we get to the good part."

Gemma felt a bubble of hysterical laughter and wondered if she was being punk'd. Nope, that show didn't hurt people. Before Gemma knew it, the person garbed like a ghost bent. Roughly, they pulled some type of hood down over her head. Wildly, Gemma struggled, feeling as though she couldn't breathe. None too gently, the hood was tied at her neck.

"Oh, fer Pete's sake, bitch," the electronic voice spewed. "It ain't lak yew gonna die— not yet, anyway."

Gemma heard weird laughter as she was yanked up by her arm. She moaned, despite the tape covering her mouth. Ouch! It felt like her shoulder was being wrenched from its socket.

"Shet up," she was told. "Now, walk."

How could she? Her ankles were zip-tied together! When she moved, they chafed and hurt, and her bones rubbed together. Trying to minimize the pain, Gemma took small mincing steps. Blindly, she fell forward a few times but was jerked back upright. Frightened, her heart hammered as she stumbled and painfully shuffled along.

Using the voice changer, the ghost ordered, "Stand here."

Wanting to run, Gemma wondered. Where was she? Inside the hood, she sweltered, in addition to not being able to see. Was she in the street? On the side of Mrs. Pigeon's house—where? Then she remembered.

Even if she could get away, she couldn't leave Heather.

Dammit, Gemma thought, had she been thinking—*going in*, she'd have counted her steps. Then she could have done the same a minute ago and know where she was. With her head covered, she twitched, hearing shuffling and sniffles. Heather! Gemma twisted, trying to face her friend. Gemma screamed too when she was hit on the side of her head.

"Told yew to stand still. Stupid." The person using the voice huffed. "Now I'm gonna do something fer you two. Don't make me regret it. If you do, I'll gladly shoot the both of yew..."

Ina, *a Polish Jew, had been hired to work in Beau's house in New York, but the winters had become too much for her ailing mother.*

Aware, Beau asked if Ina would like to leave Icebury Court.

Vacate the beautiful home in the exclusive community? "Nooo," *Ina said she had never lived anywhere so lovely. She burst into tears.* "Mister DeV—I mean Beau. This is the best job I've ever had." *Red-faced, Ina blubbered,* "That baby of yours, I love her like she's my own."

Appearing startled at the outburst and subsequent tears, tall, buff Beau stood. He patted Ina's shoulder, then he thought better. Gathering her into his arms, he spoke softly. "I—doll—I didn't mean it like that."

She looked up. He may have recently turned forty. Still, she was a bit older than the man who always smelled fabulous, the one who called her I. As she dabbed tears, she remembered why she loved him. He was a big star—who cared. Sure, Ina felt her nose was too large. She knew her legs were sturdy but not shapely. Her frizzy hair she kept in a bun, and her hands were reddened and dry from all the hard work she'd done in her previous employ. Therefore, for ages, she'd thought of herself as drab. Yet he said she had the most beautiful heart. He treated her like she was dazzling, too. He always spoke to her that way. "Darling Ina, I didn't mean what you think." *Then Beau laughed richly as he claimed,* "I'd never let you go—unless you wanted to."

"Really?" *Ina looked up, hating that her big nose was probably red.*

"Really, love. I'm just asking if you'd like a transfer to Karina Cay."

Ina's small eyes widened. Beau had a house there, on a cute little island! He'd showed her pictures. "Would I be able to...take my mom?"

She had been afraid to ask, but Beau's eyes twinkled as he said, "Babba? Of course. I can't see leaving my girlfriend here when we go."

Despite earlier fears, Ina grinned. Excited, she agreed.

"Then it's settled." *Beau again sat behind his desk.* "Since Saavion and I spend more time there with Gem, we'll need you. The coach house is big. There, you 'n Babba will both have your own facilities, like here."

Thirty years later, Ina helped JeRell serve coffee to those in the kitchen of her longtime home, DeVeaux House. As she did, she remembered when Babba died. Hugging Ina, Beau had said, "Even so, I—my doll—you'll never be alone." And Beau had been right. His family had become hers. Now Ina only prayed that *her girl*—her Bubbe, now a woman, would come safely back *to her*, and the rest of the family.

Her feet were free! The ghost had unshackled her. Although Gemma was glad, she felt apprehensive. 'Electronic voice' could still shoot her or Heather at any time. Gemma wondered why? Suddenly, she was pulled forward. It was maddening when she couldn't see or breathe through the coarse fabric. Itchy, it caused her to sweat buckets.

"Step up," she was told.

Gemma raised a foot. Feeling only air, she nearly toppled forward.

"Lift yer *other* foot. Stupid."

Gemma did and was shoved, then ordered to sit. Her hands were jerked to the side and zip-tied to a metal bar. The seat was cushy. Within minutes, she heard the same being done to Heather behind her.

Then their captor said, "We're going for a ride. Ain't that nice?" Suddenly it dawned on Gemma. She was on a golf cart seat. The cart she had driven over, most likely. Her keys! They had to have been stolen when she'd been coshed over the head and lay unconscious. She hated this, the hot and the dark, the suspense too. She especially despised the game the ghost had going. Gemma would figure a way out; she vowed it, or Lord only knew what would happen, just like in a bad movie.

Suddenly the cart jerked, and she nearly slid off the rear-facing seat.

Gemma heard gleeful laughter as the ghost—the hidden coward— used the electronic voice to call out, "Hang on, bitches!"

Trying not to pace and make his team even more uncomfortable, he crouched like a big cat ready to pounce. The man called J.B. Harden glanced out the window. The unscheduled flight from Istanbul was too long! It gave him too much time to think. He imagined the worst had happened to his wife, his kid's mom, *and* their lovely friend, Red.

Although he had repeatedly wracked his brain, Jeremy could not think of one person who'd want to harm either woman. Therefore, he believed this had to be someone's ploy, devised to extort money. Soon there would probably be a ransom demand. Whatever Gemma and Heather's captors wanted, Jeremy would liquidate the cash and pay it. He would do so on the condition that he got *bébé* and Red back first.

Arrggh, Jeremy was torturing himself! He had to stop pondering such things! Therefore, he turned his mind to business.

He had become 'the man' at Home Wares. There, he was many things, including the top dog negotiator, and he'd learned to do it well.

Throughout Jeremy's formative years, he had been groomed for this, and he'd watched. He had seen Giselle, great at client negotiations. He'd watched his dad. Gemma was an incroyable *businesswoman too. Moreover, Ms. Incredible had built her brand from the ground up by being a successful negotiator. She had even given him advice.*

"Let your employees know you want them empowered. Otherwise, you can't expect them to align with your vision, and they need to see how aligning with you will benefit them."

Jeremy had taken heed, and his employees had readily connected. Now most at Home Wares had begun to share the dream.

Gemma had also suggested that he tell them that he and they would be accountable. Toward that end, while she'd been away filming he had decided; he wanted to shed lifelong depression. That way, he could become so much more accountable. Sure, it meant he had to regularly see his physician and take his meds, but no more hiding or introverted persona for Jeremy. And his lady had cheered him all the way.

Thinking about that woman, Jeremy felt choked up. He covered his eyes. She just *had* to be okay, the mistress of his heart; she, who had mastered being present. He recalled how she could be so very *there*. That he loved; while he spoke, she never appeared to be thinking. Super busy, she had the uncanny ability to close her mind to the exclusion of all else but him. By watching her and loving her, he'd realized more; great leaders were great learners, and from her, he had learned well.

Initially, when invited to speak at French symposiums and elsewhere Jeremy had clammed up. Then Gemma had gently advised him to talk about the business aspects he knew. "Speak from the heart," she'd urged.

On other occasions, Gemma had even prompted him to speak to God that way. His wife believed everyone needed an everyday relationship with the Universe's CEO, and Jeremy had tried it. Now in the air, he would do so again. Up, pacing the Gulfstream aisle, his feet would not rest. Therefore, he paced and silently prayed. *Mon Dieu, my God, this woman you gave me...she has made me better, not just for her, but for my kid, our families, and for all those we employ.*

Jeremy faltered. Composing himself, he went on. *She and I have so much work left to do —and loving, too. S'il vous plait, please...help me get her back. Safely, that is key. Dieu merci.* Thank you, God.

When the short, wild, and winding golf cart ride ended, Gemma heard shuffling again. Years of living on the coast had attuned her to the ocean, which she could hear, too.

"Come on!" The electronic voice shouted and snatched the hot woolen hood from Gemma's head.

Ahhh, air! She could finally breathe. Oh, thank you, Lord!

"We're gonna have to do some fast walking," the captor growled. "So try anything, and bang-bang. Yew two are dead."

Gemma didn't like the sound of that, even though that voice... Despite the tinny electronic sound, it seemed familiar. She'd figure it out.

Gemma hoped it wasn't visible, but she'd repeatedly flicked her tongue while nearly suffocating under that mildewed, scratchy hood, that burlap bag. She'd pressed the duct tape that had covered her slightly parted lips. Ick. Now it was all but loosened. She lowered her head, so it might go unnoticed and made a mental note. The person in the ghost get-up was shorter than she.

Ghost waved the shotgun at the women who were no longer blindfolded. Ghost ordered them to "Go on" trek into the woods ahead of their abductor.

With her eyes darting around, Gemma knew it would soon be dusk, previously her favorite time of day—day into night. Not good. She tripped over a fallen log. In the near darkness, she deduced. They weren't close to her home or Jeremy's. Still, she would figure a way out.

Garbed in black, the ghost brandished the shotgun. Wearing heavy boots, Ghost tromped along, snapping twigs and barking orders.

Gemma and Heather both fell several times trying to navigate the vine-strewn forest floor and inky interior. With their hands bound before them, they could hardly break their fall. Yet not caring, their captor strode to stand between them. While hoisting the weapon, the electronic voice cranked out. "Blackie, yew go first."

Black-ie? What kind of racist mess? Gemma thought it as she planted her feet and stood her ground.

For her belligerence, she was hit with the butt of the shotgun, and Ghost growled. "Move your black ass! Up front, bitch! Keep thinking, and I will put you down, right here."

The disguised shorter person—whom Gemma felt moved like a woman—said basically the same thing to Heather. Somehow, the phrasing was familiar. "Do the stupid, Red, and I kill friend up there."

Gemma felt Ghost was crazy. Still, while wearing worrisome flip-flops, she had to attempt this part of the trek. Despite her taped mouth, she queried aloud what was the impetus behind the whole scenario.

Unable to understand, Ghost figured a question had been asked. Hence, an angry shove was administered, along with a reprimand.

"Yew don't git to ask me nuthin! Ya hear? No questions, bitch. Button it up!"

A moment later, Gemma winced. Darn! Taking that tumble over a felled log had bloodied her fingertips. She should not have tried to break her fall. Wearied, she breathed heavily. Didn't the ghost know it was hell trying to balance oneself while walking with bound hands? Forget about attempting to break an induced fall on hilly terrain.

Suddenly, Gemma again lost her footing. On damp pine needles, she slipped! Oh-oh! In the growing dark, on her bottom, she slid quickly downward. She knew true terror as she went. Struggling to stop, she gained momentum. She began tumbling, quickly, on pine needles and dry leaves, while her shoulders continually hit uneven rocky ground.

Thankfully, she slowed. Hurt, she wanted to cry, yet all she could pray was that they were nowhere need a cliff-side, like the one behind the manse. Then a tree stopped her descent. Aching all over, Gemma lay with a tear rolling from her eye. Hot, it trickled back toward her hairline.

When she felt she just might not slip off and into the ocean, she noticed. One of her flip-flops was gone. Her head back still ached, and the heels of her hands were scraped and burning. Her knees throbbed, and brambles stuck in her hair, not to mention the nicks and cuts on her feet and shins. Wanting to sob, she whispered. "I'm sorry little baby…"

Gemma knew. All this upset could not be good for her unborn child.

Lying on her back, she just made out faint but silvery moonlight. It peeked through lofty pines. Vowing to maim the ghost the sec a chance arose, the expectant mother just wanted a moment's peace. With her head resting on the tree's gnarled roots, she heard pounding footsteps.

Ghost tromped up, pulling sullen bound Heather along. "Get your lazy ass up!" the electronic voice screeched. "Now!"

Gemma struggled up so that Heather wouldn't get the brunt of Ghost's ire. Shaking off her remaining flimsy shoe, Gemma gamboled forward. Man, did her ankles hurt.

In time, the three wound up lurching into a moonlit clearing. It was on the clifftop. Gemma could tell from the scent and the breeze. There was a certain way the wind blew off the ocean.

Breathing heavily, she sank to the ground. Ignoring her protesting knees, she gave thanks that they had made it. But to what end? She stiffened, knowing their garbed captor, who seemed vaguely familiar, had something worse in store. That was why Gemma needed to figure a way out before it was too late.

Back at DeVeaux House, Chef JeRell fried chicken and prepared other edibles for the heaps of concerned people piling in. While doing so, he recalled having met Gemma's daddy.

At a New York gym, they'd boxed, bloodying one another. Afterward, JeRell and Beau became sparring partners. Beau offered the then-sous chef a job. That was how JeRell wound up with a lifelong friend and a new address at Beau's exclusive Long Island, New York abode.

Back then, the famous gay actor's desire for a baby had not been a secret, not in his inner circle. Amazingly, his first cousin had stepped up, wanting to make his desire a reality.

After Beau brought baby home, the Long Island residence was transformed. That tiny child, Girlie, changed Beau's life, and JeRell's. The chef learned to cook baby food, he bought organic, and he babysat. He'd never known that kind of love. With her brightness, strong will, and seemingly untamable mane, the wild munchkin had changed everyone in the household for the better. Then they'd all moved to Karina Cay. Every day, JeRell walked to and from school; sometimes, he and Beau, with the kid between them, two big dudes. Other times it was JeRell and the other dad, or he and Ina, but for Girlie, it was always JeRell.

Placing a piping hot plate before Gemma's mother, the chef remembered. *Not long after moving, he'd met his own squeeze, Ms. Nalonni, of the Fish Frying House. They became partners.*

Although it wasn't public knowledge, he and Nalonni owned one of the premier restaurants on the island, The Constellation. When Girlie became a woman, she talked her dad into becoming a silent partner, along with herself. Due to the influx of funds, JeRell and Nalonni had been able to refurbish, update, and hire a world-renowned chef. That left JeRell free to continue in his position at DeVeaux House, for his girl.

Nowadays, JeRell didn't care what time Gemma got into town; she was a priority, right after his wife. The younger woman was the closest thing that the chef had to a daughter. Not only did the crusty man with the soft center truly adore Girlie, he felt he owed her and her dad so much. If not for them, JerRell thought, he might not have his lush life.

In fading evening light, he stepped out onto the quiet, elegant back porch. He carried a lowball glass. With the outdoor room reminding him of *her*, the chef gulped brown liquor. Away from the fryer, the oven, the buzz of conversation, questions, and underlying worry, JeRell breathed.

Looking past waving seagrass, bricks, and the boardwalk, he gazed at the inky restless ocean. He saw the setting sun's faint gold, smudged just at the horizon. It nearly composed him, and JerRell sent up a prayer. He wanted Heaven to know. He needed Girlie back, safe, before full dark.

Gemma wasn't surprised when the person in the ghost garb ordered them up off the ground to march toward another nearby stand of pines. Although her heart sank, she nodded at Heather. Gemma tried to signal that they would get out of this. Somehow.

But how? Gemma wondered because the moon was now visible. Soon the sky would become indigo—and Lord, it was Twyla's bedtime. Gemma would miss it. Tears stung the mom's eyes, even as she was hit on her back with the butt of the shotgun. Angered, Gemma stumbled forward. She forgot her little girl as she was told, "Move it."

Biding her time, Gemma vowed to kick the ghost's ass—the veiled coward that she was starting to believe was a woman. Heck, even if the costume wearer didn't know who she was, Gemma would still become the character into which she had breathed life. As Warrior Woman, she would use hard-won skills to do that clown some serious damage.

Beneath the silvery light of the rising moon, Gemma ambled along as best she could. Still, she could not tamp down her anger and fear. The costumed coward had no right to keep her from her child! Furthermore, due to this stupidity, she'd missed her luncheon and the plans she'd had for it! She had wanted to announce her and Jeremy's marriage. Everyone knew; still, Gemma had wanted to say there would be a ceremony. She'd genuinely wanted to hear everyone's suggestions. Five months along, she'd looked forward to admitting what they were all guessing at; she was expecting, again. Now the time had passed. Now, she still had to find out what-all the mask-wearer had done to Heather. The biggest question was *why*?

Gemma boiled inside because it had all become insufferable. With bound hands, she couldn't help but think of her ancestors and slavery. They'd suffered far worse; from what mighty people she had descended.

Suddenly, she blinked. For a moment, disorientation replaced anger. Squinting, Gemma's heart pounded because they could not be *there*, could they? With her eyes darting, her spirits began to lift because maybe they were…near Hollow Well Lane!

The round woman approached the back porch steps. There, golden light spilled through the glass panes of the kitchen door. Briskly, she knocked. She entered in the usual Karinian way, calling, "Yoo-hoo…"

Striding into the midst of the DeVeaux House hubbub, the round woman was greeted. So was the tall man who accompanied her.

Looking over half-glasses, Jeremy's mother was not surprised that both her son's housekeeper and his houseman had shown up. Seated with Kismet, Giselle watched as a deputy made his way through the open door. Watching Mrs. O'Shea and gray-haired Gerard's progress, Giselle remembered. At times, their little island could become a hotbed of gossip. She supposed this was one of those times.

"Mrs. O'Shea. Gerard…" Giselle beckoned the longtime caretakers of Windsor Pines. The vast home had once belonged to her mother, Gwendolyn Windsor. "Come, *s'il vous plait* –please. Have a seat."

Without hesitation, the round woman did, but Gerard remained aloof.

Anyone noticing would have believed he felt bad for the new mistress of the manse. However, Jeremy's houseman felt worse for himself. He had a secret, one he prayed none of those gathered would ever know. Yet if his employer's wife did not soon return, all Gerard's friends and neighbors would know his business. Then he would indeed be ashamed.

She and Heather were prodded like cattle to walk on, to cross the moonlit clearing. So, they were going into the woods again. This time though, as Gemma stumbled along with bound and bloodied hands, she wasn't as upset as she had been. With nicks and cuts on her shins and big toe, her mind furiously worked because she remembered.

Krogan Hill, where Mrs. Pigeon lived, was inland. It was about twenty minutes from the beach. However, one could take a shortcut through the woods from that neighborhood. As kids, she and her next generation cohorts had often done so. Then they'd wound up on Beach Road, which they'd crossed. Depending on where they wanted to go, to the beach or someone's house, they'd cut across people's property. That had been back before the security gates had been erected. Now the gates surrounded most of the sprawling estates.

If they'd wanted, the cohorts had entered shady stands of pines. Then they'd worked their way to one of three different cliff-side stone staircases. There was one not far from the manse.

Suddenly Gemma's heart beat with excitement as she pieced out the puzzle. Ghost, who had to be female, must have driven the golf cart away from Mrs. Pigeon's home. If Ghost were bright, she would not have wanted to arouse suspicion. She would have quickly gotten out of the cute little enclave by swinging onto Beach Road. Still, the ghost could not have stayed on the wide street. Anyone riding by would have called the sheriff. Deputies would have been dispatched to investigate why a ghost drove a blindfolded flaming red-headed passenger. Why, too, was there a hooded, swimsuit-wearing pregnant someone else on the rear-facing seat? Red flags would have been raised.

Gemma recalled bouncing along. That was why there had been ruts in the road! She'd felt nauseous and like she would land on the ground at any moment. Ghost had turned off onto one of the little-used lanes. Very clever, Gemma thought, but not clever enough. They had traversed one of the back roads that ran parallel to the forest. Afterward, she and Heather had been coerced to unwillingly hike through the trees.

That was why things felt familiar. Gemma had grown up on the isle, so it did not matter that it was dark. Only threads of moonlight streamed through the pines. Still, now Gemma had an idea of precisely where they were! Heather probably did, too.

Both women knew. They were not far from Hollow Well Lane!

When they finally arrived at the designated spot, the ghost ordered them to stop. Having nearly worked her lips free of the covering tape, Gemma sniffed. The air was perfumed. She *knew* that smell...some kind of flower or vine, and tonight the scent seemed especially strong.

Conversationally, the ghost electronically divulged that an ax had been taken to morning glory and trumpet vines. Gemma and Heather stared. They also heard that Ghost had done so while they'd been unconscious. To make the greenery easier for them to pull down.

Both women were horrified. So that's where the ghost had been before bursting through the trees in Mrs. Pigeon's backyard! Gemma felt antsy and nearly panicked; Heather did, too. Ghost had destroyed the vines at the well—at the manse—to make their demise look like *suicide*.

The *note* she'd been forced to write! Heather remembered crying. She'd said no one would believe it. She'd blubbered that it didn't matter that it was her handwriting. Careful not to leave bruises, the ghost had repeatedly hit her in the head. Still, Heather cried that no one would buy that she and her bestie were lovers—or that she was distraught about Gemma's marriage. Jeremy was Heather's friend, too, from way back.

Curtly the ghost spoke. Using the electronic voice, Ghost claimed, "I don't wanna be out all night." Then there was weird laughter, again. "Yew two gonna die tonight. One way or another, either ya gonna do as I say, *or* I'm gonna shoot ya." Beneath the black garb, narrow shoulders shrugged. "Yer death is yer choice."

No. Heather shook her head. She became vehement, and Gemma tried to catch her eye. Gemma wanted to tell bestie that she had been so brave, now was not the time to fall apart. But Gemma could not, without giving away her tape secret. Yet she knew like Heather did.

Morning glories and angel trumpets were deadly. The first flower's seeds contained d-lysergic acid, a hallucinogen. The trumpets also caused hallucinations. Both had been known to cause fatalities.

Sounding near gleeful, the ghost sang out, "You're gonna be buried alive! Hear that, Blackie?" Ghost pointed the shotgun between the women who were poised to run. "Fire girl, now yew realize why yew had to write our little 'suicide' note." Ashlee waved it before fighting to stuff it in Heather's back pocket. "Now that yew know, git on yer knees."

Heather shook her head. Her eyes appeared wild like she would make a run for it. Willing her not to, Gemma silently pled *please don't, Heath*. Gemma did not want her friend shot in the back. If that happened, and if Heather didn't die, she could wind up paralyzed, for life.

Ghost electronically yelled, raising the gun. "On yer knees, I said!"

Using her head, Gemma beckoned Heather. *Do it*. Gemma prayed she was telegraphing too that things would be all right. Somehow.

Heather slowly got down, her eyes shooting daggers.

The ghost didn't seem to care as the electronic voice emitted. "Got bad luck, fire girl. Shouldn'a been friends with the black chick. Yew were jest bait. Ah needed *her* here. Blackie was who I really wanted. Now, these flowers'll work their magic on both'a yew."

Gemma was frightened but furious. She managed to speak around the not-so sticky tape. "No one will bee-vieve we willing-wee vid vis!"

Gerard spoke with a deputy. Now, he had to because the timeline for Heather's disappearance had been established. The vet's steps had been re-traced. People knew the point at which the women's paths had intersected. Deputies—followed by a concerned citizens search party— had scrambled to get over to Krogan Hill, the vet's last known location.

All those things were why tall, gray-haired Gerard attempted to remember something aloud. But it fled. Desperately, he wanted to answer the new deputy's question.

You know anyone who'd want to hurt Doc Garrahan or Ms. Gemma?

Gerard saw Ms. Gemma's mom walking the floor, and it came to him. Then it danced back. Still, at the edge of consciousness, something niggled. The gray-haired man wished he could stop hearing snatches of the three or four other conversations going on in Ms. Gemma's kitchen. Words floated to him while snippets wafted from other rooms. Tall Gerard wished someone would shut that back door; the air conditioning was escaping, and nobody wanted to hear loud-behind Bobby.

Out on the pretty porch, the man who worked for Buddy B blabbed. "I'd've been here earlier—if I ain't had to do the paperwork that our lil' dispatch normally does." Loud Bobby continued, "Buddy dint wanna say it, but us guys know. Ash dint call this mo'ning, dint show up, either."

Manse houseman Gerard held his head. What he mentally reached for eluded him. And doggonit! Just when he thought he'd grasped it.

Bobby's loud voice carried, "Betcha Bud don't fire his lil sweetie."

Gerard grabbed hold of the elusive. "She smelled funny!" he blurted.

The deputy looked at the firm, fit older man like he was crazy.

Gray-haired Gerard didn't care. He had known the deputy as a boy. "Stop looking like that, Tim." Heck, Gerard had even known the sheriff way back. Trip had been a rowdy teen, and his daddy had been the sheriff. The critical thing was Gerard knew what he knew. Therefore, he declared, "Tim, that girl, the one that Bobby said did not go to work today, she smelled like—"

Nearby, curly-haired Colin tried to supply a word, "Mothballs?"

"No." Jeremy's houseman became annoyed because he didn't need help. "She's not old. The girl smelled like…*flowers*."

"All women smell like flowers," the greengrocer snapped. Heck, Ms. Gemma was out there, somewhere, with Doc Garrahan, needing to be found. And here the lecherous butler was, the grocer angrily thought, talking about how some girl smelled! At a time like this.

Gerard became firm, "All girls don't smell like this—not like her." He attempted to explain. "That girl smelled like...*outside*." He'd noticed it the evening that she'd appeared in the bayou to service him. Suddenly Gerard hung his head. It was no use; he couldn't explain, and sweet pretty Ms. Gemma would probably die as a result.

On her knees, dizzied Heather felt like she would swoon. The mingling of heady floral fragrances had become too much.

Ghost noticed and snatched the tape from Heather's mouth.

"Ouch!" the redhead cried with venom in her eyes.

Not bothered, the ghost laughed. "Any last words, carrot top?"

"You're one sick bitch," Heather spat just before her lights went out.

"You *hit* her!" Gemma's yowl was muffled by the useless tape covering her mouth, "In the fvace! Vith the vutt of vat gun!"

Ghost instantly regretted it. No marks. Damn! *Suicide*, remember?

With tears falling onto Heather's peaches and cream skin, Gemma bent over her friend. Protective, she swore the tables were about to turn.

Gemma could hear her grandmother's voice, too. Softly Nannie seemed to speak, as though Nannie was alive and right there.

Patience, my love.

"I'll hit yew too," the ghost growled. Ghost pulled on a vine and then wiped her small white hand down her dark costume; Gemma noticed. Angrily, Ghost slapped at a pesky firefly, "Get outta here! Now, *yew*—skank, listen. Get them leaves down!"

On her knees, with shafts of moonlight streaming in through what was left of the hollow well's leafy overhead canopy, Gemma refused. She noted the firefly alight on her shoulder. Gemma's voice was muffled as she said, "Got a quvestion."

"What's thet?" With a flourish, the ghost ripped away Gemma's tape.

Gemma knew her captor had wanted it to hurt, but it had not. Forgetting it, she asked, "*Why*? Why all of this? And who *are* you?"

"At last!" the tormentor crowed. "The million-dollar question!"

Pulling at the crown of the ghost head, Ashlee snatched it off. A little box fell to the ground, and her voice was undisguised. "Surpri-ise!"

Gemma's eyes widened. For once, she didn't say what she thought. *I knew it was you!* The blond with the barely-there twang. As one who'd had to exact them on screen, Gemma knew voices. She vaguely also remembered the woman. The outsider had been at one of Jeremy's parties two years ago. Or whenever; still, Gemma recognized the voice, the southern cadence had given Ghost away, despite the thingamajig. Wondering *why* Gemma stared as static-ky blond hair stood at all angles.

"Whew!" Ashlee blew out a breath. "I was burning up in there."

"*Why?*" Gemma asked the perspiring woman who yet wielded the shotgun. She was...the girl from *Jere's guesthouse*! Yes. Lance's find; The one Ina had said get rid of; she had once lived in a wheeled house.

Ashlee sounded near gleeful, "Because I hate yew, thet's why, and the beauty of my plan is no one will think *I* had anything to do with this. When yer ass is finished pulling down them vines," Ashlee flicked a hand, "you'll have sap all over yew. It'll be in yer pores. You'll die. It's already on yer skin." Suddenly Ashlee shouted. "Keep workin'!"

Ashlee lowered her voice. "I'll put flowers in yer hair. How purty. People will think this was Red's doing. No one will know *I'm* the mastermind. Oh, yew 'n I know." Ashlee blinked, "But you'll be dead."

Gemma sounded skeptical. "Well... since you think I'm gonna die, I'll ask, again, who the hell are you?"

Ashlee wanted to hit the impudent bitch. Instead, she shoved her with the shotgun. "Don't question me! Jest know, yew gonna die."

"Well, if I am," Gemma insisted. "I have the right to know my killer."

Ashlee liked that idea. She twirled the mask that she had to remember to burn. "Well, since there's nothing yew kin do, now..." the bottled-blond began to talk, and the firefly flew back to annoy her. "I'm yer worst nightmare. And yew, blackie, was mine, for a little while."

Explaining, Ashlee hooked a boot in a particularly large vine and tugged. She also swatted the lightning bug. "Keep on pullin' wench."

Gemma remained on her scraped and sore knees with her hands bound, appearing to do as instructed. Moving slowly, carefully, she did not touch the actual trumpet flowers or their blood-red flutes.

Talking, Ashlee was not so careful. She just hooked a hand in greenery and pulled. Readjusting her weapon, she also said, "Ya know, since yew stole my man, all I been able to think about are them nights he crawled to me—to *me*!" She slapped her chest. "After yew left 'im!" Hatred emitted in every word, "Yew don't deserve a man lak thet."

With dried blood on her fingertips, Gemma grasped another vine, as did her captor. Watching for the chance to make any kind of move, Gemma thought, so *Jeremy* was the sore spot. *He* was the reason this person had done all of this! Again, she noticed her firefly and others.

Relaxed, Ashlee did not hide her Carolina twang. Conversationally, she stated, "Thet's not the only reason you don't deserve 'im. The biggest reason is," Ashlee spoke slowly. "Yew – are – no – good. You're a *nigger*." Ashlee shook her head. "What were yew thinkin' tramp?" Without humor, Ashlee chuckled and said, "Guess yew forgot yer place."

As she watched Gemma pull a vine down around herself and Red, who was out cold, Ashlee felt great. She even leaned to pull a large branch down herself. Ashlee did not realize the heady perfume, and the sap had already begun to seep into her own bloodstream.

Feeling mellow, Ashlee said she tried not to think about the times Jeremy had left her and the island. "I knew he was going to yew." Failing to block those images, Ashlee placed a thumb and forefinger on the bridge of her nose. Feeling her throat sting with unshed tears, she swallowed and tasted airborne flower oils. Forgetting that, she screamed. "His dick was made for my cunt! But yew," Ashlee spewed, "jest wouldn't stay away! Yer black ass wouldn't git outta his mind."

Stunned and angry, Gemma retorted. "Why would I? *I* live here! Jeremy is *my* man," despite his philandering. "He's *my* husband!"

"Shet up!" Ashlee screeched, quickly shifting to jab Gemma in the face with the gun. However, she became distracted, frantically waving at a firefly zigzagging too close to her eyes. Ashlee swatted others. Then re-focusing, she ordered, "Jest listen because soon yew will be dead."

Feeling overcome with the need to sleep, Ashlee slid to her knees. She was careful to keep her gun trained on the other woman.

"Yew don't think I know, but your mommy's in town. Saw her. Hear yer Daddy's coming too. Oh, 'n you got another one; two gay men, plooking each other. Don't look surprised. Ah know all about yew."

Ashlee's anger burned hotter because the woman on her knees had everything. "Not only do you have a mother who adores yew, ya got two daddies." Ashlee didn't even know who hers was. "Them sinners!" she screamed, doubting Maw knew either. Forgetting her family, Ashlee swiped her nose. "Some bitches want it all." Brandishing the gun, she said, "Oh well, now we won't have to wait for ever'body to come to ya funeral. I only wish I could get rid of yer kid, too. She's cute 'n all—lil half-breed monkey—but I should've said for you to brang her. Ah forgot, though. Then I could've got rid of all traces'a yew. Start fresh." Ashlee sounded dreamy, "With my Jeremy…"

Monkey? Gemma was stuck there. Baffled, she stared. The outsider was crazy, and outsider actually believed every word she'd said. Gemma suddenly remembered her mom's words. When she'd been fifteen, and she and Leez had gotten in trouble, Momma had spoken.

People aren't always nice; they may even hurt you; they have been known to do worse to children of privilege…

Down on her knees, unaware of Gemma's thoughts, Ashlee wanted to touch the kinky hair that had mostly fallen. Earlier it had been swept up. Ashlee knew her own stood out unbecomingly, but she didn't care. Later, when she helped Jeremy mourn, she would be all purtied up. Then he would not be able to resist her.

"Ya see, purty girl," Ashlee said, sounding sweet, "I knew my man would never willingly leave yew, because yew kept opening yer legs. Don't think I don't know all about *thet*. Ah do it too. The only difference is *I* git paid, and yew don't. Yew jest gi' yer stuff away. Stupid."

Ashlee spoke amiably, but her question was no less a reprimand, "Didn't yer maw ever tell yew not to do thet? Men gotta pay."

Gemma's eyes widened, but she stared at the ground. Her heart jackhammered because the blond-haired person was for-real mental.

Ashlee shrugged, and in shafts of moonlight, Gemma could see that Ashlee's eyes were beginning to glaze as though she'd smoked a blunt.

"Any hew," Ashlee continued, "I knew Jeremy had to pay. When a man misbehaves, a woman's gotta make him pay. That's why yew gotta die; yer death will be his punishment, fer cheatin' on me. Ya know?"

Refusing to answer, Gemma continued to stare at the ground, even though she was aware of the other woman's every move. She doubted chatty Cathy even realized that Gemma, the prisoner, no longer worked.

"Say yew understand!" Ashlee yelled.

"I understand," Gemma echoed, although she wanted to keep her mouth shut. "You believe what you said." Gemma knew better than to anger the psycho more than necessary. Still, she couldn't stop herself. "I understand—that you can't face that Jere loves *me*! A *black* woman. That offends you—you racist, but as a bi-racial man, he's always loved *me*. He and I grew up together. *I* know him; I know his heart. I know things about him you will *never* know or understand, and vice versa."

April Alisa Marquette
241

"Shet up. And where is he?" Ashlee sneered. "He ain't rescued yew."

Because he's out of town, Gemma wanted to scream but bit her lip.

"Yew ain't got no answer," Ashlee countered, "because the truth is, yew used some kind of black magic on 'im. Jest like thet voodoo woman, or whoever she was, used on his gran'daddy. Ah know. Ah lived in the south too, on the mainland, so don't think I don't know about all yew black whores. Y'all done it fer generations."

Ashlee struggled up. Standing, she scowled down at Gemma and jeered, "Now you wanna have another kid. Yew liked getting that kid?"

Gemma noticed the blond's eyes slowly roaming her. In her sticky one-piece swimsuit and torn sarong, Gemma felt uncomfortable.

"Ah don't blame my sweet man," Ashlee said and bent. She ran a fingertip over Gemma's shoulder, silvered in the moonlight.

Saying nothing, the expectant mother's skin crawled.

"Yew do have some purty tits." Ashlee acknowledged, roughly shoving Gemma back with a booted foot. "Did he tell yew thet? Did my man whisper sexy stuff to yew when he couldn't be with me?

"Did he kiss yer tits?" Ashlee suddenly asked, dropping down beside her prey. "Did he do it...lak this?" Using the gun, she forced Gemma back. Ashlee effectively cut off Gemma's air by pressing the barrel across her windpipe. Greedily then, Ashlee licked the creamy swell of Gemma's right breast. Swiftly then, she wrenched one swimsuit cup down. Ravenously, she fastened her mouth over Gemma's nipple.

Oh God—*ill*! Gemma flinched. However, she did not fight but protectively raised her knees. Both shielded the gentle curve of her belly. In her hands, the wrists of which were still bound, she clutched a rock.

As Ashlee noisily licked and fondled her, Gemma shivered, knowing true revulsion. Feeling violated, she wished to seriously maim blondie.

"I always wanted to taste yew," Ashlee admitted, raising her head. "Now thet I know yew sweet, it's too bad I can't keep you—for a pet. I'd have you whenever I want. But no. My man would want yew too, and I cain't share." As Ashlee moved slowly downward, her mouth hot on the brown skin beneath it, Gemma tried not to quiver with disgust.

She simply held her breath, taking Nannie's advice. *Patience, my dear...* Gemma also noticed her firefly and a host of others. It was as though, in concert, they all sang *wait*; it seemed they advised that if she would make headway, things had to be choreographed, like in the movies.

Therefore, when Ashlee raised her head to place her lips on Gemma's other sensitive breast, the expectant mother quickly brought her bound hands up. With ferocity, she caught the crazy woman in the stomach, then beneath the chin.

Ashlee's two rows of teeth clacked loudly together. *"Ompf,"* Ashlee spewed as the wind was knocked from her.

Hearing it, Gemma used her raised knees not only to protect her protruding belly but to rocket the molester off her.

Caught unaware, Ashlee tumbled to the ground beside Gemma. In the fetal position, Ashlee's face purpled as she clutched her torso.

Yet clasping her sharp rock, Gemma managed to roll over Ashlee. Using her bound hands, Gemma smashed the rock into the side of Ashlee's head. Gemma did so again as the woman screamed.

Knowing that she had better beat Ms. Delusional like Delusional had stolen something, Gemma hit Ashlee again and again. Unlike in the movies, Gemma did not stop hitting. Only when there was no movement did she relent.

Ashlee's body slowly relaxed. Her fingers stopped twitching.

Breathing hard, Gemma dazedly stared. Blood matted the moon-silvered hair. Then Gemma knew. Ashlee—the outsider who wanted the lingerie model dead—was out, perhaps forever.

Chapter 41

Jeremy burst into DeVeaux House with *le crise* on his mind. What he had not expected was all the faces turned his way. Taking them in, he realized it was nearly dawn, yet there was evidence of an all-night vigil. There were sandwich halves, and cold fried chicken, among other edibles. He saw bottled water in melting ice, half a pitcher of sweet tea, lemon wedges, remnants of a salad, fruit, and sweets. Jeremy saw a samovar of coffee had been set up, with Styrofoam cups surrounding it.

He looked from Giselle, *Maman*, holding a china cup, to his mother-in-law. Seeing the worry on the brown face, he asked, "Any word?"

Silver-haired, Kismet appeared pained. For Jeremy, that was answer enough. *Merde*! He thought, shit! *Le crise* was not over.

"Guinevere and Glenda have been alerted." Petite blond Giselle rose as she said it. She placed a comforting hand on her son's back.

Jeremy did not care about his sisters right now. They were in Europe and could do nothing for him or his wife who was five months pregnant. Further stiffening, Jeremy noticed the sheriff. Jeremy was unaware that the lawman had recently returned to pick up where a deputy had left off.

Trip was again questioning gray-haired Gerard. Just seeing the sheriff, standing in his wife's home, near his houseman, caused Jeremy to become enraged. "What are you doing, standing around?" Jeremy asked as he strode toward Trip. "Shouldn't you be out there—finding my wife? What do I pay taxes for?" *Stupide.*

Statuesque Kismet stepped between Jeremy and the taller, more solidly built man. Calmly, she explained. The sheriff and his team had been following leads since the previous day. Touching Jeremy's arm, she nodded. "Now the sheriff is here, honey, to go over more things that may be of the utmost importance."

Jeremy felt no less indignant as Trip further added, "As *head* of this investigation, Mr. Harden, I do not take orders from you. In finding *your wife*—as you so aptly put it, if you are to be involved –in any capacity, *you* will take orders from *me*." Trip stared at the other man. Levelly, the sheriff spoke. "Is that clear?"

"If I am to be involved," Jeremy repeated and could have punched Trip's lights out. "I *am* involved." *Imbécile.* "Gemma Janelle is my wife! As her husband, I must see that she's safely found and her captor brought to justice." Jeremy then dismissively stated, "I do not wish to waste precious moments quibbling." He gestured magisterially. "Carry on."

Trip stood a moment, telling himself it would not help *Gemma* if he knocked her prick of a husband on his ass.

Jeremy spoke as though to a dimwit. "As – you – were."

Knowing the alpha male pissing contest would get them nowhere, Colin spoke to his friend. "I stopped in because Red didn't show for our evening run. Then she didn't call, and I couldn't reach her."

In a strained but soothing voice, Kismet told Jeremy that everyone had been calling hither and yon ever since Heather and her daughter's disappearance. Now all the pieces were just about together.

Hearing Ms. Gemma's mother say that, Gerard remembered. Then the thought was gone. Yet he again blurted, "She smelled funny."

The sheriff looked at Jeremy's houseman and then at his notes. "Who is this now, that you're speaking of, Gerard?"

Appearing befuddled, Gerard said, "The girl in the guest house."

Avoiding Jeremy's eyes, curly-haired Colin explained. "Her name is Ashlee, or so she said."

Aware of all in his jurisdiction, Trip knew of the woman.

"She works—well, she *worked* for Buddy," the greengrocer put in. "Didn't show up yestidy, I hear. Didn't call, either, according to Bobby."

Something in summerhouse Lance was triggered. His eyes lit. "I know what Gerard means—about her smell!" Furiously, Lance's heart pumped as he picked up the thread. "She smelled like…something. On *your* property, Jere. The scent is only in a few other places on Karina." Lance found further explanation indefinable.

"Mmm…gotcha. I noticed it too, the night she was angry that—" Colin glanced from Jeremy into the women's upturned faces. Colin quickly modified, "Um, the night you turned her away from the manse. I noticed her scent as she stalked by, and it was familiar, but not perfume."

Jeremy blinked as something vague tickled his mental periphery. Suddenly his head jerked up. At the same time, he and Lance both yelled, "Morning glories!" Gerard joined them. "*The trumpet flowers!*"

The sheriff and Jeremy simultaneously swung toward the kitchen door. Lance, Colin, and others hurriedly followed, knowing they were headed back to the manse.

Slowly, Gemma opened her eyes and wondered where she was. Then remembrance crept up. Her heart erratically beat, like the wings of a frightened beast in a cage. Had she really slept—outside, on the ground? She turned her head. "Heath? Oh, God," she squawked. "Where are you, Heather G?" And had she, Gemma, really killed someone, that blond demon? "Oh Lord, oh Lord!" Gemma chanted, forcing her severely aching body up. Although it was yet dark out, dawn was not far off.

Gemma wondered. Had she hallucinated all that had happened with the woman who was nuts? Ashlee. Gemma remembered the trumpet flowers. They were known to induce hallucinations. Still, Gemma knew some things had really happened. It included blondie having slept with Jeremy. Gemma was sure the blond demon had not imagined that.

Furious, Gemma's head ached, and the stench of decay was too much. Wait until she got her hands on that man! Forgetting revenge, she scrambled among withering leaves, vines, and wilting flowers; the ground was covered with them. Gemma grasped her rock. Ignoring the dried blood on it, Gemma set out to use the sharp edge.

With the rock between her feet, methodically, Gemma sawed at the worrisome plastic that bound her hands. Many times, she hurt herself and banged one wrist or the other. Gemma felt she'd just add the new cuts and bruises to the existing ones. After what felt like an eternity, she was nearly there. It was not easy, but repeatedly she bit at the binding plastic.

With her hands free, at last, she scrambled up and grabbed the shotgun. Ignoring the body of the blond that she'd bludgeoned, Gemma hobbled over. Under the sky that would soon lighten, she made her way to Heather, whom she attempted to wake. "Please, God," Gemma moaned, "don't let her be dead." Hoping against hope that her friend had not succumbed, softly, Gemma called, "Heather?" Pushing vines aside, she was horrified to see the malicious bruises on her friend's face. "Oh Heather G... Sweetie, wake up."

The redhead woke with a start, remembering. "Where is she?" Heather's red-rimmed puffy eyes looked wild again in her injured face.

Damn that blond for hitting her! Gemma bitterly thought it as she scrambled for her rock again.

"Gem?" Heather called, trying to force her sluggish body upward. "Where is she?" That frizzed blond crazy who'd tormented her at old Mrs. Pigeon's house. The one who'd gleefully bragged about how she had killed the little dog. Crazy used the butt of deceased Mr. Pigeon's shotgun to repeatedly hit Heather on the head; the vet could not stop babbling. "Gem, she put Pug in the washer! Gem, Crazy claimed 'her landlady never let her use it,' so Crazy turned it on and drowned him!"

As Gemma tried to pull Heather upward, Gemma shushed Red. "Don't think about it, honey." It was too awful. "Just...let's go."

"That girl stuffed little Mrs. P in the dryer—I saw her teensy arm, Gem, and her leg sticking out! Crazy said she'd 'cleaned up' the place." Crying, Heather nearly puked. "Jeezsis...she made me write that note."

"Sh-shh," Gemma advised. Softly she said daylight was coming. Rousing her friend, she coaxed, "Don't lie down, Heath. *Please*. Get up."

Heather tried, but she was groggy, and her limbs wouldn't cooperate. Dehydrated, she only knew her whole face and head hurt.

Aching too, Gemma knew quite a few things ailed Heather, whose hands were yet bound. They had to move, though. "Heather," Gemma spoke to her friend like she'd have spoken to her small daughter. "Come on, baby." Gemma tugged the vet's arm. "We gotta get you outta here. You need Doc Dear. Come on, baby. I know where we are."

"Near the manse." Heather's eyelids fluttered as she heaved herself up, despite her bound hands. "That crazy girl said she was gonna dump your body in the well and leave me outside. It would look like I killed you, Gem. I'd never do that. Everybody knows it, but she wanted our deaths to allude to some twisted love story. One with a tragic end."

Gemma snorted. "She'd have been better off producing a movie." With one hand clutching the shotgun, and her other clutching Heather, bent over, the expectant mother took one painful step and then another.

Shambling forward, the best friends forever were going home.

Mere yards away, with blood matted in her now ratty hair, Ashlee opened an eye. She had a raging headache. Fighting to open the other eye, she hazily remembered. That black cunt had tried to kill her!

Ashlee dragged herself up from where she had been left, to die. Filled with unholy rage, she discarded her hot costume. Ashlee would move better in her shorts and tank top. Bleary-eyed, she noticed two figures.

Although they were hobbling, they were yet a little ways away. Those chumps! They had a head start, but it did not matter. Due to rage and being beaten down, Ashlee felt like her head would explode, but she would not be deterred. She had come too far, she was going all the way.

Upright and staggering, Ashlee's outstretched fingers itched. She would strangle Slinky—with her bare hands! Forcing stiff limbs and booted feet forward, the bloodied blond had murder in her eyes.

At his small house, Buddy B wore a tank top. He had not been able to sleep. Where could Ashlee be? He wondered again. She thought he didn't know, but her fixation with that man, the younger one, Richie Rich, who lived down the beach in the ritzy section, had grown.

Buddy B had tried to tell Ashlee that most of the beach had been the same back in the day. Only nowadays was more of it considered the rich people's section. Chickadee had not listened. She probably hadn't heard that there was a time when things had been more equal on the island. That was back when he'd been a boy, when his Pa had been the law.

Grunting while getting out of bed, Buddy B forgot about that bygone era. No sense in dwelling on the past. He pulled on socks, jeans, and a belt. He only wanted to think about now and his Chickadee.

Buddy B had offered the little blond everything; work, his home, friendship, food, his bed, his body, and them damned binoculars. He'd told her she could watch the yachts, the sloops, and skiffs as they bobbed by on the rippling Atlantic ocean. However, she had not cared about water or crafts. She hadn't looked twice. She'd gazed down the beach.

To do so was why she'd visited him after work. From her room at Mrs. Pigeon's, Ashlee had often hiked through the woods. Sometimes she'd crossed Beach Roach, and fought her way through stands of trees, just to glimpse the manse. Other times, Ashlee sat near the legendary well, just to feel like she was near Jeremy. Then when she was at Buddy B's home, she adjusted *his* binoculars to better glimpse the other man.

So Buddy B had taken the time to study *her*. He remembered all while preparing coffee. As lil blondie stood in or outside his home, he'd longed for her. Not paying him any mind, Ashlee had been unaware that Buddy B ogled her, checked her assets. He'd wondered why wouldn't she be his, willingly. They were so much alike. They could make a life together. Why did she have to long for more than she could have? His pa had done that—and see where that had gotten him.

Suddenly Buddy B smashed his mug into the sink. Eyeing the pieces, he angrily remembered what he had known. Ashlee had been yearning, but not for him. He'd known something else. Although she soaked up his substance, breathed his air, ate his food, drank his beer, and occasionally allowed him to share her body, she still thought she was too good for him. Or that he wasn't good enough for her. Whatever. She wanted Richie Rich—a black man. That one, Buddy B could not figure out.

But Pa had wanted the same thing. Buddy B remembered as he got down another mug. He shrugged because he knew something more. Ashlee thought she'd used him to get what she wanted—that other man. Yet what she had miscued on was that *he* was using *her*, to get what *he* wanted. A woman all his own. And Buddy B would have her.

Sometimes when Ashlee had been on the lookout for the other man, Buddy B had grinned. He knew: when a person wanted another so desperately, they usually did not get that person. He'd found out from Pa. Pa had been like Ashlee, blindly trying to make someone love him. Pa had wanted the priestess, the one woman he couldn't have. She'd belonged to others. Yet Pa had wanted her, in the worst way. But Pa had refused to face the truth; sometimes, a person had to move on. Pa had not moved on. Then others had moved on him.

Well, Buddy B would not wind up like Pa, twisted and stupid. Buddy B promised himself that as he sipped his coffee. He was smart. He wanted what was within reach, and what he wanted, he would have.

Unaware that the enraged blond was onto them, Heather sank down to the ground. She did so as they were about to emerge from the space where the hollow well had long been hidden. Not far from the flowers and vines that had once grown up around it, she crumpled.

Impatiently saying they would be behind the manse within minutes, Gemma urged Heather up. "Come on, baby. A few more feet. *Please*."

The redhead lifted a hand. "In a minute," she promised. Feeling dizzy, utterly unsure, ache-y and weak, she managed, "You go on, Gem. I'm just glad this is over."

After finishing his coffee, Buddy B felt ill. With a fist, he aggressively knocked on his chest. Feeling like he had gastritis, he grabbed his boots and slid his socked feet in. Then hurriedly, he exited his home. He had to get to the beach! Lil blondie was there. Connected to her, he felt it. Buddy B knew he had to save Ashlee—from herself.

Although she wanted to quickly hobble to the manse, Gemma consoled herself with being close. She promised herself she could wait a few more minutes. Thus, she leaned on the butt of Mr. Pigeon's shotgun.

Unseen, behind Gemma and Heather, Ashlee carefully slipped up. In the lessening dark, she lunged, grabbing a handful of Gemma's hair. Quickly wrapping it around her hand, Ashlee yanked, hard.

Gemma let out an ear-splitting scream. The gun fell away as she raised both hands to diminish the pain. Refusing to cry out again, her eyes watered. Twisting, Gemma kicked, and she received a punch from the back. On the side of her head, at her temple, it dazed her.

That heinous trick! Gemma thought it about not-dead Ashlee.

"Yew thought yew'd git away!" The blond yowled, "Thought ya killed me, too—well, ha-ha, bitch!" Yanking harder on Gemma's tresses, Ashlee growled, "I told yew. I'mo *kill* yew! Didn't believe, didja?"

Gemma said nothing, although she noticed that weakened dehydrated Heather used bound hands to grasp Ashlee's leg. Feebly, Heather pulled.

However, the incensed woman simply kicked the veterinarian off.

Jeremy and the others took rapid, bumpy golf cart rides through the waving seagrass behind DeVeaux House. With the sun about to make her ascent, the riders merged. All fell in line at the end of the brick walk. They swung right when it intersected, forming a T with the boardwalk. Zooming over plank boards noisy beneath their wheels, *ka-boonk*, *ka-bonk* was heard, until the riders could go no further.

Jumping from their vehicles, all clomped down the sun-bleached wooden boardwalk steps. They reached the wet hard-packed sand below. On the beach, Jeremy, Colin, and Lance ran. Trip too, as they had every day while growing up. Others followed.

It would have been hard going for anyone else, but the sand did not impede. For each man, this was his old stomping ground. They and concerned Karinians raced up the beach. Nearing the stone staircase not far from the manse, Jeremy's heart thudded nearly to a stop.

There was Gemma, Ashlee too, high up, on the flat plain of the cliff-side. Both women appeared small, as recklessly they struggled.

Gemma felt the kick back of her knee. She fell to the ground. Still, the blond would not turn her loose. Ashlee kept kinky hair wound around her fist. "Time to say bye-bye." Ashlee gave a vicious yank.

Gemma heard Nannie's voice again. *Patience, lil sugar. Patience.*

Gathering her wits and managing to rise, Gemma recalled what she had endured. To play her hardest role to date, she'd had to become *mentally* tough. In a few seconds, she remembered the aches, bruises, broken bones, and sprains. She inhaled, evoking the time she'd been thrown from a horse. Gemma exhaled, remembering ice, rain, glacial sea spray, and bone-chilling wind. All of that she'd transcended with her mind. That was why this here, this little hair-pulling psycho shit was nothing. Gemma inhaled, allowing her lungs to fill as pain abated. This was nothing; she exhaled, not for Arma fearless Geddon.

Slowly, Gemma rose. Like a ballerina, she pivoted on one leg and one foot. Feeling as though she floated through time and transcended space, she swept her other leg and bruised foot around. Deftly, she knocked both of Ashlee's booted feet from beneath her.

Jeremy and the others stood stock-still. Unable to do a thing, they all watched the tableau on the clifftop. With his heart hammering, Jeremy watched his pregnant wife struggle with Ashlee. Jeremy felt wadded up. He'd brought crazy into their lives when he should have been long past the immature. That vengeful tit-for-tat you-hurt-me-so-I hurt-you stage.

Pulling astride, the huge lawman's heart staggered as he watched the women. Angrily, they twisted, right on the cliff's edge. Holding his breath, Trip, Jeremy, and others watched as loosened bedrock showered down. Pebbles and debris ominously fell to the strip of beach below.

Mon Dieu! Without thought, Jeremy sprinted for the stone staircase.

Cursing himself for a fool, Trip wondered why hadn't he come to the manse again?! Indeed he had sent a team over to scour every inch of the property. However, that had been done, he now realized, *before* the women got there. Trip thundered inside because that girl, who did not exist, had been just a step or two ahead of him. Now he might be too late. His love might meet her demise—all because he had not done his job well! Trip had to get up there.

He noticed Jeremy. Agile as a mountain goat, the husband was already on the climb. Feeling bested, Trip felt it was *his* job, *his* duty, to stop the madness. *He* was the one who'd sworn to serve and protect.

Yet, in his vows, Jeremy had sworn to love and protect.

As he too began to climb, Trip got on his talkie. Ahead of him, Jeremy could hear the sheriff commanding his troops, and Jeremy knew. They would never arrive in time. Thus, like a madman, Jeremy scrambled. As one who'd traversed the perilous staircase since childhood, he was light-footed and nimble. Yet midway to the top, Jeremy could not see. However, he felt a *frisson* of dread.

Jeremy thought of his Gemma, who had so many sides. That was what he had always loved about her—although repeatedly, she had broken his heart. She said he'd broken hers, too. Yet as the bright morning sun burst over the cliff rise, he wondered, would they ever get it right? Continuing to climb, Jeremy did not know. Given their track record, for them, right seemed improbable. Jeremy no longer cared, just as long as he and Gemma could have another chance at being together.

Precariously balanced on the crumbling cliff-side behind Windsor Pines, Gemma knew someone was going over. She vowed it would not be her. Yeah, the blond played dirty, having grabbed the shotgun. Five months pregnant, Gemma wondered why the woman didn't just shoot her instead of using the gun to jab at her. Oh, the *suicide* theory, Gemma recalled. Blondie was still holding to that. Truly mental.

Gemma told herself there would be no crashing, for her, no fall to the jagged rocks below. There would be no surging tide, not for Twyla's mom; neither would her body wash out to sea. Gemma simply had to bide her time, for just a moment more—if she could...

Abandoning her weapon, Ashlee lunged, screaming. "We might as well both go over!"

Nearly at the top of the stone staircase, Jeremy heard a shriek. *Mon Dieu*! Halting the climb, he noticed. Movement.

Someone fell! A woman cartwheeled mercilessly in the air!

Jeremy's wife had told him about her mom's vision. He dazedly thought how accurate it had been as the actual sight sickened him. Paralyzed, he watched as *Gemma's* colorful sarong flapped in the wind... and Jeremy's heart splintered.

In that instant, she ducked, fell flat—on her belly. She felt her sarong being snatched away. She heard the thin fabric *rrrippp*. Gemma heard the bedrock give way in a manner that she never had before.

Careening over Gemma—whom she had tried to tackle—one last time, Ashlee had not connected. Without seeing, the producer knew. The receding scream meant Ashlee plummeted, along with showers of pebbles, to the jagged, jutting angry rocks in the sea below.

Afar off, but running no less, Buddy B saw all. Too much bedrock was crumbling and falling into the sea while someone was up there.

His heart hammered, and he felt like his lungs pumped fire. Putting forth a colossal effort, he felt as though he merely slogged along. Buddy B saw the movie lady *and* his little blond with the raging spirit.

Buddy B stopped short—because one of them fell.

Ohhh nooo! Something within him bellowed it. Buddy B had never known anyone to take a tumble from up there, from that height, and live.

Still, he needed to go see. He had to check the bleeding body, twisted unnaturally on the rocks below. It would be doused by ocean spray. If he waited, officials would get there. Or the tide would claim the body, batter it against the rocks, bloat it, and even carry it away. Saltwater would blanch away all color, bleach the sightless eyes and distort their hue. He could not let that happen. Buddy B could not stomach the thought of never seeing Chickadee again. Not in this lifetime.

Within Jeremy, something nearly died. Until he heard Lance and Colin. Wildly, down on the beach, they hooty-hoo-ed. Taking that as a sign, Jeremy scrambled upward. He caught *sa femme*, who raised herself to badly bruised knees. She was crying so hard. It broke Jeremy's heart. He cooed, "*Bébé*, I'm here." Grateful tears rolled from his eyes as he wrapped her in an embrace. "I am here," *for you. Dieu Merci*, thank God.

Holding her belly as he held her, Gemma loudly sobbed. She turned her face into Jeremy's open shirt collar. Hurt and dismayed, she managed to hiccup. "You, Jere." *My love.* He had been away on business. Gemma was astonished at his presence. "How?" she cried. "You—here."

Kissing the crown of her head and loving her more than he'd ever thought possible, he rocked. Jeremy murmured, "*Trésor*, I am here. I will always seek you." He kissed her tears. "Forever and ever."

Through anguish, Gemma nodded; many moons ago, he'd promised.

Moments later, Lance raced to his Irish siren, and Gemma began to tremble. "Oh God," she whispered, "So much happened, I fell—on my belly. The *baby*, Jere..." Gemma raised a hand, covered in fresh blood.

The father noticed it elsewhere too. A scarlet trickle coursed down her inner thigh to stain her leg. Swinging her up in capable arms, Jeremy raced by others and the sheriff, intent on getting *sa femme* into the shelter of his home. "Use that talkie of yours," Jeremy shouted. "Get Doc Dear!" Jeremy remembered to say, "S'il *vous plait*. Please. Godfather."

Trip blinked. Well will you look at that? His Majesty had asked a favor. He'd even said *please*. Aware that he would again have to step into the shadows and revert to loving Gemma from afar, Trip did not mind. This was a truce he could accept. Therefore, the sheriff took orders from the husband, and quickly the lawman followed through.

EPILOGUE

Buddy B slept and dreamt... During the excitement of the panty model and the vet being found, he sprinted down the beach. Quickly, he extracted Ashlee's body. Due to the commotion, he doubted anyone saw. In his dream, lil blondie loved him. Ashlee was grateful that he had nursed her back to health, although the damage to her spine he could not repair. In his dream, his Chickadee was thankful to him for the therapy provided so that at least she could use her hands. Poor thing, her legs were shot. Those she would never use again, but the 'exercises' he thought up, the ones where he made her useless hands pump his penis up and down, those did help—him.

In his dream, Buddy B told Ashlee to be grateful that she still had her mouth. It worked just fine, even though she couldn't talk.

Outside his dream, Buddy B's actual male member hardened.

In his dream, he entered her room, to do her. Maybe *she* couldn't feel it, but *he* sure could. He saw it as her way of repaying him. He had given her a home. He fed and cared for her. He often reminded her. He could have let the authorities find her. They could still 'find out' that 'somehow' she'd survived. Then instead of being free with him, she would be a paraplegic in prison.

In his dream, he told her what he often did while awake. He loved that she didn't complain, unlike other women. She just took it when he got freaky and went buck wild, backwoods style.

Buddy B woke... He rubbed an eye because that could not be; he could *not* have glimpsed lil blondie running down the hall. Grunting, he got up. Wearing only a tank top, he went to look in on her. In the pearl-gray light of dawn, she was not asleep, although she could not rise from bed without his help. Chickadee's eyes were wide open. They were brown, not blue, and she stared at the ceiling. Slowly her gaze descended to his. In her eyes, there was stark, naked hatred.

Lifting her, Buddy B inserted his mighty meat into her mouth. He thought, Oh well, he was the only one who could help her, now.

When she pressed her lips tight together, he reminded her. "I can always throw ya back in the sea, let you take your chances. I can let you try to explain where ya been all this time. Remember, you tried to kill Karina's star *and* the vet. You could explain that and why you murdered the old florist, Mrs. Pigeon. You could say why you killed her little Pug, too. People won't forgive you that one." Buddy B shook his head. "No, no. Oh, but you can't talk, can ya? Just like ya can't walk."

He pried Ashlee's mouth open while murmuring. "Now, lessee if this ol' dog'll hunt. And no biting. Ya know what happens when you do."

They both remembered. He'd used pliers to pull her front teeth.

After his morning bj, Buddy B felt great. He boogied down the hallway thinking, nothing better than a good blow job in the a.m. In the smidgen of dawn light, he caught sight of that running girl again. Plain as day, on the hall wall, the shadow raced past. Yet Buddy B wasn't frightened. His little island was full of the inexplicable and the paranormal; having lived there for most of his life, he simply knew. He had seen a spirit. It was that of the enraged girl in his back room.

When he had been a child, they'd read a scripture in church. *The spirit is willing, but the flesh is weak...* Shrugging the episode away, Buddy B knew. If she could, his Chickadee would try to get away. She, who was slowly becoming a silky brunette, would attempt to leave him. Good thing she was irreparably damaged, or she'd be out running around, maybe still trying to wreak havoc, for no good reason.

As he prepared coffee, Buddy B guessed it was good that he'd seen the running thing. It reminded him, his girl was mentally determined. So now, when he left, he would chain her, just in case. Still, it was good for his sweetie to have dreams. Buddy Barnsworth knew. He'd had them, and most of his had come true—although Chickadee had lost his baby. It was because of that tumble she'd taken. Still, he had her all to himself now. The girl of his dreams. No one would ever know, either, because it wasn't like she could walk or talk. She could only do his bidding.

Ashlee heard him going to the kitchen, and she sighed. At least now, he would now leave her alone. For a while. And to think, Ashlee had liked it when he'd recorded their lewd acts. A year ago. Now she was immobile—oh Lawd, like *Mam-maw* had almost been—and Ashlee hated that Buddy B still recorded. That animal had installed mirrors, too, all over the room where she was imprisoned. From every angle, he watched himself use her. While he slaked his unnatural desires, Ashlee could not get away. To her, it seemed Buddy B especially got off when he bent her over. Pulling her apart with his huge hands, he enjoyed every moment that she could not physically feel. Yet, she did feel, *emotionally*. Ashlee felt she'd been violated—just like she had violated others.

It hurt to realize the man with the phony, open, honest look, the one who'd seemed like her friend, really was not. But the e-books he bought her—self-help, how ironic—said she had drawn him to herself with her energy. They said the people in a person's life often mirrored them. The others reflected who and what the first person was.

Ashlee had never thought of herself as self-serving or conniving. She had not thought she was mean, mental, or a little plotter, not until Buddy B called her those things. He, who was the same, had said so while nursing her back to life. Now, Ashlee guessed she was or had been all of those things. Mean, nutso, and a schemer. It took one to know one.

In the past, she'd thought she felt trapped in a life she had not wanted. Now she *knew* she was trapped, stuck in a wheelchair if her captor decided to put her in it. She was imprisoned in that madman's home, never to be released, like a pet. Oh, Lawd, Ashlee wished to cover her face because she had killed pets, China Doll and Pug. Would the madman kill her? It might serve her right, Ashlee thought, remembering what she had said to Gemma. *Too bad I can't keep you—for a pet.*

The worst thing was no one knew. No, for Ashlee, worse was that no one outside would care. She had seen to that with her actions, starting with her choice to leave the holler. Now Ashlee saw. She hadn't had to leave the way she had. In her desperate desire to become a different person, someone bigger and better than everyone she had known, she'd turned her back on her friends and family. She'd treated them as though they were nothing. In the pursuit of becoming a lady of leisure, Ashlee had let everyone down. Now she really was a woman of leisure. She had nothing but time on her inoperable hands.

Now Ashlee could see that from whence she'd hailed wasn't so bad. She realized. She had been born poor, but it wasn't the worst thing. That Mam-maw had always tried to tell her. Mam-maw had said they had family, which was important. She'd tried to instill pride in her granddaughter. However, they had taken their 'superior' stuff too far.

Mam-maw had said they should take pride in their surroundings, too. Back then, Ashlee had thought planting flowers and beautifying their plot was foolish because they'd lived in a mobile home park. She'd thought all of Mam-maw's fix-ups were useless. Now, who was useless, literally. Thinking about it, Ashlee wanted to scream—but she couldn't.

There had been others like Mam-maw, who'd worked their parcels of land. They hadn't thought it a sin to work at the Bigmart, the Save-A-

Bunch, or to scrub floors and toilets—as Ashlee had for a brief period. Those people made an honest living, and they paid their bills. Out of doors, they chatted with neighbors and knew they had enough.

Ashlee realized she had been greedy. She hadn't listened when Mrs. Pigeon said, 'A young thing like you should be in college, or even in a trade school. Karinians would help if you wanted to help yourself." Ashlee had not heard while trying to 'get above her station in life,' as Mam-maw called it. Ironically, Ashlee had thought that of Slinky.

Slinky... Ashlee still hated Gemma, although part of Ashlee knew hate was unproductive. But because of Slinky, Ashlee had no hearing in one ear. Having lost her fetus, Ashlee wondered if Slinky had borne Jeremy's. Recalling those things caused Ashlee to remember that Buddy B often brought her the tabloids. He derived perverse pleasure from watching her madly struggle to flip the flimsy pages with her face.

Wanting to turn over, Ashlee again realized she couldn't. If only she could again be that nothing girl, the one she had been so long ago. Ashlee had despised Ursa Blank. Now, Ashlee would sell her soul to again be that flat-chested skinny Minnie. Ursa had had undamaged honey brown hair down her back, and legs that worked. Ashlee knew it was improbable, but if she could be Ursa again she would run free, between Mam-maw and crazy Uncle Jed's trailers. And she would be happy.

Tears rolled down Ashlee's cheeks because never again would she ever run or be free. *How she wished she could do it all over again.* She would appreciate her grandmother, who was indeed in her grave by now. Ashlee wouldn't hate her obnoxious brothers or pitiful Maw. Ashlee would be more like Bif, the big-boned girl who had been a real friend. Bif had appreciated her life and caring for others. Wonder what she was doing these days? Bif certainly wasn't shackled with hatred and regret as her only companions, nor was she held captive by a madman who only wanted to abuse her body; that Ashlee knew. Still, Ashlee didn't blame Buddy B. The things he did to Ashlee, she had done to herself, for years. She saw that now, a little too late.

If she could leave this place... Ashlee thought for the gazillionth time. If only she could have a different life; Ashlee knew it was the same wish that had gotten her here, in this mess. Yet, if her wish was granted she wouldn't make the same wrong turns again. Suddenly, Ashlee screamed inside, right along with the women...in the legendary hollow well.

April Alisa Marquette
257

Carrying Twyla on his arm, Jeremy stepped into the hospital room. Propped up in bed, Gemma saw him. Despite not wanting to, she got that old familiar feeling about her handsome husband. He was learning to be loving, faithful, and trustworthy. She was, too, and that she remembered.

A year after *le crise*, Gemma recalled that she had forgiven Jeremy. It hadn't been easy. At first, she and Heather had been injured and shaken. Then they had been grateful to be alive, but they still suffered nightmares. Gemma fought tremendous guilt, too, because never had she dreamed *she* would cause someone's death, outside of the movies.

Gemma had been furious. She'd felt Lance had been a pig and the man-whore who'd brought racist mental Ashlee into their lives. Gemma had refused to see Jeremy, too. During his and Gemma's hiatus, before they'd married, he had hooked up with Ashlee, thus fueling her fire. Feeling volatile, Gemma advised Jeremy to stay at Windsor Pines. She'd even refused to see her co-star, Nile, who'd ceaselessly called. Worried, he'd moaned that he'd flown down because he loved her. Gemma had asked him to give her time. Then she'd said, "Nile, go home." She hadn't wanted to see the big caramel-brown sheriff either. She told him the truth. His tenderness would only have made her cry. Trip understood.

On bed rest for months, Gemma had holed up at DeVeaux House with only Ina, JeRell, Aimee, and her fathers. When her mom returned to New York, Gemma's beloved Dad became invaluable. Day after day, Beau sat with her. Softly he'd talked, telling his baby the one thing that her Nannie had taught him; *relationships* mattered.

"Your Nannie said," Beau then mimicked her grandmother's voice, "Young man, making money is fine. Making a name for yourself is too, but *relationships* are what make life worth living." Beau patted his daughter's hand. He spoke softly. *"Relationships,* doll. Remember that."

Gemma admitted they were most important and that she shouldn't hold onto grudges. "Still, I don't know how to let go," she'd divulged. "I can't get past Jere's betrayal, Daddy—or *my* guilt. I mean, if he and whorish Lance had never brought that woman into our lives, none of this would have happened! Now *I* am a murderer!" The blond woman, who'd needed psychological help, was dead—because of *her.* That was the part that haunted Gemma, perhaps because she had long thought of herself as someone who championed women and aided the ones who needed help.

"It happened," Beau acknowledged. He spoke of the guilt he knew his daughter felt, "This sounds harsh, but you must make peace with it. *It's done, baby.* Ask for forgiveness. Then go on. Live your life, well. If not," Beau shrugged, "maybe you should have gone over the cliff too..."

Gemma had not wanted to hear any of that. Still, the day came when she felt strong enough to go to the manse. At Windsor Pines, she'd learned that her husband had the well and remaining overgrowth destroyed. It had been Gemma's intent to fight with Jeremy. Instead, she broke down in the parlor ever open to the sea. She acknowledged that people made mistakes. She took to heart what her Dad had said while quietly puttering around the home where he'd raised her. Gemma recalled Nannie's words as she allowed her husband to hold her hand.

Relationships make life worth living.

With shimmering tears, Jeremy told his wife that she was courageous, more so than anyone he knew. He said that as far back as he could remember, she had been a lioness, one who'd protected her cubs. Jeremy mentioned their unborn child and their cohort, Heather, whom Gemma had done her best to protect. With his heart aching, for fear that she would not, Jeremy asked Gemma to be courageous one more time; he asked her to forgive and grant him another chance.

This time he would not fail her. He promised. This time he'd be true.

Nannie's image faded, but her sweetness remained. It aided Gemma to forgive both Jeremy and herself. It seemed they were always hurting each other and starting over. Maybe one day, they would get things right.

Tink came along shortly afterward. Gemma knew her baby should have been dissolved in blood and tears. Yet baby was an itty-bitty fighter, just like her mom. Premature, by a month, she had been born small, but by God, she was alive, and boy was she beautiful—a tiny belle. Though incubated, Tinka Belle had held her own. Remaining in the hospital after Tink's complicated birth, one day, Gemma gazed up. A man stood in her doorway. She saw him through eyes of love. The two-time mom no longer focused on what happened and whose fault it was. She only remembered that her man had repeatedly apologized. He diligently worked on being better. She was attempting to do the same.

Gemma recalled mustering a smile for her first daughter, who'd chattered away. Although melancholy, the mom thought one thing. All that had happened was simply the script of her life. Wrenching free of the sad thoughts that would dissipate with time, Gemma answered

Jeremy's question. "Tinka Belle is doing fine. As a matter of fact, in a minute, someone's gonna wheel me down to hold her."

The businessman nodded, recalling he had learned so much, due to loving the woman who gathered her robe close. Gently, he shook his eldest. With the toddler on his strong arm, he'd whispered. "Hear that, Twyla Cher? We're going with Momma to see your sister."

Twyla softly sang her sibling's name. "Tink, Tink. Tinka Belle."

Jeremy honestly did not care that he hadn't gotten a son. Silent, he walked alongside Gemma and the attendant wheeling her to the nursery. The husband and father no longer wondered if he and *sa femme* would make it. He did not question whether they could live countless years and yet love like his parents had. Outside the neo-natal unit, the little party stopped. Nervously, Gemma glanced up, and offering courage, Jeremy ran a hand over her beautifully kinky mane, and he knew. With all that he and Gemma had come through, together—since childhood—it was highly *probable* that they *would* make it. He and his *trésor* would thrive for many decades to come, God willing. –And there'd not be many dull moments. No longer depressed, due to his meds, Jeremy nearly chuckled; it was something he still found foreign. Still, he mused, his life would be interesting, of that he had no doubt. His lioness and cubs would see to it.

Gemma remembered that in the NICU, her tiny girl rested on her chest, skin to skin. The nurses called it kangaroo care; it kept the baby warm, aided her heartbeat to regulate or slow, as well as her breathing. With Gemma's hand on the blanket covering her baby's back, the mom felt a sense of satisfaction. Although her premature infant wore a knit hat to keep her small head warm, and though baby had tubes and tape in a few places, the second-time mom was grateful. She sat there, with her own breathing slowing. With her own heart no longer racing, Gemma silently prayed, not just for the newest member of the DeVeaux-Harden clan but also for the least likely one. Ashlee. The outsider...

Now, a year after *le crise*, at home, Gemma changed her chubby, sweet baby. Nearby, pesky Twyla hovered, while motherly Ina and Aimee, the nanny, tried not to laugh. Grateful for relationships, Gemma honestly prayed—for the soul of her self-proclaimed archrival. Ashlee. Blondie had been a woman who had not received the help that she'd so desperately needed... Gemma realized it was strange, but she might always wind up praying for the woman to whom she was now connected.

For Gemma, that was okay. She was learning to surrender, to life and all its improbabilities. It wasn't perfect, but life really was A-Okay.